continued...

MIND GAME

SHADOW GAME

MURDER GAME

CHRISTINE FEEHAN

JOVE BOOKS, NEW YORK

THE BERKLEY PUBLISHING GROUP
Published by the Penguin Group
Penguin Group (USA) Inc.
375 Hudson Street, New York, New York 10014, USA
Penguin Group (Canada), 90 Eglinton Avenue East, Suite 700, Toronto, Ontario M4P 2Y3, Canada
(a division of Pearson Penguin Canada Inc.)
Penguin Books Ltd., 80 Strand, London WC2R 0RL, England
Penguin Group Ireland, 25 St. Stephen's Green, Dublin 2, Ireland (a division of Penguin Books Ltd.)
Penguin Group (Australia), 250 Camberwell Road, Camberwell, Victoria 3124, Australia
(a division of Pearson Australia Group Pty. Ltd.)
Penguin Books India Pvt. Ltd., 11 Community Centre, Panchsheel Park, New Delhi—110 017, India
Penguin Group (NZ), 67 Apollo Drive, Rosedale, North Shore 0632, New Zealand
(a division of Pearson New Zealand Ltd.)
Penguin Books (South Africa) (Pty.) Ltd., 24 Sturdee Avenue, Rosebank, Johannesburg 2196,
South Africa

Penguin Books Ltd., Registered Offices: 80 Strand, London WC2R 0RL, England

This is a work of fiction. Names, characters, places, and incidents either are the product of the author's imagination or are used fictitiously, and any resemblance to actual persons, living or dead, business establishments, events, or locales is entirely coincidental. The publisher does not have any control over and does not assume any responsibility for author or third-party websites or their content.

MURDER GAME

A Jove Book / published by arrangement with the author

PRINTING HISTORY
Jove mass-market edition / January 2009

Copyright © 2009 by Christine Feehan.
Excerpt from *Burning Wild* copyright © 2009 by Christine Feehan.
Text design by Kristin del Rosario.

ISBN: 978-0-515-14580-9

JOVE®
Jove Books are published by The Berkley Publishing Group,
a division of Penguin Group (USA) Inc.,
375 Hudson Street, New York, New York 10014.
JOVE® is a registered trademark of Penguin Group (USA) Inc.
The "J" design is a trademark belonging to Penguin Group (USA) Inc.

PRINTED IN THE UNITED STATES OF AMERICA

10 9 8 7 6 5 4 3 2 1

For Cristina Emery,
who has more courage than anyone I've ever known

For My Readers

Be sure to go to http://www.christinefeehan.com/
members/ to sign up for my PRIVATE book announce-
ment list and download the FREE e-book of *Dark Des-
serts*. Please feel free to e-mail me at christine@christine
feehan.com. I would love to hear from you.

Acknowledgments

As always I have to thank the people who really helped me. So much research goes into a book like this one, and many of the scenes or the technical data are complicated. Morey Sparks walked two miles in the Iraqi heat to get information to me. I can't thank him enough for his dedication and his help. Stay safe! Thanks to Brian Feehan, who gave up so many hours to work action scenes with me, making certain each stroke of the knife and each scene would not only work, but would be the best possible way to actually carry out the mission. For my SF team, you know who you are, thank you for all the information to help me make my men real. If there are any mistakes, they are solely mine.

The GhostWalker Symbol Details

SIGNIFIES
shadow

SIGNIFIES
protection against
evil forces

SIGNIFIES
the Greek letter *psi,* which is
used by parapsychology
researchers to signify ESP or
other psychic abilities

SIGNIFIES
qualities of a knight—
loyalty, generosity,
courage, and honor

SIGNIFIES
shadow knights who protect
against evil forces using
psychic powers, courage,
and honor

nox noctis est nostri

The GhostWalker Creed

We are the GhostWalkers, we live in the shadows
The sea, the earth, and the air are our domain
No fallen comrade will be left behind
We are loyalty and honor bound
We are invisible to our enemies
and we destroy them where we find them
We believe in justice and we protect our country
and those unable to protect themselves
What goes unseen, unheard, and unknown
are GhostWalkers
There is honor in the shadows and it is us
We move in complete silence whether
in jungle or desert
We walk among our enemy unseen and unheard
Striking without sound and scatter to the winds
before they have knowledge of our existence
We gather information and wait with endless patience
for that perfect moment to deliver swift justice
We are both merciful and merciless
We are relentless and implacable in our resolve
We are the GhostWalkers and the night is ours

CHAPTER 1

The cougar was going to turn. Tansy Meadows inhaled swiftly, biting at her full lower lip. Her heart was pounding; she could taste the familiar dryness in her mouth and feel the dampness on her palms. The rush of adrenaline made it difficult to control her shaking hands when she needed desperately to be absolutely still.

Turn, baby. She whispered the encouragement in her mind, willing the animal to do so. *If you turn, I'll make you very, very famous.*

The big cat stretched lazily, its sleek body rippling with muscle beneath the soft, tawny fur. The end of its long tail twitched.

Tansy's heart nearly ceased to beat, then began to tap out double time. *Come on, little mama,* she coaxed, *turn for me.*

Her legs had long since lost feeling; they were so numb from inactivity, Tansy wasn't certain she would be able to leave the tiny ledge where she had set up her blind some months earlier. It didn't matter; nothing mattered except getting this picture.

The mountain lion was large, nearly eight feet long, very pregnant and due to give birth any day now. The slate gray tip of its tail twitched again and again, and Tansy remained utterly still, waiting for her moment. Five long hours of waiting, anticipating. Five long hours of cramped, sore muscles, not to mention the months of preparation.

Come on, baby, a little more. You can do it. Get that beautiful face pointed this way.

The mountain lion arched her back leisurely, tantalizing Tansy with expectancy. The cat turned her sleek head, green-gold eyes glittering like sparkling jewels. Tansy exhaled slowly as she began snapping frame after frame with her camera. As if she knew she was the object of admiring eyes, the cat preened herself, lapping at her tawny coat with her long tongue. She grimaced, showing off her gleaming yellow fangs. She even managed something Tansy thought resembled a smile right before she let out a soft, whistling call.

Mountain lions hunted mainly at night. Tansy worked with both digital and film, capturing wildlife in its natural habitat. She had captured a beautiful photographic series of this particular cat bringing down an elk calf three weeks ago, but this was her first real break since. Cougars were elusive and difficult to photograph in their natural habitats. Whenever possible, they preferred a high vantage point, and their superior vision allowed them to spot humans long before humans spotted them. Tansy had been studying the female cougar, one of the most elusive animals in North America, for a long time in the hopes of capturing a cougar birth on film. She was lucky she had such an affinity with animals; even the wild ones didn't seem to mind her presence too much.

She continued taking as many pictures as she could, knowing every angle, every frame was going to yield gold.

The background was everything she could possibly have asked for. The night sky, the moon and stars, the slight wind shifting the leaves just so and ruffling the silver-tipped fur. Her subject was quite cooperative—stretching, cleaning, and displaying her long, sleek body from all angles.

Tansy particularly wanted a series of shots with a variety of lighting up close on the fur. The color was difficult to truly describe, especially with each individual hair tipped in that silvery gray, enabling the cat to disappear at twilight, to simply blend into her surroundings and move without detection through most of her habitat during night hours. She wanted to get the sense of that camouflage in the pictures, of the stealth and power of the huntress, in contrast to the playful and motherly personality.

In the distance overhead, the *thump, thump* of a helicopter, blades spinning fast as it made its way across the dawn sky, interrupted the silence of the night. The cougar froze, crouching low so the few bushes and blades of grass growing on the rock hid her. She bared her teeth in a silent snarl as she looked upward.

Tansy slowly lowered her camera and remained just as still as the cat, an inexplicable awareness of being hunted creeping down her spine. Her breath caught in her lungs, and for just one moment she was disoriented, a frightening thing while on a narrow ledge with a wild cougar just a few feet from her.

She turned her face toward the sky as the helicopter flew directly over her. Just the sight and sound of the aircraft was unsettling to her, and she bit down hard on her lower lip, peering at the craft in order to identify it, worried her parents had sent someone after her when she'd insisted she was exactly where she wanted to be. She had chosen this wilderness to be completely away from all human contact, and the helicopter above her was definitely military—not forestry, and certainly not one belonging to her father.

The undercarriage of the helicopter glowed with green lights as it moved fast over her, a large bird of prey swooping low over the tall trees and then just as suddenly dipping down below her line of vision, the noise fading quickly. She lay very still on the narrow ledge, her heart thundering in her ears. She forced air through her lungs as the lights disappeared. Her imagination was running wild—maybe she had been alone too long after all.

Movement snapped her attention back to the cougar, as the cat gave one final, almost contemptuous lick along her tawny, muscled leg and, in a single bound, leapt to the rock above her resting area. Tansy knew her den was there. The cat had chosen a small cave to give birth to her kittens.

Tansy had been able to infiltrate two caves the cat had previously used as dens to set up her equipment, in the hopes she could somehow film the event. To her disappointment, the cave the mountain lion had chosen was totally inaccessible, which meant Tansy would have to spend another year or two studying the species and waiting for the next birth cycle, after these kittens were raised. In the meantime, tonight's pictures were worth a fortune and would give her the necessary money to continue her work.

Tansy deserved a long soak in the natural pool and an even longer nap in the mid-afternoon sun. Very carefully, she stretched her sore, tired muscles. Needles and pins rushed in where before there had been only numbness. The cramps would hit soon, grabbing at her calves and thighs, a protest against the long hours of being motionless. She had no real room to maneuver, the ledge was so narrow. She breathed through the needles, breathed through the cramps, flexing and stretching with care until she was certain she was able to climb the sheer rock face as she did most days.

There were tiny crevices where she could wedge her fingers and toes. Long ago she had rigged a rope for safety. It was often an effort to remember to use it; she was so accustomed to the climb. Today, however, she was grateful for its presence. She was far more tired than usual. The natural pool would be more than welcome, and nothing was going to prevent her well-deserved catnap.

Tansy stowed her precious camera and its load alongside the diary she kept of the cat's movements, in her strongest metal box at her camp. She locked the latches with not one, but two heavy locks and stored it well away from her food supplies, on the off chance a wandering bear became curious.

She was actually happy. Tansy stretched again. She couldn't wait to let her mother and father know. They'd been so worried about her after her breakdown, and they'd been so frightened when she started disappearing for months at a time into the wildest places she could find. Dropped by helicopter with her gear, she lived with just a daily radio call to assure them she was alive and well. And she was more than well now. She had suffered through hell and come out on the other side. Happiness was a bright light spreading through her like a glow, when she honestly couldn't remember feeling happy before.

She yawned, glanced at her watch, waiting for the arranged time to call. Her mother had obviously been doing the same exact thing on her end, because when she gave her call sign, her mother answered immediately. Sharon Meadows's bubbly voice was like a ray of sunshine and Tansy smiled just hearing her.

"You should see the pictures I got," Tansy greeted. "I don't think anyone's ever managed to get so close to a cougar in the wild."

"You've always had an affinity for animals. They don't seem to mind you being around," Sharon agreed. "Even the meanest dog would turn into a love when you talked to him. But don't get too close, Tansy. You are carrying a weapon, aren't you?"

"Of course, Mom. How's Dad?"

"I'm right here, Tansy-girl. I wanted to hear your voice. Are you about to wrap it up?" Don Meadows asked.

"She's going to have her kittens any day. I thought I might be able to film the birth, but she tricked me and found the one place I couldn't get my camera into. I should be able to photograph the kittens within a few hours after birth though."

"Which means you aren't coming home." Her father made it a statement.

She laughed. "You two don't want me home. You're like a couple of honeymooners and I cramp your style."

"We want you with us, Tansy," Sharon said, and now worry had crept into her voice.

"I love it up here," Tansy explained. "I know you don't understand, Mom . . ."

Don laughed and Tansy knew he was trying to cover for her mother. "She doesn't even like to camp in an RV, Tansy. There's no way she can understand how you want to live in the wild without all the amenities of a five star hotel."

Her father had taken her camping often over the years, but her mother had found excuse after excuse not to go with them. Tansy had been about ten years old before she realized her mother hadn't wanted to come along with them and that her excuses weren't real. Tansy, like her father, loved camping, and those summers had prepared her for her current work.

"I just don't like you being so alone all the time," Sharon said, forcing a brightness back into her voice.

"Mom," she assured her, "this is good for me. I don't have all the craziness out here. I can't be around people, you know that—it's dangerous for me."

There was a small silence. She heard her mother choke and knew she was holding back tears. Tansy wasn't normal. She would never be normal, and her mother loved her and wanted desperately for her to be able to be like other women.

To get married, have a family. It was all her mother had ever wanted for her. Sharon had never been able to give birth to biological children. She'd adopted Tansy and wanted for her all the things she couldn't have herself.

"Are you certain, Tansy?" Sharon asked. "I can't help you when you're so far away. I don't know that you're healthy and happy. Are you? Are you really, Tansy?"

This time the break in her voice was very apparent, and Tansy's heart clenched tightly. "It's all right, Mom. I'm all right," she said softly. "I'm happy here. I'm productive. I'm able to make a good living at this and I really love it. My mind feels clean and clear out here."

"I just don't want you to be alone all your life," Sharon said. "I want you to find someone, and be loved by him the way your father loves me."

Tansy pressed her fingers to her eyes. She was exhausted, and even over the distance, even with radio waves, she heard the pain and disappointment in her mother's voice— not at her, she knew that. But on her behalf.

"I love both of you," Don said firmly. "And for now, that's more than enough, isn't it, Tansy-girl?"

Of course she wanted a husband and children, but she knew it was impossible. She'd accepted that and so had her father. Love for him, for his ability to understand how truly flawed she was and yet love her anyway, poured over her.

"Absolutely, Dad," she agreed, meaning it. "I'm really happy, Mom. And I'm not ill, even the headaches are gone."

"Completely?" Don asked, shock and hope in his voice.

Tansy smiled, happy to be able to tell the truth. "Absolutely, Dad." *And thank you for all the nights you sat up with me when I couldn't sleep,* she added silently.

"That's wonderful, dear." Sharon's voice was packed with relief.

"Do you need us to send more supplies? I'll get one of our pilots to make the drop."

"I'll make a list and give it to you tomorrow. I need sleep now. I was up all night."

"Take care, Tansy," her mother said, her voice back to normal, once again upbeat and happy, as if by using her bubbliest tone, she could bolster Tansy. "If you don't come back soon, your father and I will be on your doorstep."

Don snorted and Tansy burst out laughing. "Okay, Mom. Just another few weeks and I'll be home." She made kissing noises and signed off, feeling very lucky and grateful that Don and Sharon were her parents.

She had always felt loved by them, even though she was so different. She'd always been different. As a baby she detested touching objects. Even dinnerware and utensils were enough to set her off, crying and rocking, so distressed that her parents would take turns comforting her, walking her up and down, singing to her. School had been a nightmare for her, and in the end, they had hired private tutors—which had broken her mother's heart.

Tansy sighed. She had so wanted to be that girl her mother could share her life with. The proms, the late night gossip sessions, the wonderful fairy tale wedding—her mother would never have that, and Tansy wanted it for her, just as her mother wanted that life for Tansy.

Finally, after months in a hospital, she'd realized she couldn't be that girl—would never be that girl. She'd accepted herself for who she really was, flaws and all, and she'd managed to make a new life for herself. She was content, even happy, here in the wilderness.

Tansy powered off the radio and started down the trail leading to the natural pool. The hike to the basin was long and winding, but she was very familiar with it and could go fairly fast in spite of the roughness of the terrain. The rock formation was part of the reason she'd chosen this area as her base camp. The falls were beautiful, flowing down a series of smooth rocks to a natural pool below. The swimming hole was lined with rock, so it stayed clean, and it was surrounded with flat granite, so she had plenty of room to sun herself. The basin was the perfect place to spend a lazy afternoon after being up all night working.

Tansy liked to sleep in the morning, bathe in the pool, and then catch a couple of hours of sun in the afternoon before returning to her camp and preparing for another evening's shoot. As a rule, mountain lions had a large territory, the females often covered fifty square miles, but the female was staying close to her small cave, and Tansy was absolutely certain that she was about to give birth any day. She didn't want to miss her opportunity, or let the female get away from her. She'd heard of cougars changing dens at the last moment, and she needed to be watching the pregnant cat closely.

Tansy stretched out, trying to get comfortable on the smooth granite surface. Ordinarily, after a long night without sleep, she dropped right off in the afternoon sun. She tried to tell herself she was excited over her pictures, the months of work finally paying off. The truth was, since the moment that helicopter had flown overhead, she'd had a vague feeling of uneasiness, as if a storm were gathering off in the distance and heading her way. The premonition persisted and was so strong, she lifted her head to search the sky for a sign of ominous, dark clouds.

A lazy hawk floated in the cloudless sky, catching a thermal and riding it just for fun. Tansy laid her head against her arm and rubbed her cheek back and forth in a soothing gesture. It was crazy, but she felt as if she were being hunted. The area was secluded, restricted without a permit, well posted, impassable except on foot or, in winter, with snowshoes. The helicopter had shaken her more than she wanted to admit.

"Let it go," she whispered aloud.

She closed her eyes tiredly, searching for the inner

contentment she always found after a great shoot. No one else could have gotten those pictures. Well, very few. She had a way with animals, as her mother had said. If she willed something in her head, oftentimes she could get the animal to cooperate, even the most feral. She had it all: the perfect job, the wild terrain, and the peace the mountains always managed to give her. This was the life she chose, loved. More, this was the life she needed. No human contact whatsoever. At last she'd found a place she could be happy.

Tansy smiled in contentment. She was very tired and needed sleep. She only had a few hours left in the afternoon. Nights on the mountain were always iffy. Let it all go and just sleep. When she woke, she could swim in the pool and then stretch out and dry off in the hot afternoon sun before making her way back to camp to prepare for this night's shoot.

"Are you going hunting, sir?"

Kadan Montague glanced up at the crew chief, sliding his .45 smoothly into the holster at his hip and locking it down. "Something like that." He shouldered his pack and slipped his knife securely into the scabbard before glancing at his coordinates. "This is it."

The crew chief, recognizing his VIP didn't want to talk, made certain the rope was secure and moved to the side to allow his passenger to step up to the open door. Kadan caught the rope with both gloved hands and waited for the pilot's okay. The craft steadied and he went down, fast-roping, settling to earth with a slight impact and stepping clear to give the away signal. His descent had taken seconds, and the helicopter swung away, shifting toward the south, flying fast for base. It would set down at the ranger station and wait, no matter how long, for a radio signal to pick him up in the lower meadow as soon as he had the cargo ready.

Kadan took a deep, long breath of mountain air and looked slowly around him, feeling at home. Dawn was breaking over the mountain, spilling light along the ridges, turning shrubbery, leaves, and granite to gold. Pine, fir, and dogwood stretched as far as the eye could see, and huge, towering cliffs of granite jutted up toward the sky. For the first time in a long while, he relaxed. No one was trying to kill him. He might be in for a long hike, but he could enjoy his surroundings.

He moved with complete confidence, with the steady gait of a man used to being out in the wilderness and covering a large territory fast. He was at home in any environment, having trained with the military Special Forces as well as with the GhostWalker teams. Arctic, desert, mountain, and water training had given his body the fitness to hike the rigorous terrain. He enjoyed physical activity, and although he was tired from going through several time zones and being without sleep for several days, he was wholly focused on his mission.

He traveled in the direction in which he estimated he would be most likely to find Tansy Meadows's campsite. The area had several possibilities, but she had specific needs for a long-term stay, and that narrowed her options significantly. If she was anywhere in the zone he had targeted, he would run across her tracks. An hour into his hike, he found several trails leading upward into the higher, less dense forest and more toward the craggy granite, a good place for mountain lions. He worked his way steadily to the granite, where there was more brush and fewer trees.

Kadan paused on the narrow, faint ribbon of a deer trail to take a long, slow drink of his water. He had the coordinates of the range she traveled in, taking amazing photographs for *National Geographic,* and he was certain the information he had was accurate. Tansy Meadows, psychic extraordinaire and elite tracker. The girl who could track serial killers with her mind. Some said she was difficult to work with, others that she was "freaky" but got the job done, and every single report he'd read on her said she was the real thing. Of course, now the law enforcement agencies claimed she'd lost her talent in a climbing accident, when she'd fallen and hit her head. He didn't believe it for a moment, but if he was wrong, he was wasting time he didn't have on a bad roll of the dice.

He had a few questions marks in his mind about Meadows. There were no photographs of her, not a single one, and she worked for numerous law enforcement agencies. He'd tried *National Geographic*, but they didn't have a picture either. Who had that kind of power? No civilian could manage to wipe out law enforcement records—unless there was never a photograph in the first place. There were plenty of articles in newspapers, and her name was in numerous FBI and police reports across the country, and then there were her hospital records. No photograph existed there either, which meant that little Miss Tansy Meadows had to be red flagged. Kadan had high security clearance and the general even higher, yet from what they could tell, no photograph of her existed. Period.

She'd been adopted at the age of five by Don and Sharon Meadows, a wealthy couple who'd made a name for themselves in the research, design, and assembly of aircraft, specifically attack helicopters. Don and Sharon Meadows were major players in politics and frequently received government contracts for military research and design. The couple was well connected politically, but did that mean they had the clout to keep their daughter's photograph from appearing anywhere in the news? It was possible, but doubtful. It would take far more power and influence, and for what possible gain?

The first time Kadan had heard rumors of a teenager who could track serial killers was when he'd trained at Quantico. Controversy had raged over whether there was such a thing as psychic ability, and if one had it, whether it could really be channeled to track a killer. He had never entered into the discussions, because he knew absolutely that psychic ability existed, but to harness it and be able to use it were difficult things. The police Tansy had worked with swore by her, but no one mentioned her training, which had seemed odd to him.

He continued upward, his gut telling him he was on the right path. There were no tracks yet, nothing to indicate the presence of another human being, but he was certain he was heading in the right direction. He was looking for a needle in a haystack, yet he knew he would find her. Every instinct he had told him she was somewhere close. And he would bet his last dollar that she was lying her ass off claiming she'd lost her psychic abilities. If she had worked over and over with the police tracking serial killers successfully, he doubted if a climbing accident had suddenly snuffed out her talent as she claimed when she came out of the hospital, refusing to even meet with police or FBI agents again.

His gaze scanned the ground as he moved at a steady pace along the narrow trail. The path was no more than a worn deer trail, zigzagging up and down the slope, but he spotted two places where the grass was crushed and several leaves appeared bruised. Something had moved through the brush recently. He stooped to examine the ground and saw a faint track. It was nearly four inches wide and the two front toes were not lined up, with one toe farther forward, almost pointing, and four toes all together. There were no claw marks, and the top part of the heel pad had two distinct curvatures while the bottom had three separate lobes. There was no question in his mind the track belonged to a cougar. He'd found the cat; now he just needed to find the woman.

The rangers had assured him the mountain lions were up here somewhere, and that meant that Tansy Meadows would be also. His mission was to find her and bring her back to aid him in clearing the GhostWalker name. She

had the reputation with the FBI of being the real deal, and
the general needed Kadan to do damage control as soon as
possible, and to do that, Kadan needed Tansy Meadows. He
had never failed in a mission yet, and this one was too important.

He continued hiking, using the winding ribbon of a
trail. Occasionally he could see a partial track in the damp
soil, and once he found a few tufts of fur in some brush
where the cat had been rubbing. He decided she must be
female; her tracks weren't deep enough to indicate much
weight, and he hadn't come across any of the signs indicating a male's territory. This was one of the few times he had
gone into the mountains without someone trying to kill
him, and he found he enjoyed the peaceful solitude in spite
of the urgency of his mission.

He took a couple of steps and then he saw it. His heart
jumped in spite of his training, breath hitching in his lungs.
The print of a small hiking boot was outlined in the dust of
the trail and superimposed right over the top of it was the
mountain lions print. All along the cat had been stalking the
woman—and he was certain it was a woman by the size of
the shoe—probably walking parallel to her trail for some
distance before dropping in behind her.

He swore under his breath as he cast around for more
tracks. There were older tracks, indicating the woman used
this trail often, and that the mountain lion often stalked
her. He took a breath and let it out, forcing down a feeling
of urgency. If the cougar often trailed her, that didn't mean
this would be the day the cat attacked. He picked up his
pace, following the pair back up the granite slope toward
the cliffs.

The mountain lion continued her steady pacing, staying
in the woman's track, but not moving faster to overtake
her. If she was hunting, she wasn't in a hurry to catch her
prey. As the sun grew hotter overhead, he continued his
climb, taking another long, slow pull from his camel pack,

allowing the cool water to trickle down his throat so he could savor it, feeling a little exposed in the open of the granite with giant boulders towering around him.

At night it was piercingly cold. By day it could be unexpectedly hot, or without warning, a storm could move in with alarming force. He had no wish to be caught out in the open with lightning striking everywhere.

Kadan made it to the top of the rise and looked out over the spectacular view. In spite of the high altitude, he had no problem with breathing, his training standing him in good stead. He paused for a moment to take stock of his surroundings. The deep timber had given way to high ridges of granite and tall castle-like formations. It was breathtakingly beautiful. Even he had to admit it, as much as he detested wasting precious time on such things.

Above him, a long fall of frothy water spilled down, far below, into a pool of deep emerald green. The natural basin was made of granite, large boulders worn smooth from the constant assault of water. Something moved in the deepest end of the pool. He fixed his sight on the water's surface and the intriguing ripple came again. Without taking his eyes from the ever widening circle, Kadan pulled his high-powered field glasses from the case at his belt and quickly adjusted them. Instantly the emerald green of the water shimmered within touching distance. He found himself waiting in anticipation.

Closer to the water's edge, to his left and near the lowest wall of granite, the water ringed, and something silvery gold appeared to break the surface for a moment. Kadan unconsciously held his breath. An otter? Were there otters up here? Were otters silver and gold?

She rose up out of the water, long wet hair streaming, gleaming, and shimmering like skeins of wet silk. The droplets of water ran off the curves of her breasts, down her narrow rib cage, dipped in at her small waist to stream down her flat belly to the triangle of blond curls at the junction of her legs. She was naked, skin glowing in the sunlight, her tan so deep it emphasized the white gold of her hair. She tilted her head to one side and brought her long hair over one shoulder in an unconsciously provocative gesture.

The wind shifted and carried her scent to him. Kadan's body tightened savagely in response. His body knew her instantly. She looked like some wild, pagan offering. Untamed, seductive. *For him.* He went very still, his breath catching in his lungs. Instant awareness shook him. He'd certainly had his share of women, but he never reacted like this—a vicious, brutal response of his body and mind, everything in him reaching toward her.

"Whitney, you bastard," he whispered aloud. Not for one moment would he ever believe his reaction to be natural. It was too strong, too obsessive. Too unlike him.

He crouched down for a moment, feeling sucker punched. He'd joined the military, gone through Special Forces training, continued with water, arctic, desert, and even urban training, and then he'd read the call for testing of psychic ability and he had gone immediately, tested high, as he'd known he would, and been accepted into the military GhostWalker program. He'd agreed to be psychically enhanced. He hadn't agreed to be genetically altered, nor had he ever been told that they would match him chemically to a female.

As the extent of what had been done to the volunteers became apparent, Kadan had hoped he'd been one of the ones who escaped this particular hell. But he knew. His body knew. He tried to breathe away the monstrous hard-on that came out of nowhere. He pushed down the aggression as testosterone flooded his body with burning lust and a savage desire to possess. He'd never thought to ask any of the others what it was like, or even if all of their symptoms were the same, but he felt aggressive, dangerous, almost brutal, a primitive response preprogrammed into him.

Breathing deeply, he grabbed a handful of dirt, closing

his fingers around it hard, as if squeezing the life from someone's throat. And where was the cat? He had to make certain the animal wasn't about to leap on her.

Once more he lifted the binoculars, breath catching in his lungs as she came back into focus. Even the way she wrung out her hair was sensuous, tipping her head to one side, the long, golden strands rippling like silk as her hands squeezed the thick skein. Water beaded and ran from full breasts to belly and down to the vee at the junction of her legs. Her legs were slender, her butt firm as she waded toward the edge of the pool, the water lapping at her thighs. His tongue moistened his suddenly dry lips. He would have given anything to lick the droplets of water from her skin.

Reluctantly he moved the binoculars from his fantasy vision to scan the surrounding forest and mountains. Nothing. He shifted his direction, quartering the area, looking high, from branches to boulders. The mountain lion had to be there somewhere, invisible to his sight, maybe, but not to his gut.

There was no camp close by that he could see, but it had to be there. He turned his attention back to the woman. This must be Tansy Meadows. She looked almost as if swimming in the pool and napping and sunning were a daily ritual, and if so, she wouldn't be hiking too far from her home ground.

There was no doubt in his mind that she owned his body, and that meant she had to be one of the lost girls Whitney had experimented on. The demented doctor had taken infants from orphanages from all over the world and performed experiments on them. A few lucky ones had been adopted out. Kadan had her background information memorized. Her parents had adopted her when she was five years old. She had severe problems in school and other social settings. She'd worked with the police from the age of thirteen, tracking killers and kidnap victims with amazing accuracy. He should have known she was too accurate. He should have known her psychic abilities were enhanced.

Kadan took another long look around in an effort to spot the mountain lion. If it was there, the animal was well camouflaged. Every area he thought would be the perfect place from which to ambush her seemed serene and peaceful. He swung the glasses back to the natural basin.

She stepped from the shimmering emerald water, moving with grace and something else, something so seductive and innocent at the same time that his body screamed at him with urgent demand. His breath caught in his throat as she lifted her slender arms toward the sun, the action thrusting her breasts upward, the darker nipples erect from the cold. Kadan could feel the taste of her in his mouth. He took a slow, deep breath to calm the surging excitement, the exultation. His body, his mind, his very soul said she was the one. He was looking at his mate.

God help him, he didn't want to think that way—not now—not in the middle of such a huge crisis. He needed to be sane, to keep his mind and body under control. And he needed to use this woman, be ruthless if necessary. He swore softly under his breath and wiped his forehead with the back of his hand as he kept the glasses trained on her.

She lathered her body with lotion, every stroke of her hand making his body throb and jerk in need, and then she stretched out, facedown, on the flat surface of the rock, her body an offering in the afternoon sun. Her bottom was curved, well muscled, joining the long expanse of her shapely legs. It was impossible, even with the field glasses, to see her facial features; she was turned away from him, her face in the shadows. His imagination could not provide a face to go with her sensual body or the erotic way she moved. He watched her for a long while, until her breathing became slow and even and he knew she slept.

She was sound asleep and a mountain lion had stalked her all the way down the trail to the basin. It was hidden

somewhere above her, maybe watching. Again he scanned
the surrounding area, appalled that she lay naked and exposed, where any hunter or wild animal might come across
her. Fury burned in his belly, low and mean, and for a moment, the ground around him trembled. He clamped down
on his temper and forced air through his lungs as he sifted
through every possible place the cougar could hide. He'd
trained at the elite sniper school, taken the test of finding
fifty objects hidden at multiple distances, and he'd spotted
every one, but the cat remained hidden.

He lowered the glasses. He'd been too long without
sleep. He'd traveled to ten foreign countries in two weeks,
working on forming a collective pool of multinational an-
titerrorist information for an elite assassination squad. The
team would live in the shadows, travel to the kill zone,
destroy all targets, and fade away before anyone ever knew
they were in the area. Each member would be totally anon-
ymous so there could be no retaliation against families.
Each member would be a GhostWalker, able to get in and
out of a target zone like a shadow.

Kadan had been assigned the task and was pulling his
team together when he was abruptly called home and given
another mission—and this one was too important to mess
up. He was known for his coolness under fire, his absolute
calm in any crisis, his ability to lead his team and under-
take any mission, find a way to carry it out and get his team
home again, no matter the odds. He sighed. He didn't feel
cool or calm now, he felt edgy and mean. He was grateful
his fellow GhostWalkers weren't around to witness his
struggle.

Deliberately slowing his breathing, he took another
drink from his camel pack. He was going to have to
climb down to the rocks below and find a way to convince
her to join him, because in the end, she didn't really have
any more of a choice than he did. He had a feeling it wasn't
going to be easy or pleasant, but completing the mission

was necessary. And he had the feeling that if this woman had been given up for adoption years earlier by Whitney, she probably hadn't been chemically matched with him, which, quite frankly, was going to make things one hell of a mess. Whitney had kept her DNA and had programmed him, but not her.

He'd thought the task was going to be heartbreaking and difficult enough just convincing and perhaps forcing Tansy to partner with him in his investigation, but now, with the added threat of the physical pull between them, the mission had become daunting. She had suffered a breakdown, and by all accounts, it had been real. He'd read the report carefully, as well as all her medical records. She'd spent weeks in a hospital and months in seclusion with her parents. She'd been fractured, shattered by her last case, her mind splintering and refusing to relinquish the evil voices of the killers she'd tracked, or the screams of their victims. He was going to have to ask her to let other, more powerful and vicious voices in. On top of that, he was going to have to somehow explain that he was paired with her.

Kadan found himself unable to tear his eyes from her. The longer he watched her, the tighter and more urgently his body made demands. He had never experienced such sexual hunger. It seemed to fill every cell of his body, invade his brain, squeeze his body in a vise until jackhammers were ripping through him, driving out every civilized thought. He had to get some kind of handle on the link between them or he would destroy any chance he had with her.

He sat down, folded his legs tailor fashion, and closed his eyes, searching inwardly to center himself. He needed balance. The discomfort of the rocks, of his boots, of his body swarmed into his brain and he allowed it to wash over him, to form rings on the pool he focused on and disappear in the ripples of the water. He breathed long, deep breaths, searching inside himself for the truth of his strong emotions.

Fear for her safety. Both from animal predators and from human ones. This area was so isolated, it frightened him to think what would happen if she were found by some drunk hunter, or a man without scruples or principles. Any animal could stalk her while she lay defenseless in the sun; the cat already had. Anger. He examined the turbulent emotion from all angles. It was one he was not completely familiar with. Most of his life he had been cold and dispassionate in his dealings with people. That was what made him so good at his job. He had mastered his every emotion. Anger. It ripped through him. Boiled. Surged and pounded. Insisted on release like a heated volcano. Completely over-the-top, and he refused to let it to the surface. He had a mission, and nothing—no one—got in the way of a mission.

He took another deep, calming breath and stayed in the pool of sanity while insane emotions swirled and clamored and finally abated, leaving him whole again. He opened his eyes and smiled. The smile of a predator. He came to his feet, unexpectedly fluid for such a large man. His eyes found her once again. The shadows were just beginning to reach for the soft curves of her body.

He moved with sudden decision, finding the easiest way down the mountainside. It was steep and rocky and, as always in the mountains, deceptively longer than it seemed from a distance. It took some hunting to find the steep, narrow staircase that actually led to the secluded basin. He made his way down as quietly as he was able. He wanted to study her while she slept, just take his time and let the image of her burn into his memory for all eternity. He wouldn't mind throwing one hell of a scare into her either.

CHAPTER 2

Kadan was careful not to allow his shadow to fall across Tansy Meadows's body. The granite was smooth under his boots and made no sound to give him away. He stayed out of the wind just in case she possessed an enhanced sense of smell, and made certain he didn't interrupt, even briefly, the flow of air moving around her body. GhostWalkers were all sensitive to the smallest change in the energy flowing around them. Meadows may not have been trained as a GhostWalker, but if she was enhanced, as he suspected, she would be a force to be reckoned with.

He scanned the surrounding area, searching for any weapon, anything she might use to defend herself. He frowned when he realized her clothes were neatly stacked some distance from where she was stretched out sleeping. A small dart gun was beside her clothes, up against a rock. Kadan eased his way, placing each foot carefully so as not to disturb loose rock, his body moving slow to keep the air still, and reached for the dart gun. For both of their safety, he slid the weapon into his belt. She should have held the gun under her palm where she could easily defend herself against a wild animal or a hunter. If she was a Ghost-Walker, her self-preservation instincts weren't as good as they should be.

After satisfying himself there was nothing she could grab to cause either of them harm, he crouched down beside her. More than anything, he wanted to see her face. Up close she was breathtaking. Her skin looked so soft and warm, it took every ounce of his self-control to keep from touching her. Her hair was a mixture of true platinum and skeins of gold that spilled down her back and across the rock. Long lashes lay like crescents, feathery and thick. Her face was a small oval, her mouth full and inviting. He stifled the urge to bend down and wake her with a kiss. She was much smaller than he'd expected, but her legs were long, her bottom curved, and his body told him she would fit him like a glove.

His face was a few inches from hers when she opened her eyes to stare directly into his. Fear leapt, turned the deep blue of her eyes nearly violet with alarm. Her eyes glittered with a kind of reflective shine, and then she squinted, as if the light hurt them. She blinked once and her eyes were clear, cool, and assessing. She reached for her sunglasses and slid them onto the bridge of her nose with a casual haughtiness that told him she was a princess and he was a mere peasant.

Tansy opened her eyes from a peaceful dream and found herself staring into perfect cat's eyes. Cold, unblinking, so dark blue they were almost black. Focused. She was looking into the eyes of a man who had killed often. Shaggy dark hair spilled across his forehead, touching a thin white scar that ran the length of a rough face that was all angles and planes. He looked weathered and all too dangerous. There was a shadow along his jaw as if he couldn't be bothered to be civilized enough to shave. He wore no expression on his face at all, just that sweeping fixed stare, cool as a cat's.

She lifted her chin a few inches, her lashes sweeping down to veil her expression before she put on her dark glasses. She made no attempt to cover her nudity because there was nothing she could do about it and she didn't want to give him any more of an advantage by letting him see she felt vulnerable.

Rising with as much grace and dignity as she could manage, Tansy crossed to her neatly folded clothing. She had to brush past him, and he didn't budge, his frame solid and muscular, his skin rubbing against hers and causing a brief frisson of awareness. Electricity zinged along her nerve endings and tiny wings took flight along her stomach. She could feel those blue-black eyes tracking her every step of the way. Tansy was eternally grateful she'd never cut her hair. The long length of it covered her bare bottom, giving her a false sense of security. She had no idea that the silky platinum and gold mass against her dark skin was provocative, and only served to give her an erotic, seductive appearance, emphasizing her curves.

Keeping her back to him, she pulled on her shirt and stepped into her jeans, taking several deep breaths to maintain control. Out of habit, Tansy wrapped the length of her hair several times and secured it at the back of her head with a large barrette. Surreptitiously, she looked around for her tranquilizer gun. It was not in the usual place by the jutting rock, which meant he probably had it. Squaring her shoulders, she turned to face the stranger.

He was a large, heavily muscled man. The sheer brute strength of him set her heart pounding. If she had to be caught naked, alone, in the middle of nowhere, why couldn't that person have been some ninety-pound weakling? She feared more than the actual size of him. He exuded power from every pore. He looked dangerous in some way she couldn't define. She might dismiss the impression of power by saying it was his looks, but she knew better. His features looked as if they could have been carved from stone, every bit as rugged as the granite surroundings. He wasn't handsome—he was far too rough-cut for that. But he was striking in a scary way.

"I'm sorry I startled you."

His voice was smooth black velvet, the devil's tool and sarcastic as hell. Intense anger simmered below that smooth exterior. She touched her tongue to her lips, her only concession to nerves.

"It was time to wake up anyway." She made herself shrug. "This is a private preserve and you aren't allowed here." He was military, not a hunter. His eyes were flat and hard and watchful—too watchful, as if he expected her to make a run for freedom. She shifted to the balls of her feet and turned slightly to angle her body toward his, presenting fewer targets should he attack.

"I came looking for you."

Because she'd been so startled to wake up to him, she hadn't registered until now that being in close proximity to him didn't cause the headaches she'd suffered around other human beings—including her parents. The ravenous psychic energy that normally surrounded her when she was close to people wasn't present. She felt the slight breeze, heard the continual call of birds, the buzzing of bees, but no whispers in her mind.

"You came looking for me?" she echoed, feeling a little lost. Her gaze flicked over him, taking everything in the way she did, her mind cataloguing the picture, referencing the scars along with his gear—especially the knife at his side.

He smiled as if to ease her fear. He looked like a mountain lion right before mealtime. "Let's start again. I'm Kadan Montague." Deliberately, his smile almost wolfish now, he held out his hand.

Automatic reflex was nearly her undoing. Right before his hand could envelop hers, Tansy stepped backward, both hands behind her back. She didn't dare chance physical contact with him. Nor did she wish to get close enough if his intentions were to assault her.

His smile widened at her reaction, warmed the strange black eyes until they glittered like a cat's at night. "You aren't afraid of me." He made it a statement.

Anyone with a brain would be afraid of him, especially a woman. This was a man's man. There was nothing boyishly handsome in that rugged face. Nothing soft and gentle in those glittering eyes, but something else. What was it that both intrigued and repelled her?

"You caught me in a compromising position. You must admit it isn't exactly a situation that would make a woman feel safe."

Kadan studied her face—the flawless complexion, the full mouth, and the long, lush lashes—but it was her eyes that intrigued him most. There was no question that she was enhanced—he could feel the powerful psychic energy she gave off—but there was something more as well, something he'd not seen in other GhostWalkers before, and whatever the talent, it showed in her eyes. He had to resist reaching out to touch her soft expanse of skin. Twice now, her small white teeth had tugged thoughtfully at her lower lip, a habit he found sexy as hell. She wasn't reading him, and that so rarely happened to her, he could tell she that she found the experience unsettling.

She had a little too much confidence in herself, which meant she had to have some defense training. Deliberately he allowed his gaze to drift over her body and then back up to her face. She controlled the blush, and that meant she had amazing discipline and command of her body. He sent up a silent prayer that he had the same discipline and command of his body. He needed to get his mind off all that skin, her sweet curves and that damned pouty lower lip.

"What is it you want, Mr. . . ."

"Kadan," he interrupted. He kept his voice soft, but he poured steel into it. She was looking at him with those enormous blue-violet eyes, and the strange little shimmer unsettled his belly and tightened his groin. He damn well wasn't going to be the one out of control.

"I don't know you well enough to call you by your first name." She said it primly as she moved to her left, toward the natural rock staircase that led away from the basin.

Kadan kept pace, matching her shorter strides perfectly, as if they were slow dancing together. He crowded her personal space just a little, testing to see how she would react.

She stopped abruptly, but didn't move out of his strike range. "Are you purposely trying to intimidate me?"

He let a brief smile curve his mouth, giving her a short glimpse of bare teeth. "You should be intimidated. What the hell were you thinking, going to sleep out in the open without a stitch on and no weapon close to you?" He kept his voice controlled, but there was a whip in his tone, and she flinched under it.

"I'm well aware it wasn't smart. I've been out here for some time and got careless."

There was something in her tone that irritated him—no remorse, not an apology, just an acceptance of stupidity. Stupidity got a person killed. One moment of inattention could kill an entire team. He crowded her a little more, wanting her scared, because in spite of that flinch, there was no fear in her eyes.

Tansy let him come near her, not once looking at the knife in the scabbard on his belt. There was no safety thong tying down the hilt, she'd already ascertained that, and the moment he got close enough, she struck, spinning, hand going for the weapon in a blur of speed and moving away just as fast. Except . . . she didn't go anywhere. His hand clamped down on hers, capturing her fist around the hilt, his strength enormous, refusing to allow her to draw the weapon and pinning her in place. He held her rigid against his body, one arm locked around her throat, the other keeping her fist tight around the knife.

"What do we do now?" he asked, his voice low. Her scent filled his mind and body. Cinnamon. She smelled all woman and cinnamon—a lure that refused to let him go—and his body responded. Hell, he was past caring that she knew, not the way her soft body was molded against his.

She swallowed. He felt the movement against his forearm, but there was no panic, no struggle. She even relaxed into him, her free hand coming up to hook into the crook of his elbow, one finger pressed lightly against his pressure point, and that told him a lot about her.

"Now you let go of me."

Tansy should have been concentrating on getting free. Her mind and body should have been waiting for a moment when she could break loose, but *her hand was wrapped around the hilt of a knife*—one that was not new, but had gone into combat with this man and surely had been used. She didn't feel anything—*nothing at all*. There were no whispers to taunt and torment her, no tunnel sucking her in, no black oily void to drag her under and suffocate her. She'd never been this close to anyone—not even her parents—without having something rippling in her mind. She was so astonished she could barely remember she was standing in the grip of an enormously strong stranger with no one around to help if she couldn't control the situation.

"And if I don't let go?" he asked, lowering his head to inhale her scent again. Cinnamon and sin filled his lungs. Of course he was going to let her go, but not until she learned her lesson. A little fear would be good for her. She needed self-preservation to kick in. Where he was taking her, every single sense had to be honed razor-edged sharp.

The words whispered so softly in her ear, the warm

breath fanning her cheek, snapped Tansy out of her shock. *Let go!* She blasted her way into his mind, slamming her fingers hard on his pressure point, jerking his elbow down so she could slip free, even as her foot kicked back to rake down his shin.

Nothing happened. His arm remained locked tight around her throat; his body didn't even rock from hers, and her heel never touched him. Her mind actually recoiled from his, as if she'd bounced off—hard. Hard enough to set her head pounding.

"Who are you?" For the first time there was a tremor in her voice.

He let her go, stepping away from her, yet holding her hand so she couldn't withdraw the knife. "Now, you understand, you aren't the only one in the world with hidden talents."

Very carefully she flexed her fingers, indicating she wanted to let go. Instantly he responded, removing his hand from hers to allow her to drop her arm. Tansy didn't look at him, but she knew he'd felt her hand tremble. She detested showing weakness, but she'd never had anyone resist her so completely. She needed to keep him distracted while she led him to her camp, where she had a weapon or two that might afford her some protection.

"Just tell me who you are and why you're here." She started toward the trail again and this time he fell into step beside her. When he made a movement toward the inside of his shirt, her breath hitched, but he only pulled out his wallet and flipped it open, holding it out to her.

His eyes fascinated her. Midnight blue, so blue they were almost black, unblinking and intent, much like those of the predator she'd been studying for the last year. He focused completely on his prey, and right now that was Tansy. He held her mesmerized, unable to look away from him until he allowed it.

The movement of the wallet allowed her to tear her gaze

away from those dangerous eyes, and she glanced with dismay at his identification. FBI. Only she didn't believe it. Everything about him screamed military. She shook her head. "I'm not buying your story." She started up the trail with a forced sigh. "Just tell me what you want and get off my mountain."

"I need your help."

Her heart stuttered. The breath caught in her lungs and stayed there. Fear skated through her body. Her throat closed, panic rising while she battled with the sudden roaring in her mind as a door creaked open and voices began to spill out. She shook her head, afraid to speak, afraid she might scream, afraid once she started she would never stop. She counted her steps instead, placing one foot carefully in front of the other, forcing her mind to go blank, forcing air through her lungs while she mutely shook her head.

"Tansy?" There was concern in his tone.

She'd gone pale beneath her tan, and little beads of perspiration dotted her forehead. Tansy wiped them away with a leaden hand, holding the door closed while it shook and moaned, pushing hard against her will. "Go away." Her voice was a mere whisper of sound.

He kept pace easily, even though he wasn't walking on the trail, but in the rougher, thicker grass. "I'm afraid I can't do that."

"Go away, Mr. Montague. I can't help you." She continued to climb, averting her face so that it was impossible for him to see her mouth trembling.

"That's not the truth, Tansy. I've got a file on you four inches thick. You're the real thing, and whatever bullshit you've been feeding law enforcement across the country about losing your abilities in a climbing accident doesn't cut it with me."

She swallowed hard, braced herself, and turned to face him. "If you have a file on me, I'm certain it included the fact that I spent eight months in a hospital. You seem a very thorough kind of man to me, and you're not FBI, so your little badge doesn't cut it with me."

Kadan moved in behind her, crowding so close she could feel the heat emanating from his body. She might look angry, but he was far too well trained not to have noticed the hint of desperate fear in her eyes and she *detested* that he knew she was afraid. "Not of you," she murmured aloud, pouring contempt into her voice. "Never of you. Get off my mountain and leave me alone."

"What happened?"

She took a deep, shuddering breath, her fingers closing to form two tight fists. "You're a perfect stranger—a man I don't want to know. I'm a photographer, working with permits on this reserve. As far as I know, you don't have the right to be here, or to question me. If you really are FBI, then go talk to my lawyer."

"Now you're just being rude."

She felt rude. He was getting to her because she was so shaken. Tansy took another breath and let it out.

The sudden buildup of hostile energy hit her. It was hard and fast and came from just beyond Kadan.

Kadan felt the surge of aggressive, threatening energy blast him, and he caught Tansy by the wrist, whirling around, thrusting her behind him, placing his body between her and danger. She stumbled and nearly went down, but he continued moving in a circle, pulling his weapon, finger on the trigger, squeezing as the enemy attacked.

No! Back!

The voice filled his mind even as Tansy leapt over him, directly in between his gun and the attacking cougar. His finger was already pulling the trigger, his aim true. He managed to jerk just enough to miss Tansy by a breath, but the mountain lion hit her full-force on her chest, driving her back and into him so they both went down. For one moment he stared into the cat's eyes, its breath hot on his face, and then it was gone, leaping off Tansy into heavy brush and disappearing.

Everything in him stilled. Kadan locked his arms around Tansy and rolled, pulling her beneath him so he could run his hands over her body, checking for damage. "Talk to me."

The cougar had knocked the breath from her body, hitting her with the force of a locomotive. She'd likely be bruised, and she wasn't getting air, but there were no slash marks as he'd expected. The cat had pulled in her claws when she struck, and she hadn't bitten Tansy's exposed throat—and neither had his bullet hit her. He hung his head for a moment, breathing his fear away.

"What the hell were you thinking, protecting the cat like that?" he demanded, fury replacing terror. "I could have shot you. I came a whisper away from killing you." He found he was shaking her, and, shocked, he drew a deep breath, trying to pull back from the edge of disaster. He was trembling, something he never did, but he had come so close to blowing her head off. It took a moment for him to realize that his hands were wrapped around her slender throat, thumbs pressed up into her jaw, tipping her head up so her huge eyes stared directly into his.

Tansy tried to swallow, but his hands were wrapped around her throat, thumbs pressing tightly. She remained very still, shocked at the truth. She hadn't been saving the cougar's life—she'd saved his life. It had been imperative to save his life. The moment she'd felt the threat and knew the cougar was going to attack, she'd leapt over him from a crouching position, giving away another hidden secret, to keep him from harm. She blinked up at him as he slowly removed his hands from around her neck.

"You could get off of me." Her chest hurt. She was feeling every single rock digging into her back. "You weigh a ton."

He merely looked down at her for a long moment without

responding, his blue-black eyes holding heat and a raw lust, making her heart pound, but then he blinked and his eyes went flat and hard, impossible for her to read. He stood up, drawing her with him, holding her steady until he was certain she was able to stand on her own.

Tansy dusted off her jeans and then rubbed her palms down her thighs, looking around for the sunglasses that had flown off her face when the cat slammed into her. "Thanks for not shooting me." She would never admit to him that she'd leapt in front of him to save his life, not for one moment. At a much later date, when he wasn't around to confuse her, she'd take out her motives and examine them, but for now, she'd put it down to saving human life.

"You're damned lucky."

She nodded. "I know that and I really do appreciate that you're that good."

"Are you going to tell me how you made that leap from a crouch to over the top of me so fast?"

Tansy shrugged. "I don't know how I do things. I just do them." There were a lot of things about her that couldn't be explained.

"Have you ever heard of a man named Peter Whitney?"

She blinked. Her face went expressionless as she searched the ground for her sunglasses, giving herself time to think. "I think most people in scientific communities have heard of Dr. Whitney," she answered carefully as she retrieved her glasses from under some brush and wiped them off on her shirt. "I believe he was murdered." She looked him straight in the eye so he could see she meant exactly what she said. "If you've found some piece of evidence you want me to 'feel' for you, I can't do it."

"You believe he's dead?"

Tansy frowned. "It was big news. He disappeared and everyone thought he was murdered. Wasn't he?"

Kadan shook his head slowly. "No, he's alive."

"That's impossible. My parents knew him quite well. If he was alive, they'd know."

"How well is quite well? They were friends?"

Tansy shrugged. "No one was really friends with Dr. Whitney. They were colleagues and they respected each other. My father and Dr. Whitney went to school together and they had a lot of common interests."

"Were you one of them?" Kadan asked.

Tansy's mouth tightened. She pushed around him to start up the trail again. "I think this conversation has gone on long enough. It's getting personal and I don't even know what you want yet. I have work to do tonight and I need food, so if you're coming, then let's get moving."

Kadan fell into step behind her, alert for any more threats from the large cat, his gaze shifting around the area, but more than that, his every sense reaching out for information. "Dr. Whitney conducted experiments on children about twenty-five years ago. He collected infant girls from various orphanages around the world. He was looking for specific talents, female babies with psychic abilities."

Tansy kept climbing while the roaring in her head sent her pulse pounding in her temples. Counting. Ten steps.

"He named each of the girls after flowers. Tansy is a flowering herb that grows in Europe and Asia."

Fifteen steps.

"He enhanced those girls psychically and genetically altered many of them as well. When he removed the filters in their brains, he opened them up for psychic sludge. Many have a difficult time in everyday society. Most can't be around people at all. They have frequent headaches and nosebleeds. Seizures are common when there is too much psychic overload. Some can do amazing physical things, such as leap over a man from a crouching position."

He wasn't lying to her. All of her life she'd been different. All of her life she'd fought to stay sane when each time she touched an object, or sat in a chair, or reached for a door handle, the door in her mind opened and the voices poured in. She kept counting, whispering the numbers under her breath, while she tried to quiet the voice inside that was wailing with fear.

"He did other things too. He has a breeding program, matching the girls, who are now women, with men he experimented on in the military. He created several Ghost-Walker teams. I'm a member of one of those teams. I agreed to be psychically enhanced. At the time, we didn't know he took those experiments even further without our consent. He enhanced us genetically as well as paired us with the women from his earlier experiments. Our best guess is that he hopes to create unique soldiers from the unions."

Thirty steps. Things were clicking into place, and the door in her mind creaked ominously, threatening her sanity. She'd been so close to peace. So close.

"You were adopted, Tansy, and Dr. Whitney allowed some of the children he experimented on to be adopted out. He usually kept tight tabs on the girls, so I'm asking you, did you see him while you grew up?"

Had she seen him? She shivered, suddenly cold, thrown back into childhood memories she didn't want to have. Seeing Whitney was one of the few things she and her parents ever fought over. She rubbed her hands up and down her arms. She would never forget that man, the way he looked at her as if she wasn't human. He was cold and dispassionate, studying her the way a scientist might an insect. She'd begged her father not to leave her alone with him, but he would grab her mother's hand, looking upset, and walk out of the room, pulling her mother with him. It was the only time she felt vulnerable and without their support.

"Yes." Her voice was so low, she doubted he could hear. She made an effort to push back the images crowding into her mind. "He was—oily." Whitney had only to touch her skin and she would drown in a black vat of oil, suffocating under the thick stain of a twisted mind. She hadn't recognized the feeling, or identified it yet with sickness in her earlier years, but the ooze had poured into her until she couldn't breathe, until she choked, smothered by his megalomaniacal personality.

Kadan breathed in and out, hating himself. He was hurting her. He was even skating close to her edge of sanity. He could feel the pain in her like a knife through his body and mind. He'd studied every report on her. She was very sensitive, especially to violence, and he was a violent man. She didn't need to feel anything when she touched him or any of his belongings. In spite of the fact that she claimed her talent was gone, there was no way that it had disappeared. He was both an anchor and a shielder, which meant he could hold all psychic energy at bay and direct it away from her.

"You know your parents had to have known."

She spun around so fast, her aggression blasting him hard enough to kick in his reflexes. His hand closed around the hilt of his knife before he could stop himself. She was thinking about kicking him in the chest, but she controlled her temper, her blue eyes shimmering with that strange violet light that intrigued him. It had to be an enhancement, but he couldn't figure out exactly what it was used for.

Kadan lifted his hand, palm out, before she could speak. "Don't be angry with me. I'm giving you the facts. You want to hear them, don't you?" He kept his voice calm, soft, that little bit hypnotic. She was susceptible to sound; he could tell by the way she relaxed in spite of herself. "You seem like the kind of woman who prefers knowledge."

"Don't make assumptions about my parents."

He didn't want to hurt her, but he damn well wanted to do a number on her parents. They were both considered geniuses, and they must have guessed exactly what Whitney was up to. Sharon Meadows wanted a child at any cost, and she was more than willing to keep her mouth shut about Whitney in order to have one. With their money and connections, they could have had any child, why this one? Why one so damaged?

And why had Don Meadows agreed to stay quiet as well? Why not simply get another child for Sharon and blow the whistle on Whitney's experiments? He needed to look a little closer into Don and Sharon's government contracts as well as their personal lives, because their silence didn't go with the kind of picture his reports had drawn of them.

"I'm sorry," he said, allowing his voice to grow warm like spreading honey. "I shouldn't have said that."

She knew his accusation was true, but she refused to allow the thought into her mind. She needed time and he didn't blame her. If he could have, he would have spared her that, but they were going to have to work fast to figure out what was going on.

"If Whitney conducted these experiments on military men . . ."

"Specifically men trained in Special Forces," he interrupted.

"Great. That's all I need." She pressed her fingertips to her eyes. "If you're military and no one has heard of Ghost-Walkers, this information has to be classified."

"It is."

Tansy swung away from him, keeping her back to him to hide her expression. He didn't need to see her face or look into her eyes to know she was in pain. He swore silently as he followed her up the trail toward her camp.

"Don't tell me any more," Tansy cautioned. "Really. I don't want to know any more, not if it's classified. You want something from me I can't give you. There's no need to say another word about whatever is going on. Find one of the other girls."

"They can't do what you do."

He refused to lull her into a false sense of security, or lie to her, or even try to soft-soap her. She was going to be walking into hell with him. The only thing he could do for her was to try to give her all the truth, and to give his word that he'd be standing beside her the entire time. That was all he had for her.

"I can't do what you think I can."

They were nearing the top of the trail. The sun was setting and the colors changed abruptly as they topped the ridge. Orange and red poured down from the sky like molten fire. Tansy paused to survey the colors and Kadan stepped up beside her, admiring the view. Below them was a valley and then beyond that another granite peak. Stretched out as far as the eye could see was pine and fir forest. Small natural lakes and a few spilling waterfalls dotted the hills while the setting sun washed the granite in gold.

"There's a big difference between can't and won't," Kadan said, keeping his eyes fixed on the beautiful sight surrounding them. "I think if you let me explain what's going on, you'll understand why I needed to come all this way to pull you out of retirement in spite of the fact that your last case landed you in the hospital. I wouldn't have made the decision lightly."

He said it so matter-of-factly. *Landed her in the hospital.* As if it had been a small vacation for her—or as if she had been slightly wounded. Tansy swallowed the bile rising and began meticulously counting again, keeping her mind on her foot placement as she hurried along the winding trail to her campsite.

Shadows shifted as the sun dipped lower and the wind picked up, ruffling the trees. With the breeze came a rush of sound, voices murmuring, slyly laughing, the first burst of visions, blood splashed on the walls. A soft moan escaped, fear clogging her throat. She pressed her fingers hard against her eyes. "You have to go. You have to go now."

They were on the edge of her camp, her space, her sanctuary. He couldn't come here, couldn't be allowed to take it away from her.

"I want to go," he said quietly. "I would if I could, but too many people will die if I do."

Tansy shook her head in despair, glanced at the radio and then away. She could call her father and he might be able to put a stop to this. If he had known the military was sending someone with a request, he would have warned her—or would he have? In one revelation, this stranger had changed her entire world all over again.

She drank from a bottle of water, keeping her back to him, trying to sort out the things he'd told her. "Does my father know you're here?"

"Only the general. This mission is classified."

"I'm not in the military." Tansy sank down into the one lawn chair she'd brought and forced her gaze to meet his.

He spread his hands out. "Do you think I want to come here and upset you like this? People are dying . . ."

She sighed. "People are always dying, Mr. Montague."

"Kadan," he corrected. "And not like this."

She closed her eyes. "I can't do it anymore. Yes, I do have some special gifts. I can leap high and I have fast reflexes, I can feel violent or threatening energy, but I fried my talent, or short-circuited it, or something, when I fell while I was climbing. Maybe it happened when I went to the hospital. I honestly don't know, but when I touch things, nothing happens. And I'm grateful for that. I wish I could help you, but I can't."

Kadan shrugged out of his pack and stretched, loosening his muscles as he surveyed the campsite. She knew what she was doing; sheltered from prying eyes even from above, the camp was comfortable, protected, but could catch the breezes coming in.

"I have a gift for sound, Tansy, and you're lying. I can hear it in your voice."

She shrugged. "You can think whatever you like, but I can't help you. There are a few others I've heard of, psychics that can track killers. That's why you're here, isn't it? You need me to go after a killer."

"Not just an ordinary killer, a GhostWalker. I've got an enhanced Special Forces–trained killer on the loose, and I need to track him down and eliminate him immediately." Kadan reached for the coffeepot, dumped out the old liquid, and began filling the pot with water.

Tansy flicked him a glance from under long lashes. He moved with fluid grace, at home in the wilderness, completely confident in his abilities. He scanned the surrounding area several times, and she knew that if she asked he could tell her where everything in the camp was positioned and the best escape route available to them should they need one. She'd worked with men like him, cool under fire, dangerous as hell, yet he had something different, something even more. Power clung to him.

"I can't help you."

"The GhostWalkers are like you, Tansy. Their lives have been changed forever. They have the same headaches, the nosebleeds, the seizures. They're good men and women and they are under fire every minute of the day. They carry out missions no one else could touch. They put their lives on the line every day. You're one of us."

She shook her head, keeping her voice calm and firm. "I wish I could help you, I really do, but I lost the one talent you need."

He sighed softly. "I swear to you, Tansy, I don't want to do this the hard way. I want you to understand how important it is so that you at least comprehend why I had to come up here to get you. The GhostWalkers are considered too dangerous to be under suspicion like this. I'm under orders not to trust any of them. I can't confide in them or ask for help or even tell them that their lives are in jeopardy just because of what they can do. These are my friends, my teammates. Men I've trained with and gone into combat with, men who have had my back and saved my life. Some of them have families."

She recognized that he was a man of few words, that he rarely explained himself, but that he was going out of his way to do so for her. *I don't want to do this the hard way.* Her heart jumped, but she kept her face composed.

"Were you given orders to bring me back?" Men like Kadan Montague carried out their missions no matter the cost to them—or to anyone else. She waited. Holding her breath.

"Yes."

"Whether I agree or not." She made it a statement, but there was a breathless plea in her voice she couldn't stop.

CHAPTER 3

Kadan sighed. "Let's just take one thing at a time. What do you have for dinner? I'm a fairly good cook."

Tansy's mouth went dry. She couldn't sit still with the rush of adrenaline. He was going to force her to go back with him. Tansy leapt from her chair and paced across the ground to where she kept her food supplies, needing the action to hide her thoughts. There had to be a way to escape. She knew the mountain like the back of her hand. If she got out of his sight, she could get away and hide. If he really had a tight timetable, he wouldn't have the time to look for her. But she had to keep it together and not panic.

She turned from the crisp cooler and found him inches from her body. He was so silent she hadn't heard him approach. Worse, she hadn't sensed him either. She was used to feeling the energy that radiated from people, but with him, there was nothing at all to warn her he was close. She realized she was holding her breath. She inhaled and took the scent of him into her lungs. Deep inside, her body sizzled and burned in an unfamiliar way. Fear shimmered through her, not at the prospect of this man attempting to force her compliance, but because as rough and scarred as he was, he filled her senses and mind with a sensual heat she couldn't ignore.

Tansy pushed the vegetables into his hands. His thumb brushed the sensitive skin of her forearm, a long stroke that had to be deliberate. Her gaze jumped to his. "I don't like to be touched."

"You shouldn't have such beautiful skin then," he answered, sounding completely unrepentant and not in the least perturbed by her reprimand, when, truthfully, he was shocked that he'd let his guard down so far with her that he was acting out of character.

Tansy shook her head. "Don't try to flirt with me, not when you've come up here determined to drag me back down into evil."

A slow smile changed his entire face, softened every hard line, lit up the blue of his eyes, and changed his mouth from that hint of cruelty to pure sensuality. "Honey, if I was going to flirt with you, you'd know it. That was the pure truth, whether you want to hear it or not." And touching her had shocked the hell out of him.

It wasn't a few butterflies reacting; an entire forest of them took flight in her stomach. "You were flirting," she said accusingly, frowning at him.

His smile widened as he turned away to the small table where he took the chopping board from her along with the knife. "Maybe. A little. But you do have beautiful skin."

"Thank you." Tansy fired up the gas stove and put on water for rice. "I have to work tonight. And you can't come. You'll scare my cougar away."

"She follows you. I found her tracking you through the trees down to the waterfall. She's dangerous, Tansy."

"The whole world is dangerous."

"Say my name."

She touched her teeth to her lower lip and shrugged. "Kadan, then. Why does it matter?"

His blue-black eyes flicked over her. "I matter, that's why."

The way he handled the knife with efficiency, chopping vegetables for stir-fry while she pulled her frying pan out of the locked chest where she kept her cooking pots, seemed to fascinate her. He noticed she couldn't stop watching the movements of his hands, so fast they nearly blurred, each stroke deliberate, and maybe he was showing off a little. Chagrined at behaving like a kid with his first crush, Kadan forced himself to focus on his mission.

"The first time you helped the police find a serial killer, you were only thirteen years old. What in the world made you do such a thing?" he asked. "Especially when the cost to you was so high." He turned to look at her. "You do more than simply pick up an object and know what a person was thinking and feeling; you're an empath. Why would a teenager ever put herself in a position such as tracking killers? That made no sense to me." *And how could your family allow it?* The thought spilled out before he could censor it.

Her head snapped up and she glared at him, proving she could pick up his thoughts. "My family understood my reasons, and unlike you, they believe in free will."

"So you are also telepathic. Apparently that talent didn't get knocked out of your head in that climbing accident."

She didn't even blink, but flicked him a look of censure from under her long lashes. "Apparently not."

She was cool under fire, he had to give her that. "Just how many talents do you have?"

She shrugged. "How many do you have?"

He flashed her another smile. "Good girl. Don't give away too much to the enemy." He heated a small amount of oil and tossed in the chopped vegetables. "I'm not, you know."

"My enemy? Maybe not, but I'm listening to everything you say, and I think you're prepared to use force to try to get me to track your killer."

"You really don't pull your punches, do you?"

"Why would I? You came up here with your own agenda. You don't really care what my reasons are for not cooperating. My reasons don't matter to you, and quite frankly, neither do I. As long as you get the job done, that's what is important to you."

Kadan sighed. "I have no more choice in this than you do. I have orders, Tansy, and people are going to die if we don't stop this."

"How does that make you any different from Whitney? For all you know he was following orders. He's a scientist and he works for the government. He could have been under orders to develop psychic warfare; in fact, in order to conduct his experiments on you, he had to have convinced somebody high up he could do it. They had to have known about his earliest experiments."

He let the first surge of anger wash over him and dissipate while he lifted the frying pan off the heat and tossed the vegetables. Setting them back on the stove and adding a little soy sauce gave him a little more time so he was able to keep his expression exactly the same. "I've been more than up-front with you. Insulting me is not going to help anything."

Her eyebrow shot up. "It wasn't meant as an insult. I think it's a legitimate question. As I understand it, your GhostWalker program is top security clearance. You're a government secret, so secret that if you can't find out who is killing people, they want to eliminate all of you. Who has that kind of power, to play with people's lives, to decide whether they live or die? I don't see that they're much different than your killer. And Whitney maybe just carried out his orders, like you're doing now."

Maybe she was hitting a little too close to home. Of

course they'd all speculated that several of their bosses had a hand in creating them. Whitney couldn't have done it alone, and he was still working for the government, sanctioned by someone, because he was escaping every effort to capture or destroy him. He had friends in high places.

"I suppose you have a point. There's every possibility Whitney is following orders, but what he's doing is wrong in so many ways I couldn't even begin to tell you."

"And if the order comes down to eliminate your fellow GhostWalkers, will you carry it out because they told you to do it?"

He removed the vegetables from the heat and turned completely to face her, his face settling into hard lines. His eyes went flat and cold, the blue turning nearly black, focused and hungry like the cougar. "There would be a war like no one has ever seen before."

A shiver of fear crept down her spine, but she liked him a lot better for it. He wasn't joking, and so far, she was fairly certain he had told her the truth about everything. She was very sure he meant what he implied—he would go to war for or with his friends. She gave him a concession, then, a piece of herself because he'd revealed a part of his character to her.

"My parents always told me I was special. That my talent was a tremendous gift, not a curse, and that I could do things no one else could do for a reason. I started tracking serial killers when I was thirteen years old because I believed that was what I was supposed to do with my gift. I heard about somebody dumping the bodies of young girls next to schools and I thought, *I can stop him.* So I did."

Her voice was calm, remote; no expression chased across her face. Kadan knew self-preservation when he saw it. Tansy had removed herself from her past and simply recited the details as if they'd happened to someone else—and maybe they had. Her experiences certainly had to have changed her from that young, innocent girl. And she was giving him something of herself, whether she wanted to admit it or not.

"It must have been difficult, especially with you being an empath and so young. Did Whitney help prepare you?"

Tansy frowned. "How would he have helped me?"

"There are exercises you can do to strengthen each of the gifts you have and ways to learn to combat the repercussions of using psychic energy. I would have thought Whitney would have taught them to you."

"No, he didn't teach me anything. He studied me. If there was a way to combat the rush of impressions from objects, I certainly was never told. I wore gloves, of course, but the feelings, particularly emotions that were violent, often leaked through anyway. Whitney liked to observe other people's pain. It helped with his own."

Everything in him stilled. She had revealed an important piece of information without even knowing what she was giving him. "What pain?"

"He uses other people's pain to drown out his own. I think his pain stems from perceived abandonment, real or not; he feels very disconnected from everyone around him. He has rage toward his parents and teachers, people who didn't recognize his genius. He's very patriotic and has anger toward certain individuals in the government who don't share his vision, because he believes he's smarter and they should listen to him. All of that causes pain, but he doesn't recognize that it does. He can't connect with anyone."

"He has a daughter."

She nodded, chewing on her lower lip thoughtfully, frowning while she did so. "Lily. He spoke of her sometimes, and when he did, I could feel a rush of emotion in him, but it wasn't like my parents when they touched me. It wasn't the same as anything I've ever identified with as a parent's love. He views her as an extension of himself. He's a megalomaniac, has an absolute belief that he's superior to everyone else and that no one will ever measure up to his capabilities except perhaps Lily—or her children."

Kadan nodded. "That's a fair assessment of Dr. Whitney."

"You're certain he's still alive? My parents—well, my father—always insisted we use him as a doctor, but I haven't seen him since he was supposedly murdered."

"What kinds of things did he do to you?"

"He told Mom and Dad he was helping me with the headaches, but they never went away or even got better. Mostly he gave me physicals, asked a lot of questions, was very interested in whether I had sex or not, and took a lot of blood and tissue samples. He also spent a lot of time on my eyes. He was very interested in the fact that I almost always have to wear dark glasses and that I see differently than other people."

Kadan was very interested in whether or not she had sex as well, but figured this wasn't the best time to ask her. "What's different about the way you see?"

Tansy shrugged, but didn't comment.

Kadan let it go. "Did he give you injections?"

She nodded. "They hurt like hell." She frowned. "You know, I didn't always get a lot off of him, the way I do most people. Not him, exactly, his things. At the time, when I touched objects, I could read a lot about a person, but it was more difficult with him. Of course, by that time, I tried to wear gloves everywhere I went."

"You haven't felt anything even when you touch an object I've touched, have you?" Kadan asked. "I'm an anchor, which means that I can draw psychic energy away from you. I can also shield both of us from any energy and keep others from feeling ours."

He deftly added the vegetables to the rice and took the plates she handed him to serve the meal on. "My talents come in handy on missions when we need to hide from the enemy."

"But not so handy tracking serial killers," Tansy observed.

He nodded. "I'm good at working puzzles out, and once I'm pointed in the right direction, I'll find him, but I need a little help."

Tansy's heart jumped. She could never allow him to lull her into a false sense of security. "I'm sorry that help can't be me, Kadan, but it can't be. I know you've got all the ugly little details of my hospitalization. They couldn't take away all those voices, the victims—or the killers. Do you have any idea what it's like to hear screams and feel someone's desperate last thoughts all the time, and I mean *all* the time? To know the mind of a killer intimately? The delicious perverted pleasure he gets out of carving someone up, or burying them alive?" The door in her mind creaked ominously and whispers grew. She took a deep breath, controlled herself, and slammed it shut. "You're already bringing those days back and I haven't even tried to help you."

"I can keep most of the psychic spill from targeting you."

She turned her head and removed her glasses, looking him straight in the eye. "No, you can't, not and have me track him. I'd need to feel him, get inside his mind, to do what you're asking. You and I both know you can't take it out of my head once it's there."

Kadan hated that she was right. And he hated it more that she drew on gloves. She had touched him and hadn't felt anything, he'd protected her, but she didn't trust him and for a good reason—truthfully, she *couldn't*. He had to bring her back with him. There were days when his job sucked, and this was one of them.

"Sit down and let's eat. You can tell me about that cat. She's out there watching us now. I can feel her staring at us."

Tansy took the plate he handed her, careful, even with the gloves she'd put on, to keep from touching him. "She's curious about you. She probably hasn't seen anyone else in months. And her den is close. She's due to give birth anytime." Excitement flashed in her voice. "I'm hoping to get some great shots. If I'm lucky, she might change her mind and use the cave I've set up in to film the event, although so far she's been ignoring it."

"Why don't you persuade her?"

"I can't do that."

"You stopped her from attacking. If she'd wanted to do it, she could have done some major damage to you, but she didn't," he pointed out. "You have to have some control over her."

Tansy sank down onto a log and indicated that he could have the one chair she'd brought. "Maybe, but it's not really like that. I have an affinity with animals, I've always had it. But I don't really talk to them, not telepathically."

"Are you certain?"

She chewed on her lower lip. He liked that lower lip and found himself staring as her small teeth tugged at it.

"I 'push' a little to get them to do what I want, but it's not a conscious thing." She took a bite of the stir-fry. The man could cook. "Not bad."

"Self-preservation."

His eyes crinkled around the edges, tiny lines showing that he squinted a lot. His long lashes were thick and dark, and helped to cover the expression in his dark blue eyes.

"I've never been afraid of animals," Tansy said. "I've always liked being around them. I can touch them and not find myself somewhere else."

"What does that mean?" Kadan's low voice slid into her mind like soft butter. "Finding yourself somewhere else? What does that mean?"

Her expression closed down immediately and she shrugged. "When I touch objects, the world narrows and I'm in a tunnel, like an alternate world. Everything bends and curves and the energy is there, preserved for me like a recording, only I'm in it, feeling everything that is happening, no matter what it is." She looked him in the eye again. "*All* of it. Everything. If you are cheating on your wife and feel guilty, I'm there with you. If you're worried about a sick child, or paying your house payment, I'm feeling that fear right along with you."

"If that person is in love . . ."

"Then I am too."

Kadan forced his gaze away from the unconscious plea in her unusually colored eyes. Knots gathered in his gut, hard and tight, giving him hell for doing his job. He believed in what he was doing or he wouldn't have come looking for her. The vicious murders had to be stopped. And if they weren't—if the faceless names above them continued to believe that the GhostWalkers were responsible for the murders, they would never risk the controversial program ever seeing the light of day. Kadan had no illusions about their lives. The GhostWalkers—he and his friends—were expendable. Worse, they were something the government would want to sweep under the carpet like dirty laundry. They'd be sent out on a suicide mission, or quietly eliminated.

He swore under his breath and kept his gaze fixed on the surrounding forest, studying the trees and brush as if each piece of foliage intrigued him. Truthfully, all he saw was that look in her eyes.

"Why the bullshit about not having your talent anymore?"

Tansy sighed. "It's complicated. I can't actually do that work anymore. I can't separate the emotions and voices, so I'm not lying when I say I don't have the talent. Once the word went out that I had a climbing accident, I was left alone for the most part. My father handles all the calls coming in, and I think now enough time has passed that most people have forgotten me." She waited until he looked at her. "I wish you would."

"Forget you?"

She nodded, willing him to just walk away and pretend he'd never seen her.

A prickle of awareness slid down his spine, and he reacted instantly, an automatic reflex, diving for her, driving her off of the log, backward, his hands pulling her smaller body into his to protect her as he took them over the small ledge to roll down the slope. He registered the crack of the bullet shattering the tree behind his head where he'd been sitting, followed by the boom of the rifle. She went with him, keeping her body tight against his so they rolled smoothly. The rocks and brush had to hurt as she went over them, but she kept silent.

Coming to a halt, he signaled her to stay low and to scoot back into the heavier timber and brush behind them. She didn't ask questions, but stayed on her belly, easing her body backward, searching with her toes for a purchase in the dirt to help drag her into concealment. Kadan backed up with her, sliding into the brush as if he were born there, drawing a gun from his boot and slipping it into her hand in one smooth motion.

Do you know how to use this?

She blinked at him, but she shouldn't have been shocked. The moment he felt the danger, he had connected with her, so that she felt it too. His entry into her mind had been as smooth as him drawing the gun and putting it into her hand. She nodded her reassurance. They were both telepathic, and somehow that made her feel less alone—less apart from everyone. She'd never actually met another human being with psychic powers.

Stay to cover. I'm going hunting.

She didn't want Kadan to leave her. He seemed solid and safe, and exuded absolute confidence. *I'm guessing that's not some random hunter poaching.*

Not with that rifle. You stay to cover.

He was already moving away from her, and it took every

ounce of self-control she had to keep from reaching out and holding on to him.

You'll be safe, Kadan reassured her with implacable confidence. He had no other choice but to succeed. That was a sniper, and he'd tracked Kadan to this place, which meant someone very high up didn't want Kadan to succeed in solving the murders. Not that he was all that surprised; someone had wanted the GhostWalkers program gone and everyone involved dead from the beginning—and that someone worked at the White House. The GhostWalkers had been unable to pin down just whom the threat was coming from, so there was no chance to eliminate him, but if Kadan got out of this alive, they'd be one step closer to solving the puzzle. Not too many people knew he'd been sent out.

He circled around Tansy's camp, keeping his distance, and keeping his head down. Movement attracted the eye, and he wanted no part of his body showing to a sniper, or even to give away his position. Whoever they'd sent after him would be good.

He allowed himself grim amusement. But they wouldn't be good enough, because in a world of kill or be killed, there were few men like him. He was wearing clothing that reflected the images around him, making him nearly invisible. He cloaked himself, changing his skin color like a chameleon to blend in with his surroundings. And then he began to move with the stealth of a wolf.

He went up, going to high ground, continuing to circle so he could come up behind his stalker. There'd been only one bullet, and the sniper would have moved immediately, but once Kadan found the trail, he would be able to follow it.

He was taking a chance leaving Tansy. Not that the sniper could get to her; Tansy was too clever to give herself away. But she'd be making up her mind to run, and she knew the mountain. She'd been living up in the Sierras for months. She'd have confidence in herself and she was too smart to go back to camp. He sighed. He'd have to track her down again after disposing of their enemy.

He stayed low to the ground, making his way through the forest until it eventually gave way to the great granite boulders and jutting cliffs. There wasn't as much foliage, but he blended in with the rock and moved at a steady pace, not too fast to draw the eye, but fast enough to get around behind the sniper. The man would be moving toward Tansy's camp, taking the shortest route, with as much cover as possible. He would want to get the job done as quickly as he could, and that meant he had to be on the move.

Kadan skirted several jagged boulders, looking for a way up so he would have a better view of the area surrounding Tansy's camp. A giant boulder rose over the top of several granite slabs, one sitting precariously on top of the other, some leaning and a few shooting through the middle like great towers. He reached up with his fingertips and found an indentation. That was all he needed for the climb. He went up slowly, like a spider, clinging to the rock face, careful not to disturb the loose dirt and rock on his way to the top.

He had microscopic setae on the pads of his fingers and at the end of each individual seta were one thousand tinier spatulae, or tips, which were so thin as to render them under the wavelength of visible light. Not even his fellow GhostWalkers knew why he could cling to any surface, including the ceiling, but a single seta could lift nearly fifty pounds of weight. He could support his entire body weight with just one hand. It had taken him a great deal of time to learn to use his ability to "walk" over any surface, even hanging upside down, but the weeks of training had been well worth it. He could stick and unstick himself at least ten times a second as he ran up walls.

He moved slowly now, but ordinarily he could climb the

face of rock in minutes. Sticking was easy enough. Unsticking was a bit more of a problem, but he'd learned the technique over time, until he could move with incredible speed when necessary. Unfortunately, he often wore a thin pair of gloves to cover the fact that the pads of his fingers were different. The microscopic hairs were bristles, unseen but felt. He knew what Tansy felt like always having to cover her differences. He'd learned to live with the strange pads and embrace the things he could do with them, after the first wave of anger at discovering he was genetically altered as well as psychically. If the GhostWalkers' enemy in the White House knew that all the men and women in the program had been genetically as well as psychically enhanced, Kadan was certain the order would have already gone out to destroy them all. Or maybe he knew and thought of them as abominations and that's why he was so determined to rid the government of their services. Kadan had heard the term applied to them before.

Once above the forest, he lay flat and took a cautious look around the area below him. He studied each section. Tansy would have slipped deeper into the woods below. It would take a few minutes for the shock to wear off, and then she'd seize the opportunity to make a run for it. He sighed, knowing he was going to have to track her again for sure.

Kadan picked out the route that would be the sniper's best choice and spent a patient ten minutes watching the brush for movement. The wind picked up in strength as the night wore on, and the needles in the trees and the leaves on the bushes began to gently sway. Everything in him tightened. The sniper would move with the wind.

Motion just south of Tansy's camp caught his eye and he focused there, catching sight of a blur of darkness moving behind the trees before disappearing. He let out his breath. He had the man now, and he quickly plotted a course to intercept. Just as he began to move, he caught a glimpse of something sticking out from behind a fairly large tree trunk. He studied the shape carefully, wishing he hadn't shrugged out of his pack. He could have used his field glasses, because he suspected that strange shape was something commonly known as "tree cancer," a body part protruding from behind the trunk that indicated that a sniper had set up shop there and was waiting for his spotter to mark a distance.

His heart contracted painfully. What the hell were they setting up? Or whom?

Tansy, where are you? No bullshit. There's two of them. I need to know your position to know that you're safe.

Telepathy over long distance was always shaky, especially connecting with the same wavelength of someone he wasn't very familiar with. Oftentimes there could be a few seconds—or even minutes—of delay. He counted every heartbeat, wondering if she was being stubborn or hiding from him. Wondering if she knew that the more they communicated, the easier the intimacy of mind contact would become. She wouldn't want that. She wouldn't want him running around in her head. She already had too many strangers there.

Then she was there, flooding his mind with her. His body reacted to her close proximity, the sweetness of her, the feminine rush of heat and silk. The taste of cinnamon bursting in his mouth. There was fear, determination, even courage, although she didn't recognize herself as courageous. Mostly she was filled with concern—not for him, certainly not for herself—but for the cougar.

He groaned aloud. That damned cat. She'd flung herself in front of a gun for the animal. He should have known she'd be unwavering in her resolution to keep the animal safe.

I'm making my way up to the cougar's den.

Are you heading south from your camp? He knew the answer before her words formed in his mind. The spotter was edging toward the southernmost point of Tansy's camp. Maybe he saw her earlier tracks, or maybe something she'd done had tipped the man off to her presence in the brush, but the spotter was tracking her.

Yes, I'm in the rougher terrain, and circling around to make my way up into the granite to get closer to her den. I have a blind up there, and I can urge her to go to safety if they come close. They won't see the blind.

Her voice still had the little lag time that often accompanied a new connection, but already he felt more familiar with her, his mind adjusting so they rode the same wave with precision. Few were as skilled as he was, and he'd never met anyone untrained who was able to use telepathy as smoothly as he could, but although she sent out her thoughts in a slightly different way from him, she was definitely adept.

I don't want you to move. Stay right where you are, even if they come close. I'm going to draw their attention away from you . . .

No!

She sent an instant and adamant rejection of his idea, and he immediately caught the image of a cop pushing her away and going down, blood on his chest. He'd read the reports, so many of them, dating back to her teenage years, and that particular case had been vicious and bloody and took its toll on everyone. They'd lost the cop and she had been so broken up over it, and that had been in the early years of her tracking career.

He took a breath, let it out, breathing for both of them. *Listen to me, Tansy. I have skills no one else has. I'm a GhostWalker. The things I can do, psychically as well as physically, give me a huge edge. And I've had more training than most men know what to do with.* He was already on the move, soothing her as he used the granite cliff to shortcut his way to the sniper.

This time he moved fast, using the pads of his fingers to

allow him to climb around and then down. If his boots had been off, he would have gone headfirst even faster, but he just used his upper body strength and fingertips, crossing the wall of granite, moving at breakneck speed, crossing slab after slab. Several times he leapt across gaps, catching by his fingertips.

Both the sniper and the spotter should have targeted him by now, but the expected bullet didn't come. He didn't make the mistake of slowing down; he almost leapfrogged across the rock walls, zigzagging and moving up and down.

I smell him close to me.

His heart jumped again. Adrenaline poured into his body. He looked down and saw the surface of another giant slab of granite. This one had several smaller pieces jutting out from it. It was the fastest way down, but a fairly large jump. He'd have to push off from where he was, catch himself on a rock across and down from him, about five feet away, and then spring back, making another five-foot jump.

Stay still. I'll draw his attention.

He pushed off, deliberately brushing his elbow against loose dirt and rock, sending an avalanche tumbling to the ground below. The gap between boulders was wide, but his fingertips caught and held. The second jump was already planned in his mind, and he turned and leapt, just as the bullet hit the granite beside his left shoulder. Rock splintered, driving slivers into his arm, but he was already in the air, going for the surface below him. As soon as he landed, he let himself drop to the ground, rolling for cover. He kept rolling, smashing into the thicker brush and then going still.

Two more bullets hit the ground to the right of him and just in front of him. He belly-crawled backward into much heavier brush, careful not to disturb branches. Once in the small tunnels made by animals and debris catching on brush, he crawled, using elbows and toes to propel his body along the ground, making his way to where the sniper had set up his rifle.

Within minutes he could feel the violent energy coming at him in waves. The man was sweating; the scent of him carried on the wind. Kadan slid the knife from his boot, transferring it to his teeth as he crawled toward the sniper.

The man stared through his scope, scanning the area, trying to get a bead on Kadan, and Kadan could sense the man's shock at how fast Kadan had come down the granite wall. Even though the sniper had seen Kadan leap with his own eyes, he obviously was beginning to think he'd imagined it. The night shadows had lengthened and grown, and Kadan's reflective clothing and skin tones had made him virtually impossible to see until he moved. The sniper had fired on instinct, but now doubted himself.

Kadan let out his breath, shielding his psychic energy automatically. He didn't have the impression that the sniper was a GhostWalker, produced from Whitney's list of rejected psychic candidates, but he always erred on the side of caution. He had to get close. Very close. He moved again, this time out of the brush. He was more exposed, relying on stealth and his reflective clothing and skin changes to keep him invisible. Moving inches at a time allowed him to keep from drawing the sniper's attention, although more than once, as the man surveyed his surroundings, he looked right at Kadan.

Kadan ceased all movement until the sniper settled behind his rifle once more and took a careful survey around the heavy brush. Once the sniper was busy, Kadan eased his body closer, hardly breathing, not allowing a single leaf to crackle beneath his weight.

The sniper knelt beside the tree, eye once again to his scope, and Kadan rose, still nearly invisible, his knife held low, blade up. The sniper turned and Kadan struck, taking the man out quickly and efficiently, doing his best to make the kill clean. Blood splattered across the trunk and over the rifle. Kadan stepped back, avoiding the bright red streaks. He waited a few moments before reaching down, without expression, and checking for a pulse. He wiped the blade clean and then checked the sniper's hands, hoping to get a fingerprint. He wasn't surprised to find that the prints had been burned off. This man was a sanctioned killer and wouldn't be traced back to anywhere. More than likely he would have been declared dead years earlier. He was a ghost with no name and no home.

Kadan shook his head. This wasn't the life he wanted for the GhostWalkers. He left everything right where it lay, not even touching the weapon.

Kadan? Tansy's voice wavered.

I'm fine. Did the spotter turn away from you?

Yes, he's gone. He took off running back toward the camp. She hesitated. *I don't feel a wave of violence. I can't tell what happened.*

Kadan slipped the knife back into the scabbard and backed into the heavier brush. The spotter would be coming right to him.

Just stay put and let me take care of this.

He felt her hesitation and shook his head. He'd disturbed her peace just by coming to her. She knew he intended, one way or another, to bring her back with him. Now he'd brought two men who wanted them dead. She wasn't going to stick around to see what happened. He was tired. He desperately needed sleep. He didn't even know what time zone he was in anymore, but he was going to have to go chase Tansy.

I'm just too damned tired for games. Don't take off.

There was a small silence and then he felt her stirring in his mind. That same impression of heat and silk, and maybe now a hint of fire to go along with the taste of cinnamon in his mouth. Yeah, there was passion underneath all that cool. Anyone who would volunteer at the age of thirteen to track brutal serial killers had to feel passionately about life.

Do you really expect me to stay?

Her voice brushed at every nerve ending, tightening his body when he needed to remain in absolute control. If Whitney had designed his soldiers to work in pairs, he certainly hadn't taken into consideration the effect the right woman could have on a man's body.

I wish you'd give me the consideration of at least hearing me out.

There was another small silence.

I did. There was finality in her tone.

Kadan could hear the second man now. The rustle of leaves as he brushed by bushes. Breath coming in short gasps. The spotter suddenly ceased all movement. He hadn't gotten to the body, but the rifle wasn't up where it should be. He may have caught a glimpse of the barrel sticking out of the brush, lying on the ground.

Kadan crouched low, ready to spring, relying on his clothing and skin to camouflage him.

CHAPTER 4

Will you promise to leave me alone if I say no after I listen again? Tansy's soft voice held an unintentional plea.

Kadan clenched his teeth. A muscle worked in his jaw, a sure sign of agitation when he needed his usual calm. He wanted to reassure her, but he had his orders, and more importantly, he was certain she could track the killers. *Give me a few minutes here.*

He broke off abruptly. The spotter may have been a bit out of shape, but he was no fool. There was a hitch in his breath and then he opened fire, spraying the brush with bullets. Kadan dropped all the way to the ground while hell broke loose above him, smashing small branches and bushes alike, tearing up the vegetation and putting Kadan in real peril.

He scooted back, driving with his elbows to move along the ground, feeling for a depression or a slope of any kind where he could press his body even closer to the earth. The spotter was making so much noise with his automatic weapon that Kadan didn't bother shielding sound. He just wanted to get the hell out of Dodge.

His toe slipped off into space and he shifted back, feeling with his boots for a purchase on the sloping ground. The bullets slammed the ground all around him as he scooted deeper into the brush.

Tansy gasped in his mind, her fear beating at him when he needed to stay disconnected and cold.

I'm fine. Break off. I'll handle this. He knew she wasn't combat-trained, and the ugly sound of an automatic rifle spraying the brush, toppling branches and bushes alike, must have been terrifying to her. He gentled his voice. *Tansy, I'm trained for this.*

He knew that would bring up all sorts of other questions in her mind. She might not be able to get psychic energy off of him, but she picked up on body language, and as much of an empath as she was, she couldn't fail to read that he was as dangerous as hell without all the enhancements, and with them he was plain lethal.

Be careful.

Careful was part of the way he lived—some of the time—but he appreciated that she was worried when she had every reason to want him dead.

The slope wasn't as gentle as he would have liked as he backed down it. He had to dig in to prevent slipping, but the angle kept him safe from the barrage of bullets. Eventually the spotter stopped firing. Kadan could hear him breathing heavily, and then swearing as he discovered the sniper's body.

Kadan took advantage of the man's distraction and rolled to his right, before once again crawling along the ground, this time in a wide arc to come back toward the spotter at an angle. He would have one chance. If he didn't make the kill, the spotter would blow him away—and then he'd kill Tansy. He'd hunt her mercilessly and leave no witnesses.

Kadan's jaw tightened. Failure was not an option. Tansy Meadows was going to live a long life—with him. He risked a cautious glance. The spotter was crouched beside the downed sniper, one hand on the other man's throat, checking for a pulse. His gaze constantly sweeping his surroundings, he reached inside his jacket, pulled a Glock, shoved it against the sniper's teeth, and pulled the trigger, probably to ensure no identity on the off chance dental records could be found.

Kadan rose up behind the man, knife flashing toward his throat. The man must have sensed him, because he half turned, firing his gun instinctively as Kadan's blade took him across the jugular. One of the Glock's bullets shaved off jacket and skin across Kadan's shoulder, a wicked, burning kiss that stung like hell. He closed his mind to the pain and continued with a standard figure-eight kill attack, slicing down and across the torso, thighs, and then back up to finish the kill. Again he stepped back, careful not to disturb either body.

He moved a short distance from both of them and sank into a crouch, taking a deep breath. Exhaustion washed over him. The sun was long gone and another night had crept up on him. He desperately needed to sleep, not chase Tansy over the mountains. He shoved his fingers through his hair and forced his body to his feet. They would have to be gone at daybreak. He'd leave the bodies where they lay and erase his tracks, hoping the vultures and other creatures would do a lot of damage before either man was found.

He made his way back to the campsite, moving in silence, letting the night wrap him in shadows. *Tansy? You still with me?*

Again he felt her hesitation. Yeah. She was with him. She was deciding to run, but she couldn't quite make a break from him. Maybe Whitney had managed to pair them, not just on his side—or maybe he was lucky and she was genuinely attracted to him. Cursing under his breath

for even hoping, Kadan shook his head to rid himself of
the thought. She was simply a good person who didn't
want him dead.

I'm here.

He closed his eyes briefly, allowing the sound of her
voice to slide down his skin like the touch of fingers. His
throat ached and his body tightened. He was in bad shape
to let just her voice have an effect on him. He picked up the
pace, moving quickly through the trees, taking the shortest
possible route back to her camp.

The tent was tucked between a couple of rocks with
trees and brush, masking its presence. Food was scattered
across the table and onto the ground, where ants swarmed.
Wildlife had made short work of the offering.

It's safe to come back to camp now. He picked up the
frying pan and carried it to her makeshift sink.

*I doubt that. It will be much safer for me when you're
gone.*

Kadan sighed heavily, the weariness washing over him
and regret biting deep. *You know I have to take you with
me. I'm damned tired tonight. Just get back here and drop
it until I get some rest.* Kadan meticulously cleaned the
grounds, dumping the remains of their meal in her trash
can. She obviously burned most of the remains from each
day.

*How inconvenient of me to argue with you when you're
so tired.*

Sarcasm dripped into his mind, but it didn't for one moment alleviate the ache in his body for hers. *Inconvenient
is exactly the word I'd use. Thank you for understanding,*
he agreed, hoping she'd laugh. He stripped and used her
shower, allowing the water to pour over him, although it
was cold and didn't take the ache from his bones.

She didn't laugh, but a trace of amusement flowed from
her mind to his. Along with it came an impression of sad-
ness, even regret.

I'm sorry, then. But I can't help you. You refuse to take no for an answer and I'm not willing to be dragged off my mountain. I'll have to say good-bye from here. Actually though, it was nice to finally meet someone who has an explanation for what I am and how I got this way.

He caught the thought that she had a lot to discuss with her parents. *You can't do that. What I told you was classified information. You cannot take it to your parents.* He dried himself with a thin towel and dressed in clean clothes from his pack. *Come on back. Talking this way over a distance is tiring. You'll end up with a blinding headache.*

Don't pretend concern for me. Now there was an edge to her voice.

Kadan sighed. There was little point in telling her he'd rather not do his job, because in the end, he was going to do it and they both knew it. *I'm not chasing you over the damned mountain all night. I need sleep.*

That's a relief. Go to sleep and leave in the morning.

The distance was greater between them. She was on the move and had to stretch to reach him. She wasn't used to telepathic communication, because few others, probably none that she knew, actually had the ability—but several of the GhostWalkers were able to use the talent. He'd had plenty of practice honing the skill.

You're going to force me to do this the hard way, because I'm not coming after you. Just come back now before we take this to the next level. He found himself holding his breath, hoping she would listen to him. If he believed in God, he would have sent up a quick prayer for a little help, but he'd long ago learned to rely on himself. He'd seen too many fucked-up, perverted people to believe in a higher power watching over him.

Don't threaten me. I don't intimidate so easily.

He had an instant vision of her rising up from her nap, completely nude without even an attempt to cover herself and dressing right in front of him. No, she definitely didn't give in to intimidation, and he'd wanted her to be afraid enough to learn a lesson in self-preservation.

The water was hot enough to clean the dishes with. He ignored the side of him that wanted her to like him, the part that needed her, and he tapped into the ruthless, merciless side that gave him orders when he was on a mission. He began to whisper to her, commanding her to come back as he did the dishes and set them out to air dry.

He rolled out his bedding and prepared to lie down. There would be no sleeping until she returned, but he could take a look at the missing hunk of skin, sew up the torn flesh, and relax while he persuaded her to come back to the campsite.

Kadan was driving her crazy. She couldn't get the sound of his voice out of her head. She resorted to running, a dangerous thing to do in the dark. Twice she fell and rolled, but the whispers didn't let up, not even for a breath. She lay on the ground staring up at the stars, her heart beating too loud and her stomach in knots.

It was his voice, that soft, velvety rasp, in her mind. Somewhere along the way, between the insistent hypnotic commands, he began to talk to her about himself.

Come back to me. I need you to come to me now, tonight. Do you know why I have to do this? Unlike you, living with your very rich, loving parents, my entire family was wiped out. I was eight years old. My father was a drug dealer and someone wanted to take over his territory. They broke into our home and shot my sister first. She was in the living room watching television. She was only twelve and very small. I didn't think a child's body could hold that much blood in it.

Tansy closed her eyes. She didn't want to hear this. Didn't want to see him as human. She'd been to too many crime scenes where the blood ran in rivers.

Dad grabbed me and stuffed me under the floorboards, pulling out the gun that was hidden there. I could hear them all screaming. And blood began dripping into the space from the cracks. It collected all around me until I was covered in it. Until it was an inch deep in the space and I was breathing it in. Do you know what that smells like, Tansy?

She knew. She still had nightmares. She pressed her hand to her mouth to keep from sobbing. He had to stop. The images in his head were vivid, as if the crime had just occurred. His voice was without emotion, cold and dispassionate, but she was in his head and there was rage and pain and a sorrow too deep to express. She connected with those raw emotions, so that tears clogged her throat, threatening to choke her.

Come back to me. I need you to come to me now, tonight.

The pull of that demand was so strong she rolled over and got to her feet, looking in the direction of her camp. She even took a few steps before she managed to stop herself. She couldn't continue to put distance between them, but she didn't run to him the way her mind and body was urging her to do.

The thing is, now, as an adult, I realize my father was not a good man. He was a major drug dealer and involved with some very bad people, but to me, he was my father. He played games with me and loved me and tucked me in at night. Maybe, as an adult, I can even admit he was responsible for bringing a bloodbath to our home, but the child in me loved him. Always really loved him and looked up to him. I need you, Tansy. Come back to me now, tonight.

She closed her eyes, feeling ill. His voice drove her temperature up, but the things he said to her made her feel sick. He was lost and alone. And that person inside her that needed to make the world a better place, that had too much empathy and compassion to be able to even touch people, drove her to her knees at the naked sorrow in his voice.

I heard screams and shots and my mother's voice pleading not to kill my brother. His name was James and he was only ten years old. He shared my room and taught me to play ball. He never minded when I tagged along after him.

She was astonished at the cool voice he used relating such a terrible childhood trauma. Maybe he believed he had buried the whole thing deep enough that he could tell it without feeling, but she knew it wasn't so. The rage in him was frightening. The sorrow devastating. Tansy found herself moving back up the slope toward her campsite. She caught the trunk of a sapling and held on to keep from hurrying back to comfort him. Now his commands had taken on an entirely different meaning. He did need her, whether he knew it or not—and she suspected he didn't know that any more than he knew he was still that enraged, shattered, devastated child.

Come back to me. The stars are out. Do you see them? I never thought I'd see them again. Confined in that space, with blood dripping on me and pooling all around me, I never thought I'd ever be able to be inside again. I don't like walls.

He used the present tense. She took a breath and let it out. Her hands released the sapling and she began walking back toward camp, her feet moving her in spite of the fact that her brain was telling her no. Where was her self-preservation? Why did his voice affect her so strongly? She only knew she wept inside for that innocent child and wept even more for the man he had become.

I stayed hidden for hours, days, I don't know. I was terrified, not so much of being killed—I think I was long past that fear—but of what I knew I was going to find. I thought the screams were the worst, the pleading, and I prayed for it to be over. But then there was silence. Nothing broke the silence. I couldn't hear footsteps, or cries, or even breaths. After a while I wasn't even certain I was alive.

She hadn't lived through a serial killer destroying her family, but she'd been present, hearing the victims' last thoughts, their fears and cries and pain-filled whimpers, their last gasps of breath and that horrible rattle she couldn't get out of her head. She didn't need an object to touch to bring the images into vivid detail. She was in Kadan's head and the images were burned there for all eternity. Now they were in her head as well. She wasn't good at getting rid of blood and death. Tansy reached up and brushed at the tears on her face.

The first thing I saw when I pushed open the door was my brother's face. His eyes were open and he was staring at me. Sometimes I can't sleep and I see his eyes and I know I was supposed to find them and make them pay for what they did. But then I remind myself I'm not eight and he was dead and there was nothing left of him but a vacant stare, so I can't really blame anything on him. His eyes looked like glass. Come back to me, Tansy. I need you to-night.

She'd seen eyes that looked like glass. Too many eyes. She didn't sleep much either at night, which is why she chose to work and exhaust herself, sleeping in catnaps during the day. If she closed her eyes in the dark the dead surrounded her, staring with glassy eyes. She hadn't saved them. She had waited too long to volunteer. She had hesitated. She had been too slow to pick up the trail. Whatever the reason, she hadn't saved them. Maybe she needed to see it his way. They were already dead and there was nothing left but her own guilt.

My father had tried to cover my mother. I could see that. He'd tried to protect her, but they killed her and I couldn't touch her. I couldn't make myself touch either of them. You know how in the movies the kid always kisses the dead parent or loved one? Well, I couldn't go near them. I was sick. And angry. And so terrified of being alone. I dug through the blood. It was so sticky. I don't think I've ever managed to wash it off of me. Sometimes it feels like a second skin. I dug through the blood until I found my father's gun and I walked out of the house.

Her heart began to pound so hard her breath came in a ragged gasp. She was with him fully now, locked into his mind, his emotions her emotions. She was that eight-year-old boy who felt too much sorrow—and too much rage. Instinctively she tried to pull away, to separate herself, but his soft, relentless voice refused to let her go.

Come back to me now, Tansy. I walked for a couple of hours. I knew where to go. I'd recognized the men. They were business associates of my father and they'd come to dinner in our home. My mother had cooked for them. One had played baseball with my brother and me. I knew them. I stayed in the shadows where no one saw me, covered in my family's blood. I've been there ever since.

She was crying openly now. It was impossible to choke back sobs. That little boy, covered in blood with a gun in his hand. She saw him so clearly. Felt the rage with him. Knew the sorrow that still gripped him like a vise.

"Don't," she whispered aloud. "Don't do it." There would be no going back once it was done. No way to ever recover that sweetness, that innocence, that had been inside that little boy. "Don't."

I need you tonight. I'm so tired and I need to hold you close to me. I don't ever do that. Hold anyone close. I don't get close, but now there's no choice and I'm too damn tired to fight it. Come back to me.

She shook her head, but her feet kept walking and she was close now. She caught hold of the branch of a small bush and held herself straight when she wanted to fall to the ground weeping.

I walked through the front door and no one saw me. Even then I could mask my presence if I concentrated hard

enough. I slipped into the room where they were celebrat-
ing and I shot them all. One shot into each head. They
never saw me and never knew I'd done it. I didn't feel any-
thing. I wanted to feel, but I didn't. I walked back outside,
stripped down the gun the way my father had taught me,
and I threw the pieces into various Dumpsters. I wish I
could blame my brother's stare, but I have to take that re-
sponsibility. I killed them and I'd probably do it again.

Eight-year-old boys didn't walk into a house and kill
people. Not without something being seriously wrong with
them. She was in his mind, trying to find that vicious, cruel
streak, or the sense of entitlement that meant rules didn't
apply to him. She found a small boy throwing up, sickened
by his loss, terrified of his future, still filled with rage.

I've never told another living soul about that night.

Tansy turned her tear-streaked face up to the sky. A
shadow fell across her and she threw out a hand to block
any attack. Kadan loomed in front of her, catching her
wrist and pulling her into his arms, tight against his body,
burying his face against her neck. She thought his face was
as wet as hers. Slowly she brought up her arms to circle his
waist, holding him, trying to offer comfort to that eight-
year-old boy.

"I'm not that boy anymore," he reminded without lifting his head.

She slid her hand up his back to tunnel her fingers in his
hair. "I know you're not. And I'm not that thirteen-year-old
girl who thought she could save the world either."

Kadan's hands framed her face, forcing her head up so
their eyes met. His heart contracted. She was so beautiful,
her eyes shimmering violet over blue, that strange shimmer over the color almost a silver. He'd been drowning
without her and he hadn't even known it.

Need went from his mind to his body, a rush of heat that
tightened every muscle. Desire burst through him, raw and
stark and all too strong—so strong it felt like a punch in

his gut. Lust for her had been there all along, driving his body hard, but now it was so much more. He felt starved, a man possessed, craving her with every fiber of his being. Because she could take it all away, that rage, buried so deep but so much a part of him. The screams and the blood. Only Tansy could relieve the terrible cold that gripped his heart. She could drown out the truth—that he was a straight-up killer, good at hunting other killers because he could think just like them.

She touched his face, the warmth of her body seeping into the cold of his. The moment she touched him, his body reacted with brutal, painful force, filling his groin, pounding and aching with demand. Kadan bent his head to the temptation of her soft, trembling mouth. He stroked his tongue over her full lower lip, tasting that hint of cinnamon that was fast producing a craving in him. She shivered in reaction.

Even with her mind connected to his, she couldn't know how much he wanted her—how much he needed her, how desperate he was just to touch her. Kadan had never felt desperation, or need—or if he had, he hadn't recognized it. Now he couldn't think straight with wanting her. He struggled to keep his hands gentle, the touch of his mouth tender, when he felt ravenous.

"We're in a hell of a mess, Tansy. You know that, don't you?" His mouth skimmed down her eyelids, slid over the tracks of her tears, teased at the corners of her mouth.

She swallowed hard, blinking up at him, a mixture of nervous apprehension and shaken desire. Her hands on his shoulders trembled, her soft breasts pushed against his chest as his breath quickened in response to the way his teeth tugged at her lower lip. She made a small helpless sound of assent, breathy and feminine, leaning into him so that he closed his eyes, savoring the feel of her body against his.

He wasn't going to survive this night if he couldn't have her. Not now, not when the memories were so close and he couldn't bury the rage deep enough. He needed her soft body and the compassion and light in her mind. There was no other way to alleviate the darkness surrounding his soul or the piercing coldness in his heart. Salvation lay in this woman. He ached for her, for both of them. Life wouldn't be easy with him, and the things he would ask—no, demand—of her were soul-destroying, but he knew he didn't have a choice. He couldn't walk away from her. He just wasn't that strong.

He couldn't wait another minute, drawing her closer, settling his mouth over hers, sinking into her heat, the paradise of her soft, moist mouth, his tongue tangling with hers. He stroked, felt the answering shudder of pleasure in her body, the hitch in her breath. She was shy, untutored, and it occurred to him Tansy couldn't have kissed many men—if any. Something dark and possessive flared with hot satisfaction at the idea that no other man had ever touched her.

Still kissing her, he dragged his shirt open, wanting to be skin to skin. His breath strangled in his lungs, his shaft so hard he was afraid he might explode. He needed to crawl inside of her, share her skin, bury himself deep so she could pour the sun over him and steer him away from the shadows always clawing pieces out of him.

Despite his driving need, he kissed her with tenderness, savoring the taste and texture of her mouth, the soft, moist warmth that encased him as he stroked and cajoled, blatantly seducing her. Cinnamon had never tasted like sin. Skin had never felt so soft to him. Control was his code, his mantra, and few things in his life had ever shaken it, and no people, certainly not a woman, until this moment. He felt himself tremble, felt the shudder of need, the desperation in his mind.

His mouth moved on hers, deepening the kiss, while a fever ignited a slow burn in his belly. She wasn't wearing a bra. He'd been more than conscious of that all day, and now he tugged the hem of her shirt up and over her head, clamping his arm around her until her breasts were tight against the muscles of his chest. She felt like heaven.

Tansy knew she was getting in too deep. She was letting him take her over, sacrificing her body to the darkness in him, igniting a fire neither of them was going to be able to put out easily. He had used her own weakness against her to bring her back to him, and now he was seducing her. She wanted the hot pleasure of his mouth, the feel of his hard body against hers and the strength in his arms. She craved the taste and texture of him, but most of all, she needed to take the pain out of his eyes and erase it from his mind.

His hand swept over her belly and every muscle bunched beneath his palm. His fingertips felt hard and calloused, a strange bristle-like stroke that sent shivers of excitement down her spine and arousal tingling in her thighs. He kissed her throat, down her shoulder, and then covered the tip of her breast with his mouth, suckling strongly. She nearly fell, her legs going weak and her core going liquid.

"Kadan?" Her fist clenched in his hair, and her voice trembled. A breathy little moan escaped her throat. Nothing had ever made her feel like he did. Wanted. Wanton. Sexy. Frightened. She was confused. She was drowning in the sensations his tongue and teeth on her nipple created.

"It's all right, baby. I've got you," he assured her softly. "You're so soft, so perfect I can barely breathe."

She watched him through half-closed eyes, his tongue taking long licks at her nipple, his lips closing around her breast, the tongue flicking and dancing until she cried out, the sound strangled as his hands tugged at the zipper of her jeans. Every nerve ending in her body seemed sensitized as his mouth traveled farther down her stomach, his tongue swirling over her belly button. He caught her jeans and pushed them down her hips, urging her to kick them aside. She stood naked, the night caressing her skin, the moon spilling light and shadow over her.

He brought his head up, his eyes nearly glowing in the dark, shining at her with dark hunger, with an intensity that was both terrifying and arousing. As his gaze darkened with lust, sweeping over her, a groan escaped, much like the sound the cougar made before it tore into its meal. He swore under his breath and dropped to his knees, pushing her thighs apart. He caught her hips in his hands and forced her body forward toward his waiting mouth.

Tansy might have screamed. She didn't know. Maybe no sound actually emerged, but the scream of pleasure was locked tightly in her mind. He didn't look up; instead he licked at her, taking long catlike strokes with his tongue, licking at her as if he was starving and desperate for cream. Her womb reacted with a slow rolling, rippling with pleasure, spilling more rich wetness.

He growled something, the sound vibrating through her body. She caught at his shoulders, trying to steady herself when she was on the verge of collapsing, as wave after wave of sheer pleasure consumed her. Her stomach tightened, the muscles bunching, tension spreading with the rising heat.

"I can't stand it." She threw her head back, legs splayed wide, his mouth at her, tongue circling the knot of nerves, until a sob of ecstasy escaped. She pushed against him mindlessly, thrusting with her hips, seeking more as the tension never lessened. His mouth and tongue and fingers stroked and caressed and ate her alive, until she was burning up in a fever of desperate need.

The orgasm took her by surprise, racing over her, body bucking helplessly with mind-numbing pleasure as her womb and feminine channel grew hotter and hotter and tighter and tighter, until she simply fragmented, losing control, losing herself in the fiery heat, giving herself up to his mouth and hands.

Kadan was on his feet, shedding his jeans, lifting her, growling instructions. "Wrap your legs around my waist.

Hurry, Tansy. I need you." Because if he didn't bury himself inside of her, he was going to lose his mind.

She wrapped her arms around his neck, mashing her soft breasts against his chest while her long legs wrapped around his waist. She locked her ankles, nearly sobbing with need. He pressed the broad head of his shaft against her slick, wet entrance. He could barely breathe now, shocked at his own lack of control.

He felt fire blazing over his skin, lightning sizzling through his bloodstream as he began to invade her soft body, pushing through tight folds, so hot, like raw silk gripping him, burning him clean again. Inch by slow inch, he sank into her depths until he felt her wince as he lodged against a thin barrier.

"Hold on to me, Tansy," he whispered through clenched teeth. She had to be a virgin—when he was sliding away from reality and careening out of control. "Let your weight come down on me." His eyes met hers. He wanted her trust. He didn't deserve it. He'd betrayed her already by using her own compassion against her, but he still wanted her—Tansy—the real woman, giving everything she was to him.

Her eyes went dark, the shine more luminous. Never taking her gaze from his, she pushed down, while he thrust up. The ripple of pain went through her mind to his and he stopped, leaning forward to find her mouth in an attempt to kiss the hurt away. He waited until she was kissing him back, until he felt her body stop resisting his, allowing his invasion so that he sank deeper into her, until he was buried to the hilt.

He let her set the pace, urging her with his hands on her hips to ride him, to find a rhythm that she could manage while getting used to the feel of his thickness stretching her. He hadn't expected to need her so much, or that he would burn so hot. She was so damned tight, tighter than he'd imagined. The walls of her sheath felt alive, velvet soft, scalding hot, pulsing and throbbing around him, gripping him and sliding over him until he wanted to shout hoarsely with joy. Each moment inside of her sent light shimmering through him, piercing every dark shadow until for the first time that he could remember, he felt alive.

When he thought he couldn't live through another moment of her long, slow slide, she tightened her muscles even more, nearly causing him to lose control completely. He gripped her hips then, taking over, setting his own pace, thrusting hard and deep, feeling like a madman who couldn't get enough.

Her small, broken cry only added fuel to the flames. Her nails bit into his shoulders as she clung to him, lifting herself to meet his deep surges. The sound of their bodies coming together was loud in the night, but he could only hear his breath, shuddering in and out of his lungs as the world burned hotter and his body tightened and tightened until everything he ever was centered in his groin.

Her low keen shattered what little control he had left, and he began to piston into her, stretching the tension on a thin, taut wire, pushing her beyond anything she'd ever considered, until she was pleading with him for release. He kept going, plunging into her, sinking as deep as he could, never wanting to end his time with her. There was nothing in his world but Tansy, with her perfect body surrounding his. The heat and fire of her. The explosive chemistry. The soft skin and the even softer channel that stroked and gripped and held him tighter than her arms. And that scent of cinnamon that filled him with craving.

He shifted her just an inch to apply more pressure to that sweet spot, the bundle of sensitive nerves that had her sobbing out his name. And then her body rippled. Once, twice, clamped down hard, milking and squeezing. Wave after wave tore through her, taking him with her. He felt her body dragging the hot seed out of him, filling her while she pulsed around him.

She dropped her head onto his shoulder, utterly spent. He should have been. He lowered her feet to the ground, but held her, swaying, tight against him. They stayed that way for a several long moments before he felt the shift in her mind, in her body, the sudden withdrawal. He closed his eyes and held her tighter, not willing for this moment to be over. She had to give him this night. One night.

"Don't," he said softly. "Let me have you."

"I gave myself to you," she said, not lifting her face from his chest.

He picked her up, cradling her close to him. "It isn't enough. I need tonight."

She couldn't pretend she didn't want it either. She might never have another night like this one. She didn't touch men. She didn't dare risk it. Yet she'd given everything to Kadan, opening her mind, letting him feel her pleasure, share it, until he'd driven her over the edge, the sensations she'd never expected to be able to experience, hers to hold forever.

"What happens tomorrow?"

He shook his head. "I don't know, Tansy, but we have now. Tonight. This one time for us. Let it be for us."

She wavered, afraid if she took it any further, she'd never be able to get anything of herself back. She had convinced herself love wasn't for her. A man of her own was impossible, and she was too pragmatic to give herself false hope. But here he was, offering her the chance of a lifetime, one night with a man utterly and completely devoted to her pleasure. She read that in his mind, how much he wanted her to feel.

She nodded slowly, knowing she could never resist him, pushing aside every thought of the morning and what she would have to face. There was only this night for them. This one night, and she was taking it for herself.

He carried her to the sleeping bag, grateful it wasn't far. His legs were rubbery and he doubted he had much strength left. Her eyes were enormous, and he found that peculiar shine very sexy, or maybe that was just his body reacting to her scent and heat. He laid her down and followed close, massaging her shoulders and neck. That soft, vulnerable neck.

"You're so beautiful."

"You make me feel beautiful." She loved the feel of his fingers on her skin. There was a brushing stroke he used that sent the most amazing electrical sensation sizzling through her body. "How do you do that?"

"That's classified."

Tansy looked up at his face, so still and chiseled and masculine. So serious. She burst out laughing. "Your love-making ought to be classified too. You've worn me out."

"Have I?" His hands shaped her breasts, cupping the soft weight of them. "We're not finished by a long shot, Tansy," he whispered softly as he lowered his head to flick her nipple with his tongue. One hand slid along her thigh to rest on her mound. "You don't feel like you're worn out." One finger slipped into her wet channel and her muscles instantly reacted, clamping down hard. He leaned into her, blowing warm air across her breast. "No, baby, you want more. You feel very much like you want to start all over again."

He turned her body onto her side, spilling her breast into his mouth. They lay on top of the sleeping bag under the stars, his arm around her waist and one hand nestled between her legs.

Tansy cradled his head to her, her fingers stroking through his hair. Each time his tongue or teeth grazed or flicked her nipple, a flood of liquid heat bathed his fingers. She did want to start all over again. She had one night with him. She wanted to learn everything, do everything, make this night last forever. She closed her eyes and savored the feel of his mouth at her breast.

CHAPTER 5

Tansy woke to the smell of coffee. She kept her eyes closed tight, not wanting to face what she'd done throughout the night. The man may have been exhausted, but Kadan had given her everything she could ever have wished for and more. Sharing mind and body was an experience she'd never thought she'd ever have, and one far beyond anything her imagination could have conjured up. But now she had to face the light of day and what she'd done. Just about everything one could do—and with a stranger.

How could she ever look Kadan Montague in the eye? Would he expect her to just follow him down the trail into hell, now that she'd allowed seduction? Because she'd been a willing participant—she couldn't deny that, even to herself. Especially to herself.

She risked a glance at him and her heart nearly stopped. He was calmly breaking camp. Most of her things were packed, and even as she watched, he'd already opened her locked camera case and extracted her precious cameras and footage as if he owned them. The pounding in her heart roared in her ears. What had she done?

We can do this the hard way. He had warned her. She could never say he hadn't warned her. She'd allowed him to talk her into coming back to camp on her own. He'd used her own nature against her. Hell, he'd studied her, he'd admitted that. He knew exactly which buttons to push, and he'd pushed them by revealing the childhood story he'd never shared with anyone else. How stupid could she get? It probably wasn't true. She wanted to weep for her own stupidity, but there was another side that was furious at the deception.

Give the girl a night to remember. He'd been in her head. He knew how alone she'd felt, how different. She'd practically climbed all over him. Tansy suppressed a groan. She couldn't, for one moment, blame him. He'd warned her from the beginning he meant to take her back. He was ruthless, willing to use whatever means were available to him—and she'd opened the door for him to use sex. Damn him. Damn her. Now she had to figure a way out, because she wasn't going anywhere with him.

Kadan kept his head down as he methodically packed Tansy's things. It was possible she didn't realize that the more they used telepathic communication, the easier it became to slip in and out of each other's mind. He had been reluctant to separate himself from her. He couldn't remember lying with a woman in his arms and feeling utterly content—at peace. Whole. And now she was lying there, regretting their night together, the night that meant the world to him. What did he expect? Her to come to him open, with a huge, happy smile?

Her thoughts were raw and self-accusing. *He knew exactly which buttons to push, and he'd pushed them by revealing the childhood story he'd never shared with anyone else. She wanted to weep for her own stupidity, but there was another side that was furious at the deception.*

Deception? Anger and hurt wrapped up so tight he couldn't tell one from the other. Kadan, the GhostWalker with ice in his veins, felt the burst of temper rush through his system, and he turned toward Tansy, reaching into his pocket.

"Hey! Catch!" Deliberately Kadan flicked the small game piece he'd found at the last crime scene through the air toward her.

The object gleamed in the early morning sunlight as it came toward Tansy's head. She reached up in one quick motion and snagged it out of the air just as she caught his thought.

Damn me for trusting you. I told you the one thing about me not another living person knows, and you believe I used it to get you in bed. There was fury, but more than that, there was hurt.

She'd hurt him. Her fingers closed around the smooth edges of the object he'd thrown to her, and her heart sank as vicious, violent energy greedily swarmed over and into her. She tried to drop the game piece, but it was already far too late. Worse, she hadn't prepared herself. She heard herself scream, deep inside where no one could hear, as oil poured into her mind, slick and black and filled with sludge, carrying the weight of the dead and dying, the pleas and protests, the begging voices, the sickness that rose with the dark stench of blood. Kadan had said the blood was like a second skin, but it was worse than that, it seeped inside through her pores, until blood was inside her mind, sticking to everything she was, every part of her soul, dripping like wax off a candle and fusing with her like a hot weld.

Kadan heard screaming, the cry of an anguished animal, filled with pain, with agony, but she was completely mute, the blue gone from her eyes to be wholly replaced by the silver violet shine. Eyes of glass. His stomach lurched as he flung the bag he was packing onto the table and raced to her, gripping her hand, prying at her fingers. "Drop it! Drop it now."

He'd read the reports, but he hadn't understood. Damn it, he hadn't understood. Now he did, and he thought he was going to be sick. He was there with her now, in her mind, and the reality of what she felt—what she went through—was far, far more devastating than any report could ever have described.

"Damn it, Tansy, drop it now!" Bile rose. He'd been angry. He never allowed anger. He stayed in control, because when he made the decision to hurt someone, it had to be based on logic and reason, not emotion. "Tansy . . ." He whispered her name and pulled her limp body into his arms.

There was so much blood. He liked that. The splash and splatter of it. Like a painting and he was the artist. He'd wanted a different card. He couldn't use the women. Either of them. The girl was fourteen and the mother— ah—the mother. She was beautiful. And such a fucking snob. He would love to force her to watch him do the daughter first. But he'd lose points. How many points if he fucked them both? Would it be worth it? They'd all be mad at him, but what the hell, he deserved a little fun.

It wasn't his fault that he pulled the wrong card. The sound of their voices sobbing and pleading were better than any high, better than any aphrodisiac. He'd done the husband first. Macho man. Idiot, thought he could keep his family safe. Then the son. Waste of time killing the brat, but he didn't want to bother with the kid screaming. No, now came the fun. He had hours for fun, but if he indulged his fantasies, he'd lose points. Whatever should we do?

He squatted down beside the woman, smirking, high on the power. She'd do anything to live. Anything at all he

*wanted. Too bad, baby, your death is in the cards . . . He
began laughing at his own joke.*

Tansy could hear a far-off voice calling her name. The
voice sounded familiar and she tried to concentrate on it.
She was in a labyrinth of the dead. So many bodies. So
much blood. The victims begged and pleaded. Debased
themselves. Endured both physical and emotional torture,
and she went through it with them, helpless to aid them.
Sometimes she could see their faces, the desperation in
their eyes, the pleading. Sobs welled up. She couldn't reach
them. She couldn't touch them. She couldn't stop their
killer.

"Tansy, drop it! Damn it. Hear me. Feel me. I'm real,
they're not."

The voice was stern, commanding, penetrating through
the blood and gore. For a moment she was aware of being
in two places, the long blood-filled tunnel with glassy
eyes staring at her and a hand gripping hers. And then the
killer laughed and clothes ripped and women screamed. A
child pleaded, the voice hopeless, dragging her down, down
into the oily black and red sludge where she took a breath
and went under.

*Screw them all, doll face. We've got all day to get ac-
quainted. Fight me. I want you to fight me. See how pretty
your daughter looks with all those cuts over her breasts?
Nice red stripes.*

*He slowly took off his belt, knowing two pairs of eyes
were mesmerized by him.*

*Won't she look even prettier with nice wide stripes all
over her? Come on over here, doll face. Crawl on your
hands and knees, right past your old man who didn't do a
thing to save you. He would have given you up, begged me
to use you however I wanted just so I didn't kill him. He
wasn't strong. You needed someone strong. And now it's
too late. Crawl over here and put that whiny mouth of
yours to work while I teach this little girl what a real man*

is. If you'd chosen the right man, none of this would have happened, would it?

He caught the woman by her hair, yanking her head up, sticking his face next to hers. Spit ran down her face as he shouted at her.

Would it?

Kadan tried prying open Tansy's fingers. He was going to lose her if he didn't pull her back. Her face was nearly gray it was so pale. Beads of perspiration dotted her forehead. Her pulse was out of control, her eyes staring at something that wasn't really there.

"Drop that fucking thing." His voice didn't even sound like his own. He growled the command in a demonic voice. Kadan Montague, the killer who had ice for blood, was desperate, terrified he was losing her.

Swearing, he dug the pads of his fingers deep into her wrist, finding the pressure point that would open her fingers, slamming her hand against the ground at the same time. The game piece flew a couple of feet and rolled free. Tansy's body convulsed. Blood trickled from her mouth and nose. Kadan knelt in the dirt, his body blocking the early morning sun while he tried to wake her. He shook her, called her name, and then left her to get water.

Tansy choked, coughed, turned her head and then rolled to her knees, her stomach rebelling, the retching relentless. Waves of dizziness disoriented her. She wiped her face, and her hand came away smeared with blood.

"Here. Drink this." Kadan thrust a bottle of water into her shaking hands and a jacket around her nude body.

Tansy tried to raise it to her mouth, but she spilled droplets everywhere. Kadan reached around her, his hand closing on hers, steadying the bottle.

"Take a drink." His voice was gruff.

Tansy did, swishing the water around and spitting it out to cleanse the oily taste from her mouth. It didn't go away. Her mind seemed unusually calm, and she had a bad feeling she wasn't the one controlling the voices. She took a couple of more cautious sips, letting the cool liquid trickle down her throat, before she looked up at Kadan.

"They're still there in my head, aren't they? Just like always. You're stopping them."

He nodded. "Why in the hell when that fucker knew you were chasing serial killers didn't he give you the tools to work with?" Fury shook his voice.

Tansy took a deep breath and let it out. "I presume you're referring to Dr. Whitney."

"Didn't your parents call him in when you became ill after chasing a killer?"

She nodded. "It seemed part of the adoption agreement. He arranged the adoption and my father seemed to think he was the best person to treat me. I had to recount, in great detail, how each case affected me."

"He could have helped you deal with it better."

"I usually did deal with it better. If I prepare my mind for the shock, I can control the energy and voices for a short time. Unfortunately, the times became shorter and shorter, until I reached the point of really being useless. And I can't get them out of my head once they're in there." She took another drink of water, savoring the cool water when her throat felt raw.

"I'm sorry. I shouldn't have done that."

Her eyes met his. He looked as if he meant it. She shrugged. "I guess you had to try."

Kadan shook his head, refusing to take the out. "I wasn't thinking about the job when I threw the game piece. It was left behind at the crime scene. There's always a piece left behind. There seem to be eight different pieces, and one of the eight is always left at each scene."

"Because you have eight players."

Kadan blinked. Sank down into the dirt beside her. "What do you mean, eight players?"

"It's a game. A game of murder and there are several

players. It stands to reason if there are eight game pieces then you have eight players. Have any of the game pieces repeated?"

"Four of them. Two on the East Coast and two on the West."

She was silent a moment, her expression thoughtful. Blood continued to trickle out of her mouth and nose. Kadan couldn't stop himself from wiping it away. The sight bothered him more than he cared to admit. She didn't pull away from him, and he was connected so tightly with her that he could almost follow the speed of her brain as she began computing data with small facts she'd pulled from the brief glimpse she'd received of the killer's mind.

"It's possible he's on a team. He was concerned about losing points if he raped the victims." She looked up and he swore she blinked back tears. "He did rape them, didn't he? Both of them. He wouldn't have been able to stop himself. He likes what he's doing and he needs the rush of it. He needs it more than he wants to win the game."

Kadan nodded his affirmation. "They were both raped."

"Control really matters to him. He kept taunting them about choosing the wrong man. Is it possible the wife knew him? It was odd the way he acted. He doesn't like rejection and obviously feels superior to everyone, men and women. He fed their terror, and the more afraid they were, the higher he became."

Kadan didn't want to interrupt her. She was fascinating. Her mind was fascinating. He'd worked with some great minds, yet here was a woman, without training, who thought like a detective, her brain compiling data faster than he'd ever seen.

Tansy swept a hand through her hair, frowning when her fingers caught. He tried not to notice the disarray of her hair, falling like tangled silk around her shoulders and down her back. Her breasts held faint marks, marring the perfection of her skin. He'd done that. Those were his fingerprints on her. His body stirred no matter how hard he tried to control himself.

"Why don't you get dressed?"

For the first time she seemed aware of her lack of clothing, frowning, a little confused while she looked around her. She nodded and rose unsteadily. Kadan caught her arm to make certain she didn't fall. Tansy pulled clothes from her backpack and moved out of his sight. He didn't like it, but he couldn't very well insist she dress in front of him. He spent the few minutes of her absence fixing her a cup of hot coffee.

Tansy was back a few minutes later, her face a little swollen as if she'd been crying. She took the coffee mug and blew on it. "Do the murders follow one another? In other words, if one is committed on the West Coast, then does one follow on the East Coast? Are they alike?"

He shook his head. "Similar. Well planned. More than one person has to be in on the planning, but only one actually performs the kills. At least that's what I think. There's never been any evidence of more than one killer at a crime scene. The murders are connected by the game pieces. They're unusual, carved out of ivory and very distinct."

Tansy looked around. "Where are my gloves?"

"Why?" His gut protested the question and the answer in her mind.

She flicked him a reprimanding glance. "Don't be silly. I need to take a look at the piece. I haven't really examined it and I can't touch it without gloves on."

"I don't want you to touch it again."

She sighed. "Look, I've already got the voices in my head and they aren't going to leave me alone, so I may as well do what I can to at least point you in the right direction. I pick things up even through gloves if the impressions are strong enough. I have a feeling this man kept the piece with him through the entire planning stages and liked holding it in his hand."

Kadan swore as he turned away from her. She was gone from him. She had distanced herself from him and he felt the barrier even in her mind. He couldn't blame her. He even understood, but damn it all, she belonged to him, and the separation after sharing her body and her mind was unacceptable. He could barely breathe with the thought of losing her for good.

Reluctantly he handed her the game piece. It was a small stallion, anatomically correct. She took it between two fingers, turning it over and over. Her index finger began to stroke along the horse's neck, where there was no wild mane.

"He's the Italian Stallion. He likes being called that. He enjoys knowing he can manipulate women, and his friends know it. He makes the claim that it's their responsibility to keep their women away from him, not his."

"Italian Stallion is so trite. It's been done too many times."

Her gaze jumped to his face. "I'm sure it has."

He wasn't Italian, but he felt like she was accusing him of seducing her. Damn it. Maybe he had. He hadn't told her the story of his childhood on purpose. It had slipped out. He'd been horrified, but he couldn't stop talking, couldn't stop the flow once the dam had been pierced. He hadn't told the story to seduce her, or even to gain sympathy. He was in her mind. Sharing each other. He saw her. Saw inside of her. She was—*everything.*

Tansy studied the carving from every angle. "He wants this identity more than he wants his own. He encourages this one. Mostly they just call him Stallion. Who are they?"

Her finger was mesmerizing, rubbing the neck back and forth, almost in a caress. Kadan remembered the feel of her fingers stroking over his shaft. He'd been so hard. So thick. He'd never been quite like that before, full to bursting. Looking at her, with her hair all over the place, no makeup and that remote look on her face, his heart contracted. And yes, even now, the breeze carried the faint scent of cinnamon, although now it mixed with his scent.

"His friends," Kadan guessed.

"They're close but apart. They hide in the shadows. The night is ours."

His head came up alertly. "What the hell are you saying?" He snatched the game piece from her hand. "What do you mean by that?"

Tansy turned her shimmering eyes on him. Now he knew what those eyes did. They saw inside, where people never were meant to see. She was seeing too much. Where was the ice in his veins? Where was his cool?

"I didn't mean anything. I saw the words, that's all. He believes he is invincible at night." She pulled off the gloves and dropped them on the table as if she couldn't bear them against her skin.

Kadan shook his head. "I don't believe it. There aren't that many of us. Eight? Eight killers? GhostWalkers?" He shook his head again. "I won't believe that."

"So the phrase has meaning to you?"

He glanced at her sharply. She'd grown up around detectives, and her question, in that casual voice, sounded just like one.

"You're my partner," he said gruffly, staking his claim. "Don't forget that." Before she denied it, he shoved up his sleeve.

"Oh my God, how did I not see you were hurt last night?" Tansy asked. "I'm sorry. I didn't know."

"It's nothing. A scratch. I sewed it up. I'm showing you the tattoo."

There was an expectant silence. At first she didn't see

anything on his arm, but then when he released a little bit of psychic energy, allowing it to swirl close to her, she could see the strange crest.

"The GhostWalker crest. The night is ours. It's in our creed," he explained, his expression grim. "I don't believe in coincidence. But eight . . . That would be an entire team." He shook his head. "No way, Tansy. I know them all."

"They're under a lot of strain. You know it better than anyone, Kadan," she said softly, watching him carefully. "The headaches, the continual pressure of the outside world, it could drive anyone insane. I ought to know."

"But you didn't brutally kill people. And you sure as hell haven't done it for fun. These bastards are doing it for fun."

She rubbed at the frown creasing her forehead. "So why are the GhostWalkers under suspicion? I'm not certain I get that part."

She still had blood at the side of her mouth. He hated the sight of it. Pouring water onto a cloth, he closed the distance between them. "So far we have ten murders. Five on each coast. Each was somewhat similar but very different and each had a game piece left on-site, some game pieces being used more than once."

"That doesn't explain the GhostWalker tie-in."

"You jumped over me, Tansy. Right over the top of me," Kadan pointed out. "You know we're genetically enhanced and can do things other people can't. There are strong indicators that whoever is committing these crimes can do things that would be deemed impossible. Most of the murders on the West Coast have occurred in either Seattle or Tacoma, Washington. The murders in North Carolina are near the base there as well. We believe whoever is committing them is in the service."

"Where are the GhostWalkers?"

"Scattered around, on missions. They have residences, of course, but they are often on both coasts."

"Has anyone tried to eliminate them as suspects? If they're in the military, someone has to know where they are on any given day, don't they?"

Kadan noted that Tansy was swaying, her hands still unsteady, although she tried to cover it up. He stepped closer to her, ignoring the way she stiffened when he put his arm around her waist to steady her. "The GhostWalkers operate outside ordinary parameters. They don't answer to anyone but their team leader and either the general or the admiral. Both men run teams. The missions are classified and often involve travel outside the United States without a paper trail. In other words, it is difficult to tell where the truth is because once set loose, they have the ability to travel in and out of the country and even state to state without anyone knowing. Of course we're checking into that as fast as we can, but it isn't easy, especially since I can't reveal the investigation to them or the fact that they're under suspicion."

"And they were all out of the country?"

He shook his head. "No one can confirm their whereabouts but other GhostWalkers. The general consensus seems to be that they would alibi one another."

"Would they?"

He sighed. Would they? Of course they would. Another shiver drew his undivided attention to her. Up close, touching her soft skin was a kind of private hell. He tipped her face back, taking no notice of her flinch, and dabbed away the remaining blood. "Sit down before you fall down." When she didn't respond, he took her arm and forcibly led her back to the sleeping bag. Her body was trembling, but it was her eyes that bothered him. She jerked, stared off for a moment, and then came back shivering.

"I'm all right." The words were mumbled, and twice she pressed her hand to her head.

"The headache's coming."

She nodded, swallowing hard. "I'm used to them. I have pills somewhere." She looked around a little helplessly. Her body jerked again and her eyes stared.

"Damn it, Tansy, you're having seizures." He lifted her, cradling her close, holding her there for a moment, dropping his head against hers briefly, before laying her down on the makeshift bed.

"I know. It happens. The headache is worse." She rolled away from him and curled up in a tight ball. "I have to cover my eyes."

"Where are your sunglasses?" He was already up and looking for them, rummaging through the bags he'd packed, looking for her prescription.

She didn't answer, but started to rock, one hand shielding her sensitive eyes.

"This happened every time you chased a killer?"

She mumbled her reply, the words unintelligible, but he felt the assent in his mind.

"And people think *I'm* crazy."

Kadan settled down beside her, supporting her head with his palm, pushing the pills into her mouth and then holding the water bottle for her. She groaned softly at the movement, but obediently swallowed the medicine.

You don't have to stay with me. She wanted him gone, hating to have anyone see her this way. Vulnerable. Mind gone. Nearly insane. Hurting. It hurt so bad.

Kadan stroked back her wild hair, his fingers lingering in the silky strands. "Don't talk. Don't use telepathy, it only makes the headache worse. Go to sleep, Tansy."

She'd done this since she was thirteen. No training. No exercises to help her form barriers between the violent energy and her wide open brain. What possible reason could Whitney have had, allowing her to suffer? Was it another of his insane experiments? He had obviously documented each incident, insisting on examining and debriefing her each time she used her ability to track a serial killer. Had he wanted to see how long it took to break her?

She shivered, her body trembling as the overload fully hit. Swearing, he stretched out beside her, using his body heat to warm her. Her skin was cold, her eyes nearly opaque. He wrapped his arms around her and pulled her tight against him, curling so that his body protected hers. She fit. She was made for him. Whitney couldn't have done that. Kadan chose not to believe it was the pheromones. Pheromones couldn't make him feel anything but physical attraction, which he had in spades, but there was so much more.

He had long since ceased to be emotional, yet he was now—with her. Alone, with her falling into a fitful sleep, he could allow himself a little emotion. And his mission wasn't worth destroying her completely. He would find another way. There was always another way.

Her body jerked and she cried out, pressing both hands to her head.

His hands went to her shoulders, massaging gently, then moved to her neck in an attempt to ease the tension out of her. "Shh, baby, just sleep. I'm not going to make you do this. I'll find a way around all this. Just go to sleep for me."

She settled a little. He couldn't be certain if it was his reassurance, or the massage, but she seemed quieter. He moved her hair aside and bent his head to kiss the nape of her neck. "I'm going to tell them you've lost your abilities, but then you need to stay out of sight until I wrap this up." He spoke aloud more for himself than for her.

He felt her body stiffen. Her long, wet lashes fluttered, lifted, and she looked at him, her eyes so light they appeared violet.

"I mean it, Tansy, you're off the hook. You need to just sleep and not worry about anything anymore." He stroked his hand through her hair.

She closed her eyes again and relaxed beneath his hands.

Kadan sighed. How was he going to find the strength to give her up? He'd never thought in terms of a woman or a home. He'd been a loner since he was eight years old. His friends were all GhostWalkers, men who understood what it was like to be different. They were warriors, born in the wrong century maybe, men with honor and codes and a way of life that was politically incorrect. Women should never live with men like him, and he had no business staking his claim on one.

His fingers rubbed at the silky hair. He wanted her. Desperately. This woman brought sunlight to his soul. She made him believe again. Hope. Feel there was a chance at a future. Maybe a home and children. He'd been in her mind and he knew her more intimately than a man could know a woman after fifty years of living together. There was strength and determination. Independence. Compassion. She was soft where he was hard.

The sun began to climb higher into the sky, and he let himself doze while he could. He hadn't gotten that much sleep the night before. Her body had been too tempting, and he'd been starving and addicted after the first taste. Being a soldier meant you slept when you could. He woke with Tansy moaning softly, moving against him, her hand brushing his face.

He could wake up to that touch forever. A million mornings. He caught her hand and pressed a kiss into her palm. "Are you feeling better?"

"Yes. I'm a little afraid to let you out of my head. I'm not good at keeping the voices out." She brushed his hair from his forehead, her fingers tracing his scar. "I'm going to miss being able to touch you. I never touch anyone."

She didn't think she'd ever be able to touch anyone again. He should have felt bad. Instead he wanted to be the only one she could touch. Selfish bastard. He mentally kicked himself.

"I'm going to teach you a few exercises to help you

strengthen your defenses against anything invading your mind."

She frowned and sat up. "What exercises?"

"There are things you can do, practice, to help filter things out. Like meditation."

"I do that already. It's never helped."

Kadan stood up and pulled her with him. "This is going to help. Sit at the table."

She studied his face for a long time before she complied, taking the seat opposite him.

Kadan turned out to be all military and very serious as he showed her the mental exercise of building a wall in her mind, one brick at a time. It was far different from the simple mental image she employed of a door keeping back the voices and images in her head. The barrier had to be built and become second nature. When she wavered, or got it wrong, Kadan barked orders at her like a drill sergeant.

"You're giving me a headache," she finally said, glaring at him. "And I'm not under your stupid command."

His jaw tightened. "You already have a headache so it doesn't count. These exercises work and you need to learn them fast. I'm not going to be here to take away the pain."

She couldn't very well tell him it wasn't going to work, because in just an hour she could already tell her mind was calmer. If she did the exercises every day, she could strengthen her filters and barriers and keep the voices at bay.

"Fine. I didn't say I wasn't going to keep working. If you have to leave soon, let's at least try to make sense of some of the impressions I got from the ivory stallion. There've been ten murders that you know of so far, right?"

"We don't need to talk about it anymore. I don't want you involved."

"I heard you say that. Did you mean it?"

This time she was in his head. Waiting. Holding her

breath. Watching him. Kadan slowly nodded. "I can find them. It's not worth it to me to use you to save my friends."

She let her breath out. "Are you doing this to save your friends or to stop murderers?"

"Both. Someone has to stop them, and there's no way I'm letting the GhostWalkers take the fall. We have a powerful enemy in the White House and he wants all of us dead. These are good men, Tansy. I'm not going to let them down."

"Have you considered asking the other Ghostwalkers for help? If you believe in them so much and they're capable of doing the kind of thing I do . . ."

He shook his head. "No one is capable of doing what you do. And you have a mind for it. You fit puzzle pieces together at an astonishing rate."

Tansy looked around for a water bottle. "I'm thirsty." She needed time to think.

Kadan immediately got her a bottle out of the cooler. Tansy accepted it and gratefully took a long swallow.

"What are the other game pieces? Do you have them with you?"

He shook his head. "I only brought one. I thought I'd be bringing you back with me."

She tapped her nail on the small table. "So let's say we have two teams and each team member has his own game piece that he leaves behind when it's his turn to play."

He held up a hand. "Back up. What do you mean, 'his turn to play'?"

"I'm telling you, this is a game. They've established rules and it stands to reason that each person takes a turn and commits a predetermined murder. Maybe they're copying crimes from the past. Have you checked for similarities in the killings with historical killings?"

"No, but I can do that fast enough."

"I would. They might be copying murders. They have

cards of some kind." She frowned, forcing her mind to open a little and let herself remember. "Not playing cards. A little larger, like tarot cards."

"You got that from just holding that game piece?" Kadan wanted her for a partner. Her information was much more thorough and clearly presented than any report could ever be. And she had invaluable experience.

"I need to know what the other pieces are."

"Are you sure?" He didn't want to drag her in any deeper, not when he knew he had to leave her there. As it was, over a distance, he couldn't protect her mind, and those voices were still wailing. Distant, but there. The best he could hope for was that the exercises he'd given her to do would help after he was gone.

"Just tell me." She was impatient, her mind trying to solve a puzzle with too few pieces.

"Frog, there is a frog, carved out of ivory as well. If I had to guess, I'd bet the same man carved both figurines."

"I'd be able to tell you if you'd brought both." There was a slight edge, a reprimand, to her voice. "The frog and stallion, were they both left at different murder scenes on the East Coast?"

He nodded. "A frog, a stallion, a snake, and what appears to be the blade of a knife."

Her head went up alertly. "All out of ivory. Even the blade?"

"Yes." He could see her mind was working double time.

"That's significant in some way. Three animal forms and the blade of a knife," she repeated, more to herself than to him. "What were the pieces left on the West Coast?"

"A hawk, a scorpion, an anatomically correct and very well-endowed bull, and a perfect replica of a long-handled scythe."

"So already there's a pattern. We have two studs and two weapons. Let's for argument's sake say these are nicknames. Don't most military men in Special Forces get bizarre nicknames?"

His mouth tightened. She was burying his friends with her quick deductions.

She flicked him a gaze under the fringe of long lashes. "I'm going the military route because you're going in that direction. We have a stud on both teams. We can assume the weapon is the team leader. The two left are probably followers. So who is really running the game?"

"I don't understand."

She shrugged. "Someone is running the game. You have another player. Or referee. These men are highly competitive. They're thrill seekers. They want action. I need to see the rest of the game pieces and I need to hear about the other murders." She took a breath and let it out. "I'm going with you."

Kadan shook his head, his gut tightening. There it was. Complete capitulation. She was hooked. She would come with him voluntarily. "No." His voice was firm. "No way. I told you I'm going to tell them you can't do this anymore."

She waved her hand in the air. "I appreciate it, and I don't want to do it all over again, but I'm not going to be able to let this go. This killer, the 'stallion,' he's going to kill again. If not with his team, on his own. He may already be doing so. In fact, I'd bet that he is. He'll start with prostitutes, women who are very vulnerable. He needs the power and control. He's got to be stopped, Kadan, and if none of your friends can do what I do, how are you going to track him? The killings are too random."

Kadan closed his eyes and looked away from her. "Damn it. Just damn it." Because he should walk away, leave her in peace, but he wasn't going to. And not because he needed to save the lives of his friends. Not because he needed to save lives of innocent people. He was going to put her through hell because he was a selfish bastard and he wasn't willing to give her up. He didn't like knowing that about himself, but there it was.

CHAPTER 6

They began fighting the moment they entered the house where Kadan had set up headquarters. Tansy was going to call her parents whether Kadan liked it or not. And he didn't like it. She tossed her head, her eyes flashing defiance.

"You can bark out orders all you like, big man, but I'm not under your command. I'm not exactly an amateur at this business, and I don't fall under the category of your underling, so get over that notion as well. Just who do you think you are, anyway?"

Kadan stepped close to her, purposely invading her personal space, inhaling her cinnamon scent, challenging her idea of what equality was. "I'm the only man who is ever going to lie with you at night and hold you close and keep you safe. I'm the only man who is going to make love to you anywhere, anytime, any way we both need or want it. More importantly, Tansy, I'm the man who is going to kill anyone who threatens you. So you can damn well listen to me."

She blinked at him, opened her mouth and closed it again, looking confused and entirely too seductive and bewildered for him to resist. Kadan leaned his head down and took possession of that soft, trembling mouth. Kissing her felt so damned good. He wanted to get lost in her, to just have the world disappear so he could spend his life skin-to-skin, kissing her.

"You know how to take the wind out of a woman's sails," she said accusingly, when she could talk again. "What am I supposed to say to that?"

"Nothing. Just kiss me again."

Tansy turned her mouth up to his. This time he pulled her close, his hand at the nape of her neck, holding her still while he took a long exploration, savoring her cinnamon flavor. "You are never supposed to argue with me." He rested his forehead against hers, looking into her strangely colored eyes.

She laughed softly. "I hate to burst your bubble, here, buddy, but all the kisses in the world are not going to stop me from letting my parents know where I am, who I'm with, and what I'm going to do. I don't hide things from them."

Kadan jerked away from her, pacing across the room. "I can't trust them. That's the truth whether you want to believe it or not. Until I clear them, I have to treat them like the enemy."

"My *parents*? Enemies? What do you think they're going to do? Contact the killers and say we're on to them?"

He spun around and gripped her shoulders hard. "I think they'll call Dr. Peter Whitney and inform him what you're doing."

Tansy tried to pull away from him, horror blossoming on her face, but he held her with his enormous strength, refusing to allow her to move away from his solid warmth. He gave her a little shake. "Did you hear me, Tansy? Did you understand what I said? What I meant? I'm the man who kills anyone who threatens you."

She swallowed hard and shook her head. "Not my parents. They would never betray me. Never. I don't care what you think, they wouldn't do that."

"Why would they choose a damaged child, Tansy, when they were wealthy enough to buy perfection? Any adoption agency would have given them whatever they wanted right down to the color of hair and eyes. Why you? When they got you, you probably couldn't stand their touch, or even using their utensils to eat with. Come on. You have a brain. Use it here. Figure out what the hell was going on back then. They took you to a doctor you clearly didn't want to see, and in spite of your tears and pleas, they left you alone with him."

Tansy closed her eyes briefly, trying not to remember the way her mother pleaded with her father, clinging to her before he took her firmly from her mother's arms and shoved her into the room with Whitney. Kadan couldn't be right. She wouldn't let him be right. Even thinking that way was a betrayal of her parents' love for her. "Shut up. I mean it, Kadan, I don't want you talking about my parents anymore."

"Then you promise me you're not going to call them."

"I *have* to call them. We have an arrangement. If I don't, they'll come looking for me." Tansy glared right back at him. "They love me, Kadan. They won't betray me."

"Then ask them what they're relationship with Whitney is and ask them why they didn't tell you he was still alive. Do that much. Don't make me have to track them down and find out myself, Tansy. You don't want me confronting your parents."

He looked so grim, so frightening, as if he was capable of walking in and putting a gun to their heads. Her parents. Two people she loved.

"Two people who are in this up to their necks," Kadan interrupted, clearly reading her mind. "Whitney experimented on children. On *you*. And they had to have known, but they said nothing. They did nothing to stop it. At least admit they had to have known."

She pushed at the wall of his chest. "Damn you, you just can't leave this alone. You're leaving me with *nothing*. They're my sanity. They're everything in my world and you're not going to take them away from me. This is a mistake. A big mistake. I was crazy coming here with you."

His fingers dug deeper, not allowing her to escape. "You're damn right. You don't seem to have the first idea of security, even when you've had plenty of reasons to be afraid. But I'm not your problem, Tansy, and you wouldn't be so upset if you didn't already know that. Don't blame me because there's something very smelly about the way your parents acquired you."

"You're such a bastard. Take your hands off of me. I'm calling my dad."

"Put him on speakerphone. This number is blocked and will be difficult to trace, but even so, you only have a few minutes to talk. I'll be timing you. If you start to say anything that compromises our mission or your safety, I disconnect. Do you understand?"

He held her in place, his eyes blazing down into her with that relentless, implacable, very annoying expression. She had a wild urge to kick him hard. Finally she nodded. He dropped his hands immediately. She muttered a repeat of the not so nice name she'd called him earlier, only this time she added not so nice adjectives to go along with it for good measure. He simply ignored her.

Tansy swung away, stalking across the room to the phone. She stabbed out her parents' number, refusing to look at Kadan as he came up behind her and pushed the speakerphone button. Her mother answered.

"Hey, Mom," Tansy said in greeting, her fingers twisting together. "Is Dad right there with you?"

"You're on the phone, not the radio," her mother observed. "Where are you?"

"Is Dad there?" she repeated.

"He's right here. I'm going to put you on speakerphone so we can both hear," Sharon added. "When did you get off the mountain?"

"Hi, Dad. I need you to answer a question for me," Tansy said, gripping her wrist hard, digging in her nails. "Why didn't you tell me Dr. Whitney was still alive?"

There was a silence. She closed her eyes, picturing the shock on her parents' faces.

"Did that son of a bitch bother you, Tansy?" Don Meadows demanded. "What has he done? Tell me, honey, and I'll take care of it."

She looked around for a chair to sink into. Kadan shoved one under her and Tansy collapsed into it. "Why didn't you tell me about him, Dad? I've gone through enough that I deserve to know. Why do you have anything at all to do with a man like that? You've got to tell me the truth."

"What has he done? Tell me where you are and I'll send Fredrickson to pick you up. Don't trust anyone else," her father insisted.

Kadan dropped his hands on Tansy's slumped shoulders in an effort to show camaraderie.

"What does he have on you?" Tansy asked quietly.

There was silence again. Her mother choked back a sob.

"Come home now, Tansy. I'll tell you everything, but come home."

Kadan gripped her harder and shook his head when she tilted back to look at him. *They need to get out of there, somewhere safe. He's probably monitoring this conversation. Tell them that. Tell them to get out.*

"I have to go now. He's probably monitoring the conversation, Dad, and it isn't safe for you. Take Mom and go into hiding. Do it now and don't trust anyone."

Her mother screamed.

"You don't have to do that," Don Meadows bellowed. "She'll come back."

Tansy jumped to her feet. "Mom?"

"Tansy?" There was another male voice on the phone. "I'm afraid Mommy can't talk right now. Neither can Daddy. You have twenty-four hours to get back here or they're both dead. Say you understand."

Fredrickson, Dad's bodyguard, she identified to Kadan.

"What are you doing, Fredrickson?" she asked.

Her mother screamed again; this time the sound was filled with pain, not shock.

"I understand," Tansy said and hung up the phone. She didn't want to give Fredrickson, or anyone else, a chance to cause her parents further pain. "Get me a plane."

"Take a breath. Let's get a plan first."

Tansy knocked his hand away. "The plan is, I do whatever Fredrickson wants me to do. I'm not letting him kill my parents."

"He's not going to kill them," Kadan said. "As long as they don't have you, no one is going to kill them. When they acquire you, your parents' usefulness will be gone. That's when they'll be in real danger."

"You heard my mother scream."

"That was deliberate to frighten you into immediate compliance."

She glared at him. "Well, it worked. Get me a plane."

Kadan regarded her with that cool, impassive gaze she was coming to dislike. "Sit down, Tansy. We need to think, not run off half-cocked."

"Screw you, Kadan." She turned away and headed for the door.

His fingers settled around her wrist like a steel hand-cuff. "You're too emotional for this kind of work. Settle down."

She swung back, using her momentum to put power behind the punch she threw at him. Her fist went straight and true for his jaw, but he caught it, the sound loud as her knuckles slammed into his palm. He simply turned her, locking her tight against him.

"Don't be stupid, Tansy. I'm not the enemy. If you want your parents to survive, sit the hell down and let's figure out how to get them out alive. We need to know what's going on here. Is it connected to the murders? Is this about Whitney and you finding out about him? Fredrickson was obviously a plant in your house, but who put him there? Who does he work for?" He whispered the words, low and cool, in her ear. His breath was warm, his body hot, his grip too strong to break. "Use your brain."

Tansy hated that he was right. *Hated* it. She wanted to take another punch at him just for being right. "Let go. Just let go. I'm sitting down."

Kadan reluctantly released her, his eyes narrowed, watching her closely. Waiting. She felt him in her mind and glared at him.

"I need the layout of the house and grounds, with as much detail as possible, and that includes position of furniture and lighting. I need to know about security. Cameras. Guards. Alarms. Codes for alarms. Everything you can give me."

Tansy leaned her forehead into her hand. "You were right."

He was the devil as far as she was concerned, and he couldn't really blame her. He waved her admission aside. "Let's hear what they have to say before we condemn them. You just have to be very careful. Whitney is a monster."

She flicked him another quick look. "I know he's a monster and he must have something on them. Whatever it is, it has to be bad for them to go along with anything that man has done. I've been the insect under his microscope. What are we going to do to keep him from killing my parents?"

At least she had included him. "We're going to take them back. I'll make a couple of phone calls and get some help." Kadan didn't want to think too much about the way her father had said to Fredrickson, *You don't have to do that. She'll come back*, but the words were engraved in his mind and the ramifications a scary thing.

She dragged air into her lungs. "The GhostWalkers. You're going to ask them to help us." There was fear in her voice.

"And you're going to know they aren't involved. We won't be able to prove it, but you examine each of the game pieces, and when you meet the team, you'll know if any of them match any of the game pieces, right? You have strong impressions of personality."

"Of course I'll know. What happens if one of them is involved?"

"You signal me; I take out a gun and execute him."

There was another small silence while she examined his face, looking for a sign that he was joking. "We bring him in for trial," she corrected.

"There isn't going to be a trial for any GhostWalker caught murdering civilians. There's an execution order. Every GhostWalker is on the chopping block, thanks to these killers. When I know who they are, I'm authorized to hunt them and terminate."

"And you're okay with that?"

For a moment something hot swirled beneath the cool ice of his gaze. "These men are soldiers, more than soldiers. They are superweapons, sworn to protect this country and everyone in it. They are betraying every soldier who has gone before them, the soldiers fighting now, and all who come after. We have a code. They've broken that code. And more than that, Tansy, you better know exactly what we're up against."

"It's always difficult to go up against psychos."

He shook his head. "Superweapons. Never forget that these men we're chasing are not just well-trained soldiers, which would make our job difficult enough. I've had every kind of training possible. So have these men. I'm enhanced psychically. So are they. I'm enhanced physically. They are as well. If someone comes after me to kill me, they have one chance. One. They have to take me by surprise; after that, I'm hunting them and they're dead. These men are like me. Once they know we're on to them, they'll disappear and we'll never find them unless they surface to retaliate."

She nodded slowly. "Unfortunately, I have to agree with that assessment after handling the stallion. The man who owns that game piece definitely thinks he's superior and above all laws. His sense of entitlement is absolute. I believe he would come after us in a heartbeat, and it would never occur to him that he would lose."

"He's going to lose," Kadan said, no inflection in his voice.

There was no inflection in his mind either when she touched it. Only resolve and a belief that he was far more intelligent than his adversaries and that his code demanded the men committing the murders pay for casting a shadow over his fellow GhostWalkers. They would pay for betraying their country and the honor of every soldier the Ghost-Walkers represented. A shiver went down her spine. Just like the murderers, Kadan believed he was superior and far more intelligent. Faster. Stronger. That his training could see him through any situation. He believed in his teammates and he had a strong patriotic sense of duty. More than anything, these men had betrayed all soldiers, their

country, and their code. Sentence had already been passed.
To Kadan, they were walking dead men.

Kadan reached out and captured her hand, tugging until
she was close to him. A breath away. The heat of her body
meeting and amplifying the heat of his. "Tansy, don't be
afraid of me. You have access to my mind . . ."

She shook her head. "I don't. I have access to what you
let me see. You see all of me."

"You have access to all the places that belong to you.
I'm not hiding how I feel about you. I want you, not for one
night, but always."

"Because of Whitney. You think your attraction to me
is because of Whitney, and you aren't happy about it."

"I did think that," he admitted without flinching, "and I
was angry at the manipulation. But Whitney can only manipulate physical attraction. He has no power over my
emotions. And you." He framed her face with his hands.
"Have no doubt that the intensity and depth of emotion I feel
for you, Whitney could never have dreamt of, let alone managed to produce in me. I don't feel emotion as a rule. I didn't
even know I was capable of such depth of feeling. So never
worry that my feelings for you are manufactured. I could
never harm you, not under any circumstances."

Her eyes searched his, looking for something, some reassurance that went beyond what he told her, what she saw
in his mind. "My parents?" she asked softly, unable to stop
worrying. Kadan was ruthless and a man without mercy.
She knew he would execute anyone, friend or not, if they
were guilty, and he would do it without hesitation.

He shrugged. "I'm not willing to lie to you, Tansy. I
hope they aren't guilty of anything other than stupidity,
but if they try to harm you, if their intention is to betray
you and turn you over to Whitney, they'll have to walk
through me to do it."

His thumb smoothed over the contours of her bone

structure, tracing her jaw and high cheekbones, dipping down to float over her lips. The pads of his fingers felt hard, yet velvet soft, and she couldn't stop the shiver of need or the inevitable arousal that leapt from breasts to thighs. He was mesmerizing, and the lure of another human's touch was inescapable, but more than all of that was the intense sensuality, the way his gaze went hot and moved over her with such possession, the way one flick of his eyes seemed to remove her clothing.

In his head he touched her, brushing her breast or stroking a caress down her thigh at the most unexpected times. In the helicopter, earlier, when they'd been picked up, she'd huddled, knees drawn up, head down, making herself small. He sat beside her, his large frame protecting her from prying eyes, although he'd seemed to be asleep. Every now and then, she'd found him in her head and he was caressing the inside of her thigh. Stroking fingertips over her breast, leaning in to kiss her throat. He could melt her heart without half trying.

"You're a very dangerous man, Kadan."

"But not to you." He bent his head and kissed her. "Never to you."

Her eyebrow went up. She didn't smile. "You're very wrong about that." Because he was stealing her will, whether he realized it or not. She sighed. She couldn't stop her physical reaction to him, but she needed to start thinking with her brain if she was going to help her parents. "How do we know your friends will help us?"

"They'll help. We don't have a lot of time. I'll make the calls. You write down everything you can about the security and floor plans. Ryland and Nico are amazing at infiltrating hostile territory without being seen. This will be a good chance for you to see GhostWalkers in action and see what we're really up against."

"I'm taking a shower." She was still a little achy from

her mental battle with the voices, and while the water ran hot and cleansing over her, she hoped to practice the mental exercises he'd given her to strengthen her barriers.

"Take a look around," he invited as he turned back to the phone.

Tansy did just that. He'd set up a war room. Pictures of murder victims lined all four walls. Each crime was documented carefully with the camera, the body positions, the scene itself, the blood spatter, it was all there. She closed the door, refusing to step inside the nightmare without him to help shield her. As it was, her stomach rebelled, and she hastily backed down the hall to the master bedroom, where Kadan had tossed her backpack onto the bed.

The hot water felt good on her sore body. She took her time shampooing her long hair. It had been months since she'd felt really hot water on her body. Bathing in the natural pool had been a shock to her system until she'd gotten used to it, but she'd forgotten how good hot water felt. It was sheer bliss.

"I tossed your clothes into the washing machine," Kadan said, holding out a towel. He didn't avert his eyes, but rather drank in the sight of her body, noting each mark he'd put there the night before. "We're only going to be here a few hours, so I figured it was best to get it done quickly."

She wrapped the towel around her. "Thanks, I've been washing them in buckets."

He indicated with his finger for her to turn around. Tansy turned her back to him and he slipped another towel over her head, rubbing at her scalp and the mass of long hair. "Ryland Miller is married to Whitney's daughter, Lily." He ignored her stiffening shoulders and kept massaging. "Rye's got her stashed with other GhostWalkers so she'll be safe while he comes here to give us a hand. They just had a baby."

"Are you sure . . . ?"

"I'm sure of him. I've known him a long time, and remember, I can read minds. He knows I have telepathy, but not to the extent of penetrating minds. No one but you knows I can do that."

"Why would you trust me with any of your secrets?"

He rested his hands on her bare shoulders and then caressed her vulnerable neck, his fingers strong, stealing along the soft skin. "All I have to give you is the truth of who I am. You have to know what you're dealing with."

She turned her head to look at him over her shoulder. There was fear in her eyes. Excitement. Confusion. Need. "Kadan, I came here to help solve these murders, not to give myself to you."

His hand slid around her neck to her throat, his palm forcing her head back, tipping it against his chest so she was looking into his cool gaze. "Really? Because that's not what I see in your mind."

"My mind is confused." Tansy tried to lift her head, but he countered the movement, stepping back, forcing her weight against him so she was off balance. "Kadan." She said his name softly. A plea. There was pleading in her eyes. All shimmering violet again.

"We fit. You don't want to be alone and neither do I. Give us a chance, Tansy. I'm not easy, but I'm loyal, yours, all the way."

"I'm afraid of you. Not that you'll hurt me, but your code is—different. I'm afraid."

"Don't you think I know that? I'll be gentle with you."

He bent his head, tracking down her face with kisses, licking at her mouth until she opened for him. His lips settled over hers. Her heart fluttered. Her stomach muscles bunched. Liquid heat flooded her core. She wanted to cry that he could get around her mind so easily. She hadn't known she could be so influenced by physical attraction.

"Kadan, is it real? Do we dare believe it's real? I don't want to feel things for you, to love you and have it all disappear. I finally found peace in my life. I could live the way I was living. I'd never be able to go back if I gave myself to you and lost."

She'd been in his mind, saw what he was like. A hard-ass. Merciless. Ruthless. A warrior once sent on a mission, who would never stop until it was completed. A man who craved her the way he might sunlight and air. He wanted to consume her. And he wanted her body—was obsessed with knowing every inch of her, with giving her every pleasure he could think of and taking his own. He'd been a man who never believed he would have his own woman, a woman who would share more than his body. But she could take his mind, and she could be his. She could belong to him wholly, and now that he knew, he refused to back away from the one chance he had.

"Whitney cannot manipulate our minds. You see me as I am and you still want me. I see you and I'm desperate for you. He isn't anywhere in the equation."

She turned in his arms and rested her head against his chest. The way he felt about her, so completely ensnared, was both exhilarating and frightening. The fact that she could touch him, lie in his arms, make love with him, and have the added pleasure of mind-sex enhancing what was already explosive physical chemistry, was such a lure she doubted if she could resist—but self-preservation demanded she try. If she loved him—really loved him—let him all the way in, he would be so difficult to live with.

But worth it.

She shook her head. "How would you know?"

He caught her chin with two fingers and tipped her head up again, taking her mouth with much more possession this time, teasing and dueling with his tongue, sending tiny flames licking over her skin.

When he lifted his head, her eyes had gone from blue to that beautiful violet color he particularly loved. Her face flushed, breasts rising and falling, breath coming in a ragged little telltale rush. Tansy stepped away from him, wiping at her mouth with the back of her hand, shaking her head at him. He could go from ice-cold to fiery hot in seconds.

"When are your friends coming?"

"We have a few hours. I'll need the layout and security as soon as possible to plan our entry. They won't be expecting resistance. They don't know about me—yet."

His tone chilled her. His eyes never seemed to blink, cold and mesmerizing at the same time. "Someone sent a couple of assassins after you and they tracked you to my mountain; maybe they do know," she pointed out.

He shrugged. "It's of no consequence. We'll get your parents out." And he intended to have a quiet chat with dear old dad before the man would ever be allowed to be alone with his daughter again.

"I want to see the game pieces. Take a shower and then we'll see if I can find out anything that will help us before your friends get here."

He caught her wrist as she turned away from him. "Tansy." He waited until her gaze met his. "When this rescue goes down, don't interfere with whatever we do. Follow orders."

She frowned at him. "I don't know what that means."

"That means, on a mission, we run it the way we do a military op. Very precise. I can't have a lose cannon running around. You agree to follow orders or you stay here and wait."

Swift impatience crossed her face. "Oh really? And how do you expect to accomplish that?"

He dropped her wrist and began unbuttoning his shirt. "Lock you up. It doesn't matter. I run a tight op and I'm not going to have you fuck it up because you get scared for your parents. You'll be in on the planning every step of the way, but once we're hot, we go by the numbers."

"You're so unexpectedly charming, Kadan. Do you think I'm an idiot?"

He balled the shirt into his fist and tossed it toward the laundry basket he kept beside a bureau. "No, I think you're emotional. There's a big difference."

She opened her backpack. It was empty. "You put all my clothes into the wash?"

"Use my shirt. It's long enough to cover you."

Tansy tried to avert her eyes as he peeled off his jeans and kicked them aside. Okay, it was impossible. He was well endowed. And there were scars. Lots of them. Knives. Guns. Marks she couldn't identify.

"Maybe you ought to learn to duck."

A ghost of a smile teased at his mouth. "Maybe I will. It isn't polite to stare."

She had been staring. She was still staring. And his endowment was growing bigger by the moment, which meant she could be in trouble. She needed time to sort out what she was really doing with him, because he was too overwhelming and she couldn't think straight.

Resolutely she went to his closet and pulled out a shirt with long tails. She dropped the towel, keeping her back to him, and shrugged into the shirt. There was no sound to warn her and she nearly screamed when his hands came around her back, drawing her against him so that there was only the thin cotton between his rigid shaft and her bottom. His fingertips brushed her breasts as he closed the shirt, fastening one button at a time. Deep inside, her womb clenched hotly.

Kadan swept her wet hair aside and pressed a kiss into the hollow of her shoulder, the side of her neck, and then his lips whispered over her ear. "You're so beautiful, Tansy, you make me ache." His hand slipped down the contour of her back to shape her bottom. "And your skin is even softer than it looks."

"Don't seduce me." She leaned back into him, feeling helpless under the onslaught of molten lava pooling low and wicked in her body. "Not now. I've got to sort things out."

His lips skimmed her ear again. "I don't want you thinking too much. You'll realize I'm a poor prospect as a husband and run."

His words, or maybe it was his mouth, caused a shiver of awareness. Her nipples tightened and she felt liquid heat gathering. She'd never considered having a husband. She'd never thought she could ever be touched—or touch.

"Take a shower, Kadan." The words came out strangled. There was no way to hide what he was doing to her.

He nipped at her shoulder, felt the tremor that rocked her body. He wanted her to know that she belonged to him, that he could seduce her if he chose. Her eyes told him she knew it already. Satisfied, he brushed a kiss along the corner of her mouth and gently stood, her back up straight. "A shower it is," he agreed. "Don't go into the war room without me."

"I really do have a brain." She made a little face at him. "Evidently I haven't shown it to you yet, but it's there."

Tansy found her way to the kitchen. Every door had a strange device across it, and she suspected the device was some sort of bomb. Thin wires ran along the windows. She picked up the phone and found no dial tone. He'd done something to prevent her calling out. Frowning, she went back into the bedroom, to her backpack. Her cell phone should have been inside, but it was gone as well.

She stomped into the bathroom. "Where's my phone?"

The shower door was transparent glass. He turned toward her, giving her a full frontal view. Even anger didn't stop the surge of excitement at the sight of him. She swore under her breath, close to tears that she could be so stupid. He'd made her virtually a prisoner. He looked at her very calmly, his expression remote, his eyes cool, and that only added flames to the flash of temper and panic surfacing. The two emotions were twisted so tightly together she didn't recognize either one.

"I thought it best to keep it for a while, until I'm certain you aren't going to lose your mind."

Her breath hitched. The door in her mind creaked. Whispers filled her head. She barely registered his changing expression as she jerked around and back out the door.

"Tansy!" Kadan shoved the shower door open and caught up a towel as he ran after her, water flying all over the floor, his bare feet slapping as he raced through the house toward the front room. *Stop! You cannot move.* He drove each word like a nail into her mind, fear knotting the muscles in his belly and his voice unrecognizable.

Tansy halted just ahead of him, one hand outstretched toward the rigged door, her body frozen in place. He crossed the distance in a single jump, taking him over furniture and her head, to land solidly between her and the door. He dragged her into his arms, right off her feet, cradling her body against his chest, breath coming in ragged gasps. "Damn it, Tansy. You could have fucking died. What the hell is wrong with you? Why would you do that?"

His lungs burned for air, and he took a deep breath to steady himself. She was doing it to him again. In under two seconds she could destroy the control he'd spent a lifetime building. He sank down onto the sofa and caught her chin in his hand, forcing her to meet the ice in his eyes. "You ever do anything that stupid again, I swear I'll beat you within an inch of your life."

Even as the harsh words left his mouth, he was raining kisses over her face, down her cheeks, following the path of tears, and all the while he rocked her gently back and forth. "I'm sorry, Tansy. My word choice was poor. I don't believe you're going to lose your mind again, and I know that's what you're thinking. I didn't trick you into coming. I didn't seduce you into coming with me. I would have let you go."

"I can't go back to that place."

She could barely choke out the words. The fear of the door in her mind splintering, allowing the killers to escape, terrified her. For a moment she had thought he'd lied to her about the exercises, about his ability to help get her through the solving of the murders. If he believed her mind would fracture again, she had no hope left.

He felt her terror, heard the increase in the sound of the whispers. She was so fragile, and he'd brought her into this mess, and now her parents were in danger as well. "Listen to me, baby. If you can't handle the investigation, you're done. That's it. We'll sideline you immediately before anything goes too far. I'll be with you every step of the way, buffering your mind. If you work on the exercises, they'll also help strengthen your barriers. Know this absolutely. Before anything or anyone else, I'll protect you. Look at me, Tansy." He forced her gaze to meet his. "Understand I'm telling you the truth. The one thing in your life, from now until the end, is that you can always count on me."

She searched his face. He knew what she saw couldn't be that reassuring. He wasn't a handsome man by any stretch of the imagination. Several scars had added to the menacing appearance. His jaw was strong, his mouth hard. He'd long ago learned to keep his face without expression, and his eyes were as cold as the ice water running in his veins. As a rule, he felt little to nothing, until Tansy. He couldn't explain that to her, because he didn't fully understand it himself. Beneath the ice seemed to be a volcano that only erupted around her.

"Don't handle me, Kadan. I don't like to be handled."

His eyes flashed with something raw that made her stomach flip. She reached up to trace his mouth. There was always such a cruel edge there, as if he was capable of terrible things, yet one small movement, just a slight turn, and he could appear incredibly sensual. The look in his eyes held a dark lust that just intensified when he held her like this. His arms felt like steel, his body both protective and possessive. She turned soft, melting against him, into him. She lost herself in his steely strength.

His hand slid over the curve of her bare hip, those

incredible fingers, hard yet velvet soft, brushing against her skin erotically. His head dipped lower to find her ear again. "I think you're lying to me. I feel your need beating at me, Tansy. You like the way I handle you."

"You weren't supposed to seduce me."

He bent his head to her neck, his teeth nipping, first the hollow of her shoulder and then her earlobe. "Look into your mind, Tansy. You seduced me, not the other way around. How could I possibly resist you?"

She closed her eyes, knowing he was right, knowing she was enticing him, stroking at his mind with hers, enhancing his needs because she so desperately wanted to be held. To belong somewhere, with someone.

His teeth bit down, flashing pain through her body, then his tongue swirled, taking away the sting. "Not someone, Tansy. *Me.* You belong with me."

Her eyes met his and her stomach flipped.

"Say it."

She wanted to resist him, but she couldn't resist her own needs. "I belong with you."

His fingers smoothed up the inside of her thigh, teased her soft, damp mound. "Open your shirt." The fingers continued their journey, sliding into her, curling and teasing, stroking and circling her sensitive bud.

Again, she wanted to resist, just for pride's sake. She didn't altogether trust him. He was too cold, too able to turn off emotion, and she wasn't entirely certain she could trust that he would be all the things he said to her. His hunger for her was absolute, but there was a driving need in him for complete possession. She didn't understand what he wanted from her. He confused her. She confused herself, craving him desperately, wanting to escape the way he mesmerized her.

His fingers stilled. Her womb spasmed. Desperation won. She slowly unbuttoned the shirt, revealing the swell of her breasts and narrow rib cage, the flat of her tummy and finally the vee of curls at the junction of her legs. When the shirt was open all the way, his fingers did another slow curl inside her and began to stroke again, pushing deep.

CHAPTER 7

Tansy's breath caught in her throat. Her body pulsed with need. Kadan could turn her into a melting cauldron of liquid heat with one intense look. Hot excitement poured through her veins. He was all muscle and strength. And he was completely, utterly, focused on her. He made her feel as if he had to have her. As if waiting one more moment might kill him. He didn't say much. He just looked at her, his eyes dark with lust, with possession, and every fiber of her being surrendered to the demand in his steady gaze.

His calloused hand was hot on her skin, and every muscle in her body tensed. He knew every shadow and curve intimately, and she craved his touch. *Craved* it. After a lifetime of never touching or being touched, she felt like a cat, pleasured by the caressing strokes, arching her back, pushing her hips upward against his hand, needy for whatever he gave her.

The pad of his thumb, with the strange feel of velvet bristles, made lazy circles on the inside of her thigh, slid upward to caress the crease between her buttocks and her thigh. A soft moan escaped, needy and hot and so unlike her, although she was afraid that with Kadan she'd turned into a very sexual being. Blood thundered in her pulse, roared in her ears, and throbbed in her clit, in time with the mounting tension in her womb.

There was something very arousing about lying sprawled across a man's lap, shirt open, bare breasts spilling out, and his hands wandering possessively up her thighs, fingers circling and disappearing inside her body, as if her body belonged to him and not her. His face was dark and intent, hooded eyes on the rise and fall of her breasts. There was satisfaction in the carved, sensual lines of his face as he watched her breathing change to ragged gasps and the wild color flush all over her.

Heat radiated from him, and in his lap his shaft grew into a monster of need. He pressed against her tightly, letting her feel the way he responded to her eager, wet body. "Look at me, Tansy." His voice was harsh. "I want to see your face when I take you over the edge."

She loved how rough he sounded, that edge to his tone, that dark, intense desire, the lines that seemed deeper, the way her skin burned as his gaze slid so possessively over her. His fingers straightened, jabbed deep, filling her sheath, stretching the soft, slick, velvet folds. She gasped and bucked, as his thumb pressed down relentlessly on her hard bud.

"You're so tight, baby," he whispered, his teeth tugging at her earlobe. "Each time I push deep inside, you get wetter and hotter." His tongue licked along her ear, swirled down her neck. His teeth teased at her skin.

He plunged into her tight depths again, watching her face, drinking in her gasps of pleasure, the way her eyes widened and her nipples peaked. Her thighs tensed; her stomach muscles bunched. It seemed so decadent, Tansy sprawled across him, her soft body open for his every touch, receptive to his every desire.

He had never thought he'd have a woman of his own, let alone one he craved, one he felt bonded to, skin to skin, mind to mind. It had happened before he'd had a chance to think, to even know or understand, but something in her drove out the cold and replaced ice with heat. Every time he looked at her, he wanted to touch, to give her pleasure, to see her eyes glaze over with heated desire just for him. Salvation. Redemption maybe. Whatever it was, and he didn't even care, she was his and he was hers.

Moisture coated his fingers, thick and hot. Her sheath was so damned tight his cock jerked with anticipation. He thrust another finger deep, stretching her a bit, plunging and retracting, watching her face, her heightened breathing, that telltale flush, and the sheen in her eyes. He took his time, bringing her to the edge of her climax, loving her face, the beauty of need. He reveled in the way her body rode his hand almost helplessly while little whimpers and pleas escaped.

If this wasn't love, he didn't know what was. He wanted her with every cell in his body. He knew she'd been born for him. And he vowed to himself she'd never have a reason to regret her choice. He plunged deeper, his thumb teasing her clit until she went crashing over the edge, crying out his name, her body nearly strangling his fingers. He let her ride it out, feeling the powerful ripples before pulling out his fingers and tasting them, savoring the unique cinnamon flavor that was Tansy.

She was panting a little, dazed by the powerful orgasm. He slid his hand over her bottom in another slow caress and leaned down to her ear. His fingers remained tight in her hair, the heavy mass wrapped in his fist. "Slide off my lap to your knees." Even as he said it, he tugged at her hair with one hand and pushed her hips from his with the other.

Tansy found herself kneeling between his legs as he sat all the way up, one leg planted on either side of her body. Her face was in his lap, right where he'd planned all along. He caught her hand and wrapped it around the thick length of him, down low at the base, even as he used the fist in her hair to guide her mouth over him. Her tongue touched him first and his cock jerked. His balls tightened. Warm air bathed the broad head. She licked a glistening drop away and watched the shudder of pleasure go through his body, felt it ripple through his mind.

Kadan clenched his teeth as she swiped her tongue in a long, slow curl over the top of the mushroom head and then teased underneath where he was so sensitive. She looked so hot, kneeling in front of him, her shirt gaping open to give him a view of her flushed breasts and flat tummy, down to the vee of curls with shimmering moisture clinging invitingly. He licked his lips and sucked in his breath as she swallowed him.

Her mouth was hot and tight and the sight of her enjoying pleasuring him, her eyes soft and loving, was so damn sexy he almost lost every vestige of control. She didn't look away from his gaze, as her cheeks hollowed and her tongue danced and she followed the graphic instructions in his mind. His language was raw, he couldn't help it; she was killing him with the tight suction of her mouth. Her nails grazed his sac and he jerked again, the air in his lungs exploding this time in a rush of sensations.

Son of a bitch, baby, like that. Hard. His fingers clutched at her hair and he drew her closer, unable to stop the sudden thrust of his hips.

There was a moment of fear at the loss of control, but he breathed for her. *Relax. Let your throat relax. That's it, that's my girl. Son of a fucking bitch that feels so good.*

He threw back his head, a hoarse groan escaping as he caught the nape of her neck with one hand and held her there, thrusting deeper. He wanted her to drop her hands, to cup his tightening balls in her palms. He gave her that order as well. She blinked, hesitating. Her hand at the base of his shaft was her safety net.

His fingers tightened in her hair and he tugged. *I need you to trust me. Keep your mind in mine. Feel what you're doing to me.*

At once fire poured through her body like hot lava, centering in her groin. Every nerve ending was inflamed, every muscle tight, from her calves to her breasts. She knew she created those sensations in him, that raw pleasure bordering on ecstasy. She wanted more for him, for herself. She wanted it all, everything she could take or give.

She needed to take him deeper, to constrict and massage, to pour more heat over him. Her hands cupped and caressed his sac, her mouth worked, and all the while she could feel his needs, dark and erotic, tugging at her for more, always more. He needed her to give herself to him without restraint. It was the only way he had to combat the ice in his soul. She burned the arctic cold away in a firestorm of lust and passion.

He held her still, drawing back, and then pushed forward, filling her mouth, pulsing along her throat, holding her gaze captive with his. He set the pace, hard and fast until she thought she couldn't take it, then slow, each stroke long and leisurely, while his voice in her mind, rough and seductive, urged her to suck harder, to bathe him with her tongue.

All the while her body ached, begging for attention, her breasts heavy and full with need, her core wet and pulsing in time to the shaft in her mouth. She dug her nails into his thigh, desperate for all of him, even though he was intimidating her just a little, controlling her head with a hard hand at her nape and a fist in her hair as his rhythm became harder and faster.

She felt him swelling, and he immediately withdrew, breathing deep. "Not like this, baby."

"I can feel your need, see it in your mind," she protested. "I want to do this for you."

"Another day I want to feel you sucking me dry." He closed his eyes briefly, the feeling, the image, in his mind of her wanting him to finish in her mouth, her desperate for all of him, anywhere, anytime, all of him. "But not tonight. Tonight I want to be so deep inside of you that you'll never get me out. I want to brand you mine forever."

She was fairly certain he already had. She couldn't imagine doing the things she was doing with anyone else. Her body was still on fire, every part of her aching and needy.

He caught her chin, forcing her to meet his suddenly cold gaze. "I'd kill them."

"You mean me," she corrected.

He loved her. She was already in his heart, buried deep in his soul. "Never you. I could never hurt you." And he couldn't. She was one of the people in the world—maybe the only person—who was truly safe, even if she shattered his heart.

He pulled her to her feet and walked her backward until they were behind the couch. He spun her around and once again caught the nape of her neck, bending her forward over the high back, pressing her head down so that the shirt road up over her enticing curves. "I think this shirt has become my favorite." He didn't wait. Didn't give her time. He couldn't.

He slammed into her, hard and deep, through the hot, slick folds, the tight muscles that reluctantly gave way and then gripped him hard, rippling like live silk. Her cry was loud, echoing through the house, but his was hoarse, strangling his throat, pleasure ripping through his body. He couldn't believe what it was like wanting her. The intensity of his need was so strong he could barely stay in control. She was so damned hot and tight, so silky soft and slick, he had to fight to hold back his climax. Around Tansy, his control went right up in smoke.

Lightning whipped through him, scorching him. He caught her hips in his hands, and brought her back to him as he surged forward, needing to plunge deeper into the dark recesses of her tight sheath. Lust and love whirled together until he couldn't tell one from the other. Emotions surged through him, filling his mind and heart when he barely could sustain feeling any other time. Where he was cold and dark, she was as hot as the sun and bathed him in her light.

He slammed home again and stopped, feeling her tense, throb around him, tighten, and grasp with her silken muscles. Slowly he bent over her, even as he tugged on her hair, bringing her head up. His lips whispered over her ear. "You fucking save my soul, Tansy. Every time." It was stupid of him to give up so much of himself to her, but he couldn't stop himself. He needed her to know what she was to him—that he might demand her total surrender, but he was hers, all the way, and he surrendered himself completely to her.

He moved again. Long and slow, taking her to the edge, until he heard a sob escape. He wanted to do a little sobbing himself, his breath hitching, and love choking and clogging his throat. But he held on, pushing her past every limit, poising her on the edge of release, only to pull back, prolonging, building, seeing how high he could take them both.

Tansy heard the sob in her voice as she pleaded with him for release. He was relentless, burying himself deep and hard, and then just when she was certain she couldn't take anymore and she'd find release, he'd pull back, slow down, change his pace, all the while putting pressure on her most sensitive spot. Her legs shook, and her body shuddered with urgent need, aware of every inch of his thick shaft buried deep inside her.

"Hold still."

She couldn't. He couldn't possibly think she could, when she was on the verge of mind-numbing pleasure. He held it just out of her reach, and she writhed and bucked in a desperate attempt to impale herself.

"Not yet. You're going to take me with you and I don't want to end this." He pressed kisses down her spine, his hands caressing her breasts, her belly, flexing at her hips. "Not yet. I want to stay here awhile."

"Please, Kadan, I can't stand it." She felt almost crazy with need, her body on fire, her insides swollen and aching and desperate for release. She couldn't help herself, pushing back, twisting her hips, finding a frantic rhythm, grinding hard against him.

The breath slammed out of his lungs. Inside his throat—in his mind—he sounded wild, feral, a demon possessed. He buried his fingers deep in her hips, holding her still, his grip hard. He surged deep and she screamed. He pistoned forward, hard and deep, each thrust driving through the bundle of inflamed nerves so that she bucked and cried out, the sensations swamping him as her sheath tightened, strangling him, clamping down so hard he thought he'd go mad with pleasure. An explosive orgasm tore through her and took him with her, destroying all control so that he speared into her harder and faster in a frantic attempt to prolong the tidal wave that ripped up his thighs, down his belly, and centered in his shaft where her body continued to tighten around him, milking him dry. He jerked convulsively and then shuddered with pleasure as he filled her with hot semen.

He stood behind her, buried deep, his arms wrapped around her waist now while she hung exhausted over the couch. He didn't even know how they'd gotten started in the first place, only that he would never be sated. He wanted to spend every waking minute just touching her, filling her.

Kadan rested his head on her back, drawing in great deep breaths. "You know, for me, you're my woman. My wife. Whenever you're ready, say the word and we'll do it legal. There's no way you weren't meant for me." Hell, he'd never believed in God; there were too many sick, perverted people in the world, too much crime, and too many natural disasters for him to believe anyone who cared was really out there in the cosmos watching. But Tansy was a miracle. For the first time in his life, it occurred to him that if there was really such a being, Kadan owed big-time—for Tansy, because he believed absolutely that she was created for him. And he knew he'd been created for her.

"Damn it, woman, you've even got me thinking spiritual crap." How pathetic was that?

Her body shook. He straightened up, allowing his shaft to slip out of her, enjoying the ripple that ran through her belly, telling him she was having delicious little aftershocks.

"Are you laughing at me?"

She turned her head, looking over her shoulder at him, a small smile teasing her mouth. "A little, yes."

"I have what could be a revelation and you're laughing." His hands were gentle as he helped her straighten up. He drew the edges of the shirt together and rebuttoned it.

"And your revelation is what?"

"You don't deserve to know." He leaned down to kiss her because he couldn't resist her beautiful mouth. "We've got work to do. Stop distracting me."

"You can set up the game pieces while I take a bath. If I don't, I'm going to be too sore to walk."

"I like that idea."

"You're so bad, Kadan." She tossed another grin over her shoulder and left him.

Kadan listened to the bathwater running as he pulled on jeans and padded barefoot into the war room. He didn't want her here, not where the photographs of the dead

would surround them. He took the pieces out into the dining room and, wearing gloves, positioned them on the table
in the order of the murders on the East Coast and then the
West. He hated that she was going to do this, but he was
going to make damned certain she didn't have the same
repercussions as she'd had the time before.

Tansy surveyed the ivory pieces Kadan set on the table.
The game pieces were beautifully carved. Whoever had
made them knew what he was doing. Each figurine was
detailed meticulously. She held her palm over the pieces,
an inch or so above the tallest, and passed her hand over
them, feeling the waves of excitement and violence embedded in the ivory. Taking a breath, she dipped her hand
lower.

   Kadan's hand slid beneath her wrist so fast it was a blur,
his fingers circling hers and jerking her hand away before
she could pick up one of the ivory carvings. Standing behind her, he held her wrist away from the game pieces. As
he placed a proprietary hand on her shoulder, his body
curved over hers so that his heat enveloped her.

   "Wear gloves."

   "But . . ." She frowned at him over her shoulder. "I
won't pick up the details you need unless I touch the objects with my skin."

   His grip tightened, fingers digging through the thin material of the silk shirt, into her soft shoulder and into the
sensitive skin of her wrist. "Gloves." His voice brooked no
argument. "See what impressions you get. We'll start there.
If we're lucky, it will be enough."

   "You know better, Kadan."

   He pushed a pair of gloves into her hands.

   "Do the men on your team ever tell you that you're a
tyrant?"

   She pulled the material over her hands and felt some of

the tension leave his body. He'd already grilled her for an hour on the layout and security of the house, going over every single detail a hundred times, until she considered hitting him over the head with something. He was very thorough when it came to questioning—no, *interrogating*—someone.

"You're so dramatic." He slid his hand down her arm, tugged on the glove, and then splayed his fingers across her belly.

Heat spread as if he'd branded her. She felt the familiar ache beginning. He pressed even tighter around her, so that she felt him breathing in the same rhythm.

"You're distracting me."

"That's the point. Well . . ." There was grim amusement in his voice. "The point is, I want to touch you."

She was very aware of his body pressed tightly against hers. His shaft was full and heavy, rubbing along her bottom with only the thin tail of the shirt separating them. How could he be so ready so fast? A part of her was inescapably pleased. "I'm working here. Do you want to get this information or not? You're already handicapping me by insisting on the gloves."

"I'm protecting you. And I'm going to keep protecting you. I have the feeling that once you get started, you can't stop yourself."

She frowned and leaned forward to look over the game pieces. Kadan didn't move, and the action only pressed him tighter against her.

"You're going to have to go stand over there if you want this to work."

"I'm staying. Just get on with it."

Tansy sighed and forced herself to concentrate. Kadan had separated the game pieces into two groups. The first were the objects left behind at each crime scene on the East Coast. The stallion, frog, snake, and blade. There were two stallions.

"Was the stallion the first murder?"

He nodded his head.

"Then they have a sequence. Like cards or a board game, they have a certain order and each player takes his turn. If you lined them up in the order you found them, the frog would commit the next murder."

"That's right." His breath fanned her cheek, moved the strands of hair falling around her face. His lips whispered over the nape of her neck.

"Kadan. Really. I can't do this."

"Yes, you can. But you're going to know where you are, and who you're with. You're not going to be pulled down that long tunnel into a nightmare. I'll be right here, real and solid, and nothing is going to take you from me."

She shook her head. "You're so crazy. Fine. I'll try."

She had to admit to herself she was a little afraid. There were so many of the game pieces, and the energy was strong, radiating out to her palm even through the material of the glove as she passed her hand over them. In a way, she was thankful for the distraction of Kadan's hard body and gentle hands. She knew once she began picking up impressions, there would be no feelings like she had now, the arousal peaking her nipples and teasing her thighs, the feel of his hand slipping under the tail of the shirt and shaping her bottom, his fingers doing their silky slide as he stroked her skin possessively.

She wanted to stay like this forever, feeling a part of him. Sharing his mind and the pleasure he got in just touching her. He loved just being able to slide his fingers over her, slip a hand inside her shirt and cup the weight of her breast, thumb caressing her nipple. The intensity of his enjoyment at simply stroking her skin was amazing to her and she didn't want to go back to the real world, where no one ever laid a hand on her and she never dared to have actual contact.

I'm not going anywhere.

He couldn't promise that. She looked at the ivory figurines. If she touched them, and she couldn't control what happened, if the voices sank into her head, were trapped in her mind, he would have no choice but to abandon her.

Kadan swore and wrapped his arms around her, burying his face in her shoulder. "You don't have to do this."

"Yes, I do. We can't let them keep murdering people, Kadan. They have a taste for it and they won't stop." Tears burned behind her eyes. Usually there was one killer, one depraved mind she was forced to share. This time there were eight, and they were psychic, just as she was.

His lips slid over her ear. "My mind shares yours. If you're determined to go through with this, then know wherever this takes you, you won't be alone, Tansy. I'm strong. I'll find your mind and I'll bring you back."

"Last time I broke into a million pieces."

"I'll find each one."

It was the resolve, that absolute determination, that reassured her that he meant what he said. He wouldn't abandon her no matter how bad it got. It was his nature to be completely focused and implacable. He wouldn't turn back or turn away. His willpower gave her strength. Tansy settled her fingers around the frog, lifting it from the table.

The jolt was hard. The room shifted beneath her feet as the energy rushed at her with greedy claws. She hadn't expected the frog to be so strong. She'd already formed an opinion that he was one of the lesser members of the team, but his psychic energy was intense. She felt the familiar slick oil pouring into her mind, a sludge that indicated perverse sickness. He sought power. Always power. He wanted attention. Wanted his strength known when no one saw him. He was always passed over by everyone. His commanding officers thought themselves superior, but they were nothing to him—*nothing*.

Each week he took people down into his world. They had no idea he held their lives in the palm of his hand. He enjoyed that feeling, deciding—live or die by his hand. Who would he choose to let live? He wanted them to know, but only the ones who died knew, at last, looking into his eyes while he held them under. *See me.* Drowning, drowning. *See me.*

Tansy! Kadan's voice was sharp, filled with menace, with command.

She dared not disobey him. His fingers forced her hand open. She hadn't realized she was sobbing, or that the whispers had grown loud in her mind. Tears poured down her face. The screams were loud now, victims screaming as water poured into their lungs and he stood toe to toe, holding them down, forcing them to stare at his mocking, exultant face.

Revere me. I'm a god. I condemn you to death. See me. Damn you, look at me. You will stay with me and always see me.

Kadan shook her. "Look at me. Look at me now."

Her dazed eyes, shimmering with opaque violet, jumped to his. Kadan dragged her away from the table to the center of the room. He could feel the thick oil clouding her mind, hear the screams and whispers threatening to take over. He refused to allow her to look away from him. Deliberately he filled her mind with emotion, with warmth and tenderness, his hands gentle.

"Are you with me, baby?"

She moistened her dry lips, blinking rapidly. He could feel her mind clinging to his. "I'm all right. He was stronger than I expected." She shivered again, trying to drown out the sound of his voice. Thankfully, Kadan's firm, velvet-soft voice, although low, pushed over the top of the other. Kadan had established his dominance, and his power and control over her was absolute. His voice took over in her mind. *We're together, baby, one mind, one skin. They can't touch you.*

His voice was a caress, sliding over her, into her, so that she grasped at the feel of him as if he were a life preserver.

"I'm all right. I'm good." It wasn't altogether true; she retained the sludge, but it was easier to break with the voices.

"Tell me what you saw."

She took a deep, shuddering breath. "Bodies in the water. At least six, maybe more; I couldn't make myself look. He drags them down and drowns them. He likes to watch their eyes." She frowned. "He doesn't need scuba gear; he can hold his breath a really long time, or maybe he doesn't even need to do that. He breathes underwater—is that possible? Can one of the GhostWalkers actually breathe underwater? He's killed many times. But his murder in the game wasn't satisfactory to him. Something went wrong. He wants another turn."

She was breathing hard—too hard. Already he could feel the headache beating at her, piercing her skull like an ice pick. He tasted blood in his mouth and knew she was bleeding. His belly churned in response to her pain. He detested her doing this—and they had at least six more game pieces to go through.

Kadan stepped closer to pull her into his arms, but she shook her head, waving him away from her so she could finish. She looked fragile, swaying, her skin pale and beaded with tiny drops of sweat, although there were goose bumps on her arms and she kept shivering.

"He's small and slight, barely able to make the requirements for the military. Everyone underestimates him and that makes him angry. He wants women to notice him, but he can't really perform well because deep down he's insecure. He relates better when he's feeling murderous. His friends tease him a lot. He's the butt of some very ugly jokes, but after he gets over his mad, he convinces himself it's their way of showing him affection."

"And this particular murder?" Kadan began to rub her shoulders. He didn't want to share her mind while it was pounding with pain, and he had to ignore her suffering in order for her to get the rest out. He wanted to stop her, hold her, wipe her mind clean. He felt like a bastard, twisting the knife deeper, looking for more to help him uncover the killers.

She shook her head adamantly. "He was so angry, angry enough that for a moment he thought about killing . . ." She frowned, pressing her fingertips to her eyes. "Who? Someone else, someone supposed to be impartial, fair. How can he be successful at this kind of murder?"

She closed her eyes, took a breath, and let herself drown in the sludge. It wasn't as thick or as bloody, but the impression of "Frog" was strong. He didn't like killing this way. The guys were bastards, helping him plan but laughing behind his back. He knew they were laughing. Hell. He didn't want to do a couple of nerdy high school kids. At least give him jocks. He might want to cut off a few body parts while they watched him. Damn bullies shoving him around just because they could. Now he was going to have to off a couple of skinny nerds who'd been bullied all their lives. Paper-pushing bastard probably rigged the game—did one of his endless psych evals and saw this would make him sick.

Young voices rose into wails. Pleading. Begging.

I'm sorry, man, it's just a game, you know. I gotta do it for my team, but when this is over, I'll find that dickhead paper pusher and watch him die for you. He chose you, not me.

The pleading rose to a crescendo. She could see their eyes. So young. So scared. They'd never even been with a girl and they were going to die. Frog kept talking to them, assuaging his guilt at the expense of his two victims. He wanted them to understand that he had no choice. It was all part of the brotherhood. He needed forgiveness.

Girlish screams of fear. Tears tracking down baby faces. They couldn't be more than fifteen. Two young boys just beginning life. Mom. Dad. I love you. I'm sorry.

What did they have to be sorry about? Only that a killer had trapped them and was about to end their lives. Nothing else. They hadn't lived long enough or screwed up bad enough. Two boys who were intelligent and loved gadgets.

Her entire body shuddered, muscles locking. They were just babies, and Frog was going to kill them and then cut them into tiny pieces. At least he was merciful enough to kill them with a single shot to the head, to make certain they didn't suffer. And then he began to slice them into pieces. Thirty each.

Stay cool, baby. I'm here with you. Feel me. Look into my eyes. You're only far away in your head, but if you reach for me, they can't take you. I'm your anchor.

Why thirty? What's the significance of thirty? The number had to mean something. It meant something to Frog. A signal, a message, but to whom?

Kadan slid his hands from her shoulders to her wrists, holding tight, needing the contact more than she did. Her mind was amazing to him, cataloguing data, working fast, discarding theories. He'd never seen anything like it. But it took its toll.

Keep the barrier in place.

It wasn't second nature to her, holding that wall to keep a separation. As a rule she merged herself totally with the killer and victims. Maybe the details were a little blurry, but as far as Kadan was concerned, she was picking up enough through the gloves to destroy her mind.

"What's significant, Tansy?" she murmured to herself. "Thirty pieces of silver is all I can think of. What would that have to do with . . ." She trailed off, her eyes going wide. Blood trickled from her nose.

Pull away, break off completely.

She swallowed. Blinked. Her opaque eyes looked into his. Blood leaked from her mouth and one ear.

Kadan's fingers tightened on her wrists and he dragged her into the shelter of his body, thrusting his mind into hers, dominant. Controlling. *You fucking listen to me, Tansy. Break off.* He was prepared to use anything to get her back. Sex. A beating. Hell, it didn't matter. Nothing mattered but separating her from those whispers calling to her, beckoning, raping her mind, filling her full of oily sludge and too much blood, so that she was drowning in it.

His hand went to the nape of her neck, thumbs under her jaw, forcing her head up. He took her mouth brutally. Desperately. His mind vibrated with sexual thoughts, with erotic visions, with need and hunger and such a craving for the taste and texture of her he shook with it.

Her mouth moved against his, and he felt that first burst of real awareness, her mind recognizing him as the sludge receded, leaving her raw and shaking but intact. He held her close, burying his face in the hollow of her shoulder, shaken beyond anything he could remember since he was that eight-year-old boy standing alone, frightened and covered in blood.

Damn it, baby. Just damn it. He took a deep, shuddering breath, his arms locking her head to his chest as if he never wanted to let go of her.

"I'm all right. I'm with you." Her voice was small and muffled. Thin. As if she was stretched beyond endurance.

"I'm not going to survive this," he said. "I'm not. We have to do better than this or you're done." He tipped her face up to his, his gaze drifting over it, brooding, edged with icy resolve. "You're done, Tansy."

"Thirty pieces of silver. Betrayal. This is huge. It was worth it."

"Fuck that. It wasn't worth it. It will never be worth it.

Look at you. These are disgusting savages and they're rap- ing your mind. They eat you alive. You think I can't feel what they're doing inside your head?" He wiped at the blood on her face. "Like pieces of glass digging at the in- side of your mind, scraping you raw. Leaving scars. And in each of those scars, images, voices—sick, perverted kill- ers who won't ever leave you alone. You're done."

She traced the rough angles and planes of his face with her fingertips. "Shh. You're so upset, Kadan. I'm all right." The pad of her finger stroked the deep scar.

"I don't get upset." He caught her wrists, dragged her hands down to his mouth and pressed kisses into each palm. "I'm not upset. I just know this isn't right and I'm not letting you do this again."

He was trembling. He didn't seem to know it, but she'd shaken him. She couldn't remember anyone ever looking at her with that stark, raw need, the fear and possession on his face. The show of emotion wrapped him around her heart as nothing else could have, because he was, as a rule, rather distant and cold. She felt the separation, the discon- nect in his mind from everything around him—except her. It was both terrifying and exhilarating to know she could shake him so badly.

"The same man carved the stallion and the frog pieces. I think he carved all of them. I can't be certain, but I'll know once I handle the other pieces. If he did, and he's not one of the players, we'll know he's running the game. I get an undercurrent—"

His hand fisted in her hair, dragging her to him, his mouth taking hers hard. He swallowed her words and her breath, fighting for her, wanting—needing—her wholly with him. They couldn't have her. Not the killers. Not the victims. Not Whitney. Not her bastard parents, who were connected to Whitney. None of them. She was his, and he would protect her with everything he was, every last bit of training he had, every warrior's instinct, and with an ice-cold resolve that would carry him through fire, through blood and death for her.

Tansy let him have her mouth, not struggling against either his enormous physical or mental strength. He didn't realize the grip he had on her mind or her body, or the savage possession of his mouth. Even the fist in her hair twisted the strands until there was a burning sting. The combination of pain and pleasure slammed the door hard on the voices, leaving only Kadan in her mind. Kadan with his sensual, demanding mouth and his will of iron.

He kissed her until her complete submission, her absolute surrender, registered. His mouth gentled, became tender, until his kisses were slow and easy, until his breath was hers and her body molded to his. His hands slid beneath the thin material of her shirt, sliding down her back, down the tucked in waist and flair of her hips to curve over her buttocks.

"I'm so afraid I'm going to fall in love with you," she whispered when he lifted his head.

He kissed both eyelids, trailed more kisses down her face to the corner of her mouth. "Would it be so bad, loving me?"

Had there been a catch in his voice? It occurred to her that he had no family. He'd held himself apart from everyone. She smiled at him, a slow, dreamy smile that spoke volumes. She couldn't say the words aloud, but they were in her mind. Teasing him. Caressing him. *You have a tendency to be a tyrant. Can you imagine if you knew I loved you like crazy?*

She couldn't voice the words, because she was well on her way to feeling that way about him. In measurement of time, she barely knew him, but with their minds slipping in and out of each other, it was difficult to resist him. To resist his compelling need and his magnetic personality. Sometimes, like now, she felt mesmerized, hypnotized by him, just by the way he looked at her. Or maybe it was as simple as she was no longer alone and never would feel alone with him close to her.

"I prefer that you fall crazy in love with me," he said candidly.

Tansy burst out laughing.

CHAPTER 8

Tansy managed a small catnap and woke up with Kadan lying beside her, one arm slung around her waist. She turned her head to find him wide awake, staring at her face. She blinked and smiled up at him. "What are you doing?"

"Watching you breathe."

Her smile widened. His hand was beneath the shirt, fingers splayed wide, rubbing small caresses over the smooth skin of her belly. She wasn't certain he was even aware he did so. "Don't you have anything better to do?"

"I can't make love to you again; we're going to have company soon. So, no. This is just perfect doing this."

"Watching me breathe?" He was robbing her of her breath, just the way he was looking at her with those eyes and that intensity. She was drowning.

He leaned forward and kissed the tip of her nose. "That's it. Just watching you breathe. It's a great pastime."

"I would imagine it to be very boring."

He shook his head solemnly. "No. I like guarding you. When you start to have nightmares, you frown and I kiss you and you go all peaceful for me. Your breasts rise and fall, and if I put my hand right here," he flexed his fingers on her stomach, "I can feel your muscles bunching every time I stroke your skin. You're so damned soft."

She rolled over to look up at him. "You're so different when you're like this. Which is the real you?"

He framed her face with both hands and kissed her tenderly, so gentle he stole her heart. "I don't know, Tansy. Both. Neither. You've shaken me, shaken everything I knew about myself. I'm not a gentle man. I don't know how to talk to women. I don't even know what I'm doing right now, but I don't want to stop." The admission was given in a low voice, torn from him against his will.

Her heart clenched. She didn't read minds—that wasn't her gift, or curse. She read objects, and that was different. She could stop the input by wearing gloves and distancing herself. What was Kadan's life like? He saw blood and death. He killed. He fought alongside other men who killed or died. And he knew their thoughts. Their hopes and dreams. Their dirty secrets. His mind had to find a way to protect him. The coldness that he believed made him a killing machine was his mind's way of protecting him, a shield so the man didn't have to feel too much, although she was fairly certain he wasn't aware of it. There was no other choice or he would have been right alongside her in that mental hospital.

"Why did you choose the military? Why did you choose law enforcement? It must be hell, Kadan, all those killers and victims, all those battles you have to fight."

"What else for someone like me? Killing is what I do best. I've always known that."

She shook her head, locking her gaze with his. "Loving is what you do best."

A slow smile tugged at his mouth. "You're a fucking miracle."

"And you're going to have to clean up your mouth before you meet my parents." She rolled out from under him and sat up, pushing at her long hair to get it off her face.

There was a long silence. When she glanced over her shoulder, Kadan was already up, padding across the floor to the bathroom. She had sensed more than heard him. He moved like a mountain lion, all rippling muscle and silence.

He turned back, his face set in grim lines. "Your parents can clean up a few things before I do. They've got a few questions to answer."

"Look, Kadan, before everyone gets here and you decide to share with them your conspiracy theories on my parents, I want to tell you a story."

His mouth hardened into a cruel line, but he didn't say anything.

Tansy sighed. "When I was a little girl, I couldn't go to a regular school, or to a grocery store. I really couldn't do much of anything. My parents built me a play yard, basically from scratch, getting brand-new supplies. Even then, sometimes, I could get impressions from people handling the swings or bars. But I wanted a bike. A bicycle represented freedom to me. I wanted one so bad and I was willing to wear gloves all the time as long as I could just have a bike. You can imagine how my parents must have felt not being able to touch or feed me or even tuck me in at night without both of us wearing gloves. I hated the gloves, and so did they."

He tried not to ache for that little girl, but she was already in his head. He had no sympathy for her parents. Maybe his friends were right and ice water really did flow in his veins, because he wanted to gather her up and comfort her, and put a bullet in her parents' heads. Bastards. They hadn't stopped Whitney, and they had to have known what he was doing—or at least suspected something. Money was a motivating factor for a lot of people. Don and Sharon

Meadows made big bucks with defense contracts, but maybe that wasn't enough for them.

"There you are with that face, all grim and forbidding. My father made all the parts for a bicycle wearing gloves the entire time. Then he put the bike together and they gave it to me. No one had ever touched it." Tears burned behind her eyes and clogged her throat so that she had to clear it, remembering that moment when he'd wheeled the bike out of a closet and her parents had stood there, big smiles on their faces, telling her she didn't have to wear gloves to ride it.

"What parents do that, Kadan? He spent so much time on it. Anyone else would have been okay with my wearing gloves, but he made certain I didn't have to whenever I rode that bike, because he knew I hated them so much. They love me." She didn't know if she was pleading for it to be true, or pleading with him to believe her. "I know they do, Kadan, because I've always felt it. The only time I ever felt abandoned was when Whitney came around."

Abandoned was an interesting word to use. Kadan studied her face. She looked fragile. She wasn't. She was strong—incredibly strong, or she couldn't do the things she did. Bathe in blood to track killers. No one did that unless they were strong, but to him, she looked vulnerable and maybe a little lost.

Don't make me choose between you and my parents.

Kadan reached down and tugged her to her feet, drawing her into his arms. He wasn't a man who liked to retreat, but for her, for now, on this, he would. "Of course, they love you, Tansy. How could they not?" He trailed kisses from her temple to the corner of her mouth, until he felt the tension ease from her body and she grew soft and pliant against him.

"Your clothes should be ready." His voice was gruff. "Get dressed before our company comes." There was no choice. It was black-and-white. Her parents were either betraying their daughter, in which case they were both fucked, or something else he didn't know about was going on and they were going to tell him.

Tansy found her clothes folded neatly on top of the dryer. She pulled on underwear and jeans and a thin tank before wandering back into the dining room to study the game pieces. She considered going into the war room, but she didn't want the victims' impressions to override the killers'. She needed to know the killers, to figure them out so she could get one step ahead of them and stop them. And there was something that bothered her . . .

"What?"

She nearly jumped out of her skin, twisting around to find Kadan behind her. She let out her breath. "Don't sneak up on me like that. Especially not when I'm trying to pick up impressions. You scared me."

He took her wrist, his finger sliding over her frantic pulse. "I'm sorry, baby, I can't help the way I walk, but you're not supposed to be doing this anymore. I thought we agreed."

She rolled her eyes but didn't pull her hand away. He was stroking her inner wrist, his touch both soothing and sexy at the same time. "Is that what you call it? I think it was more a decree at the time, but of course, you couldn't have been serious."

"I rarely am anything but serious."

That was probably true. Tansy gave an exaggerated sigh. "I came here to give you information on the killings."

He tugged her hand to his mouth, his eyes watching hers. "Your mission has changed."

She took back her hand. "My mission is the same. You can't find them all by yourself and you know it." Her frown came back as her gaze flicked to the ivory figurines. They were beautiful, yet each represented a killer. "There's something important here, really important, that I'm missing. I have to figure it out, Kadan, because without it . . ." She trailed off, looking more distressed than ever.

Kadan touched her mind, trying to make sense of her jumbled thoughts. Her mind was racing, analyzing and discarding data, choosing pieces to put together and then breaking them apart again. Tansy had a high-speed, complex computer for a brain when it came to murder. It was no wonder the police departments who had used her had written such confusing reports. She got the job done, but it was impossible to follow her train of thought, her jumps from one conclusion to the next, or even her uncanny ability to ferret out and identify the threads of the case that really mattered.

Her mind wouldn't let go once it started. That revelation sent a wave of apprehension through him. She wasn't going to let go of it, not because she was being stubborn, but because she couldn't. It didn't matter how much he ordered her, or even if he took her away from the evidence; she couldn't back off now until the killers were caught. That had never been mentioned in the reports on her he'd studied. Not that he would have done anything different even if he'd had the information. He hadn't met her, hadn't known what she would become to him in such a short time. In some ways, Tansy was a lot like him. Once started on a mission, he found it nearly impossible to back off. Her mind was programmed the same way.

He could feel the pressure tugging at her relentlessly. An escaping thread in a larger tapestry she tried desperately to unravel to find the other end. He took a breath, let it out, breathing for both of them as he rested his chin on top of her head.

"I'm sorry I got you into this, babe." His hands slid up and down her arms in a soothing motion, but he was soothing himself, not her, and he knew it. Damn, emotions were difficult to deal with.

She waved away his apology. "Let's just go after another one right now. Maybe I can figure out what's bothering me. There are two different . . ."

Again she trailed off and he got the same impressions in her mind: a chaotic whirl, too much data triggering her alarm buttons, but nothing tangible she could grab with both hands.

Kadan glanced at his watch. "We've only got about two hours and then we'll have company. You're going to be hitting the headache just about the time they arrive."

She shrugged off his warning and reached for another of the ivory pieces.

"Damn it, Tansy." He caught her wrist and all but yanked her to the table's edge. "Put on the fuc—" He made an effort to stop himself. "Gloves. Just get them on."

She pulled on the gloves and, without pause, reached for the snake. The figurine was very detailed, the long body coiled and covered in a pattern of scales, the head up, mouth wide open to show curved fangs. Even the eyes seemed to blaze with defiance and a menacing threat. The tongue was long and forked. When her fingers curled around the game piece, the oil poured into her mind, a fast torrent, carrying malice and glee. This one liked to see pain. Where Frog wanted his victims to acknowledge his existence, his power, this one simply fed off the pain of others. And it mattered little to him if his prey were an animal, a child, a woman or man. He just needed the pain and the screams.

The breath slammed out of her lungs as the thick, bloody mud rushed into her mind, and for a moment she couldn't remember how to breathe properly. There was the terrifying sensation of being dragged under, of gasping, desperate for air, pulling in filthy, oily muck instead, so that it filled every corner of her mind and packed her lungs so solid there was no hope of breathing. She was drowning—*drowning*—and she wouldn't be able to get back. It happened too fast; her quarry was too strong.

She felt a mouth move against hers. *Feel me, baby. I'm with you.* Warm breath pushed into her lungs. She inhaled, took air in to push out some of the thick goo coating her insides. Another breath. *He can't have you. I'll breathe for both of us.*

She could do this! She accepted another stream of air, shuddering with effort, forcing it into her lungs, concentrating on pushing past that first wave of violent energy that threatened to consume her mind. Snake couldn't have her because she had her own personal guardian angel. Kadan Montague was the strongest man she'd ever known. And he was on her side—not only on it, but at it, breathing in and out, sharing air with her.

She found him there in her mind, and a tiny part of her held tight to him while she allowed the familiar expansion to push her own spirit out, to make room for the beast pouring into her, threatening to devour her.

He was eager for the kill. Couldn't wait. He wanted them alive, lasting a long time while he hurt them. The places he'd been where he'd discovered appreciation of his talents were long gone, but now he could have fun again. This cool opportunity brought back memories of the tunnel in Vietnam where he'd trapped the two farmers. They'd lasted two days. Glorious fun. Both were babbling when he ended them—and he almost hadn't. He'd been so tempted to leave their raw, bloody bodies for the rats to find, but he hadn't, and he'd thought of that ever since. Maybe this time—and he'd set up a camera where no one would find it just so he could go back later and watch them being devoured alive. Such fun. The pleas were starting, growing stronger, although Tansy tried to keep the victims away for just a little longer.

She needed to escape the snake and look for the other one, the master behind the puppets. All powerful killers, tied to strings. He pulled—they danced. The masculine whisper grew stronger. She found the thread, faint but there.

The master. She had him now. She was an elite tracker and he wouldn't escape no matter how subtle he was. She blocked out the surge of oily sludge that was Snake spilling around her and kept on track. This was what—or who—had been eluding her. Elation filled her as she targeted the thread.

A hint of satisfied amusement. No one would ever know. Genius surrounded him. Psychics, all of them, but they didn't suspect, didn't have a clue. It was his orchestra, his play, and he was the maestro conducting his performers to play their instruments with such flair. He fed the egos and raked in the cash. Millions, with millions more to be made. Untraceable millions and all for him.

Tansy struggled to stay on the thread. It was so faint, so subtle alongside Snake's violent need for pain. The victims grew louder, as they always did, demanding she recognize them. See them. Give them justice. She shook her head in an attempt to dislodge the wailing. The accusations. The oily muck swirled with enjoyment, building to a crescendo. *Ah, just give me all night with these three. Not as strong as the ones in the tunnel, but I don't have as long.* He would let the rats feast and he'd come back later to see his handiwork and enjoy the entertainment. Screams. Pleading. Begging. Tansy shook her head again, stretching for that subtle thread. The master didn't kill, so the violence edged him out, but he was there, imprinted in the ivory. Seeing it. Part of it. That subtle weave of influence feeding the killers at each site. She just had to keep pulling at the thread to unravel the mystery.

She knew him now, knew she'd seen this trail before, so light she'd missed it in the first two murder scenes, but he'd been there. How was it that he was with each one? Had he been on the West Coast too? Was he present? Was he . . .

She felt Kadan's sudden alertness, his warning system roaring in full-blown alarm. Icy fingers of fear crept down her spine. Something moved—something alive in the midst of all the blood, in the midst of all the victims. Something that was bloated and shadowy like a giant spider at the center of a web. She drew back as the shadow turned, and she knew it was as aware of her as she was of it. Terror poured into her as it—*he*—blinked his eyes and looked at her. For one instant there was a flicker of astonishment followed by grudging respect, almost camaraderie. He wasn't afraid. She got the impression of smug amusement.

Hello, beautiful. Who do we have here?

Everything in her froze. She couldn't move or speak, paralyzed by the knowledge that she was leaving just as many tracks as he was. The puppet master. And he could stalk her just as she pursued him.

You're a dead man. Kadan's voice was low, a whip of menace, startling both Tansy and the puppet master.

Tansy felt Kadan's hand on hers, prying her fingers open, ripping the ivory snake from them and flooding her mind with his *ownership*, his strength and his resolve. Kadan, the killer, icy cold and without mercy, delivering a fact, not a warning, even as he shielded her.

She felt the startled fear of the carver of the ivory figures, quickly masked. And then all awareness was gone. The puppet master had snapped the thread and was gone from her mind.

Kadan dug his fingers into Tansy's upper arms. She still had that faraway opaque look. She was pale, icy cold, her body trembling. Fear rolled off her in waves.

"It's all right, baby. I'm right here. You're safe."

She shook her head. "I'm not. He saw me."

Kadan drew her into his body, his arms tight around her. "*We* saw *him*. We can find him, Tansy. No one even knew he existed. Hell, if I hadn't been there with you, I might not have believed it."

He spoke aloud in a cool, calm voice, mostly to bring her wholly back to him.

"I've never run into anyone who can do what I do. He's a tracker."

Kadan was already aware of that and the ramifications of it. Whoever had realized she was on his trail was going to have to go on the offensive and hunt her. Kadan had felt the man's shock and then the sudden interest in Tansy. The puppet master had recognized female and a bright shining light. She didn't have violent energy, but she was a magnet for it. Kadan didn't want her to know how disturbed he was over finding the puppet master, as Tansy had dubbed him.

"Yes, he appears to be a tracker." He hadn't known they existed until he'd found Tansy and realized exactly what she could do. He kept his tone mild, realizing she was really afraid.

"Not just a tracker, Kadan," she corrected. "An *elite* tracker. I left footprints all over those scenes. If he accesses them, he'll find me there."

"It will be a faint trail, probably thinner than the one he left behind. In any case, he won't be able to identify you any more than we can him."

The puppet master had been all too curious about her, all too aware of her as being his equal. That would arouse his fascination, and that was the last thing Kadan wanted.

"Come on, baby, let this go for this evening. We have to plan a rescue." He needed to divert her attention to give himself time to think about the best way to protect her.

She shook her head. "I have to give you details before I'm all the way back."

Her response unraveled the knots in his belly. It hadn't been as bad this time. The short times she was slipping her exercises in, even a few minutes at a time, seemed to be helping. Their connection grew stronger with each time he shared her mind, and she was turning to him more and more without realizing it, allowing him to strengthen her barriers while she worked. It offered her a little more protection to lessen the adverse affects of both the killer and the victims on her unprotected brain.

Tansy took a deep breath and pushed down the fear that threatened to choke her. She would never forget that chilling moment when the puppet turned his head and looked right into her mind. Kadan had no concept of what an elite tracker could do. She wasn't at the top of her game. She'd burned out, fried her abilities, but the voices of the killers amused the puppet master. He ignored the victims. They were nothing to him, nuisances only.

"Tansy?" Kadan prompted. "You've done enough tonight. All the detectives working on these cases, the FBI task force—no one has found a link to this man. This is a huge break."

"We know he exists, but we have no idea of his identity or how he fits in yet. Let me go over everything. The snake enjoys inflicting pain. He's been in Vietnam, but not during the war. I got the impression of tunnels in a cane field." She shuddered. "He did terrible things to the farmers. A man and his son. He remembered the details very vividly."

"Don't," Kadan said. The details were in her mind, just as vivid. Every cut, every sadistic torture the bastard snake had conceived of—Tansy had it in her mind now. Kadan was already trying to push the memories behind the door for her, trying to protect her from the stubborn streak that kept her pursuing evil killers when it cost her so much.

Tansy visibly made an effort to stay focused on him, to keep the voices from scraping her mind raw. "The camera is really important to him, but he worries it will be found. He's a long way from it and has to go back to retrieve it." Her brows drew together as she tried to bring the details into sharper images. "Have your team look up, a good distance away. He camouflaged the camera so it looks like an old piece of machinery and could easily be overlooked. He worked on it a long time, and he made the metal to wrap it in. If you find it, I should get some very good impressions of him, maybe even somewhat of a description."

His fingers tightened. "That's good, baby. Now let it go so we can combat the headache before it starts." It was already swelling in her head, rolling through her like a wave. She'd used her talent too often and too close together and her mind was raw. Now she was just scraping over old wounds. Even he could hear the whispers of the victims, when the previous times he had only heard the killers.

She shook her head and he gritted his teeth, shoving down the urge to shake her hard and force her out of the half-hypnotic trance.

"The other one is the important one—the puppet master. I see him surrounded by paper. And a desk. He doesn't want anyone to notice him. He prides himself on blending into the background. He's very nondescript and strives to keep it that way, although he has a bit of a problem hiding his . . ." She touched her eyes. "He wears tinted contacts to keep people from seeing."

That sheen in her eyes, blue to violet and then a shimmering silver or opaque. Sign of a tracker. He'd never seen it or heard of it before, but now he knew what he was looking for, now he knew what that peculiar shine really was.

"He's very clever. He's surrounded by killers, by . . ." She frowned again. "I feel Whitney's taint on him. He knows Whitney. They're connected somehow, but I can't see it. Papers. That's all I'm getting. There's money. Lots of money, but . . ." She shook her head. "Whitney doesn't know. His killers don't know. He's the boss, but none of them know."

She blinked at Kadan, unable to comprehend the rush of images and impressions, shivering with cold, fighting hard to keep the voices at bay. "What does that mean?"

Kadan brushed back her hair and leaned into her, taking possession of her soft, trembling lips. "It doesn't matter, honey, come back to me." His voice was a velvet-soft lure, stroking and caressing along her skin, teasing at her nerves until she was wholly aware of him—just him.

She made a little sound in her throat, distress pouring into his mind, and she stepped into his arms. It was the first real move she'd made for comfort, and he tightened his hold around her, caging her in with a protective gesture. Lips skimming her hair and temples, he murmured soft, soothing words, uncaring what they were, only wanting to push out evil and fill her with warmth.

She buried her face against his chest. She didn't make a sound; there was no outward sobbing, but in her mind, he could hear quiet weeping, and when he lifted her chin, there were tears tracking down her face. He bent his head and licked at them, following the tracks to the corner of her mouth.

Kadan lifted her. "You're going to spend a lot of time in bed if you keep this up."

She didn't smile, just circled his neck with her arms and let him carry her without protest back to his bedroom. He undressed her, careful not to jar her, when he could feel the pain pounding in her head. He found the headache pills and gave her one with a glass of water, then stretched out again beside her, fully dressed, after snapping off the light.

"You don't have to stay," Tansy protested. "I'll be all right. The dark helps."

"I'm staying, baby. I have to chase away the nightmares if any are stupid enough to visit you tonight. Go to sleep." He flipped her onto her side, her back to him, curving his body around hers, one hand sliding beneath her shirt, palm locked over her rib cage. His breath was warm and rhythmic on the nape of her neck. He couldn't resist curling his fingers into a fist and allowing his knuckles to run along the underside of her breasts with gentle caresses.

Tansy found his touch soothed and relaxed her, easing all the tension out of her when it should have done just the opposite. Maybe because she'd spent her life without skin-to-skin contact, the tactile feeling of the pads of his fingers, the brush of knuckles, or the heat of his palm took the tightness from her muscles and melted her body.

She floated on a sea of pain, the waves crashing in her head, voices rising and sinking, the whispers loud and then soft, but instead of fighting it, curling up in the fetal position and enduring hours, or even days, of agony, she drifted also on a tide of warmth and security, feeling Kadan riding out the pain with her.

His breathing steadied her own. The stroke of his knuckles distracted her from the pounding in her temples. If the pain threatened to overwhelm her, he leaned in and brushed kisses along the nape of her neck, and then tugged at her earlobe with his teeth. She was caught between pain and pleasure, drifting . . . drifting . . . until finally the pain began to ebb and she slipped into sleep.

Kadan dozed for a while, waking every now and then when she moved. He cuddled her and whispered until she settled down. He closed his eyes briefly again, drifting a little himself, continuing to stroke her soft skin, the undersides of her breasts and down her flat belly. She didn't ever think of stopping trying to track the killers. Not once. He monitored her thoughts carefully, and once she'd started on their trails, no matter what she saw or how loud the voices called to her, even now, with the direct threat of an elite tracker, she was scared, but there was no thought of stopping.

He let his breath out slowly, his belly tight with knots, everything in him protesting her choice, when he'd been the one to draw her into the mess in the first place. And now someone had her parents. The bodyguard had been a plant, probably Whitney's, and he most likely was a Ghost-Walker. He was too cool, staying with the parents, living in their home, side by side, watching Tansy . . . And what had her father said when her mother had screamed? His voice wasn't surprised by what the bodyguard had done. In fact, he'd sounded for a moment as if he was still in charge.

Kadan rubbed strands of her silky hair between his fingers. She'd been in danger the entire time, and hadn't known it. She couldn't read thoughts, only objects, and wearing gloves had prevented her from seeing the danger. If she'd sensed that any of them felt guilt, she would have never connected the emotion to her. She believed in them. All of them. Even the bodyguard.

Fredrickson's betrayal had hurt her. Kadan had felt the piercing pain knifing through her heart. The protest in her mind. Sadly, it was Fredrickson's betrayal that had shaken her steadfast belief in her parents' love. She hadn't said anything to Kadan, and he tried not to let that bother him, when she should be sharing everything, but part of him didn't blame her. He wasn't sympathetic to her parents in the least.

Fredrickson had been around the Meadows family for years. Tansy believed him to be more than a friend, part of her family. She trusted him almost as much as she did her parents, and he'd made her mother scream in pain. Kadan replayed the sound in his head. He was sound-sensitive, and few things got past him, even over the phone. The sound had been genuine, but then the bastard part of him knew he could hurt an ally just for the necessary effect. And it brought results. If Kadan hadn't stopped her, Tansy would have delivered herself into their waiting hands. *As her father had said she would.*

If Whitney had planted Fredrickson into the Meadows' home to keep an eye on Tansy, why didn't her father know? Or had he known? Had there been a break in trust? If so, why hadn't Whitney simply killed Don Meadows? And why hadn't Meadows turned him in for the childhood experiments? Kadan turned the pieces of the puzzle over and over in his mind, but nothing fit. The moment he realized all the thinking in the world wasn't going to solve anything, he turned to the problem at hand. Tansy.

She was so unexpected. The man she called the puppet master was going to come after her. Kadan knew it with an absolute certainty. There had been shock, of course; an elite tracker was the last thing the man had expected. He must have been very shaken, although he recovered fast. There had been respect, and that made sense. Few could do what Tansy did, walk in blood and death and the filth of a killer's mind, hear the screams and pleas of victims dying, and emerge intact as she tracked the killer to his lair. Yeah, the puppet master would feel respect, but it would be more than that.

No one wanted to be truly alone. Tansy had taught him that. He'd walked the path his entire life, thinking he wanted it. He hadn't felt lonely. He'd chosen his path and kept to it, was comfortable with the way things were. And then he'd met her and he knew he never wanted to be alone again. Tansy might just be able to put up with his dominant, cold-as-ice personality and the raw need that only increased his craving for her. She had to be able to, because he wasn't going back.

And now the puppet master knew he wasn't alone. He had a companion who could tread the same minds if she chose. Tansy had noticed the smug amusement, but she hadn't caught the flair of male interest, the scent of sex. There was intrigue. Finally, someone to share his quiet genius with. Someone who would appreciate him for his camouflage. She would know what it took to control killers, to manipulate everyone around him and not get caught. The puppet master hadn't been alone for those few moments, and he wouldn't want to go back.

Kadan frowned as he buried his face in the thick mass of her hair. The puppet master wouldn't be able to stop himself any more than Kadan could. The tracker would think about it first, but she wouldn't leave his mind, any more than Tansy could get the killers out of hers. He would obsess about her. Fantasize. Want to show her he was stronger and could beat her at her own game. He'd want to show off, because finally, there was someone who truly could understand and *see* him. The puppet master wouldn't be able to resist that lure. In the end, self-preservation, discipline, and common sense would go, and he would begin to hunt her.

Kadan inhaled sharply, drawing Tansy's scent into his lungs. His. Talk about obsession. He could go from not feeling a damned thing to—*this*. Need. Hunger. His hands shaking with the desire to touch her. His mouth hungry for the taste of cinnamon and sex. He skimmed the pads of his fingers down Tansy's bare midriff, careful to keep the bristles velvet-soft, moving in the direction that prevented sticking. She liked the sensation, arching toward him even in her sleep. She was very responsive sexually, her body ripe for his with a few touches. She seemed just as starved for skin-to-skin contact as he was. When one had had a lifetime of emptiness, perhaps overindulgence and feasting were the only cure.

He glanced at his watch. They had a little time left, not much. He wanted to bring her back to the surface, replacing pain with something altogether different. He caught the sheet in his fist and pulled it down her body inch by inch to reveal the long expanse of skin. When the sheet pooled at her feet, he rolled her onto her back so he could drink in the sight of her. He'd never get tired of looking at her, never tire of touching her, or making her scream with pleasure.

His hands were big, calloused and rough, dark against her skin from so many years spent outdoors in the weather. The contrast between his hard body and her soft one gave him a monster of a hard-on, but now wasn't the time. He was going to indulge himself, but this time, it was all for her—okay, maybe not all.

He bent his head to her and licked at her soft belly the way a cat licked at cream. She tasted faintly of peaches. He inhaled her scent again just because it gave him so much pleasure, a unique mixture of cinnamon and other spices that went straight to his groin. He flicked his tongue over her, tracing her ribs and then teasing the undersides of her breasts.

Tansy moaned softly. He felt her fingers move in his hair.

"What are you doing?" Her voice was a mixture of sexy and drowsy, playing along his nerve endings, so that every muscle tightened and electricity arced over his skin.

He teased his way up the outside slope of her breast, swirled around her nipple, and then bit down gently. A broken cry escaped her throat. She tugged at his hair.

"I'm not awake yet." If it was meant as a protest, it failed miserably; excitement edged her voice.

"You don't have to be." He drew her breast into his mouth, suckling strongly. She was evidently very sensitive, because she arched into him, nearly coming off the bed.

Tansy closed her eyes, allowing the sensations to roll over and into her. His voice was pure velvet, brushing at the insides of her thighs until she was shaking with arousal. His knee roughly pushed apart her legs, allowing him better access as he kissed his way back down her belly, making her stomach muscles bunch with need.

He was fully clothed, the denim rubbing roughly against her skin, and there was something very decadent and forbidden at being totally naked, held open beneath a fully clothed man. His hands went to her thighs, pushing them even wider as he dipped his head low. His hair brushed against her inner thighs, making her jump and shiver. The shadow along his jaw scraped, sending flames dancing over her skin.

He bit at her inner thighs, his tongue bathing the tiny stings. Her hips bucked and she tried to pull his head away, squirming, moaning, rather shocked at her body's uninhibited reaction to him. His breath hissed out at being denied, and he caught both wrists in one hand and pinned them against her belly, raising his head an inch to look at her with dangerous eyes.

"Lie still."

"I can't." Her head tossed on the pillow. "It's too much." His weight pinned her down while his shoulders kept her legs spread apart, her silken sheath open to him.

He didn't bother to contradict her, but simply lowered his head again, taking long, slow licks, lapping at the spicy cream her body rewarded him with. Her hips continued to jerk and buck, as she writhed beneath his relentless tongue.

He took her over the edge in minutes, enjoying every moment of her soft body melting beneath him. He loved the look on her face, the shocked delight as waves of pleasure rolled through her. Kadan laid his head on her tummy, his arm slung around her waist, feeling the aftershocks gently rock her while he touched her mind. He'd driven out the demons, slammed the door closed on the voices, and left, in the place of cold and evil, something altogether different. There was a feeling of warmth, of love even. He winced away from the word, but it was out there now, in his mind. Love. What was it and how had such an emotion twisted its way into his heart and mind?

He pressed kisses from her belly to her breasts. "It isn't about the heart, Tansy, it's all about the soul."

She brushed the hair from his forehead with gentle fingers. "I have no idea what you're talking about."

"I know you don't. It's just as well. I'm the tough guy, remember?"

He pushed up, but Tansy caught his arm. "Are you all right? Tell me if something is wrong." He'd just sent her rocketing to the moon, and now he was already slipping away from her into a remote, distant man she could barely read, and he knew it bothered her. He hated separating himself, but he had to get her parents to safety before deciding if they should live or die.

"Everything is right, baby. I just wasn't ready for the way I feel about you, but I'm getting there." He'd accepted that she was his world. That didn't mean he was comfortable with it yet.

CHAPTER 9

Ryland Miller wasn't at all what Tansy had expected. He was definitely a force to be reckoned with, tough and scarred and built like a fighter. His steel gray eyes seemed to look right through her, his dark hair spilled in unruly waves over his forehead, but his smile was kind. She had emerged from a shower, dressed, little makeup, hair still damp, to find Ryland sitting comfortably with Kadan.

Kadan glanced up, and something in his energy chilled her at first, but then he smiled and got to his feet, and she immediately felt a shift inside of her, a melting. Kadan took her hand and tugged until she was beneath his shoulder, one hand sliding possessively around the nape of her neck while he performed introductions. Ryland's expression went from speculative to knowing, and she had to fight to keep from blushing.

"Ryland is married to Lily Whitney. They just had their first child," Kadan said.

Tansy struggled to keep her face from showing anything but polite interest. She still found it difficult to believe that a friend of Kadan's could be married to Whitney's daughter. She glanced at Kadan, but as always, his expression gave little away.

You can trust him.

Kadan's expression might be remote, but his warmth poured into her mind. She managed to keep smiling and nod at the introductions, keeping her gloved hands behind her back. She detested wearing the gloves now that she'd had months in the mountains and her brief time with Kadan without them. It was as if she'd gone from freedom back to prison, although even to her that seemed a melodramatic analogy. She couldn't help it. Her fingers felt tight and confined, itching to get out of the cramped quarters.

Three men waited in the living room, all coming to their feet when she entered. Ryland Miller might not look like a man who could be trusted; in fact, he looked like a man of few words but long on action, yet there was a steadiness in him that appealed to her. She could feel respect and even a certain friendship in Kadan's mind for the man. It would take a strong man to marry Whitney's daughter. Kadan was blocking a good deal of the energy, but he was allowing enough to slip through, and she recognized that Ryland was a psychic talent as well.

"This disreputable scoundrel is Raoul 'Gator' Fontenot. He's going to try to steal you away from me with his charm."

Gator grinned boyishly. "Ma'am, I got me a mean little hellcat at home and she'd have my head if she thought I was flirtin'," he drawled in his Cajun accent and winked at her, declaring her safe even though his smile could and probably did melt hearts.

"Is Gator some kind of nickname?"

"Yes, ma'am. In the Special Forces we often give each other appropriate handles. Kadan is 'Bishop.' Rye there is 'King,' and Sam, one of our team members, is 'Knight.'" Gator grinned at her, his drawling voice like molasses on a

Sunday. "I don' play boring chess, honey, but I wrestle alligators."

Kadan pinned his friend with a steely-eyed stare. "You keep flirting with her and you'll be wrestling with Flame. That woman is the only person who may be meaner than me."

Tansy sent Kadan a sharp glance. As a rule he could read people's minds. It was fairly clear that Gator might flirt, but he was definitely a one-woman man.

Yes, he is, Kadan agreed, *but it's good for them to know the score.*

His hand slid from the nape of her neck to her shoulder, his fingers brushing her neck, small, caressing strokes that were featherlight, but she felt them all the way to her toes.

Tough guy. She did the equivalent of mind eye-rolling, not wanting to show that even that light touch could affect her the way it did. Shivers of awareness raised goose bumps on her skin and down her spine.

Kadan merely shrugged, his hard expression and cold eyes saying it all to his friends.

Gator's unrepentant grin widened, flashing white teeth. "Flame's the better half of me and she sure keeps my life interestin."

Tansy's mind was racing with the idea of themes and nicknames in the Special Forces. Each ivory game piece had been carved obviously for a specific killer. If they were military and GhostWalkers, it couldn't be that difficult to track down their handles. There just weren't that many GhostWalkers, if what Kadan said was the truth. *Wouldn't it be a matter of just going through the teams and finding out what they call one another?*

She glanced toward the dining room. She could just glimpse the long table from the arched doorway leading to it. There were no figurines left out. All evidence was back in the war room, and she would bet her last dollar that the door was securely locked.

There is no way my teams are in any way responsible, and I would have recognized the names. I've worked with all the members of both teams. No, this is an outside team, run by Whitney or someone else. They're connected to Whitney; there was no doubt in my mind before you ever found the puppet master with Whitney's taint on him.

Tansy let her breath out slowly. Whitney hadn't been content with working on a few men; he'd given enhancements to others, and obviously their psychological profiles hadn't shown they were dangerous, or maybe it was because they were that he had chosen them. And that was very, very scary. She turned her head and looked at Kadan.

You knew. All along, you knew.

He didn't look at her, but his mind brushed against hers. *I suspected. I know these men and the others on my team. They are capable of killing, but not murder for pleasure. These killers are doing it for fun. It's literally a game to them.*

"Kadan," the third man spoke. His voice was quiet, but it drew attention immediately. "If you have something to share about all this, do it. I've been traveling nonstop and I want to get home and see Dahlia. I don't like being away from her for too long."

It was obvious the man was aware that Kadan and Tansy were speaking telepathically. She looked him over. He had that same stillness in him that Kadan did. He was tall, with longer midnight black hair, bronze skin, and truly black eyes. Where Kadan's eyes were so blue they could appear black, this man had eyes the color of obsidian.

"Nicolas Trevane," Kadan introduced. "Sorry, Nico, we're still sorting things out. Tansy's parents have been taken hostage. I think Whitney is involved, and that he has a GhostWalker present at the house with the captives. They want Tansy to turn herself over to them or they plan on killing her parents. She had twenty-four hours. Eight of those are gone."

The three men looked from Tansy's face to Kadan's. Gator grinned again, this time his drawl teasing. "I take it that's not an option."

Kadan slid his hand down the curve of Tansy's back and then slipped his arm around her waist. "No."

Simple. Direct. That was Kadan.

Tansy sighed. "I drew a diagram of the house. We do have an escape tunnel, but Fredrickson knows about it."

With his arm tight around her, Kadan led the way into the dining room, where he spread several papers on the table. "The estate is quite large and probably well guarded. Fortunately, Tansy knows all the camera positions and has pinpointed them for us."

Kadan stepped back to allow the men to study the diagram of the house and estate, complete with as much information as Tansy could remember on where the guards were usually stationed, where cameras and dogs were located. He ran his hand up and down the curve of her spine, savoring the feel of her feminine outline.

Tansy glanced at him sharply. He wasn't looking at her, nor did he appear to be paying attention to her at all, several times bending close to the table to point out details to Ryland and Gator, discussing an entry and extraction plan. She tried to listen, finding the way their minds worked intriguing, but his hand was distracting. Several times he slid his palm over her denim-clad bottom, shaping her buttocks, his thumb brushing strokes of fire while his hand caressed her.

Don't. The other men were too sharp-eyed not to notice. It wasn't so much that she objected to them seeing him caress her, it was her reaction that was embarrassing. The elevated breathing she couldn't quite stop. Her nipples hardening. His touch affected her, no matter how featherlight it was.

Don't ever tell me I can't touch you. Any time. Any place. It sounded like a command. Low. Firm. A husky, velvet promise of retaliation, sexual in nature, that sent a wave of heat crashing through her body and dampening her panties.

But Tansy was in his mind and his lack of emotion concerned her. He was disconnected. Remote. Ice water once again flowed in his veins. He frightened her that way, so distant he didn't seem aware of any of the emotions a normal person would have. It was only his hand on her, the shape and texture of her, the scent of her, that kept a trace of feeling running through him. He clung to that small connection, but didn't seem aware that that was what he was doing.

As if to make certain she understood, his hand moved over her hips and up her rib cage, sliding along the side of her breast, back up to the nape of her neck. His fingers tightened until she turned her head. He leaned over. Casually. In charge. Taking his time. Daring her to defy him and pull away. If she hadn't felt that small flicker of need in him, she might have kicked him in the shins and told him to go to hell, but instead, she stood there quietly and waited for the touch and taste of him. There was an aura of sexual intensity surrounding him, and the moment they were close, his sheer magnetism overwhelmed her self-preservation and she seemed to just give herself to him, drawn like a moth to flame.

He took her mouth gently, not at all like the threat in his mind. She tasted his hunger and knew his need of her was elemental and deep and beyond even his understanding.

Kiss me back.

She wasn't certain why he needed her so much. Reassurance? He seemed so completely confident, she could barely believe that he felt in any way threatened by the presence of the other men. That seemed out of character. Her arms slid around his neck and she opened her mouth to his, feeling him inside her, stroking and tasting with that same gentleness that was so disarming.

Are you all right? She touched his cheek.

He lifted his head and smiled at her. *No problems.*

She wasn't sure she believed him, but he was already bending over the drawings. To the others he pointed out the gate with the cameras and guards.

"This booth is manned at all times. Cliffs back up to the house and they'd be difficult to climb, but not impossible from the ocean side. Fredrickson is bound to be looking at an entry from that side so he'll most likely step up the guards there."

"You don't think he'll believe I'll walk right in and give myself up?" Tansy asked hopefully.

"We have to assume he knows I went looking for you and that you're with me. You didn't use the radio to call your parents, you called from an untraceable, secure line. Fredrickson will know that. He'll be prepared for an assault team."

"So entry up the cliffs isn't going to be a good plan."

"We can wait for Tucker and Ian to report in, but let's assume not," Kadan said. His gaze shifted for a brief second to Ryland.

The dark-haired man eased his shoulders a little. "I could use some coffee, Kadan. Do you have any around here?"

"In the kitchen," Kadan said.

"I'll get it," Tansy said, glad for something to do. Planning assaults wasn't her forte. "Anyone else want some?"

Kadan waited until Tansy had taken their orders and left the room. He kept his voice low. "The package is expected to be hostile. There's a tie to Whitney. I want to bring them out quietly to a house only we know about and keep them under guard. If they don't tell us what we need, I'll have a private talk with them."

Ryland stirred, his gaze flicking toward the kitchen. "Kadan. Not if she's your choice. I'll take care of it."

Kadan shook his had. "My woman. My responsibility. I can live with it."

"She won't be able to."

"I have no problems doing whatever it takes to keep her safe, and she'll never know."

Nico shrugged his shoulders. "Your call, Kadan, but women have a way of finding out things you don't want them to know, and any one of us would do the job for you. Just give us the word."

"Appreciate it," he said gruffly, but he wouldn't shirk his responsibility. Not when it came to Tansy's safety, and especially because they were her parents and she loved them. If it came down to it, he'd take them out as quickly, painlessly, and humanely as possible.

Tansy returned with a collection of mugs, sugar, and cream. Kadan took the tray from her and placed it on the table.

"How's it coming?" She glanced at her watch. "And how soon do we leave?"

"I think we've about got this, baby. You'll stay in the safe house we're setting up for your parents. I'll have a couple of my men there with you."

She scowled at him, shaking her head quickly. "No way. That was never part of the plan. I'm going with you. If something goes wrong, I have to be there to—"

"No." Kadan said the word quietly, his voice so low it was barely audible, yet it cut like a razor, demanding immediate compliance.

Tansy jerked away from the fingers that had settled gently around her wrist like a bracelet—except instead of getting away, she felt the fingers tighten into shackles, preventing her from moving anywhere.

"You won't be sacrificing your life for theirs. That's never been an option." His voice whispered like velvet, but cracked like a whip, lashing across her mind, burning his decree into her brain. He made a small effort to soften the order with an explanation. "We can't take you into combat, you'd be a liability."

This was the other side of Kadan. Immovable. His blue

eyes were nearly black now, unfathomable, impossible to read. His expression remote.

The three other men drifted from the room, leaving her feeling more vulnerable than ever. She couldn't be alone with him, not when his mind held hers, determined to force his will on her.

Tansy went very still, refusing to struggle against his grip. Kadan was enormously strong, and there would be no getting away from him until he wanted to let her go. If he wanted cool and remote, well, she could do that as well. She locked her gaze with his, refusing to be intimidated by the dangerous edge to him. He wore the image of a warrior like skin, the fit natural and impressive. Perhaps this was more the true Kadan then the one in her bed, but she couldn't let him see that her stomach had bunched into knots and her heart beat too fast.

"Fortunately, I am not in the military and not under anyone's command."

He didn't change expression, but she swore a shadow moved across his face. Her heart skipped a beat. She would have finger marks on her inner wrist.

"Really?"

He said one word. Only one. A soft inquiry that sent fear skittering down her spine whether she wanted to be in control or not. Why? After all, what was he going to do?

She found she couldn't look away from him. His eyes darkened even more. Something hot flickered in the depths so that through the black, his eyes burned with blue flames. She caught her breath as he pulled her hand to the front of his jeans and rubbed her palm over the thickened bulge there.

You're taking a big chance, baby, arguing with me when you can't win, but the result is one hell of a wicked hard-on.

He leaned close, his tongue flicking over her ear. *I'll bring them home to you safe. That's a promise, Tansy.*

He wouldn't guarantee beyond that, but if she looked into his mind, she could see his word was gold. Unless her parents were already dead, he'd find a way.

He'd disarmed her completely with one breath. That small promise. Maybe if she hadn't been able to touch his mind, feel his assurance, his total commitment to returning her parents to her, she would have snatched her hand away. Instead, she stayed still, her heart beating too fast, her body and mind belonging to him whether she wanted it or not.

A part of her hated the way he made her weak, but defiance and argument seemed stupid. What would it get her? In the end, she would be a liability to them if she went along. They were a team and they were used to working with one another. She knew teamwork, and an outsider could easily ruin their rhythm and throw them all off. And that might get her parents—or the team—killed.

She just wished everything he said didn't sound like an order. Worse, she hated that there was a part of her that went soft and slick and hot at the sound of his voice when he talked that way. She was crazy to be in any way attracted to a man who wasn't in the least civilized.

His teeth bit down on her earlobe. *You can't fault me for protecting you.*

She closed her eyes as he rubbed against her hand, unsure how to reach him when he felt so distant from her. *Is this all there is between us?* Explosive chemistry.

She ached with wanting him, but it wasn't enough. Not now. Not when she'd been in his mind. Not when she could remove the hated gloves and touch his skin.

Not for me, he assured her.

She couldn't imagine being with another man, wanting to touch him, or have his hands all over her. The things he wanted with her seemed wrong with anyone else and so intensely right with him. She had no idea why, only that she wasn't ready to walk away from him yet.

Not ever. Deliberately he removed her palm from the front of his jeans and sank his teeth into the center, scraping back and forth, his eyes never leaving her face.

She swallowed hard. "You can't talk to me like that. I'm not one of your soldiers."

"I don't talk to my soldiers like that. Only you. I stand in front of you."

"I want to be beside you."

He kept her gaze captive while his tongue swirled over the center of her palm, teasing, reminding, driving her temperature up when she needed to be cool. "I can't give you that right now, Tansy. I can only give you what and who I am, right now this minute. I have to shield you, because that's who I am. You have to decide whether or not you can live with that. Whether you can love me, and not just a sliver of me, because the biggest part of who I am is the man standing in front of you." He kissed her palm and closed her fingers around it. "Even if I could wrap myself up in pretty lies, I'd never be able to pull it off. I don't know how to be anything else."

His voice was the same. Absolute confidence. Velvet-soft. Skimming over her body and teasing her inner thighs with excitement. But in his mind, where he didn't know, where he never looked, there was an edge of despair, a belief that it was impossible for her to love him. She caught a glimpse of his commitment to her, of his intention to hold her to him with any means he had for as long as he could.

He would make every moment together memorable, the sex incomparable, and he would do everything within his power to make her happy while keeping her safe. It was all there for her to see. But that part of his mind was the only part she could feel warm in. And that warm, compassionate side of her, the need to soothe and help others, instantly gave herself to him, even though she recognized he could be every bit as dangerous as those she hunted, or even more so.

She took a breath, let it out, and then leaned in to brush a kiss over his stubborn jaw. "Just try a little harder not to order me around so much."

He didn't respond. The others were returning, one by one, looking disinterested when she knew they had to be very engrossed. Instinctively she knew Kadan had never shown a fascination with another woman to them. They had to be somewhat concerned, but they were polite, getting back to business as though nothing had transpired.

"When you put out the call and told us what you needed, Lily found a house near Tansy's parents' estate," Ryland said. "If we get through the wooded area and use the canyon to make a run through the heavier terrain, we'd be less likely to be spotted."

"There's a Humvee in the garage. The keys are in all the cars," Tansy offered. "Of course there's also a tracking device in it. It's the real deal. Dad's taken it in the canyon lots of times."

Gator shrugged his shoulders when they looked at him. "Piece of cake. It's ours."

"So we'll bring them out with that and take them to the safe house," Ryland said. "Gator, check the best route through. Nico will cover our back trail."

Kadan tangled his fingers with hers. "Ian and Tucker are reconning the estate right now. They'll give us the most up-to-date intel as soon as possible. When they get back to the safe house, they'll wait for us to bring them Tansy." He brought her knuckles up to his mouth, distracting her from panic with a scrape of his teeth. "You'll have to stay out of sight. My gut feeling is Whitney was watching your parents, and when his cover was blown, Fredrickson had standing orders to pick you up and bring you in. The men who came at me in the mountains were trying to kill me. If Whitney sent them, they wanted me out of the way so they could acquire you."

"If that's true, Kadan," Ryland said, "it doesn't fit with

Whitney's breeding program. He would want both of you, not just Tansy."

Kadan shrugged. "Maybe my genes are just not as upscale as Tansy's."

"He's had all these years to come after me," Tansy pointed out. "Why now?"

"That's an excellent question. Let's find out if anyone has the answer to that," Kadan said, his voice changing from light to grim, as if the very idea of anyone trying to take her from him put a murderous edge to his mood.

"I don't need two men to babysit me, Kadan. Over the years my father kept adding security to the estate, and I don't think four men are going to be enough. We used to have rent-a-cops, but in the last couple of years, Watson, our head of security has made a few changes."

"Watson?" Kadan turned his head sharply. "You've never mentioned him before. Who is Watson?"

"Benny Watson. He took over security for Dad about two years ago, when Dad decided to beef things up."

"Why did your father replace his security detail?"

"Dad and my mother do a lot of work out of their home. Most of their research is classified. He got very nervous after a story came out about them in *Newsweek*. He wanted to just make certain that no one could get to them or any of the plans they were working on."

"Did Fredrickson recommend Watson to your father?" Ryland asked. "Ordinarily two GhostWalkers will work an assignment together, and one of them is an anchor. I'd be surprised if Whitney assigned Fredrickson to infiltrate your household alone."

Tansy frowned. "I don't honestly know that much about him. Fredrickson is part of the family. He lived at the house, ate with us, even sat around with us some evenings and watched movies. Watson was always in the background. He didn't ever talk to me. I always thought he regarded me as a pain in the neck."

"Did you ever get vibes off of either him or Fredrickson that they could have psychic abilities?" Kadan asked.

Tansy shook her head. Kadan's gaze met Ryland's over her head, just for a brief moment.

"Watson increased the security at the house?"

She nodded. "For several years we just had a local security company, but Watson fired them all and brought in a different group. They didn't ever interact with us, but they were courteous at all times. I'd say hello and ask how they were doing. They'd answer briefly and go about their job. That's about the same time they brought in the dogs."

"Did you ask your father why?" Kadan asked.

She shook her head, her gaze shifting away from his. She withdrew her hand and even stepped back from him. "I was in the middle of some pressing problems of my own, and whether my father decided we needed added security or not didn't really matter to me." She sounded defensive to her own ears and moved farther away from him, out of reach, not wanting questions—or sympathy.

She had known she was losing her mind. She hadn't slept in weeks, afraid to close her eyes, terrified she would drown in blood. The whispers never stopped. The voices spoke night and day, and ugly, haunting images crowded into her mind. She felt covered with oil, unable to draw a clean breath. There had been no reprieve, no Kadan to kiss and stroke her until her vision focused solely on him, until her body became his, until her mind was so full of warmth and caring and desperate need that there was no room for anything unclean.

"My mom is very fragile, Kadan. We've always sort of protected her. She's a brilliant woman, and too caring. Things can crush her very easily. Fredrickson's betrayal will have devastated her." She took a breath. "She might not be able to walk out of there." She made herself look at him over her shoulder. "And you'll frighten her."

She really hated admitting that to him, but his expressionless mask and cold eyes would terrify her mother. She didn't want to hurt him, or to present her mother in a bad light, but she shouldn't have worried. Kadan didn't even blink, shrugging his powerful shoulders as if whatever her mother thought of him mattered very little.

"I'll get her out."

"I'm saying she might get hysterical," Tansy confessed.

"I got that, baby. You don't have to worry." His voice soothed her, that same warm velvet that made her ache with need. Now she felt caressed and touched, although he was across the room.

The phone rang. Kadan snatched it up and listened, scribbling notes as whoever was on the other end talked. Curious, Tansy moved back to Kadan's side, very conscious of the other men huddled around the table. She wore the gloves, but even so, she avoided touching their coffee mugs or anything else she'd seen them handle. These were men of violence and each of them had killed. She would have picked up some impressions whether she wanted to intrude on them on not.

They were silent for the most part, no unnecessary talking. Once in a while, Gator broke out in a grin and nudged one of the others with a teasing comment, but they stayed intent on their plans, committing the diagram and layout of the house and security to memory.

"Tucker and Ian are back at the safe house. We have a go. The security near the cliff has more than doubled, and Ian says it looks like they may have brought in some mercs. They aren't rent-a-cops, for certain. All of them handle themselves as military or ex-military." Kadan pulled the estate diagram to him and began marking X's at various points.

Tansy looked over his shoulder, watching the growing number of red X's with dismay. There were too many of them. Four men against so many trained guards. Not just trained, men probably trained in Special Forces. Her breath hitched in her lungs.

Kadan. She breathed his name in fear, not meaning to, but terror gripped hard.

He was going to save her parents when he didn't even trust them, risk his life because of her. She didn't want that from him. She didn't want to use him that way, use the cold, driven part of him that always demanded justice or revenge.

She felt the flicker of warmth in her mind grow and blossom until he filled her with . . . *him.*

Kadan, you can't. We'll do this another way.

Kadan turned from the map of the estate, away from the other men who were talking over various plans, and looked down at her, into her enormous, frightened eyes. She was afraid for him. That struck him as amazing—that anyone could worry about him. And it was genuine. He searched her mind, because even with the stark look of fear for him on her face and in her eyes, he couldn't quite believe it.

Damn it, Tansy. You're turning me inside out.

He knew his voice was too gruff. He was growling at her to keep from pulling her into his arms and burying himself in the haven of her body. To keep from giving it away that she had consumed him and he was nothing without her. He didn't know any other way to show her, didn't know how to say it; there were only his hands and his mouth and his cock. There were no words inside of him, and if his body couldn't win her, couldn't let her see he was loving her with every touch, every stroke, he was damned. Truly damned.

He stepped in to her, crowding her even though he knew he shouldn't, needing her warmth when inside he was as cold as ice. His veins were ice, rivers of it, small chips floating like small shavings on the surface. He could feel the cold deep inside, the stone that was his heart, the space that was never filled, never warm, unless her heat surrounded him. He put his hands on her hips, that sweet curve that could only be Tansy. Deliberately he ran his palms up under the hem of her tank top to that small strip of bare skin. He rested his hands there, letting her heat soak into him, feeling it pour into his heart and soul and melt the ice in his veins.

Thankfully, she didn't pull away from him, sharing her body even in a room full of strangers. He loved her all the more for that sacrifice, her shoving aside her embarrassment for him. Her gaze clung to his.

"What am I going to do with you, Kadan?" she murmured softly.

He knew her question had nothing to do with sex, but he filled her mind with a graphic answer, complete with graphic images—her sprawled naked on his bed, his mouth and hands all over her, his cock buried deep inside her—and yet really, truthfully, for him his answer had nothing and everything to do with sex.

She blushed, glanced at the other men, who were staring at the drawings, not paying any attention, and shook her head.

"I don't want you to go."

He took her hand, tugging until she followed him out of the room. "I don't think they'd kill your parents after the twenty-four-hour deadline, Tansy, but they might wound one of them. And if they move them, it will make a rescue much more difficult. Once they've moved them, they could do anything to them. We have to go now."

"Then use the other two men. I'll be fine. I know they're part of your team. They've seen the layout of the estate. Let them go with you."

One hand cupped the nape of her neck, his thumb sliding over her jaw in a little caress. "If something happened to you, Tansy, there wouldn't be much point in any of this. I'm not so far away from that edge myself. And you've seen it. Don't pretend you haven't. There would be a bloodbath the likes of which no one has ever seen. I refuse to take chances with your life—or my honor. Are we clear?"

She swallowed hard, tears burning behind her eyelids. "I don't want anything to happen to you or your friends."

"This is what we do, baby. And I've got someone to come home to. I wouldn't blow it now." He leaned down and took a tear from her face with his tongue. "Don't be afraid for me. I want you to pack up everything you'll need just in case we have to move fast. We'll keep this house as a base, but we'll need to go at a moment's notice. I want to be on the next scene the moment we get word."

He wanted there to be no mistake: She wasn't going to be staying with her parents. She'd be with him.

Tansy nodded. "I travel light, Kadan. I'm used to the life, remember?"

He didn't want to remember the horror in her mind, and he sure didn't want her remembering it either.

"It won't be like that. I won't let them take your soul again."

She rested her forehead against his. At least he understood. Her parents had tried to understand her, but it was impossible when they couldn't know what was happening in her head. *Just don't think about it, Tansy-girl,* her father had said. *Why can't you just push the bad things out of your head and think good thoughts?* her mother had chimed in. As if somehow, if she just tried, she'd stop the killers and victims from sticking in her head and sucking out her soul.

She looked up at Kadan. He seemed so strong. Invincible. Standing between her and evil. She believed him. She believed that quiet confidence, the implacable resolve she found in his mind, but most of all, the ice running through his veins and in his mind and heart. Because he could match the killers move for move, like players on a chessboard, and they couldn't defeat him with their immoral, malicious inhumanity as they had her. They couldn't eat him alive and take him over. And he was standing in front of her.

"We really have a chance of stopping them, don't we?" she asked.

"We will."

Tansy nodded. "Okay then. I'm with you."

"Then let's get your parents back."

Kadan squeezed her hand and let her go. There would be no more touching her mind until it was done. Maybe once, maybe one more time when he kissed her good-bye and left her with her guards at the safe house across the narrow canyon from her parents' house, but that would be a luxury. She couldn't be anywhere near him when he ran a mission—especially this mission. Because if her parents were in any way involved with Whitney, he would fulfill his promise to her: She would see them one more time, and then they would disappear.

Kadan still had possession of her cell phone, a fact she had long forgotten, and he hoped it stayed that way, because there was no way she was getting it back until this thing was over. As a precaution, there was no phone in the safe house he was taking Tansy to, so if things went wrong she couldn't try to call and make a deal with Fredrickson, exchanging her life for her parents'. Ian and Tucker had strict instructions on what to do if the mission went south. They would get Tansy out of the area fast, that night. They had the necessary drug and would use it if push came to shove.

Kadan had given orders that they weren't to tell her, just drug her and get her out. They could deal with the grief and anger later, but they weren't to let Whitney get his hands on her. Tansy was not going to end up in his macabre breeding program, not if Kadan could do anything about it, and that was a promise he'd made to himself.

CHAPTER 10

The three GhostWalkers waited patiently while Nico went to high ground, establishing a position where he could cover them all and give them the location and movement of as many guards as possible. The wind had picked up a little, coming in off the ocean, rustling the leaves in the trees and bringing with it the smell of sea and sand. The moon was a mere sliver, spilling very little light on the ground, although the night was clear and that meant stars were out in full force, illuminating more of the landscape than any of them wanted.

The estate was on five acres overlooking the ocean. A high privacy fence surrounded the beautifully landscaped lawns. Weeping willows formed graceful sentries around a shimmering pond where a low, arched bridge spanned the water, lending it a fairy tale quality. The house rose up with majestic grace, surrounded by balconies, columns, and inviting porches. Masses of flower beds and carefully trimmed hedges led up the stamped walkways and surrounded the house itself. The estate looked the picture of elegance and tranquility.

From the outside, it was impossible to see the second set of fences where the guard dogs patrolled, or the artfully hidden cameras that were scattered around the grounds. At night laser beams crisscrossed the grounds along the walkways. Guards at the front gates were alert and visibly held guns cradled in their arms.

Kadan made certain to shield his team's presence from any other psychic in the vicinity, keeping the waves of energy close to him. He stood very still, his breathing slow and even, his heart rate normal, his mind calm. This was his world, and there was no anxiety in it for him, only a strong sense of purpose and resolve.

The air moved in and out of his lungs in perfect rhythm. This was when he was most alive—when he was hunting. He could inhale and scent information, sort through data with the same precision as a jungle cat. Men moved along the inside of the fence, staying within sight of the dogs, on alert for the slightest reaction from the canine guards. They patrolled the grounds, along the garage and house, making it difficult to keep the laser beams on. They turned them off while conducting a manual search and turned them back on when they left the area.

"In position," Nico's voice sounded in Kadan's ear.

Nico could shoot the wings off a butterfly if he had to, even in a high wind. Kadan had every confidence in the sniper.

Kadan pointed at Gator, and the Cajun instantly went to the ground, belly-crawling across the open space between their position and the first fence. They'd chosen the southernmost part of the estate as an entry point. From there, they had access to the helipad and garage, two places absolutely necessary to control if they were to succeed.

Gator made it across the rocky terrain, pushed through the saw grass and rolled up against the privacy fencing. He lay quiet, his mind reaching out until he found the dogs. There were eight of them. Big German shepherds. Intelligent. Well trained. They paced along the fence in strict formation, each dog so many feet apart from the next so they could complete the circuit of the property so many times per hour.

Gator's first touch was tentative, finding the leader of the pack. There was always one. The good handlers always recognized that fact and dealt with the most alpha of a dog team a little differently. Each dog was trained to make decisions, but none had been exposed to Gator's talent. He could influence animals fairly easily, matching his brain waves to theirs and bending the dogs to his will. In this case, he wanted no alarm raised as they went into the compound.

It took a few minutes to connect with the alpha, to find it in the midst of all the animals, each with its own personality. The moment he merged, Gator was in a different world. His sense of smell was instantly heightened a hundred times. He scented the individual guards, the squirrels in the trees, and even a rodent that had made a home in the nearby grass. Colors dimmed, the spectrum narrowing, so that his sight was altered.

He could see the grounds now, his connection with the alpha strengthening by the moment so that he was seeing what the dog saw as it paced in between the chain-link fences. The guards moved systematically over the yard in a typical sweep, making certain no one had penetrated the interior. The dog continued moving at a steady pace, alert and a little confused with Gator sharing his mind.

He calmed the animal, joined forces, and dominated, taking control and issuing orders. One by one he connected with each animal. They were not to give away, by sound or alertness, that a stranger slipped through their ranks. He was one of them. A member of the pack. They were to continue their patrol and alert only when told.

Once he was certain the dogs would obey him, Gator signaled to Kadan. "Green light."

Kadan had dressed for the occasion, his clothing reflective, his skin mirroring the color of the ground, and his equipment locked in place for quick use. Drawing his skin-tight hood over his hair, he made his way to the fence. It was about twenty feet high, straight up, no toe- or finger-holds. He studied it for a moment and then leapt high, catching with the pads of his fingers. He went up the smooth side easily, using his enormous upper body strength to climb, only the sticky pads of his fingers preventing him from falling.

"Guard twenty feet from your position. Hang tight," Nico reported.

Kadan clung to the side of the fence, his skin matching the darker tones, his clothes blending seamlessly. Even the hood mirrored the images around him, so he simply disappeared. The human eye couldn't spot him. The dogs knew he was there and reacted with a restless sidestepping, but Gator's outpouring of influence kept them from giving the GhostWalker's presence away.

"All clear. He went around the side of the building. Laser's down near the helipad. You have a go now," Nico murmured.

Kadan pulled himself to the top of the fence, changing skin color to match the surroundings as he took a quick look before he vaulted the double chain-link fences holding the dogs. He landed in a crouch, waited a heartbeat, and then began moving through the dense shrubbery, relying on Nico to be his eyes as he crossed to the back of the garage.

"Coming at you, thirty yards. Two guards and they know what they're doing."

Mercs. Kadan's lip curled as he sank down and went still. Fredrickson had blanketed the estate with mercenaries, and either Don and Sharon Meadows knew and approved, or they had gotten themselves into a mess they couldn't handle, but it was fairly difficult to hide the kind of men guarding the estate. Kadan watched through narrowed eyes as the two men covered the ground fast. Every now and then their gazes touched on the dogs pacing in the fences. The men's gazes shifted constantly, on the alert. Fredrickson definitely was expecting trouble.

One merc paused only a scant few feet from Kadan's hip, talking into his radio. "Everything is quiet, Boss. The dogs aren't showing signs of nerves."

"Keep everyone alert," a voice, probably Fredrickson's, snapped.

The two men rounded the corner of the garage and were out of Kadan's sight. He remained where he was, his breath moving through his lungs with a steady rhythm. A third man emerged from the garage, looked left and right, and then walked over to the chain-link fence to stare at the nearest dog. He muttered something, picked up a rock, and flung it through the open links. The rock hit the other side of the fence and the dog showed teeth. Kadan slipped the knife from his boot and waited.

"The son of a bitch is teasin' the dog," Gator complained, his voice a whisper in Kadan's ear. "Can Nico put a bullet in the bastard's head?"

"No," Kadan hissed firmly and eased his body out of the brush, his gaze on the man who now jabbed at the dog with a long stick. "We need complete silence."

"You kill him, Kadan, and our surprise is gone. I'll take him out after you get Fredrickson," Nico said, his voice cool and confident.

Kadan cursed under his breath. He wanted to do the bastard. He detested men who preyed on anything or anyone who couldn't fight back. Looking at the dog, with its snarl and bared teeth, he realized the dog just needed one moment for revenge. It was obvious this man tormented the dog on a regular basis.

Another time, buddy, he promised and sent the dog a silent apology before he began to inch his way across the yard. He was running out of time. The moment the guards moved their sweep to the other side of the estate, they'd be activating the lasers.

Nico whispered in his ear, letting him know when to move and when to be still. He made it to the edge of the shrubbery at the far side of the house, but it took several minutes of painstaking progress before he was clear of the laser field.

Kadan moved into the wide bed of flowers close to the house, looking up at his chosen point of entry. It was two stories up and Tansy's bedroom window. On this side, there were no balconies, and she often left the window open a couple of inches because she needed to feel like freedom. Her hands, encased in gloves, always made her feel like a prisoner, and she would slide her hands out the window and wave them in the night air. If he was lucky, no one would have remembered to lock her window, as she'd been gone so long.

"Now," Nico's voice whispered in his ear.

Kadan leapt up as high as he could, going from a crouch to a full extension and reaching high above his head. His finger pads caught and held, gluing him to the side of the house. Again his skin tone changed, taking on the hue of his background. He began to move upward in silence. Fredrickson was a GhostWalker and their strongest opponent. He had the ability to sense their presence, and they had no idea of his psychic talents. He had to be neutralized before a rescue could take place.

At a soft go from Nico, Ryland moved into position, penetrating on the opposite side of the grounds, to get through the laser fields as the guards swept that area. When he made it through the yard and neared the house, he would hold at his location waiting for Kadan's entry and the all clear, signaling Fredrickson was dead.

Kadan climbed to the window, anchored his body with one hand, and, as he carefully raised his body to peer over the sill, felt with the other for trip wires. His hearing was particularly acute, and he became aware of the faint hum that often accompanied a live wire. Fredrickson had not only known about the slightly raised window, he'd anticipated an entry and left it invitingly open that scant inch and a half, but had laid enough traps for ten mice.

"I'm going up, Nico. This is a trap."

"Two men on the roof," Nico reported. "One just above your position and one about ten feet to his right. Both look likes mercs. I can take them both, but Fredrickson will know."

Kadan had already begun his descent. "No. I'll get in."

"I can rile up the dog. We've still got the bastard guard poking at him with a stick," Gator offered. "Let me get the dog going and that will draw them to this side. Fredrickson will go on alert, but he'll want to know what's going on."

"That's a go."

Kadan could use the diversion. If he was lucky, once Fredrickson knew his own guard had screwed up, he'd send someone personally to chew the man up. And that meant a door open. He just had to be in the right place at the right time. Moving with the speed and precision of a spider in a web, Kadan chose a door on the side of the house close to where the guard was teasing the dog. He went down the wall headfirst, much like a gecko might, held by the sticky pads on his fingers and his enormous strength until he was hovering just above the door, in plain sight on the side of the building.

Within minutes the German shepherd went crazy, slamming into the chain-link fence, roaring a challenge, snarling and barking, hitting the fence repeatedly in an attempt to get to his cruel handler. The yard erupted with guards, men running, calling out to one another, rushing toward the fence. One caught the guard with stick in hand, still tinged with blood where he'd driven it into the dog's side. Lights burst on overhead, turning the grounds into daylight. Alarms shrieked as the lasers were set off.

Within a couple more minutes, enough time for the message to be relayed to Fredrickson, the door below Kadan burst open and a man went running out. Kadan swung his body through the opening, landing in a crouch inside, gun already out and tracking. From the drawings Tansy had provided, he knew this was an atrium that opened into the living room. Huge plants grew nearly wild, rising to the high ceilings, the mist kicking on automatically every few minutes to provide the atmosphere of a rain forest.

Kadan took his time. He was in enemy territory now. Not just any enemy, a GhostWalker who would feel the slightest change in the energy around him. Kadan could shield, but the closer he got to his prey, the more difficult it would become to do so. And he was close. Fredrickson was also a shielder—surprising, but it had to be true. That gift was somewhat rare, just as being an elite tracker was.

Kadan went to his belly again, green now, like the plants around him. Using his elbows to propel him forward, he slithered through the jungle of foliage to the edge of the glass. The atrium was huge, bringing the rain forest indoors. Completely glass, the room could be enclosed and kept separate from the rest of the house, or, with the double glass doors opened as they were, the sweeping, dramatic plants could become part of the enormous sunken great room.

Tansy had been raised in this opulent home. She'd lived there as if it was an ordinary, everyday house, probably taking the beauty and uniqueness for granted. Kadan had spent a lifetime on the streets, in foster homes and one-room apartments, before moving on to the military life of jungle, desert, and sea. What was he thinking? How could she go from this to what he could give her? The moment the thought entered, he pushed it away. Tansy had no place here. She couldn't screw him up any more than she'd already done by turning him inside out.

Kadan forced his mind back under control and slid through the doorway into the great room. Fredrickson was just ahead of him, staring impassively at Tansy's parents, who were sitting in two high-backed chairs, both with their hands tied behind their backs. Sharon Meadows was a small woman, very thin, with a wealth of blond hair. A bruise had formed just below one eye and there was swelling near her mouth. It didn't take a genius to figure out Fredrickson had used her to try to control Tansy. She wept silently, casting little glances at her husband, who looked as if he might have a stroke any moment.

"She's dead if they come in here," Fredrickson said to Don. "You'd better hope your daughter loves you both enough to give herself up without bringing help."

Sharon shook her head hard, but only sobbed louder.

Don bared his teeth and struggled to loosen his bonds. "You don't need to touch my wife. Tansy will come. You tell Whitney she'll come. There's no need for this."

Fredrickson shrugged. "We'll take her back, one way or the other. And we're doing you a favor. They know about her and she's marked. They'll kill her if they find her before we do."

"You keep saying 'they' as if that's supposed to scare me," Don hissed. "I don't believe that anyone wants her dead. Whitney made that up because he wants her back."

Kadan propelled himself forward on his belly over the smooth, rich marble floor, gun in one hand, knife in the other. He slid forward, inch by painstakingly slow inch. Each centimeter counted when he was out in the open and Fredrickson had only to turn his head. Kadan gathered his strength, his resolve, and he flowed from the floor, rising like a demon summoned from hell, hurtling the knife straight to his enemy's throat.

The knife buried all the way to the hilt. Fredrickson

gurgled, eyes wide, one hand half rising in reflex, as if to examine the instrument of his death. He swayed and then toppled to the floor. Instantly Kadan felt the psychic shield come down and lethal energy flowing toward him. He spun, already diving in front of Tansy's mother, instincts screaming at him that she was the target. The bullet caught him higher than he'd have liked, slamming into his bullet-proof vest like an explosive fist to his chest, half spinning him and driving him backward hard.

Sharon's high-pitched shriek hurt his ears nearly as much as the punch to his chest, but his gun hand was already up, finger squeezing the trigger, one, two, three, precise shots, dropping the second GhostWalker even as Kadan fell. Blood sprayed across the marble and spattered the walls. He saw the red droplets showering down as his body slammed hard into Sharon's, driving her chair over backward.

The blow to his chest had ripped the breath from his body, and it felt like every bone was broken, smashed beyond repair. For an instant, the edges of his vision blurred and then went black. He woke with rage and panic seconds later, his chest on fire, burning as if a hot iron was branding him, and Sharon screaming nonstop in his ear. He fought the need to rip his vest off and shut the woman up at the same time.

Movement caught his eye, and his legs still tangled with Tansy's mother, he rolled, the gun rock steady in his hand, instinct staying his finger on the trigger. Don Meadows froze from where he was trying to slither across the floor, his gaze fixed on the knife at Kadan's waist.

"I'll fucking put a bullet in your throat," Kadan warned, feeling deadly with his chest on fire, fighting for every breath. "Go, Gator," he managed to order into the radio while he extricated himself from the woman's flopping limbs.

Sharon's screams would draw everyone for miles.

Calmly, Kadan pulled out an air syringe and pressed it against her neck. He didn't bother to untie her hands. The drug worked fast, halting her scream in mid-shriek so blessed silence fell.

"You bastard. What the hell have done to her?" Don demanded.

Kadan sent him one quelling look, and the man was smart enough to stop talking. Kadan's chest hurt like a bear, still painful with every breath he drew, but the fire was beginning to subside a bit. He still wanted to rip his vest off, along with the shooter's head. He pushed down his need to put another bullet in the dead man's head, most likely Watson's, and instead, he took care to insure the room was cleared of all enemies so he had only to contend with Tansy's parents.

"Any more guards in the house?"

"Most are outside. Several are on the roof."

"Then they'll be coming at us eventually. Are you going to give me trouble?" As a rule Kadan could read minds in close proximity, especially in a situation like this one where fear and anger were strong emotions, but Don Meadows had some kind of barrier that blocked his thoughts and emotions from escaping.

"Not if you're getting us out of here."

"Tansy sent me."

"She all right?"

Kadan liked him a little better for that. "She's fine." He slipped another knife from his belt and cut the tape binding Meadows's wrists. It was a calculated risk since he couldn't read the man's mind, but they had to move fast.

"Coming in." Ryland's voice floated over the radio.

"Come on then," Kadan replied in greeting. "Gator, you clearing a path for us?"

It wasn't difficult for Gator to scale the fence, using the prongs on his boots and the spikes on his gloves. He went up and over and then signaled to the dogs, stirring them up, commanding them to bark, to roar out challenges from every point in the yard while he sprinted for the helicopter pad. He'd just made it to cover when the guards burst out into the open from every direction, lights once again flooding the compound. This time, the handlers released the dogs from the double fence and brought them leashed, searching for enemies on the grounds.

Gator did a hasty job of planting the explosives, first on the helipad, more on the helicopter, a third along the fence just beyond the pad. He used the blurring speed of the enhanced GhostWalker, cutting through the acreage to get to the opposite side of the estate, throwing voices as he sprinted, disrupting the dogs so they went crazy, howling and barking, raging at their handlers, so that chaos erupted in several hot spots, keeping guards running in every direction but toward Gator or the house.

A guard on the roof must have spotted him, because Nico's gun boomed and the man nearly toppled at Gator's feet. Gator kept running. A second shot rang out, and he caught a glimpse of a man falling from the roof to a balcony. The Cajun didn't hesitate; he put on a burst of speed and zigzagged, just to keep the odds in his favor.

"Thanks, man."

"No problem." Nico sounded the same. Matter-of-fact.

It took Gator several minutes to get to the opposite fence, two acres from the helipad, and even he was a bit out of breath after his run. Whipping out a can, he sprayed an entire section of all three fences. A man shouted hoarsely at him, but Gator kept spraying and didn't turn when Nico's rifle coughed up another kill.

"Where are you?" Ryland's voice buzzed in his ear.

"Heading for the garage," Gator answered and whirled back to make another run. This time he was going to have to first get through the ranks of guards and then enter the garage, where Nico would no longer be able to help him.

He drew two guns and headed for the garage. The guards

were gearing up to make a move on the house, knowing through radio silence that their bosses were most likely dead. They were between him and the garage, and he had to get to the Humvee. "I'm on the move now."

The moment Kadan heard Gator was making a break for the garage, he skirted around the woman on the floor and pulled two guns from his belt. "Search him, Rye."

He didn't look back, but broke out of the house on the run, firing relentlessly, choosing his targets as he cleared a path to protect Gator. He could hear Nico's rifle and the resounding crash of Gator's guns as they joined in the fight.

"I'm in." Gator's voice was a little out of breath. He swore. There was more gunfire and then he spoke again. "Son of a bitch, get out of my ride." More gunfire came from the vicinity of the garage. "It's an original, and man, she's a beaut."

Kadan gave a small sigh of relief. The intel on the vehicle had been hastily researched, and Tansy hadn't paid attention to it, she'd never even ridden in it. Don Meadows had the real deal, the military-issue, four-wheel drive, high-mobility, armor-plated, go-over-and-through-anything vehicle. And they were going to need it.

"Blow the helicopter," Kadan ordered.

Instantly the aircraft lifted into the air, exploded into several large pieces, and settled back down in a fiery orange and black cauldron of flames. The explosion had the desired effect of sending the guards scurrying toward the ocean side of the property.

Kadan counted to thirty and gave the next order. "Take out the helipad."

The second explosion rocked the estate. Smoke billowed into the air along with a tower of flames.

Kadan retreated to the doorway of the house. Ryland would have to pack Sharon out on his shoulder, but Don . . . now, Don was another matter. Kadan didn't trust him. He had to have some psychic ability to have such a natural barrier in his head. Given a psychic talent and his long-standing friendship with Whitney, Kadan didn't trust the man any further than he could throw him.

Ryland came up behind him, gun out, Sharon draped over his shoulder. Don had been herded in front of the GhostWalker and was clearly unhappy.

"I can carry my wife."

Kadan turned cool eyes on him. "You can be quiet or you'll go out the same way she's going out."

Meadows flushed. Kadan doubted anyone ever talked to him like that. As a future son-in-law, he wasn't racking up the points, but he didn't really give a damn.

"At least give me a gun to defend us," Don demanded.

Kadan swung around, drawing the air syringe from his pack and slapping another liquid cartridge into it.

Don held up both hands and backed up. "I'll be quiet. Seriously, you don't need that."

Kadan ignored him, turning back just as the Humvee burst out of the garage and bounced over the flower beds. The few remaining guards scattered, dogs roared, and the vehicle slid sideways to the atrium door.

"Blow the back fence," Kadan ordered calmly as he stepped back, jerked Don out of the line of gunfire, and shoved Tansy's father behind him.

The third explosion shook the house again.

"Go, Rye," Kadan ordered, calmly shooting two men who were aiming at Gator. Nico's rifle barked at the same time, and the bodies jerked twice as they went down.

Nico was firing steadily now, providing cover as Rye ran, Sharon's limp body bouncing like a rag doll against his back. He slung her into the waiting vehicle and took up a position to cover Kadan and Don.

"Let's go," Kadan said. "Make a run and dive inside. Get on the floor and cover your wife's body."

To his credit, Don didn't hesitate. He looked neither

right nor left; he just took off sprinting, leaping for the open door and draping his body over Sharon's.

"Get out, Nico," Kadan ordered. "Go, Gator."

The Humvee lurched forward and then picked up speed.

A guard rose up on the driver's side, sighting down his barrel at Gator. A red hole blossomed where his left eye had been just as Kadan put one in his chest.

"Nico," Kadan said, reprimanding him.

"I'm out," Nico confirmed. "Catch you at the rendez-vous point."

"Did you get the tracking device, Gator?" Kadan asked.

"Dismantled," Gator said, his eyes on the fence looming ahead of them. The double chain-link with the privacy fence just beyond it. He kept his foot on the gas, building up their speed.

Don Meadows lifted his head trying to peer out, saw the fence coming at them. "Stop!"

Kadan's boot found the back of his neck and shoved him low as the front of the vehicle hit the chain, weakened by the acid bath Gator had provided. The Humvee tore through the second fence and struck the third at full throttle. The splintering crash was loud as the boards gave way and the vehicle passed through unscathed.

Gator had a map of the rough terrain imprinted in his head. The property backed up to the steep canyons. The dense foliage and trees would provide them with cover as they made their way to the safe house. The Humvee went up and over a slope and down the other side, and they were dropping off the earth, with mountain peaks rising above them and wilderness surrounding them.

Kadan took his boot off Don Meadows's neck and indicated for him to get in the seat. "Get your wife strapped in so she doesn't get hurt."

Meadows glanced out the window and then around at

the three grim-faced men. The Humvee bounced over rocks and brush, and although Gator had slowed considerably, the motion was intense, jostling the passengers, throwing them from side to side and up toward the roof. Don reached down, his grip gentle, to turn Sharon over and up into his arms. Ryland and Kadan were guarding each side of the vehicle, guns out, waiting for signs of pursuit.

"Nico should be coming at us anytime," Gator called, slowing more. He turned the wheel hard to his right, the wheel jerking violently as they went up and over a series of rocks and then dropped down a brush-covered slope into a creek bed.

"Movement to the right," Ryland reported.

"Hold your fire," Kadan cautioned. "Nico? Are you seeing us?"

Static was the only answer.

"Incoming," Ryland announced.

Don automatically covered his wife, trying to press her limp body against the seat as tightly as he could.

Gator took the Humvee into a fairly thick stand of heavy brush, smashing through leaves and branches while Kadan shifted to the right. A four-wheel-drive Jeep burst through the trees, coming at them fast. Kadan calmly fired three shots through the window at the driver while Ryland took out the passenger with a head shot. The driver slumped to one side, and the Jeep hit a rock and bounced into the air, crashed down, and hit a tree, coming to a stop. Gator drove a few yards deeper into the brush and once again made a hard right to try to get to the point where Nico should have been waiting.

He brought the vehicle to a stop, and Kadan signaled to Ryland to watch their packages, while he yanked open the door and leapt out, running low along the ground, his skin changing, his clothing reflecting the surrounding brush. He went up the slope, leaping over downed, rotting tree trunks and a few brambles to land back on a narrow trail.

He could hear the sound of a small motorcycle and knew Nico was in full retreat. Behind him came another much larger engine and the sound of gunfire. Nico was trying to lead them away from the Humvee.

"Bring them to me," Kadan ordered, hoping the command got through to Nico.

The canyon was steep, narrow, and covered in dense shrubs and trees. Nico had to be taking a beating on the small bike as he tore through the underbrush without protection. The whine of the engine grew louder as Nico seemed to circle back toward him. Then he burst through the bushes just a foot or so from Kadan, his face and arms covered in angry scratches, bleeding from a hundred tears in his skin. He abandoned the bike, leaping off it and rolling into the brush while it was still moving forward, his rifle protected by his body.

Nico came up on one knee, the butt of the rifle fitting snugly against his shoulder as he sought a target. Kadan looked him over once to ensure none of the wounds were too bad; most looked like brambles had ripped the sniper up as he traveled through the brush. Then the pursuing truck topped the slope and bounced over it. The guards in the back were thrown from side to side, making the shots difficult.

Nico, of course, had no problems taking out the marksman steadying his rifle, but Kadan's first bullet took the man behind the shooter high in the shoulder, spun him around, and knocked him out of the truck. He was still moving, and Kadan had no choice but to waste a second shot, giving the third guard a chance to get off a shot. The bullet whistled past Kadan's face, and he felt the burn along his cheek, although it never touched him.

Nico's rifle bucked again and the shooter went down.

Kadan took out the driver and without a word, the two GhostWalkers raced back toward the Humvee. Ryland threw the doors open and they climbed in. Gator gunned the engine and they were on the move.

"You look a little worse for wear," Nico said in greeting. "That woman of yours is going to get all mushy over you."

Kadan didn't change expression or look at Tansy's father, but inside, his heart did a peculiar little flip. No one had ever had a mushy reaction to a few wounds on him. Would she? Even with her parents present? He hadn't considered that. The thought warmed him a little. He didn't want to think about her when he was working. She had no place in this part of his life. He was born to fight, born to kill, and someone as compassionate as Tansy would never understand the need and desire that drove him to take on the assignments he did—or maybe he was wrong. Maybe that same desire was in her—that thirteen-year-old girl offering herself as a sacrifice in order to track evil—maybe the need simply manifested itself differently.

He wiped his hand across his face and was surprised when it came back smeared with blood. He didn't even know whose blood he wore, only that he was going back to her covered in it. He seemed to spend a lot of his time with blood on his skin.

Ryland prodded him with his boot. "You've got a hole in your shirt. You hurt?"

Don Meadows cleared his throat. "He took a bullet when Fredrickson tried to kill my wife. They said if there was a rescue, they'd kill her and they meant it."

"Fredrickson was an idiot. He should have taken me out first and then killed her," Kadan said, shrugging his shoulders. It was what he would have done if the situation had been reversed. Take out the badass and then do your work.

Nico handed him a bottle of water from his pack. "Drink up, man, you look like you could use it."

He must look worse than he'd thought for Nico, the one covered in raw scratches, to point out that he looked bad. He took the bottle and downed half of it in one swallow.

"Who are you?" Don asked. "Where's my daughter?"

"She's safe. I've got a couple of good men guarding her."

"Guarding her, or keeping her prisoner?"

Kadan thought that over. She had no access to a phone. Ian and Tucker had orders to keep her close. She couldn't leave, and if things went wrong, they would forcibly remove her to a safer location. Technically, he supposed, she was a prisoner. He didn't bother to reply. Damn if he'd explain himself to this man.

He shifted his gaze, let it drift over Meadows. The man was in good shape, strong, fit, intelligence in his eyes. He was thinking, assessing the situation, and Kadan bet the man knew where every weapon in the Humvee was. Meadows also read accurately that any of the GhostWalkers was likely to kill him before he ever got off a move.

"What did you give my wife?"

Kadan glanced down at the sleeping woman. She looked very fragile, her pale face covered with bruises and her mouth swollen. She'd probably have a few more bruises where Kadan had slammed into her.

"She'll wake up in a few minutes, before we get to the house," Kadan assured him. "A little headache maybe and very thirsty, but she'll be fine." He reached over and sliced the tape binding Sharon's wrists. Her skin was swollen and raw.

"Who sent you?"

"Tansy."

That surprised Meadows. He blinked, but kept the same expression. He looked the way Kadan had seen so many in his position look before. Superior. Waiting to take charge. Angry at the loss of control.

Kadan fished in the small pack at his belt and came out

with a small tube of salve. He tossed it to Don. "Put that on your wife's wrists. It should help." He kept his eyes on the man's face. "You have some psychic ability, don't you?"

Ryland and Nico both turned to look at Don. Even Gator took his eyes off the faint ribbon of a creek bed he was following to look in the rearview mirror.

For one moment Don's eyes went hard and sharp, then he frowned and shook his head. "I don't know what you're talking about."

So it was going to be like that. Kadan kept his sigh to himself. It was no surprise, but he'd hoped for a different outcome. He shrugged his shoulders and kept silent as they bounced through the canyon toward their destination.

CHAPTER 11

Ian McGillicuddy was very tall and heavily muscled, with chestnut hair that gleamed red when the sun hit it. His dark brown eyes were very intense, and as big as he was, Tansy could have found him intimidating, but his infectious smile kept that from happening. He was very gentle and polite with her at all times, even when she was pacing, probably driving him crazy.

Tucker Addison was nearly as tall as Ian, with rich, dark skin, muscles that rippled every time he moved, cool brown eyes that seemed to see everything, an engaging smile, and close, military-cropped hair that didn't hide the springy curls Ian teased him relentlessly about. He seemed very patient and calm, although he often would shoot Ian with rubber bands for some teasing remark.

Tansy liked both men, but it didn't help make the time go by faster. A feeling of dread built, and several times she found herself reaching for Kadan, only to find—nothing. Intellectually she knew she couldn't reach over distance, but that didn't make the fear subside. She probably asked

Tucker a thousand times if they'd heard anything, and he was always gentle and patient with his answer.

After a while she couldn't take the compassion in their eyes and went into the kitchen on a pretext of making tea. Tucker followed her into the room and perched on the table, folding his big arms across his impressive chest and regarding her with his ever present calm.

"The hardest part of any mission, even when you're the one participating in the action, is the wait. You learn, over time, that everything takes longer than you want it to, to sleep whenever you can, and above all, to not play the odds in your head. You just live in the moment. Action, no action, it's all good. Right now, we need to be living in our moment and let them have theirs."

Tansy filled the kettle. "You can really do that? You don't worry about them? Or yourself when you're going into combat?"

He flashed her a smile, and there was a dangerous edge she hadn't seen before. "No, ma'am, I don't worry so much. It's not going to get me much but lines on my face. I can't change what's happening to them. Anything our imagination conjures up is probably worse than what's actually going on." He waited until she looked up at him, pausing in the act of putting tea in a small teapot. "I have faith in them. In Rye and Kadan and Nico and Gator. I believe in them. They'll do what they say they will do."

She let out her breath and tried to calm her chaotic mind. "They aren't invincible."

His smile widened. "Sure they are. That's where you go wrong in your thinking. You have to believe in them. There is no other outcome than success—total success. Once you believe, you don't spend all your time tied up in knots."

"I let him go to get my parents. It's wrong to trade one person's life for another, as if he's not as valuable. I should have just gone myself."

"You know better than that. Kadan's trained for this

work. It's what he does and who he is. He'll go out over and over on missions, Tansy. You have to be okay with that."

"Why does he do it? Why do you do it?"

His white teeth flashed at her. "Why does anyone do anything? We're good at it. We're *very* good at it. He'll bring your parents back to you."

She ducked her head. "I don't want anything to happen to him."

He drew in his breath sharply. "You're worried for Kadan?" His smile widened. "Man, I'm slow." He slapped his forehead. "All this time I was thinking you had this moral issue going, or that you were all concerned about your parents . . ."

She scowled at him. "I am concerned for my parents."

"It's Kadan. You're all worried about our boy Kadan." Tucker raised his voice. "Ian. Get in here. You have to hear this."

She put her hands on her hips. "You're having way too much fun. I'm not talking to you anymore."

Ian stuck his head in. "What's up?"

"Our girl here is all worried over Kadan. She thinks he might fall down and skin his knee."

Ian hooted. "You're nervous because of Kadan? All that pacing is over that big badass?" The two men exchanged a long look and then burst out laughing. "Honey-girl, you have no reason to think that man is going to get hurt. Feel sorry for the other guy."

"Keep laughing, you hyenas," Tansy sniffed. "I'm not making either of you tea."

"Come on, now," Tucker said. "You can't blame us for laughing. Kadan's like the hound from hell."

Ian nodded. "The devil himself."

She made a face at them. "You're both awful. You know you don't have to stay with me. I can look after myself."

She'd been considering trying to put some more pieces

of the murder puzzles together, but she needed to be alone to do it. She was certain Kadan hadn't told his friends anything. They were suspects, although Kadan didn't suspect them for one moment. She couldn't imagine that she wouldn't have some reaction even through her gloves if they were serial killers, but one never knew. She placed a mug of tea in front of each of them.

Tucker drew back, looking at it as if it might bite him. "Ma'am?"

"You're supposed to drink it."

Tucker exchanged another long look with Ian before delicately picking up the mug as if it might bite him.

"You too," Tansy demanded when she caught Ian smirking at his partner. "It's good for you. I carry a special blend in my backpack. It will soothe your nerves."

Tucker screwed up his face. "I have nerves of steel. I don't need this sh . . . *stuff*."

"Maybe we can find some whiskey to dump in it," Ian suggested, staring down at the brew with evident apprehension.

She was fairly certain their outrageous reactions to a cup of tea were meant to distract her, and she let them, teasing both men about being such babies.

"Are either of you married?"

"Nope," Ian said. "Women just don't appreciate my particular charm."

Tucker shook his head. "Got no problem with the charm, but they're too danged high-maintenance for me." He winked at her. "Course now that Kadan's taking the plunge . . ."

Her head went up. "What do you mean he's taking the plunge?" It would be just her luck that Kadan would be engaged. The moment the thought entered her head, she realized just how much the possibility of her parents betraying her with Whitney really had shaken her. She'd been in Kadan's head numerous times. There was no doubt his feelings, confused though they might be, were still genuine, still raw and strong and true. He couldn't fake that; no one was that good. She would have known.

Tucker hooted again and slapped his thigh. He even took a healthy swallow of tea.

Ian nearly spewed his. "Getting married. Hitched. The old ball and chain."

"Are you implying that Kadan's getting married to someone? Just who would that be?" She knew now; how could she not? It was so like Kadan to tell everyone but her.

"You, of course," Tucker said.

She noticed his eyes had gone cool and watchful, as if he was waiting for a sign from her that she wouldn't let his buddy down.

"He told us you were his fiancée and he planned on snapping you up the moment this is all over. Said he'd do it before, but he couldn't chance the paperwork."

"He said that, did he?"

"Yes, ma'am."

"How odd that he forgot to say it to me."

Tucker shrugged his massive shoulders. "Not so odd when you might rip his heart out. He'd be smarter to just get the deed done before you think too much on it."

Yeah, that sounded like Kadan, although it surprised her that Tucker could see into his soul like that. But then Tucker was an interesting man. All of Kadan's friends were. She felt a little guilty making small talk and waiting for them to leave the room so she could wash up, but she was leaving these men to guard her parents while she went off hunting a killer. She had to be absolutely certain she wasn't leaving the killer with the people she loved. She filled the sink with soapy water, carefully watching the door until they were gone, before peeling off her gloves.

Tansy sank into a chair and studied Tucker's mug from

every angle before cupping her hands around it, palms not quite touching, hoping she wouldn't have to actually touch the thing to gain impressions. She closed her eyes, allowing the energy to wash over and through her. He'd been lying to her—he was worried about Kadan and the others and wished he was there, guarding their backs. He was very uneasy that he wasn't with his team, at his usual place, watching over them, protecting them in the middle of a firefight. He worried that Kadan might be in over his head with her.

She had an immediate impression of strong loyalty; this was a man who stood by those he loved, his friends, and was honor bound and very patriotic. Flashes of his past ran through his mind, missions that had gone sour. The Congo. Colombia. She saw images of Kadan, streaked with blood, crashing through a door, face grim, guns blazing, shouting hoarsely. Smoke curled around them, thick and dark. Tucker, a man draped over his shoulder, ran through a gauntlet of flames and gunfire while Kadan and Nico, providing covering fire, ran on either side of him. Ryland led the way, automatic stuttering, and behind Tucker and the wounded man were Gator and two others she didn't recognize.

Tucker wasn't a serial killer, and she didn't need to know anything more about his past. She forced her hands away from the energy field and curled her fingers in her lap, waiting for her mind to clear. The familiar throbbing at her temples warned her she'd been using her gift too often and too close together, but, although she was certain she would find that Ian wasn't any more guilty of murder than Tucker, for her parents' sake, she had to be certain.

She took another deep breath, blew on her palms, and leaned forward to surround Ian's empty mug. His energy was fainter than Tucker's, and for a moment her heart jumped, afraid she might have to actually grasp the mug. That would plunge her in far deeper than she wanted to go. She inched her palms closer, until she was a hairs-breadth away. Then she was in the wave of energy, and impressions raced into her mind.

Like Tucker, Ian was worried about his unit, particularly Kadan. The man rarely shared personal information, and Ian was certain a lot more was going on than Kadan was telling them. Ian didn't like the fact that he'd never heard of Tansy and that he had the feeling she was one of the "lost" girls; that was bad news because it would mean Whitney would be hunting her.

That sent a shiver down her spine. She forced herself deeper into the impression, wanting to get it over with. He wasn't a killer, but he'd certainly killed. There was Kadan again, this time dressed in jungle combat gear. The team was sitting, buried to their noses in mud, down in a swamp with alligators and snakes, barely breathing, sharing telepathic communication that Kadan and Ryland seemed to maintain together for the rest of the men. Saw grass waved above their heads, but even so, they each used a straw to breathe through the mud and few inches of water above their heads.

Ian's disgust was strong. He glared at Gator, who kept poking him. *You say alligator one more time, I'm gonna feed your body, piece by piece, to one.* There was no real malice in the words; she could even detect affection.

She had the impression of others moving around them, nearly stepping on them. No one moved, everyone stayed quiet, even Ian, when Gator made a swimming motion through the mud with one hand like an alligator, right toward Ian's belly.

That's it, Rye, I'm doing it. I'm gonna cut his throat and leave him here.

Grim amusement swept the circle. *Yeah and you can answer to Flame. She'll eat you alive, Ian,* Ryland replied.

Tansy made a note to meet Gator's wife. The woman

seemed able to strike fear in the men when a swamp full of enemies and alligators only made them laugh.

Why is it every time we rescue someone, something goes wrong? Ian demanded. *From now on, take the missions where we get to kill everyone. We need to be taking down targets, not sitting here in the mud with Gator's little play pals.*

Tansy heard the words, but felt his emotions. He preferred the rescue missions even though nearly every time something did go wrong, and for that reason, he desperately wanted to be with his team, providing cover, watching their backs just as Tucker did. She realized that Tucker had been thinking about a rescue that hadn't quite gone by the book as well. She took a deep breath and moved her hands away from the cup.

At once she felt the dizziness and headache that accompanied using her gift. She'd been careful not to go too deep, but still she was shaken. She touched her face and found a trickle of blood by her mouth and another along her nose. Just as she was pushing to her feet, Ian rushed in.

"They've got your parents and are running clear. They should be here anytime." He stopped in the middle of the floor, took in the two tea mugs in front of her, the blood on her face, and the fact that she was no longer wearing the gloves she'd been wearing since the moment he'd met her. "What the hell are you doing?"

She felt her color rise. It was embarrassing to be caught, like a Peeping Tom staring in a window at someone's private life. She wiped at the blood, succeeding in smearing it as she walked without haste to her gloves. "I'm sorry. I felt I had no choice."

Tucker pushed in behind Ian, frowning when he saw the blood. He moved quickly to the sink and soaked a small towel. "Come here. Let me see what I can do."

The headache was pushing forward and she didn't want it, not with her parents and Kadan on the way. She shouldn't be feeling guilty that she'd used her gift without Kadan present, but she had the feeling he'd be upset, and for some strange reason, that disturbed her. Her life was already twined with his in such a short time she could barely believe it.

Tucker tipped up her chin and dabbed at the blood, while Ian continued to stand with his hands on his hips, glaring at her.

"You may as well confess," Tucker said. "Ian might stare holes through you. He's scaring the hell out of me."

"You're guarding my parents," she explained. "I had to know what kind of men you are. I tried not to pry too deep."

Something dangerous flickered in Tucker's eyes, but his hands remained gentle on her face as he removed the blood. "Did you find what you needed?"

She nodded, flashing a tentative grin. "Ian doesn't like alligators." She looked up at the tall Irishman. "I'm really sorry to have intruded. I was careful."

Ian made an effort to keep from looking affronted. "I might have done the same."

Tucker sent him a look, clearly reminding him they were there not only to keep her safe but to prevent her from leaving if she had a mind to, so they were just as guilty. "Do you get headaches along with the bleeding?"

She nodded. "I have some medicine in my bag."

"I'll get it," Ian said and stalked out.

"I don't blame him for being upset," Tansy said. "No one wants to have their private thoughts read."

"You can really do that?" Tucker asked.

She nodded. "I'm careful to wear gloves so I don't handle things. It keeps a barrier between me and everyone else unless the energy is particularly strong, such as violent energy. Then I read it whether I want to or not."

He studied the weariness in her eyes. "It takes a toll."

"Yes. Does it on you?" She shook her head hastily when

his gaze went hard and dangerous. "I didn't pick up any national security secrets. I have no idea what you can do, but your energy and Ian's both indicate strong psychic ability. Without Kadan here, I can read that just standing in the same room with you."

Tucker nodded. He'd read her energy as well.

Ian came back in and handed Tansy her bag. "You look pale. Maybe you ought to sit down. If Kadan sees you looking like that he'll kick our asses."

Both Ian and Tucker were very large men with defined, bulging muscles. Neither looked as if he could get his ass handed to him very easily.

"He really isn't as scary as you make him out to be," Tansy said, swallowing the pills.

They looked at each other. "Honey-girl," Ian said, "don't you go deceiving yourself. Kadan Montague is hell on wheels in a fight. I don't want any part of him."

A strobe light flashed, and both men went from easygoing to alert, their demeanor changing abruptly. Tucker glided on silent feet, catching Tansy by the arm and pulling her with him to the living room. Ian plunged the house into darkness, drawing his weapon.

"Coming in," Ryland's voice came, and the front door opened.

He came through first, sweeping the area with his cool, hard eyes, gun out just in case they were walking into a trap. Ian relaxed and put his weapon away. Tucker released his hold on Tansy. The rest of the rescue team walked in, Don and Sharon Meadows in the center.

"Mom! Dad!" Tansy eluded Tucker's grab and rushed her father, charging across the room, nearly knocking him down as she flung herself into his arms before anyone could stop her.

Kadan stood close to Don, inches from his side, the hilt of his knife already a part of his hand, and knowledge burning in him that he could stab deep, severing the jugular before Meadows would know what hit him, if Tansy's father made one wrong move toward her.

Tucker and Ian moved to cover Kadan, and Nico and Gator took up positions in back and front of Meadows. Each had a knife blade up against his wrist where no one could see. Ryland was stuck with Sharon, still woozy from the drug Kadan had injected into her system to quiet her. He moved her to the side, making a show of placing his body between Meadows and his wife.

Even as Tansy kissed him, Don caught the movement, correctly interpreting the threat. He gently put Tansy away from him, holding her shoulders at arm's length.

"Are you all right, Tansy-girl?"

"I'm fine, Dad, but I was so afraid for you. I heard Mom scream and I thought the worst. Are you hurt? Did he hurt you?"

"No, he just knocked us around a little. It was just such a shock finding out he'd been betraying us all of those years. I considered him family."

Don Meadows was lying to his daughter. Kadan flicked a glance at Ryland. Meadows had known Fredrickson belonged to Whitney.

"What did he do to Mom? And how could he, after sitting down with us all those years eating and watching movies and being a part of our family?" She looked beyond her father to her mother's delicate frame.

Her eyes darkened when she saw the bruises. "Mom! Oh no. What happened?"

Kadan looked from Don Meadows to his adopted daughter and then to his petite wife, Sharon. Tansy's hair was a thick mass of almost white gold, an unusual color at her age, almost a silver gold. Sharon's hair was dyed the same color, but Don's hair was prematurely silver gold, lending the parents a similar appearance to their adopted daughter.

Tansy hadn't once looked at him, not even a stolen

glance, not a hint of recognition, and part of him felt dead inside. He kept his hand curled around his weapon, not speaking, not interrupting the reunion, when he really wanted to drag her against him and make her notice him.

Sharon touched the bruise on her face. "Fredrickson hit me very hard when he took over the phone call. I nearly fainted."

"I'm sorry he did that, Mom. He was a horrible person. What happened to your mouth?"

Sharon glanced at Don. "He was angry at your father. We didn't know Watson was in on it, and when he came in, Don tried to jump Fredrickson. They didn't touch him; I think they knew it wouldn't do any good."

Don swore. "Damn cowards. Hitting a woman."

"They knew if they threatened me, Don would do whatever they said. They hoped you would too."

Tansy was more careful with her mother, hugging her gently and kissing the bruises on her face. "Come sit down." She caught her mother by the hand, tugging, leading her to the couch. "I would have gladly exchanged my life for yours, Mom, but fortunately I have friends who were willing to help."

Don made a sound that was suspiciously like derision. Tansy didn't look at her father. She wanted to go to Kadan. He was all she could think about. He filled her mind, but she needed to comfort her mother. She needed to touch her and know she was all right before she was selfish, before she acknowledged to herself, to everyone, that Kadan was her heart and soul. Because if her parents were involved with Whitney, she'd lost them and she needed this one last time to be wholly loved by them and love them back without reservation. Once she saw Kadan's face, nothing else was going to matter to her for a long while.

She let out her breath, running her glove-covered fingers over her mother's arm, feeling inexplicably sad. She wanted to touch Sharon skin to skin. To be normal. "I love you, Mom," she said, her heart heavy. "I've always loved you so much. I'm sorry for all the letdowns over the years, but mostly for this. I don't know what they want, but you got this," she touched the bruise again with trembling fingers, "because of me."

"No!" Sharon drew her daughter into her arms. "I love you more than anything. Your father and I both do. There are no regrets." Surprisingly, her voice was strong, fierce even. "There never will be, no matter what happens. And I'm grateful your friends came instead of you. I would have been furious with you if you'd tried to exchange your life for ours."

Tansy kissed her mother again and took another deep breath, before daring to look up at Kadan.

Kadan saw her breath hitch in her throat. He swore he felt her heart stop beating. The color drained from her face and her eyes went that peculiar shade of violet.

"Kadan," she whispered his name and he felt her move in his mind. *Kadan*. A breath. A caress in his mind.

Suddenly for him there was no one else in the room. Only Tansy. Only that look on her face that was worth all the waiting in the world. She didn't take her gaze from his as she crossed the few steps to him, seemingly oblivious to her parents' curious stares. Her hand smoothed, featherlight, over his scar, then skimmed his chest, finger touching the rip in his shirt.

"Look at you," she said softly. "Just look at what they did to you."

He should have been embarrassed with the other Ghost-Walkers looking on, especially when he caught sight of Gator's grin; the man was going to have fun tormenting him later, but nothing else mattered but that look in her eyes. All the teasing in the world was worth that moment.

She was completely focused on him, soft inside, worried, her heart in her eyes. Her lips trailed down the side of his face to his chest.

How bad? Her fingers went to his shirt, dragging it from his jeans in an effort to get at his chest. *I have to know how bad it is.* There was desperation in her voice, in her mind, and—God help him—tears.

His heart clenched. His belly knotted. How the hell did men survive women loving them? Because he honestly didn't know. He framed her face with his hands, unable to prevent himself from seeing the blood staining his skin and the rough, scarred backs against her smooth, rose-petal-soft cheeks. The pads of his fingers, topped with microscopic velvet bristles, brushed against her mouth. That beautiful, full mouth that terrified him when nothing else could, smiling at him, kissing him, taking him to paradise, *loving* him as no one else had ever done or could do. She was such a damned miracle.

He bent his head to hers, uncaring that her parents watched, uncaring that his friends could probably see the caveman desperation in him. The claiming. The possession. The love that he couldn't hide. This was coming home. Her soft mouth, hot as hell, sexy as could be. He closed his eyes and savored the cinnamon taste of her. It wasn't enough. It never would be. His hands slipped to her shoulders, ran down the sides of her body to rest on her hips, fingers digging deep to pull her close against him. The true miracle was—she kissed him back. She didn't step away, she pushed tight against him, pliant and soft and yielding, as if she belonged.

Thank you for bringing my parents home safe. And for keeping your promise that you'd come back to me.

You never have to worry about that, baby. I'll always come back to you. And God help them both, he meant it.

Reluctantly he lifted his head, searching her eyes for a

moment, needing to feel the connection between them when, without her touch, he felt so much empty space between him and his emotions. He couldn't quite bridge that gap without her.

Tansy tugged at his shirt. "Take it off. I need to see."

If she'd said she wanted to see, he might have ignored her, but the need in her voice, in her mind, in the stark admission, had him pulling the shirt one-handed over his head and removing the vest. His chest was one black and purple bruise.

Behind him, Sharon gasped. "Watson was going to shoot me," she whispered, her fingers going to her trembling lips. "I saw him aim for my head. I didn't realize he shot you."

Tansy closed her eyes for a moment, her fingers barely touching the massive bruise on his chest. *For my mother?*

She knew he didn't believe in her parents' innocence.

You took this for my mother? She looked up at him, love and awe mixed in her expression with pride and something so sexy he wanted to throw her on the floor and bury himself deep.

Kadan was so out of his depth he didn't know how to respond. Hell no, he hadn't done it for her mother—he'd taken the bullet for her. For Tansy. Okay, maybe it had been instinctive on his part, protecting the package, but if he had to think about it, he'd say the risk was all for his woman. He was so far from a saint it wasn't funny, but if taking a bullet made her look at him like he was the best man in the world, he'd do it again.

It's nothing, Tansy. I'm perfectly fine. He skimmed his mouth from the corner of her eye to the corner of her mouth, scowled, touched his tongue to the side of her mouth, and pulled back with suspicion at the coppery flavor.

"What have you been doing?"

She couldn't help the small guilty look she shot Tucker and Ian. Kadan followed the shift in her gaze, and his hands slid up over her hips to her waist. "You're in trouble."

Why in the world that sent a little electrical thrill through her, Tansy didn't know, but suddenly her breasts ached and she felt the familiar dampness between her legs.

"I had to make certain . . ." She trailed off at the look in his eyes.

Kadan caught her chin and tipped her face up. "You don't take risks. Do you understand me? You don't risk yourself like that. If you wanted to know, you could have waited for me."

He looked tired, weary, covered in blood, his chest black and blue, but his gaze held hers, steady and firm. Tansy smiled at him, leaned her body a little into his. "I hear you. I'll be more careful."

"Tansy," Sharon said. "Please introduce us to these men. They certainly saved our lives. Thank you." She smiled at each of the men and they squirmed a little under the attention. "Thank you all so much. I don't even know your names. And, Tansy, this man is obviously very special to you. Don't you think you should introduce us?"

Sharon looked at Kadan as if he was a hero, but one glance at Don Meadows told Kadan that the man didn't have the same opinion of him. He sent Tansy's father a hard look. No, they weren't going to get along at all, but Daddy didn't realize Kadan didn't give a damn whether he was liked or not. Only whether the man meant harm to Tansy.

"I'm sorry, Mom, I was just so happy that everyone managed to get out alive," Tansy said. "This is Kadan Montague, my . . ."

She looked so confused that Kadan took her hand and brought it to his mouth. "Fiancé, Mrs. Meadows. I'm the man who is going to marry your daughter."

Tansy's eyebrow shot up, her gaze still held captive by Kadan's. *You sort of forgot to ask me.*

I'm asking you now.

Her heart jumped. He was covered in blood, looked weary as hell, had a torn shirt and a smashed vest, bruises on his chest, but he stood in front of her, head unbowed, eyes flickering with blue ice, holding his breath. She felt that. The air caught in his lungs. Need beat at her. Desire pounded at her. *His.* His emotions that he barely recognized, frozen he thought, volcanic she knew—those emotions were for her.

Well, okay then. How the hell could she ever resist him? Not with his hands running up and down her arms and that stark look of need in his eyes whether he knew it or not.

"What the hell is going on here, Tansy?" Don Meadows demanded, breaking the spell.

Tansy glanced at her father. "I'm introducing you to the man I'm in love with, Dad."

Don scowled and took an aggressive step forward. The moment he moved, Kadan shifted, his body angled to protect Tansy. As a unit, his team went into position, Nico circling behind Meadows, Tucker and Ian flanking Kadan. Gator sauntered over toward the door, giving himself a clear line of fire to both Sharon and Don. Ryland slipped behind Tansy.

Don froze instantly. "We don't know the first thing about this man. We've never even heard of him before. I hardly think you can be in love with him, Tansy. Tell him it's all a mistake and you'd like him to leave."

"What you mean is I'm not good enough for her." Kadan goaded him, using his quietest voice, knowing the contrast between his low, mesmerizing tone and Don's harsh manner would be grating on Tansy.

"Hell no," Don burst out, clearly furious. His face went dark with anger, and he took another step toward his daughter, unable to stop himself, in spite of the threat of

Kadan's team. "This is bullshit, Tansy. Who are these men? What do they want? I don't believe you'd take up with this . . . this *mercenary* for a moment."

Tansy gasped in outrage. "I suppose mercenaries are good enough to employ to put their bodies between yours and a bullet, but not good enough to marry your daughter."

"Keep quiet, Tansy. You're in enough trouble."

"Don," Sharon interrupted. "What in the world is wrong with you? This man saved our lives. It's obvious Tansy has known him."

"Nothing is obvious," Don snapped, his tone dismissive. "You don't have a clue what's going on here, either of you."

Don Meadows was clearly a man who ruled his world and was used to obedience from those around him. They certainly addressed him in tones of respect, and Kadan was certain no one had ever put a boot on Don's neck. The tread patterns were still there, faint, but discernible.

Kadan settled gentle fingers around Tansy's arm and drew her completely behind him, shielding her from her father's wrath. "Settle down, Mr. Meadows. I'll admit that I'm nowhere near good enough for Tansy, but fortunately, it doesn't seem to matter to her. Right now, before we get into anything personal, we have to clear up a little business."

Meadows's lip curled with contempt. "Of course. Now the truth comes out. How much?"

Kadan remained silent, simply raising an eyebrow. When Tansy would have moved, Ian and Ryland moved up on either side of her, caging her in without seeming to.

"To make you go away. How much is it going to cost me?"

Kadan smiled and there was no humor in the baring of his teeth. He looked what he was: dangerous, predatory—and mean. "You don't have enough money to make me go away, Mr. Meadows. I suggest you sit down and answer a few questions for me."

"Dad! Why are acting this way? These men risked their lives to get you free. Fredrickson and Watson would have killed Mom and maybe you as well. You owe them your lives and you're embarrassing me."

"You don't know the type of men you're dealing with, Tansy, but I do." Don made every effort to soften his voice. "Honey, these men are employed by Whitney. They have to be." He snapped his fingers at her, beckoning her to come to him.

None of the men moved, making it virtually impossible for Tansy to go to him even if she'd been so inclined. Instead she glared at her father. "You're wrong, Dad," Tansy said. "Fredrickson was employed by Whitney, not Kadan and his men."

"Actually, Mr. Meadows," Kadan said, his voice pitched very low. "I'd like to ask you about *your* relationship with Dr. Whitney."

There was a small silence. Don's face reddened more, as if his blood pressure was climbing. "That's none of your business."

Kadan kept silent, simply waiting. The tension in the room grew thick.

Sharon pressed a hand to her mouth and shook her head. "We despise Peter Whitney."

"Sharon." Don's voice was a lash.

His wife flinched, but she stared at him defiantly. "I said it aloud. I don't care if he knows. I despise the man and want him out of our lives. I want him out of our daughter's life."

Kadan reached behind him and tangled his fingers with Tansy's. *Your mother is telling the truth.* He had to give Tansy that much. She was appalled at her father's behavior. Appalled and embarrassed that he would dismiss so casually the men who had saved his life. She was also terribly afraid that he was very mixed up in Whitney's business. Kadan wanted her to know that even if her father was guilty, her mother wasn't.

"Did you know Fredrickson worked for Whitney?"

Don pressed his lips together in disapproval, refusing to speak.

Sharon shook her head. "We were so shocked. Whitney is a madman, and he's been attaching himself to our family for years. We hired Fredrickson because Whitney began to scare us—well, scare me. I was afraid of him, and I didn't understand what he wanted from Tansy. He arranged our adoption, and at first I was so grateful, but even when she was little, Tansy didn't like him, and I wanted her to see another doctor for her . . . disorder." She glanced at her daughter in apology, but Tansy was looking at her father with open shock on her face.

"Why didn't you get another doctor for her?" Kadan asked quietly.

"That's none of your business!" Don roared. "Sharon. I forbid this. Our private life has nothing to do with these people. You're exhausted and scared. There's no need to continue this discussion right this moment." He looked at Kadan, openly challenging him. "Is there? Your men look like they could use a shower and a good night's sleep. You've got blood all over you. I suggest we take this up in the morning."

He wants the chance to talk to Mom alone and tell her not to say anything to you—or to me. He hired Fredrickson when Mom was so scared for us. He had to have known all along Fredrickson worked for Whitney.

There was quiet acceptance in Tansy's voice and that hurt more than tears. She didn't need to hear anymore.

Kadan shrugged. "Good enough. We have a room ready for you. The place is well guarded, Mrs. Meadows, and we've got alarms on all the doors and windows. The phones aren't working at the moment, but we have plenty of food if you get hungry. One of my men will be around, just ask him to show you whatever you need." He took Tansy's hand and tugged. "We'll say good night now."

She didn't look at either of her parents, but went with him without a word.

CHAPTER 12

Kadan padded on bare feet out of the bathroom to the bedroom, rubbing his hair with a towel, another slung loosely around his waist. Tansy hadn't said much, other than to order him to go take a shower, once they'd gone to the master bedroom. He wasn't certain what he was going to say to her, or how he would reply when she asked him what he intended to do about her father. He had no acceptable answer to give her.

He stopped dead when he entered the bedroom. The room was lit with low, flickering candles and smelled like heaven. Tansy sat on the bed naked, only her long hair covering her golden expanse of creamy skin. She looked sexy, a fantasy creature, lifting her eyes to his even as she rolled a bottle of oil between her hands to warm it.

"Where did you get all this?" He wasn't even certain that was his voice, husky and low and already groaning with desire.

"I have my secrets."

She flashed a mysterious smile, tipping her head to one

side, her hair sliding over her one shoulder and down her back to pool on the soft sheets. Her breasts gleamed invitingly in the candlelight, her nipples already tight, tempting him to devour her.

"Come here." She patted the bed. "I want you to lie down on your stomach."

He opened his mouth to protest; lying down wasn't what he had in mind, but there was something so secretive, so sensual in her expression, he lost his voice. He tossed the loose towel aside and shed the one around his waist, his shaft already growing hard in anticipation. He'd treated the small abrasions and lacerations over his body, but there was little he could do for the bruising. He just hoped she wouldn't notice too much in the soft light. He stretched out facedown and cradled his head on his hands, eyes open to watch her every move.

Tansy leaned over him, her long hair brushing seductively over his back and sides. The feel of the silky strands sliding over his bare skin had his body tightening instantly. She began a slow massage at his neck, rubbing the scented oil deep into his skin. She paid very careful attention to every line of his muscle, every hard knot. She moved down his neck until he was groaning with pleasure, his body relaxing under her hands.

Her fingers traveled down his biceps with slow, mesmerizing strokes; she tugged until he straightened his arm, and she continued along his forearm, until she twined her oiled fingers with his. Each finger was lubricated and rubbed until he felt almost boneless. She started down the other arm, until once again she'd locked her fingers with his and then begun a slow, individual massage of each digit.

"Are you planning on putting that over my entire body?"

She began working his back muscles, rubbing harder in some spots and with a sensual circle that nearly drove him out of his mind in others. "Yes," she answered softly. "Everywhere."

His shaft jerked hard. "I'm leaking all over the bed," he said, his voice going velvet. He was as hard as a rock, almost painfully so, even his balls tight. She was going to kill him, yet he'd never felt so completely at peace and happy.

Her hands followed the slope of his flank, kneading the tight muscles. Her hair brushed along the back of his thighs, and he jerked in shock when she bit him. The small sting sent lightning careening through his bloodstream and arcing over his skin. For a moment her oiled hand slid under him. He lifted his hips to accommodate her and her fist closed around his shaft, slick with the heated oil. He groaned in satisfaction as she stroked him several times, but when he went to turn over, she stopped.

"No, stay still." Her hands went to the backs of his thighs, kneading and massaging the heavy muscles and then down to his calves and even his feet.

Kadan wasn't certain he would survive. Her hands were exquisite on his muscles, and the oil grew warmer, heating more with the manipulation of her fingers, until his skin began first to tingle, and then to flicker with electrical shocks, charging deeper into tissue until fire streaked through his bloodstream and pooled low and sinfully wicked in his groin.

When he was groaning, so full and heavy he was afraid he would burst, she licked up his thigh to his flexing flank, biting again. "Turn over."

He moved fast, wanting to drag her under him, but she shook her head and caught at his arms, bringing them over his head, leaning in, her breasts tantalizingly close to his mouth as she positioned his hands on the pillow.

"I'm not finished. You're supposed to be enjoying this. I know I am." She bent to brush a kiss along his mouth, then caught his lower lip between her teeth and tugged. "It's only fair that I know every inch of you. If I'm marrying you, I should see what I'm getting."

Her hands slid down his chest to find his heavy erection. She wrapped both well-oiled hands around his thick shaft, stroking, drawing the head toward her, leaning in to lick at the pearly drops she extracted. The velvet rasp of her tongue sent lightning lashing through him again. Her hands slid lower, beneath his sac, stroking upward, massaging the oil into his sensitive balls until his hips bucked nearly uncontrollably.

He reached for her, but she sank back onto her heels, kneeling just out of reach, shaking her head. "You're supposed to do what I want tonight."

"I am?" He lay back, watching her through half-closed eyes. She was so beautiful to him, there in the candlelight, taking the control, giving him more pleasure than he'd ever known in his life, than he'd ever known existed.

She nodded slowly and poured more oil into her hands. "Yes. You scared me tonight. I think that calls for a little cooperation, don't you?"

Instead of massaging the oil into him, she began a slow massage into her shoulders and then down her arms. Kadan's breath stilled when her hands cupped her breasts, slid over the creamy mounds, thumbs rubbing the oil into her nipples and kneading it into her skin until she gleamed in the soft candlelight. Her hands slid lower, tracing along her ribs and down her belly.

He touched his tongue to his lips. "I could help."

She shook her head. "I'm watching you watch me."

Kadan took a deep breath. He'd never seen anything so sexy in his life. Her hands slid over her body, taking her time, massaging the oil into every single square inch he wanted to taste. He could almost taste her now, a hint of cinnamon in his mouth mixed with wild honey. Her skin glowed in the soft light, her curves accented, her body open to his hungry gaze. Her skin loved the oil, absorbing it quickly until only the glow, scent, and that heightening awareness, the growing heat rushing through his system, remained.

She crawled over the bed, over him, a sensuous slide of skin against skin, her head dipping to lap at him as she moved over the top of him. Her long hair teased his hips and chest as she began to rub the oil into his front. She paid particular attention to his bruises, adding featherlight kisses to help with healing. She dipped her head again to trace circles with her tongue over his chest and nipples, teeth scraping gently, teasing and tugging while his stomach bunched into tight knots and his shaft swelled to bursting.

She moved down his flat belly, rubbing along the defined muscles there, following with strokes of her tongue. His breath hissed out when she moved over his thighs, the insides, the backs of her hands sliding over his sac, now so tight and coiled, so ready he couldn't stop the little pulses rocking his cock.

Her hands finished with his feet and moved back up his legs in a slow glide. His breath strangled in his throat, trying to anticipate what she might do next. She reached casually for the glass of ice water she'd set on the small table by the bed and took a long drink. His entire body went on alert, every nerve ending coming alive, as her naked body slid up his. She wrapped her arms around his hips and lowered her head, again with that painful slowness, her long hair teasing his skin.

Her mouth slid over him like a glove, and his entire body arched in reaction, hips bucking wildly at the explosive combination of fire and ice. She sucked hard, flicking at the sensitive mushroom head with her cold tongue. The cinnamon burst around him and through him, inflaming his senses. If it was possible, his shaft thickened, every drop of blood in his body racing to gather into one point.

He caught her hair in his hands, tangling his fingers in the silken strands in warning. He couldn't take much more without exploding. His breath came in ragged gasps, and he knew that in another minute he wouldn't be able to stop himself from taking back control. Her mouth was too effective, driving him beyond all limits.

Just as he reached for her, she sat up and straddled him, dropping her body, so slick and tight and hot, over his, so that he filled her, pushing through glorious silken folds and lodging deep. She rose above him, the shadows from the candlelight flickering lovingly over her body as she began a languorous, sensuous ride. He could see the lines of her body, her head thrown back, eyes closed, throat exposed, and an expression of pure ecstasy on her face as her muscles worked him, while she rode up and down with that same slow purpose she'd been taunting him with since he came out of the shower.

"You're so fucking beautiful," he whispered, his hands going to her breasts.

He'd never forget this night or the way she looked. She'd loved him with every touch of her hands, with her mouth and now her body. She'd loved him and he felt it and knew what the word meant, what the emotion was. *Love*. He tasted the word and it tasted like cinnamon—like Tansy.

I have nothing else to give you. Only me, only my body, only the way I feel about you.

Tansy wanted this night to be perfect, her gift to be the ultimate expression of love. He had sacrificed for her, risked his life, and come back to her expecting nothing in return. This was all she had to show him what he meant to her.

You're everything to me. And he meant it, filling her mind with the way he felt, with the overwhelming intensity of his emotions for her.

She lifted her body leisurely, as if she had all the time in the world, rolling one way and then the other, moving her hips in small circles as she slid up and then down, inch by inch, filling herself with the hard, thick length of him. His shaft was scorching, fiery-hot, hard, like velvet over steel, stretching and filling her to bursting. Going so slow, she could feel every inch of him, the friction sending streaks of pleasure up through her body, spreading to her thighs and breasts in waves.

She opened her eyes to look at him and found him watching her through half-closed, glittering eyes. The emotion was stark and raw and so intense her vaginal walls rippled in response and her heart gave a funny flip. He looked at her with more than just dark lust; he looked at her as if she were the only one in his world. She could see a kind of worship in his eyes. His breath came in ragged pants and she felt the dig of his fingers into her hips.

A slow smile teased her mouth. "You really like this, don't you?"

Kadan wasn't certain he could get a sound out through his clenched teeth. *Hell yeah.* It was the best he could do when her tight sheath gripped and suckled, hotter than he'd ever known. He wanted the ride to be hard and fast, to grip and pound into her; the slow pace was killing him by degrees, but how could he give up the sensation of pure pleasure washing over and over him as she lifted her body and worked her muscles?

She rose again, a sultry, sensuous move that took his breath as she lowered herself again, her hips twisting into a tight roll that nearly destroyed him. His fingers dug into her hips hard, thighs bunched as he drove hard upward to meet that downward spiral. Lightning streaked again and his balls tightened painfully, her muscles tight and hot and strangling him.

He was done. At his end. He flexed his hands once, her only warning, and then he took control, lifting her with his enormous strength, driving her down onto him hard, tearing through those tight folds over and over, pounding into her the way he needed. He hit the back of her cervix and kept plunging deep and hard, using his strength and his speed. Her womb spasmed around him and the walls rippled and pulsed. Still he drove into her, hammering out a rhythm that took her over the edge fast.

He felt her shudder, felt her body clamp down on his. He refused to let it end for either of them, driving her to a second orgasm before the first subsided. Her muscles locked down, milking him hard, so that he couldn't stop the violent explosion, tearing up past his legs, centering in his groin, flooding her deep with his hot release. Her keening cry echoed more in his mind than through the room, but his hoarse cry of satisfaction joined the soft sound.

Kadan wrapped his arms around her and pulled her down over him like a soft, living blanket as the walls of her sheath continued to ripple powerfully around him.

Tansy. He whispered her name, his soft voice shaky with emotion even in her mind. *How can I ever go back to living without you?* He couldn't. He wouldn't.

She'd given him more than the most erotic experience he'd ever known; she'd given him a gift that was beyond measure. She hadn't held back anything from him. She'd poured everything she was into their lovemaking. She'd given the gift of herself—of her love.

He rocked her gently, trying to regain control of his breathing, of his scattered wits. Around his, her body continued to rock with small aftershocks. He could feel the little shudders that went through her and the way she struggled to breathe. He rubbed his way down her back, massaged the curves of her buttocks, kissed his way along her shoulder and neck.

When she was quieter, he rolled her over, still buried deep, and found her mouth with his. His kissed her with everything he was, with every bit of tenderness he could manage. He was never a gentle man, and he certainly could never articulate in words the depth of his feeling for her, or his appreciation of what she'd given him, but he tried to show her, kissing her over and over, taking her mouth and giving her his own while his hands stroked caresses in her hair.

"Where in the hell did you get that oil?" He rolled to his side, allowing his body to separate from hers, tucking her close to him.

"I made it." She brushed his hair from his face. "Did you like it?"

He turned his head to kiss her fingers. "You know I loved it, Tansy. What do you mean you made it?"

"I don't suppose you noticed all the flower gardens on the estate? When I was a little girl my mother tried to think of things we could do together that would be fun, girly, and didn't involve touching. So we gardened at first. I had my own little garden that really grew into a huge project. I loved being outdoors with her. She'd talk about all the different plants and their different uses historically. She mentioned perfume and oils and I was intrigued. She always smelled so good, and she told me how my dad took her to this perfume shop and had a special scent made just for her. I decided I wanted to do that myself."

He nuzzled her neck. She smelled delicious. "So you did."

She nodded, turning her head just a bit to give him better access. Maybe it was because she'd been deprived of human touch for so long that she craved his hands on her, but she wanted to feel his palm cupping her breasts, his thumb stroking back and forth over her nipple and his mouth skimming the hollow of her shoulder.

"I did. And I discovered that different oils could be bases used for different purposes. Arnica can help with bruising and is great for massages. Grapeseed is a great moisturizer. There are so many natural oils and herbs and flowers that can be used for all sorts of uses while also creating great fragrances. The cinnamon is my favorite, and fortunately I found a way to make it absorb, taste, and smell good."

"And you just happened to carry candles in your pack as well?" He leaned over and blew them out, then lay back, licking at her shoulder and then teasing with his teeth, producing a little shiver.

"I was camping and light tends to hurt my eyes, so as a rule I keep a box in my backpack. They aren't terribly fancy, but they do the trick."

There was a small silence. He could hear the clock ticking. He inhaled the scent of her, taking it deeper into his lungs, and nuzzled her breast. She never pulled away from him, as he half expected her to do. Instead, her body welcomed his, warm and so soft, always inviting. He could barely breathe with loving her. She thawed something frozen in him when she was close. He hadn't expected it to be like this, but there was no going back.

Thank you. He couldn't say it out loud. He would have choked on the words.

She looked at him, her gaze drifting over his face, seeing more than he wanted her to. "For what?" Her fingertip traced his lips.

For making me feel like I have someone to come home to. Hell. He was choking up anyway. Fuck it. *For loving me.* He despised being so inept with words, not when she deserved so much better, but it was the best he could do with his throat raw and his eyes burning.

"I do love you," she said, rolling over to sprawl on top of him, framing his face with her hands. She kissed him, sliding her tongue along his lips, and, when he opened, into his mouth, to tangle in a slow, leisurely dance with his. "I didn't think I would, but who could ever resist you?"

"I want to be inside you again," he whispered. "I need to be. Slide down my body and get me hard, baby."

He was already coming back fast, but she didn't hesitate, kissing her way down his chest until her hands cupped his sac, stroking upward, and her mouth closed over him, tight and hot.

Kadan came alive instantly under the growing experience of her fantasy mouth. He made love to her again, as gently as he could for as long as he could, but inevitably, he grew rough and hard, plunging deeper and faster, riding her with everything he was. It didn't matter that he took them both over the edge again. His body might be temporarily sated, but his mind would never be. Touching her, loving her, was a miracle.

He curled his body around hers, his arm possessively around her waist, and listened to her breathing. He could spend a lifetime holding her close. He waited, there in the dark, with the scent of cinnamon and sex hanging in the air, until she was in a deep sleep. Very gently he pressed a kiss against the nape of her neck and removed her hand from over the top of his. Rolling carefully off the bed, he pulled on his jeans and a shirt and dragged his belt with his weapons and a few supplies around his waist before slipping out of the room.

Ryland was waiting for him in the hall. "Took you long enough."

"I wanted to make certain she was asleep in case this goes bad."

Ryland nodded. "We'll have to make entry from outside. He's barricaded the door."

Kadan shrugged. "He's not stupid, but he's so full of shit. He's up to his ears in Whitney's mess. The wife is clean though. I could read her and she despises Whitney. I think the only real source of contention in their marriage has been Whitney."

"So she wanted to take Tansy to a different doctor and her husband refused," Ryland said. "I wonder why he would do that." He frowned and leaned close to Kadan, sniffing. "Cinnamon?"

"Shut the hell up," Kadan snapped and pushed past him.

Ryland took another whiff and gave a low whistle. "You smell yummy. I'm getting hungry. Maybe cinnamon buns."

Kadan flipped him off rudely.

Nico stood waiting by the front door. As always he was their backup. He frowned when the two GhostWalkers got close. "What the hell is that smell?"

"Kadan's new spicy cologne."

"Go to hell, Rye," Kadan said and shot him a look that should have withered him on the spot. "Both of you can go to hell."

"I think his blood sugar's dropping," Ryland explained. "Must have been all the cinnamon candy he got tonight."

Nico put on an innocent face. "That woman of yours smells a little like cinnamon."

"Makes you hungry, doesn't it?" Ryland said.

"Yep. Can't wait to tell Dahlia about this one. The ice man gets all hot and bothered around cinnamon spice. Who would have guessed?"

"Don't make me shoot you." Kadan yanked open the front door. "Because I'll do you both in a heartbeat and never look back."

Ryland smirked at him, not in the least intimidated. He began humming a tune overly loud under his breath.

Kadan shot him a look of intense irritation. "What are you doing now?"

Nico nudged him. "Don't you know that tune? I'd think it was your favorite. You're such a music cretin. Neil Young wrote some great songs." When Kadan still looked blank, Nico sang the lyrics while Ryland hummed. *"I wanna live with a cinnamon girl . . ."*

"I really am going to shoot you both." Kadan shook his head.

They'd never let him live it down. By tomorrow both of the clowns were going to buy him a Neil Young album with the song "Cinnamon Girl" on it. He shook his head and kept his grin to himself. He'd probably play it too, but hell if he'd ever tell either of them that.

He gave a small salute to Tucker, who was making the

rounds and emerged out of the bushes as if he'd just materialized.

"Everything's quiet. Gator ditched the Humvee on the other side of town. He'll be back in a while," Tucker said.

Ryland nudged him. "You smell love in the air, Tucker?"

Tucker inhaled. "Kadan. Man. High-five me, bro."

"I'm going to make every one of you eat those smiles," Kadan groused and pushed through them to stalk around to the side of the house, ignoring the soft, taunting laughter that followed him.

He crouched just below the window of the bedroom they'd given Don and Sharon Meadows. It was time to pay the man a little visit. They'd told him the window was wired, but there was no alarm on, not until Kadan knew exactly what he was dealing with. Just in case Don had his own method of alarms, he checked all around the window and listened for the telltale hum of a live wire. It was silent, other than a few soft snores from Tansy's father.

Kadan slipped his blade along the windowsill before levering the window up. He'd made certain there would be no noise when he opened the window before he'd ever put the couple in the room to begin with. He went headfirst into the room, creeping down the wall to the carpeted floor, knife in his teeth, Ryland right behind him.

They split up, one on either side of the large double bed. Ryland pulled out the air syringe and made certain Sharon would stay asleep. When he was certain she was out, he signaled Kadan and slipped into the shadows where Don wouldn't detect him. Nico took up a position just outside the window where he could train a gun on the man at all times.

Kadan crept up the wall at the head of the bed and slipped behind Don to settle his weight carefully. He didn't bother with a knife; if he had to kill Don, he would do it with his bare hands. He didn't want blood for Sharon to wake up and find.

He placed his hand carefully on the man's throat and pressed hard enough to wake him.

Don's eyes snapped open and he stiffened.

Kadan's fingers dug deeper, letting him feel his enormous strength. "I wouldn't move if I were you," he said quietly. "I'm a patient man, Mr. Meadows, but I'm tired tonight, and I've got a long day ahead of me tomorrow. I'm going to ask a couple of questions, and whether you live or die in the next few minutes depends on your answers."

Don flicked a quick glance at his wife, his lips compressing tightly.

"She's fine. I can read minds, and hers was fairly open. She loves you and Tansy. The two of you are her world. She despises Peter Whitney and can't understand why you insist on having him in your lives when you know he's a monster." Kadan leaned close. "I can't understand why you would ever risk your daughter with that man. You know she's one of his experiments."

Don jerked, his eyes widening in shock.

"You think the government doesn't know about all the little girls whose heads he fucked up? He did the same thing to a bunch of Special Forces men. I'm one of those men. I don't have a lot of love for Whitney and you shouldn't either."

"I don't," Don snarled. "I despise the man."

Kadan stared down into the defiant, angry eyes and read guilt. He didn't let up on the pressure at all. "You despise him, yet you force your daughter to see him even when she says he makes her uncomfortable."

"It was part of the adoption agreement."

"You knew what he'd done when you adopted her." Kadan made it a statement.

Don's gaze shifted. "Damn it, this isn't any of your business."

Kadan leaned down, staring into the man's eyes. He wanted no mistakes, because this time, Meadows had better understand fully what and whom he was dealing with. "Tansy's mine now, and I take care of my own. I will kill you and never look back, Meadows. Give me a reason not to. I don't much like you and you sure as hell don't have to like me, but if you want to live, you'd better answer my questions. I can smell lies and deceit all over your sorry ass."

Don pressed his lips together harder.

Kadan gave him one last chance. "Do you know what he's doing with those girls now? Do you know why he wants Tansy back? He has a breeding program. The women don't have to be cooperative, just get pregnant by the men he chooses for them. He wants the babies. That's the man you're protecting. That's the man you're giving your daughter to."

Don stared up at him with shrewd eyes. The man had an enormous IQ. He was successful in a highly secretive world, quite brilliant and much respected in his chosen field. He might be arrogant, but he had some cause to be. Kadan remained silent under the close scrutiny. There was no doubt in his mind that Don was making up his mind about his future son-in-law. Kadan knew what he was seeing. Rough, cold lines etched deep. The picture wasn't pretty and it shouldn't be. Kadan would kill him if it was necessary and he wouldn't lose sleep over it. If Don Meadows saw nothing else, Kadan wanted him to see that.

"I went to school with him. He was elite. Tons of money. His parents were billionaires, you know. The school was full of people with money, but few in his class. I was there on a scholarship. It was a private boarding school and I was young, wanting to fit in without a hope in hell of doing so. I was homesick, but this was a chance of a lifetime and my parents were so proud that I'd been chosen for the honor of attending such an elite school."

Don sighed and shifted slightly, glanced at his wife and then back up at Kadan. "If I'm going to tell you this, can I at least sit up?"

Kadan held his gaze. "You've got a sniper who never

misses pointing a gun at your head. You have one of my team sitting across the room from you holding another gun in his hands and he doesn't miss either. And just so you know, I'd kill you before either of them got off a shot." He pulled his hand away from the man's throat and backed up a few steps, completely confident in his speed and ability to carry out his threat if Don made a wrong move.

Don rubbed his throat, sliding his body cautiously forward and folding into a sitting position. He reached for Sharon's hand and checked her pulse. "My wife has nothing to do with any of this. If you kill me, give me your word you won't harm her."

Kadan's eyebrow shot up. "You'd believe me?"

"You're a hired killer, Mr. Montague, but you're not a liar."

Kadan kept his expression blank. That wasn't exactly the truth. He'd do whatever it took to complete a mission, but he shrugged his shoulders. "Your wife won't be harmed."

For a moment relief showed in Don's eyes, then his gaze flickered away. Yeah. There was guilt there. The man was knee-deep in dirt.

"Peter Whitney is an incredibly intelligent man. I admire intelligence. We gravitated toward one another. I was younger, and in a school where everyone has money—and degrees of it—it's difficult to fit in. I wanted what they all had."

Kadan remained silent. He might understand it, but he had a bad feeling, and a part of him was already mourning for Tansy. As he watched Don talk, taking in the shape of his eyes and the silver hair, things began to click.

"Whitney has this built-in radar for psychic ability. He can pass someone in the street, and even if they don't know it, he does. He can shield his brain and he can spot psychics, but that's the extent of it. He's many things, Mr. Montague, but he's a patriot as twisted as his visions for the country are. Of course in the early days, I didn't see him as twisted. He was older, smart, which few people were, and he had more money than anyone else on the planet. Everything he said sounded golden."

Kadan stayed patient when he wanted to shake the man. His revelations were going to hurt Tansy—and she'd have to be told. Damn this man for his childish greed.

"Whitney envisioned a world without men dying in battle. He said we could create supersoldiers. I honestly didn't think the psychic abilities were strong enough in people. Mine weren't. I feel things sometimes. When I see a helicopter or an airplane, I can redesign it for better function and speed and maneuverability because I 'see' the flaws."

"And you have a natural shield."

Don nodded. "I didn't know it for a long time. How many people can read minds? I met Sharon while I was in graduate school. She was so small and fragile, with a weak heart. I fell like a ton of bricks, but she comes from the same kind of money as Whitney, and although I was making a name for myself, I was nowhere in her league. I didn't think she'd look twice at me."

Kadan was beginning to put the pieces together. Don Meadows was a fool. This was all about his wife.

"I managed to get her to go out with me, and in the end, she married me. Her family was furious and threatened to cut her out of her inheritance, but she married me anyway. Eventually her father backed me in my business, and we've been lucky and have established enough government contacts to be more than successful."

"But . . . ," Kadan prompted. Don Meadows was circling the subject, hoping it would be enough without disclosing his ties to Whitney. Kadan wasn't about to let him get away with it.

Meadows sighed heavily and stroked Sharon's limp hand. "Long before Sharon's father would take a chance on me, I worked for Peter. He had a huge research center and

I was given my own department. I had visions of maybe becoming partners with him one day and showing Sharon's family that we didn't need them. Peter and I took a business trip to Europe. I was twenty-six. Sharon was ill and couldn't come with me." He shook his head, his expression rippling with pain. "Her health is very fragile."

Kadan nodded. He already knew what was coming.

"I don't know what happened." Don rubbed at the lines in his brow. "I think about it all the time. I was drinking and there was this girl. She couldn't have been more than fifteen." He looked up at Kadan, pain in his eyes. "Thirteen. She was thirteen." He shook his head again. "I don't remember much about that night. Only that I must have gone crazy. The sex wasn't consensual. I know because I've seen the videotape a hundred times and it's ugly. It's damned ugly to know that you're capable of something like that when it's so repugnant to you."

There was bitterness in his voice, even self-loathing. Don brought his wife's hand to his mouth. "Peter cleaned up the mess—his money, of course—and we came home. He swore no one would ever know."

"And you trusted him? You weren't suspicious that he might have had something to do with you acting so out of character?"

"I had to trust him. He was my friend. It didn't occur to me until a long time after, and by then, I had so much to lose. Sharon couldn't have children. She knew I wanted them. I was afraid if she found out I'd not only cheated on her, but that I was capable of rape, of animal brutality, she'd leave me. She'd think I married her for her money. There was a part of me that wanted the money and I had forced a child. *God!*" He dropped his head into his hands. "You have no idea what it feels like to know a monster lives inside of you."

"Have you ever done it since?"

Don's head jerked up, eyes flashing with anger—with denial. "No! I'd shoot myself first if I ever had such an inclination. I don't know what happened that night, but I saw myself. It was me raping that child. The video wasn't tampered with."

"But someone set the camera up in the first place."

Don nodded. "Yeah. But I didn't know there was a video until five years later."

"When Whitney brought Tansy to you. She's your biological daughter, isn't she?"

Don swallowed hard and ducked his head again, shaking it from side to side. "Whitney called me into his private lab and brought Tansy out. You should have seen her. All white hair and those eyes. She had the same mouth her mother had. I knew she was mine the moment I laid eyes on her. Whitney showed me the tape. And he had tapes of the girl in what looked like a hospital during her pregnancy. She sold the baby to Whitney. Later, he claimed she died in a car accident, and maybe she did; I searched for her, but couldn't find her."

"And Whitney had Tansy for five years."

Don nodded. "He'd enhanced her psychic abilities. Apparently the girl, her mother, was psychic and Peter wanted to see what he could do with the baby. She wasn't the only one he had. He told me they were orphans he'd collected, unwanted children. He had nurses for them and said he was getting rid of them, adopting them out. He told me I could take Tansy on the condition he continued to be her doctor so he could see her progression."

"And you balked."

"Hell yes. The son of a bitch. He had my daughter. He'd set me up. And when he produced the video, I realized he had to have been the one behind the camera, that all those years earlier, he'd been a party to what I'd done." He sighed heavily and leaned back against the headboard, still stroking Sharon's hand. "He wasn't always a madman. I saw the signs, but didn't want to. He was my friend and I didn't have too many of them."

"And he opened doors for you," Kadan wasn't going to let him off the hook. Don Meadows was an intelligent man. He also was ambitious. He wanted the respect, contacts, and money that came from his association with Whitney.

"I can't deny that."

"So he came to you with his proposal. He wanted you to adopt your own daughter. And if you didn't play ball with him, he was going to destroy the life you'd so carefully built."

"He would show the video to Sharon and her family. He said he'd go public with it. That video is sick," Don said. "It would have destroyed all of us."

"And the other children he had in his laboratory. He was experimenting on them and you knew it."

"He was adopting them out. They all had problems, just as Tansy did. He promised he'd give anyone who took them enough money to take care of their special needs."

"And you wanted to believe that."

"I had to believe it, for my own sanity. She was my daughter. My own child. I wanted her living with us any way I could get her. And I knew Sharon would take a damaged child, no matter how bad she was. Sharon desperately wanted children."

"You're a selfish son of a bitch, aren't you?" Kadan said, his tone mild.

CHAPTER 13

"Damn it! I'm a victim here too," Don insisted. "You have no idea what it was like."

"You didn't want to face up to the music. Whether or not Whitney drugged you, and it is probable he did, you still participated in the rape of a thirteen-year-old girl and you got her pregnant."

"She had no one. Whitney told me she was a street girl there that night to try to steal from us."

"I believe she probably didn't have anyone to protect her. Whitney wanted her genes. The rest of her was an inconvenience. He must have found her on another trip, recognized that she had psychic ability and 'bought' her, just like he did the others. He probably offered her money to stay in a nice warm room and she waited there, thinking she had a good gig, a place to stay and food to eat. Hell. For the first time in her life, she wasn't on the street. And then Whitney brought you to her."

"I don't remember."

"You didn't want to remember. And you may have put

out a few feelers to try to satisfy your guilt about what happened to her, but you have enough money and enough contacts to find anyone in the world. You didn't want anyone to ask questions about why that girl was important to you."

"She's dead. Whitney told me she was dead."

"And you wanted to believe that."

Don glared at him. "I don't think someone like you has a right to judge me. Do you think I can't take one look at you and know you're a killer?"

If he meant to make Kadan wince, he was mistaken. Kadan knew exactly what he was; cold as ice and willing to get the job done. "Then we understand each other," he said, his voice pitched low. "There is a difference though. I know I'm a bastard and I don't deserve Tansy. I fully admit it to myself and to her. I'm taking her anyway because I'm selfish and I'll work every day of my life to make her happy, and at the end of our days, I hope she'll have no cause for regret. You pretend you're a good guy. You deceive yourself and your family. And you left those little girls with a madman so you could continue your life just the way you wanted."

"I'm telling you, he was putting them up for adoption. The damage to them had already been done."

"He didn't put most of them up for adoption. He's using them in his breeding program."

There was another shocked silence. Kadan could tell by the man's expression that the shock wasn't feigned.

"Are you certain of your information?"

"Yes. And there were other girls as well."

Ryland stirred for the first time. "What about Lily? You had to have known he kept Lily." His voice was very low, almost a whisper, but his tone was pure menace.

Don started, his gaze jumping to the man he couldn't quite make out in the shadows. "He was good to Lily."

"He experimented on Lily. What do you think it did to

her when she found out about him? When he let her believe someone murdered him? You knew, didn't you, that he was alive?"

Don nodded. "Someone high up, someone really connected wanted him dead. They knew he was enhancing Special Forces soldiers and they thought it was an abomination. Peter wanted superweapons for his country. He didn't know who it was, but they'd made several attempts to kill him and they'd hit at his soldiers. He told me they'd murdered at least one of them and he was afraid for the others. He had to disappear until he knew who his friends were."

Ryland shifted again, as if he might pursue the subject of his wife, but he let it go. He'd been the man targeted for murder by the faction who thought Whitney's experiments were abominations. He'd seen several of his men die and he'd barely escaped with his own life.

He knows more than he's telling us, he sent silently to Kadan.

"We were locked in cages," Kadan said, "in Whitney's research center. We were the men Lily helped escape."

"Her father wanted her to help them escape. He told me he maneuvered her into the position with the hope that she could do what he couldn't," Don said hastily. "For all of his sins, he wanted all of the soldiers he'd worked on to survive and serve their country."

"Did he know who wanted him dead?" Kadan asked.

"Someone very high up in the food chain. Whoever it is works in the White House and Whitney couldn't touch him. Fortunately, Peter has a lot of friends who covered for him and helped him carry on his work . . ."

"His breeding program," Kadan said. "The one he wants Tansy to participate in."

Don shook his head. "He doesn't want any harm to come to her. I know that. When he got word that his enemy was forming a coalition to wipe out his soldiers, he insisted

I hire Fredrickson to guard Tansy. Someone got to Fredrickson."

"Fredrickson worked for Whitney," Kadan pointed out. "No matter how you spin this, you aren't going to make Whitney into a saint just so you can condone the fact that you let him get away with experimenting on children. He experimented on your own child, and kept it up as she grew. You allowed it. And you hired Fredrickson at his command. His orders were to take Tansy if she ever discovered what was going on. She asked you the wrong question and Fredrickson did his job. He was going to take her to Whitney."

"I know he's a bastard, but he would have kept her safe."

"He would have forced her to have sex with a man she didn't want to have sex with, just like he forced that little teenage girl to have sex with you." Kadan remained absolutely still, a statue carved in stone. Even his stillness seemed a threat.

Don's face crumbled. "Damn you, you're leaving me with nothing."

"You would have given her up." Kadan's voice was as cold as ice.

Kadan, Ryland warned softly, clearly fearing what his friend might do.

Kadan didn't know himself. The thought of Don Meadows even contemplating turning his daughter over to a man like Whitney after he'd seen the experiments, the rape of a teenage girl, his wife hit by Fredrickson . . .

"All for what?" Kadan asked softly. "To keep your image and your money, your cushy little life. You would have traded Tansy into a lifetime of slavery."

"No! Damn you, no!" Don denied the accusation. "I wanted her safe from the coalition. They're much stronger. They've established themselves and are trying to kill every soldier and woman known to have been enhanced."

"And you know this how?" Kadan's voice was still cold, still remote, as if the jury was still out on whether or not he was going to reach across the bed and rip out Don's throat.

"Whitney has friends who tip him off, and he told me Tansy needed to be in a safe house. We had a terrible fight about it. I told him I could protect my daughter."

"That's when you hired the mercs."

Don scowled. "Fredrickson found Watson for me, and they hired men who could keep her safe."

"They were Whitney's men. When Tansy asked the wrong question, they did as Whitney ordered them. They were to secure her immediately and bring her to him. They were willing to torture your wife to get her there."

"Fredrickson told us there was a hit out on her." Don looked Kadan straight in the eye. "He said an assassin was sent to kill her."

"Two men showed up in the mountains. I thought they were after me. How would anyone know Tansy was enhanced?"

"She worked with the police and the FBI solving serial murders. There's been a series of murders that a reporter speculated were all connected, and her name was brought up. We didn't tell her because we didn't want to upset her, but the reporter knew she was a photographer and suggested she was in the Sierras. He implied she was helping the FBI with the murders. The article even gave a report about her being hospitalized and that she might taint the evidence."

A chill went through Kadan's body. If someone had dug up information on Tansy and reported it, the elite tracker she had accidently run across would have her identity. He took a deep breath. "Give me a name and a newspaper."

"What? Are you going to kill him too?" Don asked, a hint of bitterness, mixed with sarcasm, creeping into his voice.

Kadan's hand snaked out so fast it was a blur. He grasped Don by the throat, cutting off oxygen and nearly lifting the man off the bed. Don choked, gasped, turned red and then purple, desperately prying at Kadan's fingers to release him. He stared into impassive eyes.

"Kadan." Ryland said his name. Low. Firm. No inflection. *Lily will get all the information we need on the reporter. Let it go.*

Kadan dropped Don in disgust and turned away from him, pacing across the room, while the man coughed and dragged air into his lungs.

"I'm glad you find this amusing," Kadan accused through clenched teeth. "I find it distasteful."

Don used his heels to push himself back against the bed to prop himself up. "Damn you," he choked. "You don't know what you would have done in my shoes."

Kadan crouched down beside the man, looking him straight in the eye. "I would have killed Whitney the moment he showed me that tape. He had you rape a child. He stole your child. He tortured her, experimented on her, and continued to do so to other children. He had a man strike your wife, and believe me, Fredrickson would have gone to any lengths, including killing Sharon. Watson certainly tried to put a bullet in her head . . ."

Don covered his face with his hands. "I don't kill people."

"Maybe not, Meadows, but you're willing to leave a monster loose in the world so you can keep your precious world intact." Kadan was nearly choking on his disgust. "And you hired killers and let them stay in your home."

He's weak, Kadan, not malicious.

Fuck that. He would have turned Tansy over to Whitney to protect his world. Kadan abruptly stood again and put distance between himself and Don. He didn't trust himself anymore. He wanted to break the man's neck. "Where's Whitney? And don't tell me you don't know every one of his hidey-holes, because you've had twenty years to gather intel on him. A man like you has files on people."

"Whitney has places all over the world. He has more money and more connections than you can imagine. You can't beat him. And at least he isn't trying to kill you. Your enemy is his enemy. And he's the only man capable of protecting Tansy. I couldn't do it, and I don't think you can either."

"We'll see. I want your file on Whitney."

Don shrugged. "It won't do you any good."

"I want it."

"It's in my house. I have a safe in my office under the floorboards where I keep it. The one on the wall is for thieves to think they're getting useful information."

Kadan was done. He couldn't bear to be in the man's presence for even another minute. *Rye, take over. I can't look at him anymore. Send someone for the file.* "I'm taking Tansy with me. You stay here with my men and don't be stupid enough to give them any trouble."

"Whitney will release the video."

Kadan turned cold eyes on the man, looked him up and down, and then shook his head. "You still don't get it, do you? He won't release the video. He has as much to lose as you do. The government and the military still consider him a good guy. He isn't going to risk jeopardizing that for a little payback. He got what he wanted from you. Your genes. Now he'll come at Tansy and he'll have to go through me to get to her."

"What about my wife?"

Kadan dropped the temperature by several degrees just staring at the man. "I have no wish to cause your wife pain, Mr. Meadows. You're free to continue lying to her, but I will tell your daughter everything. I have no intention of deceiving *my* wife."

"Are you going to tell her you threatened my life?"

Kadan smiled, and there was no humor at all in it.

"Tansy has access to my mind. I don't think she's going to be very surprised at anything I ever do."

"You self-righteous son of a bitch." Don scrambled to his feet, his face red and twisted with anger. "You tell my daughter she's the product of a brutal rape. You tell her that she's been deceived for years, destroy everything she loves and believes in, and then feel good about yourself because you're such a fine, upstanding man."

Kadan flung the chair that had been placed under the doorknob against the wall with enough force to smash it into several pieces. Jerking open the door, he stalked out of the room, afraid of the cold in his veins, in his mind. He needed to see Tansy. To touch her. To make certain she was okay. He just wanted to hold her and keep her safe. Damn her father and his weakness. Telling her everything would destroy her world. Not telling her would leave a huge chasm between them.

Tucker and Ian came running down the hall toward him, guns drawn. The crash of the chair had been loud enough to alert them to potential trouble. Kadan just shook his head and kept moving toward the other end of the house, where Tansy slept. He picked up the pace without even realizing he was doing so, shoving open the door and standing there, framed in the doorway, drinking in the sight of her as she lay sleeping.

The room was dark, with only a small bit of light spilling through the curtains at the windows. The air still held a hint of cinnamon, and his stomach tightened as he drew a deep breath. Her hair fanned across the pillow, a cascading fall of white gold silk that tore at his heart. She looked so young when she slept, innocent and sweet, as if all the bad things in life hadn't touched her yet. She sighed softly and turned, reaching—for him? He hoped it was for him. He hoped he represented something good in her life in spite of all that had happened.

He crossed the room on silent feet and crouched down

beside her. "Baby. You need to wake up for me." He bent his head and trailed kisses over her face. His hands slipped beneath the blanket to find the curves of her warm satin skin. "Open your eyes."

She blinked, the twin crescents of thick lashes batting at him while beneath the covers her body stirred, moving more fully into his hands. "Hey you." Her smile shook him, filled with welcome. With something soft and inviting. "Is it morning already?"

She sounded so drowsy—so sexy. His body tightened more. He couldn't help cupping the soft weight of her warm, soft breasts in his hands, or sliding his thumbs over her responsive nipples. "We have to go."

"I need a couple more hours of sleep."

He nuzzled her throat, kissing his way down the curve of her breast. "You can sleep in the car, honey. I need you to get up now."

She gave a soft little groan of protest. "It's dark."

"I know. Come on. Come with me." His fingers tugged the blankets down just a little more, exposing her breast to the cooler air. He licked her nipple, then drew her breast into his mouth and suckled, sliding his arm around her waist to pull her more fully to him. She felt soft and pliant in his arms, offering herself to him, the way she did.

Kadan closed his eyes, savoring the moment, the knowledge that she so completely gave herself to him. He kissed his way back up her throat to find her mouth, losing himself there for a few minutes. She gave him everything, with no hesitation, without reservation. There was no resisting her, not when she just opened herself up for him and took him in. He pressed his forehead to hers, sharing breath.

"I'm sorry to wake you, Tansy. I know you're tired, but we're running out of time on this thing. Your parents are safe here and we need to get back so we can get the job done."

"I thought I'd have time to visit with Mom and Dad. I

haven't seen them for weeks," Tansy protested. "And after what happened . . ."

"I know. But I need you to come with me now."

She drew back and searched his face, looking for what, he didn't know. What could he say when he wanted to rip out her father's heart? Anything he said might shatter her.

Tansy studied Kadan's grim face. So tough. So rugged. So uncompromising. He looked dangerous, but when he touched her, his hands were gentle and his mouth loving her whether he knew it or not. Something was wrong. Not the murders. This wasn't about the murders. She took a deep breath and let it out, wrapping her arms around his neck so he could pull her into a sitting position.

"You're upset."

The love in her voice shook him. As if he mattered. As if it mattered that he might be upset. If he was, it was on her behalf, not his own. He lifted her into his arms. "I'm taking you out to the car. We're heading back to the other house."

"I'm naked. I can't ride naked in the car," she protested.

His blue eyes slid over her, dark as midnight. "Yes, you can. Cuddle up next to me, I'll keep you warm."

She wiggled and he put her down. "It will only take me a minute to dress and pack, but, Kadan?" She waited until he looked at her. "When we're in the car, you're going to tell me everything."

"You won't like it, baby. Make certain it's what you really want."

She caught the nape of his neck, raised herself on her toes, and kissed him. "It's what I want." She turned away to pull on a shirt, not bothering with underwear.

Kadan watched her through half-closed eyes: the graceful, efficient movements, the lack of hesitation as she padded across the room in front of him to retrieve her jeans. He loved her. The words were in his mind, but they didn't manage to make it to his mouth. But his soul moved. He felt it.

Tansy smiled at him. "I'm ready."

He stalked across the room, long, purposeful strides that might have cowed someone else, but she stood her ground, just looking at him. He caught her face in his hands and kissed her again. Telling her. Saying it without words. Loving her.

He let his hand slide possessively down her shoulder, then her arm, until he could tangle his fingers with hers. "Let's do this." He pulled her beneath his shoulder and walked her through the house.

Tucker and Ian were waiting by the back door. Tucker leaned in close to brush a kiss over her forehead. "We'll take good care of the parents," he assured her. "No one knows they're here, so we won't have problems."

"You'll check in with us?" she asked anxiously.

"You got it," Ian told her.

"Thanks, both of you," Tansy said.

"I owe you," Kadan added, his voice gruff.

He opened the passenger-side door for Tansy and she slid onto the seat. Tossing her bag in the back, Kadan slipped behind the wheel and reached for the key. Instantly the back doors opened and Ryland, Gator, and Nico piled into the backseat.

Kadan looked into the rearview mirror, at their set faces. "What do you think you're doing?"

Ryland shrugged. "Covering your ass, like always."

"I have to do this alone, but I appreciate the offer."

"No way are we bailing," Gator said. "You're up to your ears in a mess and we're goin' to back your play the way we always do, bro, whether you want it or not."

"This is one of those classified—"

"Bullshit," Ryland said. "You have the girl. You think I didn't click on it the minute her old man mentioned the murders? They suspect us, don't they? That's why you dragged her back here, to help clear our names. They're after us, aren't they?"

"Who the hell are *they*?" Gator asked.

"*They* are the ones who have been trying to kill us off from the beginning. Once it got out that Whitney made supersoldiers, the technology was worth billions to other countries," Ryland explained. "With us dead, no one can do a snatch-and-grab and try to dissect us and get the answers for free. No one can find Whitney and get the information, so they have to find a way to bring us out into the open, where they have a better chance of killing us. If Ghost-Walkers are accused of murder, there isn't going to be a trial, is there, Kadan?"

Tansy tangled her fingers with Kadan's. "We're not going to let that happen." She spoke with supreme confidence. "I'm an elite tracker. I'll find them and Kadan will take the proof back to Washington."

"I've never heard of an elite tracker," Gator said. "What is it that you do?"

Nico leaned forward over the seat and there was respect tinged with awe in his voice. "You're the serial killer girl. You track murderers using your mind."

She smiled at him. "That would be me."

"How the hell do you do something like that?" Ryland asked.

She shrugged. "All of you do unusual things. It's a gift."

"It isn't easy," Kadan snapped. "She ended up in the hospital the last time." He brought her hand up to his mouth. "Don't make it sound like it's a breeze."

"They helped my family."

"You were willing to do it before they helped your family."

Color rose, staining her cheeks. "It's no different. Don't make it be different."

Ryland touched her shoulder. "We appreciate it, Tansy. You should have told us, Kadan. We could have helped."

"I'm under orders. The general called me back, explained the situation and told me to clear it up fast. So I found Tansy."

"Well, now you've got some help. We're going with you."

There was a stubborn streak a mile wide in Ryland—in all of them. Kadan knew they'd just follow him, now that they knew what he was doing. They were tenacious like that. "Find the reporter. Tansy has to handle a couple more objects. I think we can find at least the East Coast team."

"Team?"

Kadan explained the theory of a murder game. "Tansy's hoping to profile each of the players and maybe get a handle on how the game is played and who is running it."

"Do you think this coalition, the ones who want us dead, is behind the murders?" Ryland asked.

Kadan shook his head. "My gut feeling is that they're simply taking advantage of it. The coalition Meadows mentioned has a major hard-on for the GhostWalkers," Kadan said. "They had to have given some of the details to the reporter, knowing he'd run with it. He found out Tansy was working in the mountains and led them right to her. And they sent a couple of assassins after her. I thought, at the time, that they were after me, but they didn't know I was there until they started tracking her. Bad luck for them."

"We'll track down your reporter and find out who put him on the trail," Ryland said. "And then we'll meet you at the other house. And Kadan?" He waited until Kadan met his steely gaze. "You'd better be there."

Kadan sent him a faint grin and saluted. "I understand. And I'm grateful for the company."

Gator dug into his pocket as Nico opened the door.

"Want an Altoid, Kadan? They're cinnamon." He tossed a tin of the mints onto the front seat.

Kadan choked. If it was possible for him to blush, he might have done it. He didn't dare look at Tansy as his friends got out of the car. He just started the engine, put the vehicle in gear, and drove away, flipping them off through the open window as he pulled onto the street.

Tansy laid her head back against the seat as she picked up the little tin and turned it over and over before dropping it back on the seat. "I take it they have an enhanced sense of smell. Have they been giving you a bad time?"

He could have sworn there was amusement in her voice, but when he glanced down at her sharply, she looked sober and innocent, which raised his suspicion more. He put the tin in his pocket, not wanting it out in the open as a reminder of his friends and their highly developed sense of smell, or their bad taste in humor.

"I'll get them back. Why don't you go back to sleep? I'll put some music on."

He turned on the CD player. Tucker and Ian's voice came over the speakers, singing off-key. *"I wanna live with a cinnamon girl . . ."*

"Bastards." He turned the player off immediately.

Tansy burst out laughing. "I don't think they're going to win any contests."

"I'm sorry if they embarrassed you."

She leaned over and nuzzled his arm with her chin. "Why would I be embarrassed? Are you?"

"Hell no. I wouldn't give a damn if they walked in on us, but I don't want you uncomfortable." He was adamant.

She shrugged. "I'm not going to be embarrassed because I have sex with you, Kadan. I like having sex with you. I like how you make me feel and I especially like how I make you feel. So let them say anything they want. It doesn't bother me."

She meant it. He felt a surge of pride, of awe, that she

could belong to him. He wasn't even certain how it had happened, but damn, he was grateful.

"You left the room tonight."

"You knew?"

"Of course I knew. I like having you curled around me, and the moment you left, I felt alone. You went to see my father, didn't you?"

"How did you know?"

"You weren't satisfied with his answers. He knew about Whitney's experiments, didn't he? You would have told me right away if he hadn't."

"I'm sorry, baby." He laced his fingers through hers and brought her hand to his heart. "I really am. I wanted it to be different for you."

She was silent, staring out the window for a few minutes before she took a deep breath and looked at him. "My mother?"

"She has no idea. She despised Whitney. I could read her mind, but I can't read his. I made certain she slept through our talk. I didn't want to cause her any more distress than she already has been through."

"What was his explanation?"

"If I tell you, Tansy, I'm going to tell you the entire story. Be very, very certain you want to know," he warned.

"That bad?"

"Yes." He kept possession of her hand when she tugged at it to pull away from him. He wasn't going to let that happen. Her father had hurt her, not him.

"Was he going to give me to Whitney?"

"Damn it, that's not fair."

"They hit my mother. He would do anything for my mother. If he thought they'd hurt her, he'd give me up and never look back." She turned toward Kadan. Lights from oncoming cars played over her face and then left her in shadow. "I know he loves me, Kadan, but it's always been about my mother."

"And that's all right with you?"

"I grew up knowing that. It was normal. I don't know what it's like for a child that isn't adopted, but . . ." She trailed off. He was so still. His mind was still, even when she touched it. She turned the pieces of the puzzle over and over in her brain. She was good at solving puzzles. Things clicked into place for her. And the click wasn't what she'd expected. She shook her head in denial. "I remember being in Whitney's laboratory. It was horrible. There was so much pain. There were other girls there and nurses. He had this little soundproof room he'd take us into. Some of the girls would have seizures and we'd all get nosebleeds. He'd just record everything, with this strange little remote smile on his face. If he frowned, you were in trouble. I even remember the day he brought me to see my parents for the first time."

"Both of them together?" Kadan asked.

"No. Just my father. I remember the way he stared at me. He reached out to touch me and I flinched away. I was wearing gloves, but it was so hard to control impressions and they hurt my head, so I didn't want him touching me."

"How was he looking at you?"

There it was again, that note. A piece of the puzzle. He wanted her to see for herself, but she kept turning away from the truth. She tightened her fingers in his, wanting strength. She was asking for the truth. She was causing him distress by insisting he tell her, yet she didn't want to see. She pulled up the memory.

She'd been so frightened. All the girls were frightened. A couple of the nurses tried to comfort them, but never around Whitney. He looked at them as if they were insects, and he didn't want the nurses "coddling" them. A couple of the girls were outwardly defiant, and that made him harsh and cruel. Even as a child she recognized the taint of madness, even though she couldn't really read him.

And then the girls began disappearing. Whitney would

never respond when they dared ask where one of the girls had gone. When he'd taken her out of the laboratory, she'd been terrified, her imagination running wild. She didn't know what the outside world was like and it was so huge. Enormous. The sky was frightening; the noises overwhelmed her. He'd dragged her into a room and shoved her toward a man who had been sitting quietly in an office chair.

She stumbled and looked up at the man. He was tall and fit, with white gold hair, and he turned his eyes on her and she had been afraid to move. Shock. Absolute shock registered on his face. For a moment something fluttered in her mind. Recognition? But she'd never seen him before. She thought . . . *I belong.* She hadn't known what a father was before then. Now she did. She moistened her lips and glanced up at Kadan's stone-set features. "He's my birth father." She continued to look up at him. "Tell me how."

He told her then, all of it, holding on to her hand, his voice a soft, compassionate caress, his thumb stroking back and forth across the back of her hand.

She kept her head down, long hair spilling around her face so he couldn't see her expression, but he was in her mind, trying to surround her with warmth, with love, with everything protective in him. She remained very still, even in her mind, as if she was afraid that if she moved, she'd shatter.

Baby. He breathed the endearment, tempted to pull the car over to the side of the road and hold her tight. She didn't want him to though, he read that much. She needed time to assimilate what he'd told her.

"You're absolutely certain?"

"He told me himself."

"Mom doesn't know any of this?"

"No." He brought her hand to his chin and rubbed his jaw back and forth in an effort to comfort her.

"Good. I don't want her to ever find out." She looked at

him then and he saw raw pain in her eyes. "Can you find out if my birth mother really is dead?"

"Whitney keeps files, and Lily has access to them using some complicated back door to a computer I don't understand. I'll ask her to start looking. If he has records on you, and I'll bet any amount of money that he does, she'll find them."

She gripped his hand tighter. He felt her in his mind. "Did you kill him? Is that why we had to leave so fast?"

"I wanted to," he admitted quietly, wishing he could feel remorse or shame. The man was her father. "For a minute I thought I might. But I think he's punished himself more than I ever could. And he does love you, Tansy. He certainly loves his wife."

"Don't tell me he loves me. He didn't love me."

"It feels that way right now, baby, but when you look back over the years you had with him, you'll know he couldn't fake the way he treated you. He loved you."

"But he didn't want to risk what he had to save the rest of the girls, or to find out if my birth mother was alive or dead or even murdered by Whitney." Her fingers fisted in his shirt. "He would have had Fredrickson turn me over to Whitney if I'd gone back."

"He wouldn't have had a choice. Fredrickson would have been willing to kill everyone to take you back to Whitney."

"You wouldn't have wanted to kill him if he had been trying to save my mother. You would have understood. It was more than that."

He didn't know what to say to ease her pain, and he cursed his lack of words when she needed . . . *something*. "I'm sorry, Tansy."

He wished he could take her pain on himself. He would have done anything for her, but instead he could only feel helpless. "I put a pillow there between the seats so you could lie down if you wanted." He willed her to close her eyes and rest. They had a long day ahead of them and she was worn out.

Tansy didn't reply, but she did straighten the pillow and lie down, her head against his hip. He stroked little caresses over her hair while he drove through the night. She didn't sleep for a long time. He had been afraid she'd cry, but when she didn't, it felt worse to him.

In her mind, Tansy withdrew from him. Even connected as he was, he could feel her huddling in a corner as far from him as possible, too hurt to trust anything or anyone. And he couldn't blame her. Don Meadows had been her hero, the man who rescued her from Whitney, and all along he'd been keeping Whitney's dark secret.

Kadan drove through the night, keeping one hand on her, insisting on the one connection when she was so far away. It took her a couple of hours to drift into a fitful sleep. By the time he'd pulled up to the house, she was in a much deeper sleep, and he was able to carry her inside and put her on the bed. He stretched out beside her and finally closed his eyes, wrapping both arms around her to keep safe, even in her dreams.

CHAPTER 14

Kadan woke with his arms filled with warmth, and the scent of cinnamon and sin surrounding him. His body throbbed with a monster hard-on, his shaft full to the point of pain as he lay curved around Tansy. He kept very still, breathing through need, disgusted that he could be dripping like a rutting animal, hot and thick, pressed so tight against the soft, tempting curve of her bottom, when she was still reeling in shock from the devastating revelations of her father's betrayal.

What was wrong with him that he couldn't give her the comfort she needed? He pushed his forehead against the back of her silky head, for the first time in his life really wishing he was different. He'd never cared before. It had never mattered to him to articulate his thoughts and feelings to another human being. He had no family or home, and he'd never believed he would either. And now here she was, soft and warm and smelling of heaven, feeling like paradise against his body, and all he could think about was riding her for hours, instead of finding the right words to comfort her, the right way to hold her, without seeming like all he really wanted was a fast, hard ride.

Sometime in the night he had wrapped his arms around her, his hands cupping her breasts so her nipples pushed into the center of his palms and the soft weight of her lay in invitation. He realized he was rocking his hips gently against her, rubbing his shaft along her buttocks, and he forced himself to stop, breathing deeply to stay in control. Cursing under his breath, he pulled his arms free and rolled away from her. With his groin so full and aching, it was a kind of torment to sit on the edge of the bed and just breathe her in.

He felt her move, felt her awareness, heard the small hitch in her breath as she woke. He didn't look at her, because if he had, he wouldn't have been able to stop himself from sliding her body under his. Instead, he padded to the bathroom on bare feet and took a long, cold shower that didn't seem to do anything but make him more uncomfortable.

His jeans seemed tighter than usual and his body didn't want to cooperate; there was no comfortable place to tuck his hard shaft, but he did his best. Tansy was already up and in the other bathroom, obviously taking a bath. He could smell the fragrance wafting out from behind the half-open door and hear the splash of water as she bathed. He closed his eyes, trying not to see an image of her nude, rising up out of the water, long hair flowing around her like a silvery waterfall.

He stalked into the kitchen and put on coffee, trying to keep his imagination from running wild, thinking about the water beading on her skin and where it might be running. And what the hell had he ever thought about before she came into his life? He used to have a brain; now all he thought about was sex.

He tapped his foot, determined not to go look at her. All that soft skin. The silky hair. Her enormous eyes. Mouth to die for—a mouth made for sin. He found himself at the bathroom door, nudging it open with his foot. He stuck his head in and lost his breath. She was rising up out of the tub, wrapping her hair in a towel. She looked at him, not even making an attempt to cover up, one eyebrow raised in inquiry.

"Uh. Breakfast." His voice sounded rusty. "I figured you'd be hungry. What would you like to eat?" Because he'd like to eat her. Or have her eat him. Hell. He was losing it. He had to solve a murder, not turn into a teenage walking hard-on.

"Oh, that sounds great. I'm really hungry." She bent over to pick up the folded towel resting on the vanity, her breasts spilling forward. Small beads of water ran down the soft curves and dripped from her nipples to the floor.

Kadan licked his lips. There seemed to be a strange roaring in his head, and if he didn't adjust his jeans soon, the seams were going to burst. "Egg preference?"

She straightened and shook out the towel. Tiny droplets of water traveled down the valley between her breasts, across her tempting belly, to find the vee of white gold curls at the junction of her legs. He caught himself staring, wanting to drop to his knees and sink his tongue in her. She seemed oblivious, running the towel along the curves of her body, soaking up the tiny water drops.

"Anything is fine, but I really like scrambled."

"Scrambled it is, then."

Kadan left her because she had a small, sexy smile on her face, and was barely rubbing the towel over her skin, and he was going to ruin a good pair of jeans and embarrass himself. He stomped down the hall back to the kitchen, wishing he smoked. He slammed a frying pan onto the stove, muttering to himself. His radar went off and he spun around.

Tansy stood in the doorway, one towel in her hand, the other wrapped around her hair, and nothing else. "Have I upset you?"

Kadan shook his head, keeping his gaze on her face, willing his wayward eyes to focus. Unfortunately they focused on her mouth, which did little to help his situation. "Of course not. I'm just feeling a little out of sorts."

"I don't mind cooking. I need you to put the game pieces back on the table for me anyway. I'm not a great cook, but I manage."

Naked. She was going to cook for him without a stitch of clothing on. He wouldn't survive. "Like that?" Now his voice had dropped to pure smoke.

Tansy looked startled. She glanced down at herself. "No, of course not. I was planning on getting dressed first." She turned and stormed off, her shoulders stiff.

Now he'd really upset her, and all he could think about was the sway of her ass as she stomped down the hall. Relationships were complicated when they really shouldn't be. He sighed again and went down to the war room. He may as well set up the pieces before cooking. He needed to get his head straight, and walking into a room with so many victims screaming for justice had a way of reducing everything else to nothing. He might not be good with women, but he knew how to track killers.

She joined him when he'd finished separating the small figurines, using his gloves to ensure no prints or impressions of him transferred to a game piece. She came up behind him, so close he could feel the heat of her body. She smelled so good he wanted to breathe her in.

"I may as well finish the East Coast pieces. I've only got one left."

"Not yet. You need to eat something. Come have your coffee while I cook you some breakfast." He captured her fingers and tugged, taking her with him, wanting to put off the inevitable as long as possible.

She went with him without protest, making him feel a little better. Nothing had ever rocked his world or gotten under his skin until Tansy. Feeling shaken was a new experience for him. He pulled out her chair, brushing a kiss on top of her head. For the first time she sent him a real smile, one that lit her eyes, and he breathed again. When she was settled with a cup of coffee in her hands, he broke the eggs and began beating them into a frothy brew.

"How does your job work?" Kadan asked. "Did *National Geographic* hire you to take pictures for them?"

She shook her head. "I do freelance work. In this case, they picked up an article and photographs I did for them last year and loved it, knew I was still studying the cougar, and agreed in advance to help fund me. I was pretty thrilled. I had a great tutor in photography, and I've slowly been acquiring a reputation, but this was a huge break for me. But no, technically, they don't employ me."

"Who knew you were up in the Sierras?" Kadan asked. Now that his brain was working again, something was nagging at the back of his mind.

She took a sip of coffee and frowned at him over the cup. "My parents knew. And Charlie, at *National Geographic*. Well, he didn't know where I was exactly, only that I was filming mountain lions." She put down the coffee mug and leaned her chin into her palm. "How did you track me to the Sierras? I mean, it's a big mountain range. How did you know I was at that exact location?"

"There was no way you were going to go anywhere without contacting your parents. Everything I read about you told me you wouldn't go more than a few days without letting them know you were okay, even if you were in Africa somewhere shooting pictures."

Tansy swept her hair back from her face. "So you just waited until I called home and traced the signal back to me."

He shrugged. "It was easy enough. But no one else was watching your parents. I would have known."

"Why is it important?"

"Your father said something to me that just keeps nagging

at me." He put the eggs in front of her and placed the other dish across from her. He sank down across the table from her and picked up his fork. "For just a moment let's set aside the killers we're tracking. They can't know I was sent to find you. But someone knew where you were, and I don't think they followed me."

"Why? You can make mistakes," she teased.

He forked eggs into his mouth, frowning as he chewed. "Not like that. I thought, at first, that they were after me. They were there to get you. To kill you. They weren't going to bring you back to Whitney."

She sat up straighter. "I thought they were men Whitney sent to get me, or someone who wanted you dead because of this investigation."

"I imagine a lot of people would like to see me dead, but as far as I know, only the general asked me to clear up this murder mess. Everyone else thinks I'm involved in a different type of mission. So no, the killers weren't there to stop me, they had to be there to kill you and I just happened to be in their way."

"Who would want me dead besides Whitney?"

"Whitney doesn't want you dead, honey, he wants babies out of you. And if I'd been thinking with my head and not my cock, I would have realized that immediately. He wants a baby out of us. You might not have been paired with me, but I was definitely paired with you. He wants our two talents bred into a child."

She swallowed hard. "That's sick, Kadan. What if I do get pregnant?"

He laid his hand over hers. "He'll never take our child. We're building a fortress in the mountains. We'll have escape tunnels and routes and protections, so much so that it will be difficult for anyone to get to us. You'd be safe there and so would our child."

His tone was the same as always, that low, velvet conviction that made her a believer. "So if the murderers we're tracking didn't know you were investigating them and Whitney doesn't want me dead, who does?"

"Your father mentioned a coalition, a group that has formed. We've run into them before, and we thought we'd broken them up when we killed their leader. Evidently he wasn't the only head of the organization. They have a lot of help. Someone in the White House who has access to a high security clearance has been targeting the Ghost-Walkers for death. They leaked the information that the East Coast and West Coast murders were connected, and they gave a reporter your name. He did a little investigating and realized you were the same Tansy Meadows who had tracked serial killers. The moment he found you, the assassins were on your trail."

"But how did he find me?"

"That's what I want to know. Did whoever tip him off give him that information as well? And if so, how did they come by it?"

Tansy ran both hands through her hair. "I don't have any idea, Kadan, and truthfully, I just can't find it in me to care that much. I want to solve these murders and get the killers off the streets. All the rest of it will just have to take a backseat until we figure out what's going on."

Kadan glanced at her half-eaten eggs. "You didn't eat much."

"It's enough to get me through this. I'm going to do this one right this time."

He took both plates to the sink and left them there, turning to lock his gaze with hers. "You'll do what I say, Tansy. It's my job to keep you safe—and sane. Wear the gloves. If they have to come off, fine, we'll cross that bridge when we need to, but start off with the gloves and see what kinds of impressions you get."

"You're handicapping me."

"I don't really give a damn, now, do I?"

They stared at each other for a long moment, and Tansy

shook her head. "We're never going to find them if you don't let me do my job."

He refused to argue with her. He simply followed her down the hall and picked up the gloves, shoving them into her hands.

Tansy pulled on the protective gloves and stood at the table, peering down at the ivory game pieces. She'd already felt the surges of energy, some much more potent than others, and now that she was tuned, the collective pieces gave off a frightening vortex of energy, whirling into one violent mass. Even with the gloves covering her skin, the violence was tangible as she leveled her palm over the top of the last ivory piece from the East Coast.

Without actually touching it, Tansy studied the intricately detailed knife. The blade was sharp and had tiny notches in it. She frowned. Ordinarily she would think the notches might be imperfections, but the carver was too good and had too big of an ego to let anything he worked on be less than perfect.

"The puppet master believes he's smarter than everyone else and he wants them to see him without really seeing. He wants his genius to be in front of them, easy to read, but not to really 'get' it. That way, he can gloat and prove to himself over and over that he's superior, even to enhanced psychics."

"Is he enhanced?"

She drew a breath, allowing her palms to be so close only a piece of paper could separate her from the game piece. The surge of energy was potent and filled with violence. The one she had dubbed "Blade" was definitely a dominant. She wondered what Kadan's energy would feel like if he wasn't shielding her. She imagined it would be something like this. Waves of force, relentless and sure. Blade had to be the East Coast team leader of the game. She didn't want to read him right now; she was trying to get a feel for the puppet master.

"I can't tell. Not like this. His energy is very subtle, but I think he weaves it that way."

Tansy concentrated on the ego, the biggest part of him. The man was fastidious; she had the impression of someone who was very conscious of his clothes and style. He wanted to look well groomed, a *GQ* man. He wanted to appear cool and sophisticated without drawing attention to himself. He had money . . . She pulled her hands away abruptly, another piece of the puzzle falling into place.

"This is about money."

Kadan frowned. She was already pale, the drain on her tremendous, and they'd barely gotten started. He could feel the energy in her mind, dark and violent, swirling with edges of red, but she hadn't immersed herself in it at all. "What's about money, Tansy?" Sometimes he thought she put herself in a trance, her eyes opaque and distant, gleaming with that violet-silver shine.

"The murder game. It's all about money. That's your connection."

He shook his head. "I looked into insurance payoffs. A few of them had insurance. One or two left a hefty inheritance for a family member, but the majority don't have enough money attached to raise a flag."

"The two boys. The ones Frog killed. Did they have insurance on them?" Tansy sank into a chair because her legs felt rubbery.

"Why question that particular murder?"

"There couldn't be another motive. Who would want to kill two high school boys who were smart, weren't robbed, and probably had never done anything to anyone in their lives? I got the impression from them that they had barely started their lives. They were shocked. Frog didn't want to kill them; in fact, he was upset with the puppet master and the others on his team and the other team. Really upset. He asked forgiveness and even went so far as promising revenge. He didn't want to kill them, yet he chose those two boys. They weren't random victims. You're going on the assumption that each of these murders was random, but Frog's murder wasn't. He had to fulfill some contract . . ." She broke off and looked up at him in shock. "Contract murders? Could this game be about paid hits?"

Kadan automatically shook his head. How could that be? A *game*? But even as he was denying the possibility, her reasoning somehow fit. Her mind worked differently, taking pieces, discarding them, and trying them in ways no one else might think of. Another gift. A talent she didn't recognize.

"Don't touch anything until I get back." He didn't want to leave her, not when information was pouring into her mind, and he was afraid she might grasp the game piece now that she had a trail to follow. "I mean it, Tansy, wait for me."

Tansy found it difficult to resist the lure of the ivory blade. The notches meant something to either the carver or the owner of the piece. Which was it? Her mind refused to stop racing for more details. Once she was on the scent, she found it nearly impossible to focus on anything else, and the energy of both men was much more potent in this piece.

"Tansy," Kadan's voice was sharp. "I said no."

He caught her wrist, the sound of his palm hitting her arm loud in the silence of the room. She blinked up at him, a little distracted by his presence.

"I need to . . ."

"No." He kept possession of her hand. "I went to check on the file in the war room. The boys were half brothers and the insurance on them was heavy for kids that age. Mother inherits. She'd only recently remarried. Boys had different fathers, and the third husband seems to have gotten along with the boys and was broken up about the whole thing."

"Did you interview them?"

He shook his head. "I haven't had the chance. I got my orders, read everything, and knew I needed you, so I went looking for you."

"But either the mother or the stepfather could have hired someone to kill the boys." Tansy made it a statement, but she was frowning, shaking her head. "Something is just a little off kilter, Kadan. I need to get stronger impressions. I need to actually handle it."

"With gloves."

"I won't get what we want. You said we'd have to solve this fast. I know your friends didn't do this, but whoever wants all of you dead is going to use the murders as an opportunity to get rid of them. By the time the real murderers are found, it will be too late."

He didn't want her pulling off the gloves. She'd be annihilated by the violent energy. He could feel waves pushing at her mind, and she merely had her hands close to the game piece.

"We need to know."

He pulled her off the chair and sat down. "Sit on my lap."

"Kadan." It was a protest. She frowned at him, pushing at the long blond hair falling around her face. "What are you doing?"

"Protecting you. Sit on me. I'm going to keep my arms around you, my hands on your wrists. If I tell you to drop that thing and you don't, I'll be in a better position to force it out of your hand. We both know this is dangerous to you."

"I don't know if I can concentrate like that."

Kadan shrugged. "Take it or leave it, but you aren't touching that thing without me surrounding you with as much protection as I can give you."

He had that tone again. Tansy sighed. There was no moving him from his position when he used that tone. Very slowly, breathing deep, she removed the protective barrier of the gloves. She sank down onto his lap and his arms immediately circled her, his hands resting lightly over hers, which gave her added confidence.

She cupped her bare hands around the ivory knife. The energy swarmed to her, violent, almost angry. Smug. Superior. Oily sludge poured into her brain, dripping with blood, with the need for more blood. Beneath the muck, hidden, she found that small vein that ran under, nearly overwhelmed with the dominant strand, but flowing subtly, a monster at work behind the scenes.

She took a breath and worked at separating the two threads. Blade needed followers, needed them to see him dominate every situation. He looked for fights. Wanted others to argue so he could hurt and frighten them in front of others. He was cruel to his girlfriends and those who loved him, usually subtle cruelties, but he enjoyed the pain in their eyes—and the fear. Ridiculing others and making them look small in front of his friends was a favorite pastime.

Distaste. Smug satisfaction that someday . . . She almost had the puppet master, but Blade wouldn't give up the spotlight. Something important eluded her as it moved by. She couldn't focus properly because the violence in Blade was his primary characteristic.

More oily sludge coated her mind as he pushed deeper into her brain, determined to imprint himself there when she was really looking for the more subtle thread. Looking big mattered to him, almost more than anything else. He despised having to salute. He wanted to take out some of the officers and their families. He fantasized about it all the time.

The son of a bitch who wrote him up for beating the crap out of the stupid private that dared to contradict him. Yeah, he wanted to show *Officer* Showoff just who really was in charge. Damn the rules of the game. He'd agreed to them, but no one would know if he spent a few hours carving Mr. Officer up. Of course, it wouldn't be nearly as much fun if the others didn't know what he was doing.

Another voice began to rise, one she couldn't push down. A woman, pleading. Begging. Stirring Blade to further action. He loved the begging. The victim had no idea she was rousing him to further acts of torture for his own pleasure, and Tansy had no way of warning her.

Shut up, bitch. Stop sniveling. Whiny, stupid bitch. Of course I'm going to kill you. I'm going to gut you and leave you hanging on a meat hook in the cooler. What did you think I wanted with you? Your fancy jewelry? Your grotesque body? No, I want you dead. But don't worry, you'll be like one of those fine fat pigs your family slaughters and butchers; I'll leave you hanging there for the world to see. Or maybe your husband will carve you up and sell you to the markets to make a few extra bucks.

Blade laughed, the sound wholly evil, and Tansy's stomach lurched. She would have problems getting his vile imprint out of her head. The stain was thick and intrusive, coating the walls of her mind and finding every niche and crack, until it seeped beneath the door where the other voices wailed to be let loose.

Look for the other one, Kadan murmured, his voice a breath of fresh air, like a cool breeze running through her brain.

Tansy made an effort to push the evil Blade to the back of her mind, ignoring his insistence on sharing his handiwork with her. His voice receded a bit, allowing her to find the lighter tracks buried beneath his thick, oily presence. The puppet master. There he was. She had to be careful, very cautious not to alert him to her presence. She tried to keep her touch light, but she'd never had to worry about her own back trail before when she'd tracked.

She drew another deep breath into her lungs, fighting to keep her stomach from churning. She leaned against Kadan and drew his masculine scent into her lungs. For a moment her world righted again, as she breathed him in, the clean outdoor spice of him. Blade receded a bit more, his voice dimming, and she seized the thread that was the puppet muster.

The impressions she received from objects such as this one often seemed like a giant spiderweb, thread after thread wrapped intricately around one another until the killer and victim were bound together and it was difficult to tell the threads apart. The puppet master had carved the game pieces, leaving a great deal of himself in the ivory long before he'd given them to the players and he'd left his own threads. They were light and subtle, but they permeated the entire web.

In all the years she'd tracked killers, none of the threads had been attached to a mind. There was no way to backtrack and find them; she had to piece together information until she received a large enough picture to get the killer. She wasn't certain how the puppet master was still attached, but he had found her particular thread and backtracked. She had to be very careful to step lightly and cause no vibration of her own to warn him she was seeking him again.

She allowed the killer and his victim to wail and gnash around her, as she waded through the blood and gore to examine each thread until she found the strongest impression of the puppet master. She matched the flow in her mind to that subtle energy, taking care that there was no signal as she examined it. Yeah. He was there all right. She just couldn't quite get him. Without hesitation, she closed that breath of a gap between her skin and ivory.

Heat seared her palms. The screams of the victim nearly shattered her. The killer was so strong she had the impression of him bursting through the door, his mouth stretched into a grin, his face shadowy, but there was no facial hair and no mask. The woman fell backward, trying to crawl away as he loomed over her. Tansy jerked herself away from the sight, trying not to hear or see, but looking for the shiny radial that formed the support of the web. It was several strands thick, the shiny primary thread, from the handling and carving of the knife.

The notches were made with care, each one exact and polished as per request. *Idiot smug bastard wants the world to see how scary he is, but he's a child wanting attention, wanting to be feared when he should be hiding. They'll catch this one first, openly showing his kills on his game piece. And he'll turn on his friends because he really isn't so tough. He doesn't like women, but he despises men, mostly because he's afraid of their strength.*

Tansy breathed away the thoughts the puppet master had while carving. Her fingers stroked over the blade, trying to pick up the puppet master's essence, not his thoughts on the killer. A desk. He sat at a desk, stacks of paper all around him. She had the impression of movement, as though others flowed around his desk or were near it. The sound of muted voices. A telephone ringing. She caught a glimpse of a leg clad in a uniform. A military base. He had to work at a military base.

She breathed through her mouth, trying to keep from smelling the blood that thickened around her mind as she concentrated on her prey. The killer wanted to show off, terrifying the woman deliberately. Tansy shook her head, trying to rid herself of his evil nature. There was no conflict in him, only an eagerness to appear larger and more terrifying than anyone else. He wanted the world to fear him, thinking that would get him the respect he deserved.

She shivered, pushing the killer away from her to grab at the anchoring thread. The puppet master, so the opposite of the killer. He wanted no fame or recognition. He pulled the strings and made the others dance. If they were caught, he could walk away, no ties whatsoever to the killings. His concept, his handpicked killers, and no one knew, not even

Whitney. His bank account grew and the homicidal maniacs had their fun. It was all a nice little game any way you looked at it.

Tansy held her breath. He sat at a desk, his clothes impeccable, even the pleat of his trousers exact. He had a strong physique, took good care of himself. His hair was trimmed short and he wore glasses, which made him look distinguished, but not handsome. He had to take care with his image that no one focused on his appearance one way or the other.

"Drop it, baby," Kadan hissed, alarmed. "You're too close." His hands closed hard over hers, prying at her fingers to release the ivory knife.

She could almost smell the puppet master. The sounds of his world crowded in, and if she could just catch that elusive scent. It smelled like . . .

Cinnamon.

"Shit! Damn it, he's found you." Kadan dragged her up, knocking her hand against the table in an effort to dislodge the game piece. Her eyes had gone all the way opaque. She was deep in a trance, caught in another world.

The puppet master turned his head, removing his glasses as he did so. She found herself staring at pale blue eyes. Shiny eyes.

Hello, beautiful. You took the bait and came to visit me again. I'm delighted to meet you. He held up a file with her name on it. *I've been reading about you. Such a gorgeous girl. Too bad you let those sick bastards get to you. Are you feeling better now?* The voice was pitched low, solicitous. He believed he was stronger than she was, that he could control her too.

Kadan popped open the tin of Altoids Gator had tossed onto the front seat of the car, and he shoved one into his mouth. He caught Tansy's chin and ruthlessly brought his mouth down on hers, his tongue demanding entry, sweeping inside to claim her. She was lost in the labyrinth of a spider's web, and he needed something stronger to bring her out. The only thing he could think of was him and the way he showed love. Feeling desperate, he kissed her, pouring everything he was into that kiss. His personality, such that it was, dominant and controlling, ruthless and dangerous, protective and loving her with every fiber of his being. He shared the taste of cinnamon, the wild call between them. *You belong to me. He can't have you.* It was a command, hard and firm, demanding absolute obedience. *Come to me now.*

No! You fuck. She's mine. The puppet master screamed the words in Tansy's mind, trying to hold her to him, his web of threads wrapping her up in a cocoon.

Tansy tasted cinnamon and heard the demand in Kadan's voice. There was no way to defy him or ignore him. This was Kadan at his most dominating, his tone promising swift retaliation if she didn't listen. She shivered and reached for him. The moment she did, the sticky hold on her loosened. She felt Kadan's strength yanking her to him, his mouth hard and aggressive. Then she felt his hands on her, the force of the blow against the table.

Drop it now, baby. Drop that fucking thing now.

Don't you dare! The puppet master lost his smooth edge and snapped his own command, two dominants determined to control her.

No matter how rough his hands, how hard his voice, Kadan's mouth was tender, loving her. Craving her. Needing her. Nothing else mattered. She became aware of the ivory piece digging into her palm, the cries of the victim, the killer mocking the woman as he gutted and lifted her, still alive, to the meat hook overhead. She heard the insidious whisper of the puppet master, calling to her. And then Kadan flooded her mind, filled her with—*him*.

Strong arms. Broad shoulders. Heavily muscled chest. The scent of the outdoors and danger. His mouth, sensual or cruel. His eyes filled with love and desire. She leapt, throwing herself to him, giving him everything she was, turning her back on everything else in her life until there was only Kadan, trusting him to catch her.

Kadan watched the ivory piece fall to the table as he wrapped his arms around Tansy, preventing her limp body from hitting the floor. Blood leaked from her ears, mouth, and nose. He'd expected that, but not from her eyes. She was hemorrhaging internally and there wasn't a damn thing he could do about it. Hell, he'd probably broken her hand trying to break the seal of the tracker. He could see it was already swelling and turning color. Her palm was imprinted with the blade, the details etched into her skin.

He lifted her, cradling her high against his chest, detesting that he had been the one to bring her back to this life. Nearly running, he took her through the house to the bedroom they shared, placing her carefully on the bed.

"Tansy. Wake up, baby. I'm afraid to let you sleep." He didn't know how powerful the elite tracker was, or even if he could find her like this, but the voices were still trapped in her mind and that meant there was every chance the puppet master was there as well. "Come on, honey, open your eyes for me."

Kadan soaked a washcloth and wiped the trickling blood from her face and ears. He had the pills for her headache as well as a glass of water. This was going to be a bad one. She was shivering continually and when he touched her mind, he found chaos instead of awareness.

"All right, baby. It's going to be all right." He said it more to comfort himself than her. He sank down onto the edge of the bed and pulled her into his arms, wanting to surround her, wanting her to breathe him into her body. He rocked her gently. "Wake up for me. Open your eyes."

She remained limp, although tremors rippled through her body repeatedly. He lifted her swollen hand, examining it carefully to see if any of the bones were broken. Ordinarily he could open her hand easily, but when she was in her hypnotic tracking state, her pressure points didn't react as readily as he would like. If they continued, he would have to figure out some way to get rid of the object she was reading without injuring her.

He turned her hand over and opened her fingers to examine her palm. The details of the knife were pressed deep, but there was no burn, just the imprints as if she'd been holding it so hard her skin had picked up the impressions—and he didn't want them there. Kadan used the pad of his thumb to rub gentle caresses back and forth over the knife etched into her palm. The bristles were hard, but velvet soft, and he was careful to keep the sticky side from touching her skin, wanting only to soothe her.

Something moved in her mind and she winced, but he was there first, standing guard, standing in front of her. He would have to insist she do more exercises to strengthen her barriers, especially now, with the puppet master actively hunting her. Their enemy knew who she was. And he would have the details of her life, including the names and address of her parents. Fortunately Don and Sharon Meadows were under guard, but the man might try to find them, using his military contacts.

Tansy stirred, the heavy fringe of lashes fluttering. Her stomach lurched and her muscles tightened beneath his hand. Blood trickled from her nose again and she shuddered. "My head." She mouthed the words rather than spoke them aloud.

"I've got your medicine right here." He held the pills to her lips and then, half sitting her up against his chest, held the water for her.

Tansy swallowed with her eyes closed tight. "It hurts worse this time and it's growing stronger. I'm in for a bad one. Will you make certain the drapes are closed and there's no light in here?"

"Is it safe?" He didn't want the puppet master visiting her in her sleep. Was it even possible? He doubted if she knew, but it worried him.

She was shaking and turned her face away from him, not wanting him to see her so sick and vulnerable. She was afraid to be alone with the voices in her head, afraid if he left her he'd take his shield with him, but she didn't ask him to stay.

He leaned close to her, his lips against her ear. "You don't have to ask me to stay, Tansy. I'll always be here." He stretched out beside her and pulled her close, pillowing her head on his shoulder, his arms holding her. "Go to sleep." He brushed kisses in her hair. "Don't dream, Tansy, just sleep. I won't leave you."

CHAPTER 15

Tansy was back in the swirling, chaotic world of pure energy. She loved it and hated it, drawn back in spite of herself time and again to a world no one else shared. When it was good, it was paradise, all stars and floating on a sea of happiness, a kind of euphoria unlike anything she'd known—except maybe sex with Kadan. When it was bad, it was the thing of nightmares, blood and gore and vicious, evil sickness.

She reached for the stars, but knew she'd missed again. She'd been doing that for years now, missing paradise and grabbing hold of hell with both hands. Blood poured into the sky and seeped through the ground, rising like the tide, so thick there was no way to swim and keep her head out of it. Hundreds of heads bobbed with hers, eyes wide with terror, mouths gaping open as they silently screamed. She wondered if she looked the same, desperate to keep from drowning in the red muck.

And then the volume turned on, and she could hear the screaming, feel it vibrating through her bones. She clenched her teeth and shook her head as fingernails scraped at her skin and bony hands clutched at her arm. Just below the surface she could see a woman looking at her through the murky red veil, her eyes pleading for mercy. Tansy clenched her teeth and reached through the sludge to take hold of the woman's arm. She pulled and pulled—pulled until she felt her arms were being torn out of their sockets, but she couldn't budge the woman.

She steeled herself and dove, head down through the lake of blood, diving deep in an effort to find what was anchoring the woman below the surface. Something bit at her ankle and she looked down. The woman was tied to a round cylinder of metal, left alive to stare toward the surface and safety until the air ran out in her lungs.

Tansy looked around her, the bloody water so murky she could barely make out the other bodies, all standing straight, eyes raised toward the surface that eluded them by no more than a few inches, all held down by wire tied to their ankles. Fish ate at their flesh as if they were swimming through a drive-through sushi bar.

She choked. The air exploded out of her lungs and she kicked her way to the surface, her head bursting through the oily sludge, gasping for air, screaming, fighting as hands tried to drag her back down.

You can't get away now. The whisper was a soft taunt that ran through her mind. She recognized that voice. She fought harder, crying now, pummeling the force holding her down, desperate to get away.

You're safe. You aren't drowning in blood, baby, you're safe with me. Kadan's voice slipped into her mind and then he was there, filling up every part of her soul until he was the very air around and in her.

She realized she was pounding at his chest and kicking blankets onto the floor, and she made herself stop. Her own cries echoed in her ears, and she stopped that too, taking in great gulps of air in an effort to calm herself.

"I'm sorry. I'm sorry, Kadan." She pressed her face against his chest.

He rained kisses over the top of her head and stroked one hand down the length of her hair while he held her tight against him. "There's no reason for you to be sorry."

"I can't save any of them."

He swallowed hard. "They're already dead, Tansy. Long dead before you ever touch the object that holds the violent energy. They're gone and no one can save them. All we can do is to try to stop their killers from murdering again."

"Frog tied her just below the surface of the water so she could see freedom, but couldn't reach it. There were several people, like a colony of them tied down just like that. I saw a cylinder, like an air tank, and there was a logo on it, only it wasn't me seeing the actual logo. It was *him*, Frog, he was whistling as he prepared an air tank, grinding the logo from the side of the tank." She pressed her face closer to him, trying to crawl inside of him to escape her own mind.

Kadan stroked her hair several times in an attempt to soothe her. "How did you access Frog when you were handling Blade's piece?"

Tansy's voice receded, her mind clouding even with Kadan firmly in it. "The puppet master was thinking about him when he carved Blade's piece. He doesn't like Blade, but has a certain empathy for Frog." Her voice trailed off and she began to rub at her arms. "I have to get it off of me." She began to struggle, trying to wriggle away from him, rubbing harder at her arms. "Oh God. I have to get it off of me."

Kadan held her at arm's length, inspecting her as she writhed away from him. She fought in earnest, tearing at her skin, scrubbing at her breasts and belly, scratching and rubbing frantically.

"Help me. Why aren't you helping me? Hurry. Get it off of me." A sob welled up in her voice. She choked.

"Tansy, you're safe," he repeated. "There's nothing on you."

She erupted into violence, punching and kicking, trying to shred her clothes, tearing long scratches in her arms. He caught both wrists in one hand and pinned them together while she fought like a wildcat. He used the weight of his body, not wanting to risk hurting her, but she was gone again, her eyes sliding from awareness to opaque. Once again calmness receded a little to let fear slide in. He didn't want her anywhere near the puppet master in her condition.

"Tansy, look at me." He used his most commanding, his most compelling voice. For a moment she went still, her gaze locking with his. "What's all over you?"

"Blood." The one word was chilling.

His heart nearly stopped. He could hear the voices in her head screaming, the victims pleading, the sound of their sobs. Over the top of the dead came the taunting laughter of the murderers, so many of them, their vile sickness spreading like a cancer.

She began to squirm again, her breath coming in ragged gasps, tears welling up. "Why won't you help me? I didn't do this." She flung her head back and forth in denial.

"No, baby, you didn't," he agreed softly and stood up in one easy motion, flinging her over his shoulder, her head draping down his back. He took her through to the bathroom, his face grim, a vise gripping his heart. As soon as he had the water temperature right, he stood her struggling body on the floor and began to strip her.

Tansy tore at her clothes, desperate to remove the thick coating on her skin and hair. It was under her fingernails and in her eyes. She ripped at the material of her clothes, never wanting to see them again. In the shower, the moment he placed the washcloth in her hand, she began to scrub, hot tears pouring down her face, mingling with the water raining down on her. She was so cold, her body shivering uncontrollably, her teeth chattering until she was afraid they'd chip or shatter. She reached for the hot water tap, but Kadan's hand caught her wrist.

You'll burn yourself. It's gone now, Tansy. You're clean.

There he was. In her mind, protecting her. The relief was overwhelming. *I couldn't find you. I thought you . . .* She trailed off, unsure where she was or what she was doing. She was so confused she reached for him again, not understanding what was happening to her.

I'm right here, Tansy. His voice was calm, mesmerizing, soft and low, filling her mind with warmth. He seemed an anchor, very steady and strong when she was so confused.

Tansy became aware of the water pouring down on her. Of her naked body hurting, of her hand scrubbing at her skin, causing abrasions, nearly taking off the top layer. Startled, frightened, feeling disoriented, she knew this had happened before. She'd stood in a shower, tearing the skin from her body. Her parents had wrapped her in blankets and taken her to a hospital, where she'd spent weeks locked up for her own protection. She was lost again, trapped inside her own mind with such evil beings the world would never comprehend their behavior, and they would never let her go.

No! Damn you, no! Kadan dragged her into his arms, holding her tight. *You aren't lost. You aren't with them. You're here. With me. Look at me, Tansy.* He caught her shoulders, shaking her gently, staring down into her eyes, determined to bring her back to him. "Look at me now." His fingers bit deep enough to cause pain, to override the trance and drag her back to reality.

Tansy knew she was reeling back and forth between her hypnotic state and actual time. She concentrated on the bite of pain in her shoulders. She felt each individual finger digging into her flesh, nearly to the bone. Recognizing Kadan's touch brought her a little more into the present.

She grabbed at that, at his warmth and the solidness of him.

"Look at me."

She heard that note distinctly—the edge to his voice, the absolute authority and command that often annoyed her, yet now was her lifeline. She obeyed him, because one always obeyed Kadan when he used that tone. She struggled to look beyond the veil coating her eyes, the one that imprisoned her in her own mind, so that she could comply with Kadan's demand. It took strength and determination, but she managed to raise her gaze to his.

Immediately his eyes locked with hers. Kadan's eyes blazing with sheer force. Her breath hitched in her lungs and she choked, but didn't look away. The water poured down on her. She could feel the heat and sting of it on her raw skin. Vapor curled around them, and it was real, from the water temperature and not in her mind. He stood there, a warrior of old, fully clothed and soaking wet, his blue eyes so dark they were midnight blue, his mouth set in grim lines, his fingers still digging into her shoulders, connecting her with reality.

"Are you back with me, baby?"

His voice. She wanted to melt into a little puddle at his feet the moment she heard that soft, velvet voice caress her, stroke her body, slip inside her to wrap around every cold spot and warm her. She didn't dare speak. If she continued crying, she'd never stop, and speaking would bring another flood of tears. She knew what had happened. She couldn't hide it from him. She'd been standing on the brink of madness and he'd pulled her back from the edge.

She nearly crumbled, humiliated and ashamed, wanting to tear her gaze from his, but he refused to release her, stepping forward to close the gap between them, still looking down at her, still commanding her gaze. One hand slid up her shoulder to the nape of her neck, sliding around her throat to tip up her chin with his thumb.

"Say it, Tansy. Say you're with me."

She swallowed, knowing he felt the movement in the palm of his hand. "I'm with you."

"You're mine. You belong here, with me. Say it."

She touched her tongue to her lips. They stood there, water pouring around them, her clothes torn and strewn on the floor, her skin practically scrubbed off, her mind damaged almost beyond repair, and he wanted . . .

His hand closed tighter around her throat. He gave her a small shake. "Say it."

"I belong here, with you." She wanted to belong with him, but he was so strong and she was so falling apart. Her mind was shattered, the pieces scattered everywhere. She had the mad desire to look around for them, but his gaze continued to command hers, refusing to allow her look away from him.

"Who do you belong to, Tansy? I want you to say that you're mine. Say it out loud so that you know it. So that you believe it. I'm not letting you go. I refuse absolutely to give you up. Not to someone else, not to your parents and certainly not to a bunch of murderers. Who do you belong to?"

She was lost in his strength. Lost in his eyes. "You. I belong to you." She barely whispered the words, her throat clogging.

He still held her gaze, refusing to release her. "And who do I belong to?"

She blinked. Warmth poured into her. She was aware of him filling her mind, pushing out every ugly thing that had been there. He was there, slamming the door closed on the voices, building a brick wall across it. Kadan. Of course. She felt a ghost of a smile, of hope. "Me. You're mine and you belong to me."

He crushed her to him, so tight it drove the breath from her, nearly cracking her ribs, but she only wrapped her arms around him and held on. He buried his face in the soft hollow of her shoulder, and it was impossible to tell if the water from the shower soaked into her skin or if his face was wet with tears. He didn't move for a long time. When he did, his hands were gentle.

"Let's get you out of here." He reached up and turned off the water, then pulled a towel around her. "The others should be checking in soon, and I want to get a hot cup of tea into you."

She stayed still, allowing him to rub the water very gently from her skin. He seemed to need it even more than she did, his hands sliding over her, the roughened calluses feeling good in spite of the abrasions on her arms. Her hand throbbed, and when she looked down, she saw that it was bruised and swollen, but she didn't remember what had happened and was afraid to ask.

"I have to tell you the details or I could leave something important out."

The towel halted movement abruptly, just below her breasts. He looked at her, his face more grim than ever. "Fuck that, Tansy. This is ended right here."

His crude and immediate reaction made her want to smile all the more. Inside her, where he couldn't see, light burst through her, driving out more of the ugliness. He was like a breath of fresh air sweeping through her.

She caught his face in her hands and kissed his strong jaw, nibbled her way from his scar to the corner of his mouth and teased at his sensual lower lip, tugging with her teeth. "Why didn't you want me this morning?" She couldn't keep the hurt out of her voice. "Why didn't you make love to me? Was it this? The things in my head? The damage? Or was it the fact that my father's involved with Whitney?"

Kadan's head came up and his eyes blazed down at her, hot and hungry, filled with burning lust and something else that made her go soft inside. "I was being nice, giving you time."

She frowned at him. "Time for what? One moment you were lying next to me and I could hear your breathing change and feel you hard against me, and then you just rolled over like you couldn't stand being next to me."

"Couldn't stand being next to you?" He echoed her, his gaze narrowing.

His hand snaked out and caught the nape of her neck, dragging her against him, mashing her breasts against his wet chest. He fastened his mouth to hers, a brutal, almost angry kiss, devouring her, staking claim to her mouth while his hand slid possessively down the long curve of her back to her hip. He ground his body hard against hers. "Don't fucking *ever* tell me I don't want you," he snapped, eyes blazing.

"But you . . ."

"Never doubt that I want you every minute of every day. Night and day. I'm always hungry for you." He tossed his wet shirt aside. "If I had my way, you'd just walk around naked waiting for me to bury myself in you." He peeled the wet jeans down the columns of his thighs and kicked them way, and his shaft sprang out, hard and thick and so ready for her he was already leaking little pearl droplets from the broad, flared head.

"Kadan." His name came out in a breathy little moan that was half fear, half desire. She backed up at his sudden aggression, but he just followed her, stalking her across the room until the wall was against her back and she had nowhere to go. She drew in a deep, shuddering breath and held up one hand.

He ignored it and caught her up, his strength enormous, lifting her naked body and taking her back to the bed, uncaring that they both were wet and soaking the sheets as he positioned her at the edge of the mattress, her legs over his shoulders so that she was entirely open to him.

"Don't tell me I don't want you." This time he growled it, the sound rumbling in his throat. "I fucking want you all the time. Just like this. You understand me? Just like this."

There were no kisses, no foreplay; he buried himself deep, hard, and fast, pushing through the tight folds like a battering ram taking him home. He said with his body everything he couldn't say aloud. Every stroke was hard and deep, his hips frantic, plunging into her over and over, driving her up fast, taking her breath, forcing her higher and higher as he claimed her, as he made her his.

He let himself lose control, wild with primitive need, the desire to show her the truth. This was where he belonged, *in* her. That she could question his desire for her was shocking to him, and he took her with an animalistic pleasure, riding her with heat until it felt like flames were licking up his legs and over his buttocks and into his groin. She was hot and tight and felt like a silken fist gripping him, squeezing and strangling until he thought his head might explode from the sheer pleasure.

When she was gasping and thrashing beneath him, he leaned forward, applying more pressure to her hard, sensitive bud, more intense friction as he pistoned into her. He kept bending until his mouth found her nipple. He flicked his tongue twice and then bit down gently. She screamed, her body imploding around his, melting and gripping his with fierce need until he emptied himself into her, filling her with hot seed, collapsing over the top of her, a little shocked at the fury of his body taking hers when he thought of her as fragile.

He could feel the rippling of her body, the aftershocks shaking her as he moved in more gentle strokes, hating leaving the haven of her body. He waited until he could breathe again before he looked at her, half-expecting her to be angry with him, but she cradled his head, her hands in his hair, stroking caresses over him. Accepting him. Accepting his dominant nature. Just accepting him, and that was more humbling, more frightening than all the guns in the world aimed at him.

"I have to touch you." His admission came out rough. A demand instead of the way he'd wanted it to sound. He wanted to share with her his own weakness, give her something of himself that mattered. He let his breath out and tried again. "I need to touch you."

"I love when you touch me, Kadan." She pushed back his hair, her touch gentle.

Kadan shook his head, straightening, stepping back. "No. I don't mean now. I mean all the time. I need the contact with you." He shoved his hand through his hair. "Damn it. This isn't coming out the way I want it to."

Tansy slowly lowered her feet to the floor and sat up. "Tell me." She threw back the wealth of long hair over one shoulder in a sexy slide.

Her breasts drew his immediate attention, jutting out at him invitingly. He couldn't stop himself from leaning down to suckle for a moment. The craving was so strong it shook him. He stepped back, shaking his head, wanting her to understand.

"I *need* my hands on you. I can't tell you why, only that I have to know you're all right with me touching you anytime, anywhere. In my head, I have to know you're going to accept me, want me touching you or to have my mouth on you or your mouth on me." His hand slipped over his shaft, already semi-hard. "That you're going to want me inside of you, a hundred times a day. The thought is going to be there that if I really needed to, you would find a way with me no matter what's going on around us."

"I'm not certain why you think that's such a bad thing, Kadan."

His eyes darkened more. "You think you need me more than I need you. You think I'm stronger and that I'll grow tired of your dependence. I'm in your head. I know what you're thinking, but you aren't really seeing me, Tansy. I want you to see me." He let his breath out in a little rush. "You're home for me. You and your body. You're home."

"All right." She lifted her gaze to his, to make sure he knew she meant it. "I'm absolutely all right with you touching me. I love your hands on me. I especially love your mouth on me, and if you want to be inside me, say the word and I'm there. Just try not to throw me on the kitchen table in front of everyone and we'll be fine."

The knotted muscles in Kadan's stomach unraveled and he could breathe freely again. He hadn't scared the hell out of her, but then, Tansy didn't scare all that easy. She stood up to killers and she willingly faced hell and madness to track murderers. She wasn't a shrinking violet, and if any woman could handle his needs, he was betting his heart it would be Tansy.

"The kitchen table is fine, but no audience. I've got that."

A slow smile tugged at her mouth. "I'm glad you made that distinction."

"I can exercise discipline when necessary."

Tansy laughed, and the sound was music to him. Kadan pulled her up and kissed her thoroughly on her mouth, just because the sound of her laughter sent warmth careening through the ice in his veins.

"Come on, baby." He gave her bare bottom a swat and then rubbed caresses into it when she yelped. "Let's find you some clothes before the others get here."

She looked at the mess in the bed and sighed. "I'm sorry you had to deal with that."

"I'd walk through hell barefoot for you, honey, so a little shower is no problem." His heart would never beat the same, but if that was the price of bringing her back from the brink of madness, he'd accept it.

"You said something about a cup of tea. Would you mind making me one while I clean up?" She didn't want him in the shower while she retrieved her torn clothes; it would just be too humiliating. He might have thought his dark secret was a match for losing one's mind, but she didn't think so, and she needed a few minutes to pull herself back together.

His gaze slid over her, assessing her pale face. "Is your head still hurting?"

She sidestepped the question. "I'm much better. I really would love a cup of tea."

He could feel her will pushing at him. He didn't want to leave her. She looked very pale. There were red patches, scratches, and bruising marring her skin. Her hair was wet and dark, sliding down her back in a long tail, still dripping a little water onto the floor. He could see her thighs wet with his seed. The vise seized his heart again and he turned away, emotions too intense when he was so unfamiliar with them.

"Tea it is," he said gruffly and yanked jeans out of his pack.

Tansy padded barefoot into the bathroom and looked at herself in the mirror. Haunted eyes stared back at her. She was a mess. She lifted her swollen hand and stared down at the mark embedded in her skin. It was beginning to fade, but it told her volumes. She had come too close this time. She'd been lucky that Kadan had fought for her. Her mind was still healing from too many battles with violent energy, and she needed to be more careful if she was going to survive intact.

She threw her torn clothes away and took another shower, washing her hair and rinsing the abrasions on her body. She'd done that to herself, nearly taking her skin off. She couldn't think about it too much, because the sensation of blood coating her skin crawled over her the moment she looked too hard at her body. Rubbing her familiar, soothing lotion into the scratches helped some, and she braided her long hair to get it out of the way before dressing in jeans. She didn't bother with a bra, but just pulled on a dark-colored T-shirt before stripping the bed and throwing wet sheets into the washing machine.

She stood in the doorway of the kitchen watching him. He was an amazing specimen of a man, heavily muscled and quiet on his feet, a tapered waist and a great butt. He was too rough to be called handsome by any stretch of the imagination, but he was striking, compelling, a man one paid immediate attention to.

He knew she was there, she could tell he did. There was always something remote about him when she first came into a room, but then he gentled, the glacier thawing so that he sent her a warm smile over his shoulder.

"I've got your tea. I put a little honey in it. It's good for you."

"You're lucky I like it with honey," she said and sat in the chair he pulled out for her.

His gaze slid over her, clearly saying he didn't give a damn if she liked it or not. He would have poured it down her throat if he thought she needed it. She made a face at him as she wrapped her palms around the warmth of the mug. Her hand was very sore and she flexed her fingers.

"We have to find another way to open my hand when you want me to drop whatever object I'm handling."

He shot her another piercing look. "It's a moot point because you're not doing it again."

She forced back her protest and took a sip of the tea, allowing the liquid to warm her before answering. "I know it must have been frightening for you to see me like that, but we can't stop now. I know with what I got on Frog I should be able to find him. He has some kind of water business on the side. Fishing. Whale watching. Taking people down in a shark cage, who knows, but it's the ocean and the business belongs to him. He loves to be underwater. I think the cylinder was a scuba tank."

"You just won't stop, will you?" There was warning in his voice.

Tansy met his glittering eyes, not flinching from the arctic chill in his stare. "No, absolutely I won't, not after seeing these men. They aren't going to stop, Kadan, and the police aren't going to find them. They've had all this evidence, and yet no one can find a print, or a motive, or anything but the game pieces. You didn't even know there were eight players before I started helping you."

"Your sanity isn't worth it to me."

She held his gaze, refusing to back down. "It is to me. If I can save one life—prevent a child, a parent, anyone at all from suffering at their hands, you bet it's worth it to me. You're willing to trade your life for your country; well I've got this talent no one else seems to have, and whether it's a gift from God or a mutation, I don't know, and frankly, it doesn't matter. I choose . . ." She looked him right in the eye. "I *choose* to use it to stop killers. For me, the sun may rise and set with you, you may rule me in the bedroom and every other place, but not in this. In this, I say when I stop, not you."

Kadan tipped his chair back, not saying anything, regarding her through brooding, half-closed eyes. He looked frightening, his face a hard mask, his mouth tight. Her heart began to beat very fast. Kadan would never hurt her, certainly not for taking a stand, not when she was right—not *ever*. She forced herself to remain silent, not to appease him, although she wanted to. She lowered her eyes and sipped at the tea, holding the mug tight against her throbbing palm, hiding the knife impression from him.

"Your choice was to stop. I dragged you back into it."

She shook her head. "You walked away. You were going to tell them you didn't find me, or that I'd lost my abilities. I chose to come with you."

His jaw tightened. A muscle jerked and his eyes were

twin chips of blue ice. "You have no idea the lengths I'd be willing to go to keep you safe."

There was no give in him and he didn't sound loving. He sounded cold and hard and terrifying. She caught a glimpse of that eight-year-old boy who found a gun in a river of his family's blood and chose to pick it up and seek his own brand of justice. He was ruthless and merciless, and he would be even more so protecting her.

"I'm counting on you to keep me safe while I do this, Kadan. But we have to stop them. Not for your friends, but because they're evil and we can't leave them running around loose on innocent people. You know it as well as I do. You have no intention of stopping."

"That's different."

She nearly snorted tea out her nose. "Why? Because you're the heap big man?"

He leaned forward then, the chair legs coming back to the floor with a crash as he bent over the table, catching her chin in his palm. "No. Because you're my woman and I'll be damned if anything happens to you. I didn't feel a whole hell of a lot before I met you, and now that I do, I don't like where it can take me if something bad happens. You don't want to hear this, Tansy, but I'm not all that far removed from the men you're hunting."

"That's not true, Kadan."

"Lie to yourself then, but don't ever be stupid enough to think that I wouldn't kill for you, or die for you. You want to do this, then you do it my way. I mean it, Tansy, you do it my way. That's all I'm going to give up."

"That's not giving up a thing."

"The hell it isn't. I don't want you anywhere near this mess. I can slap your ass in a safe house with ten guards on you around the clock and there's not a thing you can do about it, so don't tell me I'm not compromising here."

"You're being a bastard."

He put both hands on the table and leaned in close again,

his voice pitched low, his eyes turning glacier blue. "I *am* a bastard. It's time you figured that out."

She sat back in her chair, glaring at him over her tea. After a moment of silence she heaved a sigh. "Fine. Tell me how we're doing this."

"You will give me your word of honor that you won't touch anything to do with the murders or the killers or the victims, nothing at all, without me present, and only with gloves. No handling anything without protection."

"I may not be able to track the puppet master," she protested.

"Then it won't happen. Gloves and me, or no handling. Your word."

His implacable tone set her teeth on edge. "Kadan, try to be reasonable. Do you realize how much information I got this time? We haven't even had a chance to go over it."

He didn't reply. He simply stared at her, unyieldingly.

"We can find a way to make it safer."

"Take it or leave it."

She growled at him. "You're so stubborn. Fine, then. You have my word. I could shake you sometimes."

"Well I could paddle you sometimes. So I guess we're even." There was no give in his voice, no triumph, just stating a fact in that wicked, black velvet, suggestive tone.

She had the feeling he was really contemplating turning her over his knee, and something perverse in her had her tingling with unexpected arousal. How did he do that, turn everything into sex with just a tone? She was in for one wild ride with him, but she couldn't let him just take her over. She had to learn to hold her own.

Tansy leaned her chin into her hand. "You've got that look in your eyes."

"What look?"

The one that took her breath away and made her panties damp. And they were arguing over something important.

"The argument is over. We both compromised," he

pointed out, reading her mind. His lips curved into a sensual smile. "I'm fortunate that I make your panties damp. Lift up your shirt for me."

She regarded him steadily, wondering if he was challenging her or testing her. She didn't care which it was, she'd told him the truth. If he needed access to her body, she was more than willing to give it to him. She pulled the hem of her shirt up over her breasts and held the material out of the way. His eyes darkened from ice blue to midnight. His fingers trailed over the creamy slopes, brushed over her nipples, and followed the red marks down her body.

"Did you put something on this?" He stroked a caress over one angry streak on her belly.

She nodded. "It looks worse than it is. My skin marks easily."

He tugged her shirt down and leaned over the table to kiss her. "Do you want more tea before we do this?"

"No. Do you have a recorder?"

"It's on the sink. I knew you weren't going to let this go." A ghost of a grin touched his mouth.

She wadded up a paper towel and threw it at him. "I can't believe you."

He placed the recorder on the table and turned it on. "Why was the puppet master thinking about Frog instead of Blade when he carved the knife for Blade?"

"He despises Blade and men like him. He thinks Blade is a bag of hot air and dismisses him even though he runs the team." Triumphantly she glanced at Kadan. That was a confirmation that she'd been correct and Blade was the leader of the East Coast team. "If you can track Frog, using the water business, scuba gear, and being able to hold his breath for phenomenal amounts of time, you should be able to find Blade. They work together."

"In the military."

"I believe they are, or they were. They might have another business, something to do with security." She caught her breath. "Yes. They all run a security company together. That was the puppet master's idea. He made them think it was their idea. He's good at manipulating people. He manipulated Whitney. How? How did you do that? I'm so on you," she whispered. "And you're not going to get away from me."

Kadan stayed in her mind, intrigued by the speed with which she gathered pieces of information from images and thoughts and put them together with amazing accuracy. Her brain amazed him.

"He handpicked these men. For his own purpose. He duped Whitney. Whitney the all powerful." Her eyes lit up and she stabbed a finger toward Kadan. "He worked for Whitney during the testing process, Kadan. Can you track him that way? There have to be records. Whitney couldn't have run the testing. He had to interview only those who got through the first few rounds. And he was testing for psychic ability at that point, not whether or not these men were psychologically suited to be enhanced."

"We believe Whitney enhanced a few men who were screened out of the program for his own personal army. A group of men who were tested were listed as missing or dead over the next couple of years, but we found one or two of them very much alive and enhanced. Could these men be part of Whitney's army?"

She shook her head. "No. They had nothing to do with Whitney after he enhanced them. These men belong to the puppet master. He got them through the screening and then somehow through the interview with Whitney. He did it for his own personal gain, no other reason. He had a plan from the beginning. Can you track him?"

"Lily might be able to find out who he is through Whitney's records. Almost all documentation the military had on us was destroyed. What is there is behind a million flags. Whitney experimented on us at his research lab, not on a military base, and only a few people knew."

"You'll have to find those people if you want the puppet master. He's good. Really good if he can slip past Whitney's guard."

"What does he want with the killers? Does he get his kicks out of planning the murders?"

She frowned and rubbed her temples. "He doesn't plan them. The teams do."

Kadan reached across the table and erased a trickle of blood from her nose with the pad of his thumb. "We're done here, baby."

She shook her head. "I can keep pulling out more."

"We're done. You're going to get a brain bleed and then we'll be in trouble. I've got a lot to go on. I think with what you've given me, I might be able to find Frog. Ex-military, or still in it, a security company with his teammates, and an affinity for water."

She leaned her head into her hand again, rubbing. "Don't go in the water with him, Kadan. I can feel that's what you're thinking of doing, making him lead you to his underground colony, but he's at home in the water."

He took her swollen hand and brought it to his mouth. "Don't you worry about me, honey. I know how to take care of myself."

CHAPTER 16

"What's wrong?" Tansy asked as Ryland, Gator, and Nico entered the house.

The sun had gone down, leaving shadows over the windows. She'd had to sleep on and off throughout the day, waiting for her headache to let up. Without the glare of light, her eyes felt better and she was beginning to feel alive again.

The three men collectively winced at her question and then exchanged a long look with one another.

For men who were normally inscrutable, Kadan found it surprisingly easy to recognize trouble the moment he saw the faces of the three GhostWalkers. They looked grim, angry, and very upset that Tansy was in the room with him. There was nothing wrong with Tansy's radar. She picked up the signal almost at the same moment he did.

Kadan. She won't like hearing what we have to say. Her father's involved, Ryland warned. *She's in immediate danger.*

Kadan felt the blow to his gut, but stayed outwardly impassive. Immediate danger. *How?*

"Don't!" Tansy said sharply. "If you think you can cut me out of this now, Kadan, I swear I'll walk out of this house. I deserve better than that."

"I thought you were shielding," Ryland said a little sheepishly. "Sorry, Tansy."

"I am shielding. She's very sensitive to vibrations." Kadan reached out and shackled Tansy's wrist, pulling her beneath his shoulder so he could circle her waist with one arm. *Don't threaten me like that. You try to walk out and see what happens.* He didn't give a damn if all three Ghost-Walkers knew he was talking telepathically. Her threat had shaken him more than he wanted to admit. In place of ice, there was suddenly a cauldron of fire roaring in his belly.

"We wanted to protect you, *chère*," Gator added in his thick Cajun drawl.

Tansy shoved at the wall of Kadan's chest, not even rocking him. That took her temper up another notch. "I'm putting myself on the line too. If you have something to say, just tell me. I don't break so easily, and I don't need to be wrapped up in cotton like a doll."

"Settle down, Tansy," Kadan said without looking at her. He couldn't look at her. She thought she was going to walk out of the house? What the hell did that mean? His grip on her waist tightened. "You need coffee, Ryland?"

"I'm not sure we have time for coffee. How well guarded is this place? You have an escape route?"

"Of course. We can defend fairly easily, that's why I chose it. We have a way to the roof and another below-ground if need be. If the bastards want to come for us, they'll get more than they bargained for."

Gator and Nico were already moving to the windows, checking alarms and drawing the drapes. Gator flicked off the lights and went to the next room to do the same there.

"Who's after us?" Kadan asked.

"Our friend in Washington."

"The same one who sent the first team after Tansy?"

Ryland nodded. "They know where she is."

Kadan felt the breath slam out of Tansy's body, but she stayed still, waiting for Ryland's explanation. "Here? They know she's here? How?" He drew her closer, his arm going to an iron band of protection.

"I spent some time with the reporter who broke the story on the murders and how they might be connected." Ryland didn't go into how he'd spent the time with the reporter, but Kadan knew his friend and his patience when it came to getting information. "He was also the one who wrote about Tansy's whereabouts in the Sierras. It seems he was tipped off by a friend of his, a secretary to Senator Freeman's wife, Violet."

"Violet Freeman. She just keeps turning up. You'd think she'd have enough to do with her husband on life support." Kadan shook his head. "We should have capped her when we had the chance."

"Are you talking about Violet Smythe-Freeman? What does she have to do with this? She and the senator are good friends with my parents. I've been to their home any number of times," Tansy said. "Her husband was a presidential candidate and someone shot him in the head, leaving him on life support. It's a terrible tragedy."

"Yeah, a real tragedy," Kadan said. "We all held a candlelight vigil for him."

Tansy frowned. "He was a friend."

"He was a slimebag. He sold out his country, Tansy. He sent a team of GhostWalkers to the Congo, where a particularly vicious rebel leader was waiting to ambush them. The torture a couple of them endured was immeasurable. He then toured Whitney's breeding facility with Violet— yes, she not only knows about Whitney, she's one of his enhanced girls, and she allows his work to continue so that she and her husband can get into the White House. He was shot at Whitney's compound, not as the newspapers reported."

Tansy sank onto the couch. "Are you certain? They've been at my house. Violet and my mother go shopping together. They play cards. They . . ." She trailed off and looked up at Ryland. "What else? Just tell me."

Kadan stood behind the couch, dropping his hands to her shoulders, fingers easing the tension from her. He ached for her. Her world was turning upside down.

"Whitney put a tracking device in all the girls. He surgically implants it in their hips."

Tansy gasped and looked up and back at Kadan, her eyes locking with his.

It's okay, baby. We'll deal with it. He wanted to hold her, rock her, take her somewhere else where all the ugliness was out of her life. Unfortunately, this was their lives and always would be. He had no choice. He was enhanced and so was Tansy. He couldn't change that.

"Your father apparently found out about the tracking device when you were about fifteen or sixteen and had it removed. He told Violet about it. According to the secretary—"

"You talked to the secretary?" Tansy asked.

Ryland shrugged. "We had a little meeting. It seems she enjoys knowing secrets, so she often listens in to Violet's conversations with her guests. She claims Violet initiated the topic of tracking children with your father."

"She's taking a huge risk, spying on Violet," Kadan said. "Violet would have no hesitation killing her."

Ryland nodded. "I did suggest that Ms. Harris get a different job immediately and destroy any tapes she may have. Whether she listens or not is up to her. Meadows knows Violet was one of Whitney's experiments. My guess is she confided in him to gain his trust."

"And then when Whitney lost his tracking device, he

sent Violet to find out why," Kadan guessed. "That would be like him. She's playing both sides."

Ryland nodded, avoiding looking at Tansy. "And Meadows planted one of his own when he had Whitney's removed."

"In me?" Tansy leapt off the couch and paced across the room, whirling around to face Ryland, her fingers closed into two tight fists. "My father planted a tracking device in me? They can actually use GPS to find me?"

Ryland nodded. "I'm sorry, but yes, that's what he told Violet. They apparently had a long conversation about how all parents should put them in at birth, and she was interested because the senator might want to bring this up and back the idea. Kidnapped children could be found easily. The conversation was all about what tracking devices could be used for, the good they could do. It also got a little technical on how they work. Violet knew how to find you." Ryland looked at Kadan. "I spent some time with Ms. Harris, and as it turns out, Violet wanted the information about the murders and Tansy given to the reporter. Violet had her secretary leak the information."

Tansy's hand was still over her mouth, her eyes wide. "And the secretary just gave you all this because of the generous good heart that she has?"

"I persuaded her that if she wanted to live a few minutes longer, she'd better tell me the truth," Ryland said without flinching away from her steady gaze.

Tansy glanced at Kadan's impassive face. "You all play for keeps, don't you?"

"Yes, ma'am," Ryland answered. "We've dealt with these people for a long time. Our friends end up dead or tortured. Sometimes both. Violet traded your location, and basically your life, for something big that she wants. What it is I don't know, but the reporter heard a rumor that Senator Freeman was going to undergo some kind of new, experimental brain operation. If that's true, I'm guessing your life is the price someone was asking in order for the senator to be a candidate for the surgery."

"So they're going to come here and kill me." She swallowed hard. "And all of you."

"I would think that was the plan," Ryland agreed. "But we have a few plans of our own."

"Great." Tansy swept a hand through her hair and looked at Kadan. "Can we get rid of the tracking device?"

"Yes, eventually. For now, the best we can do is jam it. I don't want to cut you open to take it out. We need a doc for that."

"No, we don't. Not if it's in my hip where the first one was. I remember having stitches in my hip. Dad told me I fell and hit my head and tore a laceration in my hip but—" She stopped abruptly and turned her face away from them. "I'm going to make tea. Does anyone want a cup?"

Kadan filled her mind with him, wrapping himself in her. He wanted to pull her into his arms, but she kept space between them. The only thing he had was his mind and he used it, pushing inside her where she was silently weeping, where the pain of her father's betrayal cut like a knife. Even when he willed her to look at him, she kept her head down, her arms crossing her breasts in a protective gesture. He hated the separation. And he hated more that his reaction went from being about her and the pain her father caused, to him and his own need to be complete with her.

He watched her walk out and felt like she took all the warmth in the room with her. His eyes met Ryland's. "I've never wanted to hurt anyone in my life the way I want to hurt her father," he admitted.

"Man," Ryland set the heavy bag he'd carried in onto the couch and unzipped it, "I'm sorry to have to tell her. And he bragged about it, bragged he could find her anywhere in the world. He may not have realized he set the assassins on her trail, but he did. He led them right to her."

"She'll handle it," Kadan said.

"Yeah, but she shouldn't have to," Ryland said, dragging weapons from the bag. "I brought a few supplies. Thought they might come in handy. And I've got transport standing by just in case we need it."

"Isn't Gator's wife really good on a computer?"

"She can hack just about anything," Ryland confirmed.

"I'm going to need her to work on a few things for me. With her help, I think I can find and take down killers on the East Coast team, but not until Tansy handles the other team's game pieces and gives me enough to find them. I'm going to have to eliminate them all fast so no one has time to disappear."

"Tansy can do that? She looks a little worn."

Kadan shook his head. "I almost lost her with the last one. We'll have to be careful. But I can't eliminate anyone without the others going underground. I have to know who they are."

"I can ask Lily if there are any other trackers, but I've not heard of it, not legitimate ones anyway." Ryland began pulling guns and ammunition out of the sack and spreading the cache across the couch. "So she has to handle how many more objects before we can go after them?"

"Four."

"That burns." He added grenades and claymore mines to the mix. "You better pack up whatever evidence you have and get it ready to move fast. We secured another house, and partially set it up. We can use this one as bait, but I doubt if they'll be very far behind us. They've had the information for a while. They'll be trying to find out who is with her."

Gator and Nico came in and scooped up the claymores. "We'll handle the setup outside," Gator drawled.

"Don't kill the neighborhood dogs," Kadan warned.

Gator flashed him a grin. "Hey, man, they shouldn't be on my property. Where's that good-lookin' woman of yours? You don' much let her outa your sight."

Kadan sent his friend an ice-cold stare that failed to wipe the grin from Gator's face. The Cajun just shrugged his shoulders, shouldered his weapon, and followed Nico out with a handful of claymores.

"Does he ever stop smiling?" Kadan asked.

"Not in all the time I've known him." Ryland shoved a magazine into an automatic. "This woman is the one?"

"The only."

"Then we make certain she's safe," Ryland said.

A muffled noise, like something thumping against the floor, came from the kitchen. Kadan whirled around, inhaling sharply, and caught the coppery scent of blood. He sprinted, using his enhanced speed, his heart in his throat. *No! Damn it, no!* He knew what Tansy was doing. He should have known from the moment he saw her face when they'd told her.

He halted at the kitchen entrance, his heart nearly stopping. He stood for a beat of time staring almost uncomprehendingly at the blood soaking into the kitchen tile and the knife in Tansy's hand. He moved with blurring speed, gripping her wrist, twisting hard to remove the weapon and toss it across the room with so much force it dented the wall where it hit, before clattering to the floor.

"What the fuck were you thinking?" Pressing his hands tightly to the gushing wound in her hip, he raised his voice. "Ryland. Get the emergency medical kit now."

"I want it out of me."

"Shut up." Kadan's piercing eyes slashed at her face as he put pressure on the wound. "Don't talk or move. Damn it! Just damn it. *Ryland*. Fucking get in here."

Ryland came at a run, the medical kit in his hand. He threw himself on the floor beside Kadan, ignoring the blood soaking into his jeans.

"Okay." Ryland took a breath. "Okay," he repeated, waiting for his heart to start again. "We've got Nico. He can deal with this shit. He's good, Kadan. I've called him in."

"I need more pressure. She's losing too much blood." Kadan tried to detach himself, to find that calm that was always at his core, but there was only fear. He'd never been so shaken by fear. There wasn't enough air in the room to breathe.

Nico and Gator came rushing in, and Nico pushed his way in between Kadan and Ryland, indicating for Kadan to let him see the damage.

Kadan caught Tansy's face in his blood-soaked hands. "I swear I'm going to beat you within an inch of your life for this. Damn you for this, Tansy."

"You're not helping," Nico said. "Back off and give me some room. I need hot water and some towels fast. Ryland, get me the iodine."

Without a word, Kadan positioned himself at Tansy's head, so that she was pillowed in his lap. He tried to keep his mind blank, for once in his life, allowing his teammates to do the work.

"Normally when I use healing energy, Dahlia is with me to focus the crystals. Somehow she can get what's inside of me to flow much more easily." As he spoke, Nico dumped the antiseptic into the wound.

Tansy screamed and nearly came off of Kadan's lap. It was liquid fire pouring through her flesh. Kadan held her down and she clutched at his arms. "Make them take it out."

He swore savagely. Kadan, the ice man, who was about to go off like a nuclear blast. "Can you do it and still stop the bleeding? Can you get it out of her?"

Nico muttered to himself, but he wiped at the wound and peered into the deep slash. "I can see the edge of it. It's close to the bone, Kadan. Maybe. Give me the small knife in the kit, Rye." He held out his hand for the instrument while he looked at Tansy. "Can you take the pain?"

"Anything to get it out," Tansy said. She looked up at Kadan, tears swimming in her eyes. *I know you're angry with me.*

Damn it, just stay quiet right now. His chest was so tight it burned. He couldn't lose her. Thunder roared in his ears. Fire burned in his belly. His gut knotted tight and hard and dangerous—oh so dangerous. His mind actually went numb, blank, except for the protest, the litany. *Don't take her. You can't take her. Whatever you do, don't take her.* He didn't even know who he was pleading with, but there was too much blood.

Tansy wanted him to understand how desperate she felt. Killers crowded into her head, victims shared the space. There was no way to tell him, not now when he was so angry with her. She almost wished for his cold mask. He looked frightening, a dangerous man on the edge of sanity. She should have thought before she'd decided to take the tracking device out herself. How deep could it be? Her hand had slipped. There'd been more blood, the shock of pain; her hand just slipped. She couldn't stand the thought of anything else foreign in her body. And she couldn't bear the idea that she might cause the death of Kadan or any one of his friends.

Kadan gripped her shoulders hard and Gator thrust a towel into her mouth as Nico took the tip of the blade and sliced deeper around the small tracker. She heard her muffled scream, her body arched in torment, but she fought the reaction, wanting Nico to succeed.

Kadan swallowed bile and bent over her. *You're all right, baby. He's getting it out of you. Just breathe through it. Almost there.*

All the while Kadan soothed her, he kept shifting his gaze back and forth between Tansy's face and Nico. Ryland put tweezers into Nico's hand, and Nico carefully inserted the tips into the wound. Sweat beaded on Tansy's forehead; there were white lines around her mouth. Her lashes fluttered and her eyes turned opaque.

Kadan wanted her to pass out. Her fainting would be good for both of them. He willed her to let herself go, and thankfully, she did, slumping in his arms, making it much easier for Nico.

"Got it." Triumphantly, Nico held up the small chip. He handed it off to Gator and turned back to the deep slice along Tansy's hip and thigh. "I'm going to need to stitch this. Do we know her blood type?"

Kadan nodded. "It was in her file. She has the same type I do."

"That's not a surprise," Ryland said. "Lily found documentation that Whitney's been trying to make us universal so we can all give to each other. With pairing, he tried to make certain. Remember, we're all supposed to be the ultimate weapons in combat situations, so that means we have to be able to heal each other."

"Yeah, well, if I can't do my thing with her, she's going to be out of commission for a while. We may need to take her to a hospital."

"Do your thing then," Kadan said, ice creeping back into his voice, "because protecting her in that public a place will be nearly impossible."

Nico didn't reply. He simply began the intricate and difficult job of meticulously repairing the damage Tansy had done to her leg.

"Do we move her? We're going to have company and she probably needs a transfusion," Ryland said. "It's up to you, Kadan."

"We fight here. Get fluids in her and see if we can hold off the transfusion until we move. If we're lucky, maybe she won't need one." Kadan wanted a battle—even needed one. He felt the familiar calm settle over him. The warrior was stronger than the lover, more recognizable. The persona fit him. "I've got the escape routes ready. If you have to go up, there's a rope ladder as well as a cable to shoot to the roof on the west side. I don't want to let it get that far."

"I'll be outside then," Nico said. "When I'm done here, I'll find myself a spot."

"They'll send a team," Kadan warned. "I took out two of them in the mountains. They aren't going to be happy about it."

"I'm feeling a little mean about now," Nico said as he took another stitch.

Gator nodded, and the smile not only faded from his eyes, but his mouth had gone tight and grim. "I'm getting damn tired of our women having to suffer."

Kadan looked at Ryland, who shrugged his broad shoulders.

"I've been looking for a little action ever since I found out Freeman was involved. She's a traitor of the worst sort, turning on her sisters to further her own cause. I could use a little combat time."

"Set up an IV in the bedroom," Nico instructed. "I'll try to heal her. Don't worry, bro, we'll get her right."

"I can't do what Dahlia does," Kadan said, "but I'm fairly accurate at focusing energy. I can take a shot at helping you."

Nico nodded and kept working. Ryland added more light while Gator found a mop and a bucket to try to clean the mess.

"What are we going to do about her clothes?" Ryland asked.

Kadan sighed. "She'll run out at this rate. I'll cut off her jeans. They're ruined anyway. She'll have to be ready to go once we take out the team. I'll get her ready, don't worry."

Nico sank back on his heels and wiped his face, smearing it with Tansy's blood. "Get her ready then. Are you set otherwise?"

"No. Rye, you'll have to pack up the war room. Don't touch anything with your skin. Use gloves, double them up if you can. I'll need everything out of there, and be especially careful with the game pieces on the table. She handles those to track the killers."

Kadan lifted Tansy into his arms. She flinched and murmured a protest, instinctively trying to pull away. "Do you have painkillers in that bag?"

"Yeah. Hurry, Kadan. We'll need you for this. They'll be coming in when they think you've gone to bed." He glanced at his watch. "We've probably only got an hour before they come at us." He threw a towel on the bed as Kadan jerked a knife from his boot. "I'll get the equipment, but if she ends up needing a transfusion we could be in trouble."

Kadan appreciated Ryland giving him a few minutes of privacy to strip the bloody clothes from Tansy's body. He cleaned her as best he could and wrapped her in one of his shirts, but left off the sweatpants he'd found in her bag until Nico gave healing a try. He was covering her when Ryland returned with the IV equipment.

They worked fast, pushing the fluids while Nico knelt beside the bed. He unwrapped a crystal from a soft cloth he kept in his pocket. "This is amethyst for focus, Kadan. You want to direct through this. I'll use the rose quartz for healing." He unwrapped the second piece.

"I'll place my hands over the wound and you gather the energy using the amethyst. Try to pull it to you and then focus it over my hands. I've never done this without Dahlia."

"I can do it," Kadan said. He had to do it. He had no choice. "Energy swarms to me, and as a rule I can focus, direct, and even bend it to my will. Give me the image of what Dahlia does and I can grab it out of your head."

Nico extended his hands over Tansy's bare hip, directly over the long gash. He wanted the inside of the torn wound to heal, the tear to repair itself. His hands felt cold, as they always did when he started. He used a Lakota healing chant his grandfather had taught him years earlier, the steady rhythm helping to block out everything around him but the task at hand.

Kadan reached for Nico's exact brain wave, found where

he could merge, and slid respectfully in. He saw the image of Nico's wife, Dahlia, with the two crystals in her hands, and he picked them up, closing his fingers around them. The air around him instantly charged, crackling with electricity as the energy rushed to him, filling him, so that his core temperature rose and, with it, heat invaded the room. The crystals in his hands glowed hot, and he felt a jolt and then the sizzling tingle of an electrical current. He placed his hands over Nico's, palms down, the crystals between them.

The current hit Nico hard, slamming into his body with much more force than when Dahlia conducted. The whip of electricity sizzled through him, white-hot, almost frightening in its strength, and then it jumped back to Kadan. Tiny sparks rained down around them.

"Rein it in," Nico hissed between clenched teeth. "Too much power."

"I'm trying." The heat the crystals gave off burned against his rough palms. He hated to think what that would do to Dahlia's hands.

Kadan took a breath and forced his mind to stay connected with Nico's. He heard the man's heartbeat, the flow of blood through his veins. It took a moment for him to realize it wasn't Nico's heart he was hearing, but Tansy's. He took a breath and called the energy to him again. It swelled in answer, a hot burn that went through him, once again gathering strength, until it boiled and seethed in a violent mass as he focused and aimed it through the crystals. Mimicking the images of Dahlia in Nico's mind, Kadan pressed the amethyst crystal into Nico's hand.

There was a moment, a breath between time. Kadan saw prisms of light burst from beneath Nico's hand and radiate through Tansy's hip. Another beat of time and they were gone, but the heat was there, rising around them, white-hot. Sharing Nico's mind allowed Kadan to feel power uncoiling, shifting and moving, coming from a tight core to spread and grow.

The universe unfurled, stretching out before them, so that both men seemed to become an integral, fundamental part of it. Atoms and molecules burst around them, lights like cosmic stardust beckoned from every direction and gathered inside of them. Power moved through their bodies, sizzling in veins and arteries and even in their brains. Kadan placed the rose quartz in Nico's hand.

At once the force grew, gathering into a huge collective pool of electrical energy. Kadan felt the change in Nico, the sudden focus. Immediately the energy surged toward Nico's hands and the crystals he held. Light burst bright and radiant beneath his palms, saturating the wound, cauterizing the tears, and speeding the healing process. Ghost-Walkers already possessed a natural ability to heal faster, but Nico's healing energy visibly repaired damage.

The flow only lasted a few moments, but the light was blinding and the heat intense. When Nico dropped the crystals back into Kadan's palms, they were warm, almost to the point of being hot. Nico slumped forward against the bed.

"That's all I can do. I hope it's enough. She nicked an artery, and I'm no vascular surgeon. If that didn't repair the damage, she'll have to go to a hospital."

"If that didn't work, no surgeon is going to be able to help her."

"I tried to direct the energy to her artery, but this is the first time I've worked like this without Dahlia, and the power is much stronger coming through you and harder to work with." He glanced up at Kadan. "You're one scary man, my friend."

Kadan shrugged. "I wouldn't mind having your talent."

Gator stuck his head in the door. "Nico, you need to be getting outside. I don't think we've got much time. I hear dogs in the neighborhood acting up, and the word is we've got strangers drifting from house to house."

"'The word is'?" Kadan echoed. "Seriously, Gator, talking to animals is making you nuttier than ever."

Gator flashed his ever present grin and winked. "Yeah, you remember you said that when the animals take over and I rule the world."

"Rule outside, where you can call your army in to help," Ryland suggested.

Gator saluted and followed Nico into the living room, scooping up weapons and ammunition as he went through.

"Do we have a vehicle ready for a quick escape?" Kadan asked as he checked the IV. He crouched down beside the bed, taking Tansy's hand in his.

"We're ready for them. The neighborhood's going to hell though." Ryland went out, turning off lights as he went, plunging the house into darkness.

Kadan pressed his forehead to Tansy's. "You awake, baby? I need you to wake up."

"It hurts. I'm not sure I want to be awake." She'd been aware of Nico sending fire through her body and not much else. Everything around her had taken on a dreamlike quality.

"I'm putting a knife under your pillow. Use it on the enemy, not on yourself." There was a bite to his voice, suppressed hurt under the layer of coolness.

She caught his sleeve and turned her head, her lashes lifting so he could look into her eyes. "I wasn't leaving you, Kadan. It was an accident. Really an accident. I wouldn't do that. I was hurt and upset and angry at my father, but I wouldn't do that to either one of us."

"We'll talk about this later." He pulled out a gun. "Keep this in your hand, and don't shoot me when I come for you. We'll have to move fast when we leave."

"Take the IV out then." She tried to sit up.

His arm was a bar across her chest. "You're going to just lie here and rest while we take care of you. Don't give me any problems right now, Tansy, because I'm willing to tie you to the bed to keep you out of trouble. You scared the hell out of me and I didn't much like it."

"It was an accident."

His hand spanned her throat, tipping her head up. Cold blue eyes stared down at her. "Accidents are fucking out of the question from here on out. Are we straight on that?"

Tansy's eyes searched his. She swallowed against his hard, calloused palm before nodding.

Kadan leaned down to kiss her, brushing feathery kisses all over her face, throat, and neck. When he got to her earlobe, he tugged with his teeth and then pressed his lips against her. "Never scare me like that again. *Never.*"

"I won't."

Kadan didn't much care that he was demanding the impossible. He kissed her again and pushed the gun into her hand. "Don't move until one of us comes for you." He waited until she nodded again before he turned away and strode out of the room.

The moment he was in the living room, he went into warrior mode, gathering his equipment and slipping out of the house through a window. He went up where he could have a better view of the neighborhood and the yard. He didn't want anyone to get close enough to enter the house, or even get where they could fire into the bedroom where Tansy lay. On the outside Kadan had Nico, who could hit anything in his crosshairs, and Gator, who had an army of animals and the capability to walk through enemy lines and dispose of anything coming at him with his knife. Ryland was inside, prepared to evacuate with Tansy at a moment's notice.

"I want a full count, Nico," Ryland's voice hissed in Kadan's ear. "We're taking this one to them. They've been coming at us, and this time we send a message back to Violet. Bring it hard."

Kadan took a long, slow look around. He'd chosen a house far back from the street in a quiet cul-de-sac. The streetlights didn't reach the edge of the property and the nearest house was yards away. Down the street, only a half a block away, was a park, well manicured but with several stands of trees. Behind his house was his escape route, a Jeep trail through an undeveloped lot that dumped into a street near a freeway.

"I have six. They think they're being very stealthy and they're definitely loaded for bear."

"Give me positions," Kadan snapped.

"Six o'clock, between two houses. Coming toward the backyard," Nico responded.

"I've got him," Gator said into his radio. "You can move, Kadan; none of the dogs are going to bark."

"Second man coming over the roof, third house on the right. I've got him marked," Nico droned. "Third running along the fence just about a block away, but coming fast."

"He's mine," Kadan said, and slipped over the edge of the roof, dropping into a crouch in the grass.

"Make the targets quiet, if possible," Ryland said. "Nico, can you hold off on your man until we locate the other three? Once you take your shot, the others will know we're hunting them."

Kadan went through the front yard in a crouching run, using blurring speed. Motion drew the eye, but with the night and their enemies a distance away, he was confident he could make it to cover before he was spotted. He flattened against the SUV parked in front of the house, waiting again.

"Position," he whispered.

"Closing fast, about ten yards."

Kadan went up the side of the SUV and gained the roof, lying flat, knife in his fist. Gator crossed the open meadow at the back of the house, a shadowy figure that flitted from one lone tree to the next, taking him closer and closer to the neighbor's yard. Kadan had always admired the smooth, stealthy way Gator moved. There was never a sound, as if even the wind held back when he was on the move. He could make himself part of anything, until it was impossible to see him when he went still, and then he just flowed like water over rock.

Gator stretched out on the lawn, lying prone out in the open. Kadan marked where he'd gone down, but still had trouble spotting him. Footsteps forced him to look away. His prey was drawing close. He shifted, the movement barely discernible. Out of the corner of his eye he saw the first man emerge between two houses and rush across the open space of the lawn, directly in Gator's path. The Cajun rose up like a specter, his knife hand flashing in a swift slash, across, down, and back up. He stepped back and the body fell forward. Gator was already moving fast for the shadows. The hit had taken less than two seconds.

Kadan concentrated on the runner approaching. He counted the steps, lifting his head to watch the man emerge from the tree line and burst along the walkway coming straight at him. He reversed the knife and threw, using a sidearm technique, keeping from exposing himself at all as he lay flat on the roof of the vehicle. The man staggered backward, clutching at his throat, gurgling. He went to his knees and fell face forward onto the walkway.

Kadan immediately slid from the roof to the house side of the SUV, away from the street, and crouched low to minimize any target he might present. He glanced around in a wide sweep. Nico had his eye to a scope, sighting down on the sniper on the roof several houses down. Behind him a man rose up, all in black, gun in hand. Kadan drew and fired in one swift motion, squeezing the trigger three times.

Nico rolled, came up, rifle to his shoulder, and fired off a round at the sniper. The man went down, his gun skittering across the roof, followed by his body.

"Thanks, bro."

"Four down," Kadan reported.

"Find the other two," Ryland snapped. "No one goes home on this one."

Nico kept rolling to the edge of the roof and disappeared as he leapt to the ground. Gator skirted some hedges and came out fighting hand to hand with a fifth man. It was impossible to get a clear shot at him. Kadan sprinted, covering the distance fast to back the Cajun, just as Gator went inside and sunk his knife into the man's thigh. Kadan shot the man as he lurched back.

"Five, Rye," Kadan reported.

"I've got six. He tried the window. Clean up and let's get out before the cops arrive. We're on the clock," Ryland said. "Gator, don't leave behind any of those mines. Let's move, everybody."

CHAPTER 17

Naughty, naughty girl.

The voice was chilling. It sounded taunting and disembodied, as if coming from a great distance, down a long tunnel, but carrying untold menace and a dangerous threat—of what, she had no idea.

Tansy turned her head to try to catch a glimpse of the speaker, but no one was there. Goose bumps rose on her skin. Fear skittered down her spine. She swallowed hard and remained very still, trying to determine where she was. It was difficult to see; there were no lights, but she had the impression of people moving around her.

She shifted, wanting to find light, but her leg didn't work properly. Her hip and thigh throbbed with pain. A dark, almost inky black substance ran down her leg, in a long stream to pool on the floor. The ink dripped steadily from above her, as if the ceiling was a sieve. One fat drop plopped onto her shoulder. She frowned and tried to brush it off.

It won't come off.

Tansy took another look around her. The walls were

leaking the same inky black stuff. It was sticky and thick. Her feet were covered. *What is it?* she asked, puzzled.

There was a moment of bursting triumph. She felt it resonate through her, a kind of wild elation that was both victorious and smug. She pressed her lips together, determined to remain quiet and not give the hidden watcher more ammunition. She had the feeling he was feeding off her fear, wanting her to recognize his superiority.

Tansy squared her shoulders and forced confidence. If he had to hide his identity from her, he was no doubt concerned about her abilities. All she needed to do was find her way out of this strange maze she seemed to be in. Her feet were weighted down with the thick goo, and it was rising, now ankle-deep. Shadows moved in the ooze. She bent to peer at them. Her father's face stared back at her, eyes wide open in terror, mouth gaping wide.

Tansy drew back, her heart leaping, air slamming out of her lungs. She touched her leg, and her hand came away with the inky blackness on it. She lifted it and saw that it wasn't black, but red. Blood coated her hands.

Daddy!

She reached for him, trying to grip his shoulders, not understanding why he was drowning and she was now only up to her knees. She tried desperately to pry him free, yanking at his shoulders and arms, but he was trapped. She couldn't dive in—her leg refused to move—she could only hold him, watching in horror as the blood rose and he continued to drown right before her eyes.

She heard screaming, the keening wail of anguish, heard her father's last desperate gurgle for air, and then he went under, and she could only hold his shoulders, her arms buried deep, refusing to let him go, even though she knew he was already gone.

Daddy's girl shouldn't be so naughty. Look what happens when she's bad.

The screaming filled her mind, burst through her head, roared in her ears to consume her. She became aware that she was fighting, punching at something solid with her fists, pummeling hard, kicking, and writhing, until something caught her wrists in a vicious vise and slammed her arms hard to the mattress.

"Tansy! Stop. You're safe. It's a bad dream. You're safe. Look at me. Look at me, baby. You're safe, here with me." Kadan's voice cut through the screams.

She realized that she was the one screaming. Her throat felt raw and sore; her heart was beating wildly, her mind chaos. She clung to the sound of his voice, pushing through the layers of her mind. "There's so much blood."

Kadan pressed kisses along her face. "There's no blood. Open your eyes, honey. Trust me. There's no blood."

"My father?" Her voice hitched. She forced herself to pry open her lashes.

Kadan's face was above hers. Real. Solid. So strong. She looked beyond him to see the other three GhostWalkers, guns drawn, crowded in the doorway. She didn't recognize the room, but it was light and there was no evidence of blood anywhere.

Ryland, Gator, and Nico turned and went out, closing the door behind them, leaving Tansy staring up at Kadan's face again. She could see the lines there, the stamp of hard authority, the cut of his mouth, so grim, his eyes, watching her intently, wholly focused on her, but more important, he was there in her mind, filling her up until there was no room for horror and fear.

His thumb slid along her wrists and he reluctantly let go of her arms. "Are you okay now? Let me look at your leg and see that we didn't open that gash."

She remembered the hurried exit from the other house the night before, although she'd been drowsy and suspected he'd put painkillers and something to make her sleep in the

IV. Shockingly, her leg hurt less than her bruised hand. Whatever Nico had done had really helped.

"It's fine." She felt shaky, wanting him to hold her. "I think he was there."

Kadan's gaze jumped back to her face. "He? Who?"

She moistened her dry lips. "The puppet master. I think he found me."

"It was a dream. Last night was very traumatic, Tansy. There was blood everywhere. It stands to reason you'd have a nightmare."

She shook her head. "I think it was more than that. Please make certain my father's all right. He was in my dream, drowning in blood, and I couldn't save him."

Kadan rubbed his chin along the top of her head. *Rye. Check in with Tucker and Ian. I need to know her parents are safe.* It stood to reason she'd have nightmares about her father; after all the revelations, how could she not?

"Rye's calling now, honey." He kissed her forehead and moved back to examine her hip. Her screams still echoed in his mind. He'd known more fear in the last twelve hours than he had since his childhood. "Tell me why you think the puppet master found you. Tell me about your dream."

She did, in a hesitant voice. It occurred to him, as he watched her face, that she didn't expect him to believe her. She must have had nightmares before her breakdown, very similar to what she was suffering now, and no one believed that the voices wouldn't leave her head. She could still hear the victims and their killers long after the police had closed the case. He had to be very cautious in his reaction. Her fingers plucked nervously at the sheet, and that small telltale action tugged at his heartstrings.

"The last dream I had, for one moment I thought I heard his voice, but then it was gone and it was all part of the nightmare. This time I'm sure it was him."

Kadan let out his breath, his mind turning the possibility over. "Can you do that? Talk to one of the killers in a dream?"

She shook her head. "No way. I get impressions, sometimes very strong ones, but it's always of things they've done in the past, not present. The puppet master is a tracker and he can follow my impressions, but he shouldn't be able to enter my dreams."

Kadan frowned, trapping her injured hand beneath his. Her nervous plucking at the sheet was making him want to drag her into his arms and rock her. He needed to stay cool and think. "Have you heard of dreamwalking?"

Tansy sat up. When she did so, Kadan caught her waist and moved her up into a more comfortable position. She didn't protest his help, although her leg didn't hurt that much. She knew, on some level, that he needed to help her, to feel as if he was doing something for her. "I've heard rumors of the talent, but I don't understand it and I certainly can't do it."

"One of the members of our team, Jeff Hollister, is a major talent when it comes to dreamwalking. It's dangerous. If you're killed in the dream, or caught there, you can't get back to your body and it eventually dies. I think it's a very rare talent, but then so is being an elite tracker. We have to face the fact that there's every possibility that the puppet master is a dreamwalker. Nico can also dreamwalk, but he claims Jeff is far stronger."

"How does it work?" Now she was even more frightened. Her fingers tangled with his and clung. "Can he get to me?"

"Maybe, but we've got Nico and I'll get Jeff to come on board. He had a stroke some time back, but he's recovered and has wanted to go on a mission. This might suit him."

"I don't understand."

"They can protect you while you're sleeping, maybe even kill him if we set it up right."

"In the meantime, going to sleep isn't a good idea?"

"Let me talk to Jeff and find out what he thinks. Do you need help getting up?"

She tugged at his hand as he stood. "Thank you for believing me. I could be wrong, but I don't think I am."

"I hope you are, baby, but I'd rather be prepared if you're not." He lifted her off the bed in one easy movement.

"What are you doing?"

"Carrying you to the bathroom so you don't have to walk on that leg."

"No you're not. I'm fine. Really. I'll get dressed and make breakfast, and then we'll try to see what we can find out about the West Coast team. If we're lucky, we can pick up impressions on how the game works and what the stakes are, along with identifying the killers."

"Lily, Rye's wife, and Flame, Gator's wife, are researching the East Coast suspects. It shouldn't be difficult to identify members of teams who took the psych test and served together. If they have a history, and they used those nicknames in the service, then even if they are out now, we'll find them."

"Put me down." She wasn't going in the bathroom with him.

Kadan set her down reluctantly, allowing her body to slide against his, hands skimming down her sides to hold her hips against him. He rested his forehead against hers. "Be sure, Tansy. I don't want to find you on the floor."

"I'm sure." She was even more certain she needed a shower and actual clothes to face the other GhostWalkers after screaming her guts out. "Go make sure my father's okay."

"Don't lock the door."

"I have no doubt if I did and I fell, you'd have no problems breaking it down," she said, teasing him.

Kadan wasn't certain he was in the right frame of mind

to be teased, but he managed a faint smile as she closed the door in his face.

"She all right?" Ryland greeted, snapping closed his cell phone as Kadan entered the room.

"Yes. I want to get in touch with Jeff. We may need him. How's he doing?"

"He's strengthened his right side, that was the damaged side, and he's walking now. The right leg was unresponsive for a long time. He's working out daily, sometimes too much. The tremors stopped in his hand and he's no longer numb in his face. Lily thinks his right leg will always be a little weak, but his talents are stronger than ever. He's had more time than any of us to practice, and Lily was particularly hard on him, working him as much as possible on exercises to keep him from seizing when he uses psychic ability."

"If I needed him for dreamwalking, do you think he's up to it?"

"I'll double-check with Lily, but we're not going to keep him on the sidelines much longer. You know Jeff, he's a kamikaze, high IQ, needs a lot of stimulation. He's thrown himself into his recovery, but he wants action."

"Talk to Lily then. What did Tucker say?"

"Says all quiet, but if you're worried, they can bring in Sam."

Kadan frowned. "Not yet. Let's see how things play out today. She's going to try to lift impressions from a couple more pieces."

"You're not happy about it."

"No, it's dangerous. I might not be able to pull her back if the impressions are too strong. And we've got an enemy we can't identify trying to track her. He knows who she is thanks to the news story. He's smart, this guy. And he's patient. He flies under the radar."

"Is he working for Whitney?"

Kadan shook his head. "It doesn't feel right to me, and

Tansy picked up that he had worked for Whitney sometime in the past. She thinks there's the possibility that he ran the psych testing for the candidates for the GhostWalker program. Can Lily access those files and get us names?"

"She'll try. It's much more difficult. We're using a back door into Whitney's computer as well as searching the computers he left behind, but most of those records were destroyed when the GhostWalker program was supposedly disbanded. No one wanted the news to get out that the government's top scientist, still working for them, experimented on children that he bought and sold. We now know there were more girls than the ones he held at his home. This experiment has been ongoing for too many years, and you and I both know others had to have known about it."

Kadan led the way to the kitchen. Nico had brought in groceries earlier, so there was coffee made. He set about making breakfast. Tansy wasn't going to be standing on her leg, and she sure as hell wasn't serving breakfast to everyone before she handled the game pieces. Ryland pitched in and helped him, and by the time the others came in, breakfast was ready.

Tansy came in, limping a little, very pale, her eyes taking up most of her face, but the fragrance of cinnamon and sin drifted through the air. She was barefoot, wore no makeup, and her mouth was devoid of lipstick. She wore a soft pair of sweats and a thin tank that hugged her breasts, and Kadan thought she was the most beautiful, sexy woman he'd ever seen. He went to her immediately, wrapping his arm around her waist and pulling her against him, inhaling her scent while he dropped a kiss on her upturned mouth.

You smell great. He couldn't say it out loud, not in front of everyone, and he couldn't stop himself from running his finger down the length of her arm, taking in her soft skin. Aloud he said, "Your father is fine."

She looked up at him and smiled. "Thanks."

He craved that look in her eyes. Soft. Loving. Reserved only for him. His hands found her hips and slid upward, shaping her body. She didn't even flinch as his palms caressed her tucked-in waist through the tank, found her narrow rib cage, and went up the sides of her breasts. She wasn't wearing a bra, and he resisted cupping the soft weight, but he couldn't resist teasing her. *No stripping you naked on the kitchen table and having my way with you?*

She nibbled on her lower lip, her gaze holding his boldly. *You'll probably have to wait on that one until we're alone.*

The way her eyes ran over him, touching on the bulge growing in the front of his jeans, had him grinning like a fool—and he rarely grinned.

"Sit the hell down," Ryland growled. "The two of you are killing us."

Kadan pulled out her chair for her, waiting for her to adjust her leg for comfort before sliding into the seat next to her.

"I appreciate all of you for what you did for me last night," Tansy said. "I had no idea those men could find me, and I'm very ashamed of my father for the part he's played putting your lives in jeopardy. Believe me, if I could find a way to repay you . . ."

"You have," Ryland said gruffly.

"I have?"

Gator winked at her. "Yes, ma'am. That goofy look on Kadan's face is worth all the bullets in the world." He leaned across the table toward Kadan and sniffed. "And he sure does smell pretty now."

Kadan hooked his foot around the leg of Gator's chair and jerked, dumping him unceremoniously on the floor.

"Kadan's family. That makes you family," Nico said solemnly, as if nothing had happened. He didn't even glance down at Gator, who sat on the floor, laughing.

"I see," Tansy said.

Kadan dropped his hand beneath the table to her thigh. *Does it hurt?*

She shook her head. *My hand hurts more.*

He immediately took her hand and turned it over to examine the palm. "Take a look at this, Nico. When she took the gloves off, the ivory piece branded into her skin, although it's not a burn. I tried opening her hand to get her to drop the thing, but not even using pressure points helped. I hit her hand on the table edge. Do you think it's broken?"

Tansy attempted to pull her hand away, but Kadan tightened his grip. The men crowded around, looking at the impression of the knife embedded in her palm. Nico turned her hand around and murmured to her to open and close her fingers.

"Her hand's not broken, Kadan, and the impression is fading. How does your talent work, Tansy?"

Again she tugged at her hand, but Kadan kept possession of it, although he did lower her arm, taking her hand beneath the table, out of sight. His fingers brushed back and forth over her palm in long, slow caresses where no one could see.

"I'm not certain. I've had the ability as long as I can remember. I touch something, and I can sense the impressions left behind by anyone who has touched it before me. If it's strong energy, such as violence, the impressions are equally as strong. It's rather like always being in on private conversations."

"So you wear gloves most of the time?"

She nodded. "Always. I don't wear them when I'm camping up in the mountains, but as a rule, unless I want to stumble onto someone's secrets, I'm careful."

"I'm shielding for her," Kadan said. "Which is why she's able to be okay here with all of you and in this house." His fingers continued to stroke her injured hand beneath the table.

"We really should get started," she said.

Kadan sighed. She was right. If he was going to eliminate both teams quickly, he needed this information. "Let's
do it then."

"I'll clean up," Gator said.

"I'm going to button down the house and set up a couple
of escape routes just to be safe." Nico shoved back his
chair.

"That leaves me to talk to the ladies about what they
can give us on your suspects," Ryland added.

Kadan appreciated his friends' discretion. It was difficult enough to watch Tansy suffer while she worked, but
he also knew her inevitable reaction embarrassed her. She
didn't want to try tracking in front of an audience. He held
her hand as they went into the bedroom where he'd set up
the pieces. He'd placed the four pieces side by side on the
dresser.

"Sit. I don't want you screwing up your hip."

She nodded, almost without hearing him. Her gaze was
already fixed on the small, perfectly detailed bull. He kept
his mind in hers, wanting to understand what she was doing so he'd have a better chance of helping her when she
needed him. She was already half-gone from him, tuning
everything out around her but the object that she was going
to handle. She pulled on the gloves almost absently, not
even glancing at him.

There was only Tansy and the ivory game piece and the
information it would yield. Her breathing changed first.
Kadan watched Tansy's face rather than her hands. He
knew the moment she picked up the ivory bull with her
gloved hands. The jolt of violent energy was strong. He felt
it blast through her mind to encompass his. Along with the
violence was a sexual energy that didn't surprise him. Tansy's record of tracking was 100 percent, and if she thought
a piece represented the highly sexual nature of the owner,
he believed her.

"He's very involved in the rodeo. He likes the power of

the bull and craves it for himself. He enjoys his prowess with women. His buddies want the details, and he tries to top his record of several women in one day, all begging for his attentions. He often has a couple of women at the same time. He enjoys that he can get them to do anything he wants more than he actually enjoys the sexual act. He's a total adrenaline junkie, needing the high all the time. The murder doesn't give him his fix, but the idea of getting away with it, the planning, carrying out, and walking away clean—that's the rush for him. The more public, the greater the risk, the better the high."

Her eyes deepened in color, going from blue to violet. He could see the silvery lines begin to form in them, and his belly hardened into tight fist-size knots. She moved farther and farther away from him along the thread of the cowboy, where he couldn't really follow. He could see blurring images, coming and going fast, but his mind's eye couldn't grasp them. He could only pick up the impressions from her.

"This was a chance to pull ahead of Team One. The idiot Stallion couldn't keep it in his pants and lost points for the other team. If he could pull this off, they'd surge ahead. The target was everything they could possibly want. High-profile. In public. The method was up to him, just get the job done. His kind of scenario. The thrill of walking into the courthouse with cameras everywhere and chatting with his target had been amazing. Hell, he nearly came in his jeans. Bodyguards everywhere. Stupid rent-a-cop mentality. Maybe for fun he'd take a couple of them out as well, but he had to make certain it all went down exactly as instructed, making sure the correct targets were taken."

Tansy swallowed hard and forced herself to slow down, to try to make sense of what she was seeing and feeling. "He wants to do the murder publicly; it's almost a euphoric feeling, very sexual, although sex has nothing to do with the crime, even if his target happens to be a woman.

He isn't at all like Stallion, where the murder is all about raping and dominating a woman. It's the thrill all the way with this one."

She took another breath, let it out, and slipped deeper into her hypnotic state. Kadan could see the silver spreading through the violet, so that her eyes began to shimmer. "You loved being in the military and didn't want to leave. Why did you then? You hide your true nature so well. Why? You were forced to leave or you would have stayed on forever. You could do whatever you wanted and not get caught. Oh God."

Kadan saw her hesitate. Her finger began to slide back and forth in a mesmerizing stroke over the back of the bull. "You killed more than one teammate, slipping up behind them and breaking a neck or shoving your knife into their side. You slit the throat of a commanding officer just a few feet from your team just to see if you could get away with it—and you did, blaming it on an enemy you killed. How did he know? No one saw you. No one ever suspected you, yet he knew. Who knew, cowboy, who knew you were a serial killer before you ever played the game? Of course. The puppet master. He knew and he stroked your ego and manipulated you into playing his game. But why? And why did you leave the military?"

Kadan moved closer to her, sensing she was being drawn farther away from him. He didn't touch her, but kept his body an inch from hers, watching her hands now, watching the way she stroked the bull.

"An injury. Something bad. Something we can catch you with. You're on disability. A decorated vet from special teams that rides bulls even though you're on full disability. What is wrong with you? And how did he know you killed?"

She drew a deep, shuddering breath. Kadan stiffened. She was reaching for that other thread, the subtle one that was potentially more dangerous than any other.

"He knew you would kill. He knows you so well. He got you through, got you the . . ."

I have your favorite teddy bear. The one you kept from that old nurse who rocked you at night when your head hurt so bad it felt like someone was pounding spikes through it. Your energy is embedded deep in poor little teddy.

Kadan reacted instantly to that taunting voice brushing at the walls of her mind. He swept his arms around her, shoving his much larger fingers between her thumb and forefinger, forcing her hand open so the bull dropped free. He jerked her around to face him and settled his mouth over hers, kissing her long and deep, pushing himself into her mind, filling her full, so full of himself that there wasn't room for anything or anyone else. He allowed images to fill his mind, to push into hers, images of the two of them making love, hot and sweet and fierce, just the way he was kissing her.

He gave the killers and the victims no chance to settle anywhere, sweeping them aside and staking his claim. Her lashes fluttered, and when he lifted her head, the color was back to violet, the opaque veil gone. He kissed her again.

"We did it." There was a smear of blood by her nose. He removed it with the pad of his finger. "You picked up a lot even through the gloves." Her body was trembling and she still seemed far away, but he'd brought her out of the trance and pushed the killers from her mind. "Let's get you into the other room. You're going to need your headache medicine."

She shook her head, her fingers tightening on his arm. "No. I have to go after another one. I want the one with the faintest impressions. I have to do it now."

She was swaying with weariness, and he could already feel the beginnings of the headache beating at her. They hadn't even debriefed the first game piece or talked about the puppet master. And Kadan sure as hell wasn't going to let her anywhere near that bastard. "It's too soon. You're exhausted and drained."

"Exactly. He'll believe I can't do it again so soon. He won't be looking for me. This is my chance. He's so arrogant he thinks he's way stronger, that I can't possibly find him before he finds me. He went to my parents' home, Kadan. He knows who I am and he went to my parents' home, somehow got in and went through my things. I have a teddy bear I had with me before I was ever adopted. He has it. I'm going to find him now, today. He'll think I'm done and he won't be lying in wait to ambush me."

"I don't like this, Tansy," Kadan said, uneasy with the idea. She was exhausted and shaken; he could feel her body trembling against his.

"I can do this, Kadan." Her eyes met his steadily. "I can. We have a chance to track him right now. It might be our best shot at it."

He took a deep breath and pushed down his need to protect her, his desire to wrap her up and keep her safe from any harm. She wasn't a woman who played it safe, and just as he wanted her to accept his nature, he needed to accept that she was far too courageous for her own good—and he loved her that way.

"Damn it," he said, capitulating. "Which one?"

Tansy leaned against him for strength while she passed her palms above the three remaining game pieces. Energy pulsed off of the scythe and she pulled her hands away quickly. "Move that one for me."

Kadan picked the carved scythe up with a cloth and set it to one side.

Tansy tried again. The two remaining ivory pieces were side by side, so she could judge their potency. The scorpion hit her fairly hard, sending impressions of rage into her mind. She quickly pulled her hand away and stared at the last one—the hawk. "I think this is my best shot at it, Kadan. The others throw off so much violence I get impressions when I'm inches from them. This one is much more contained."

"Let's do it then," Kadan said. He stroked his hand down her back, the curve of her spine, and over her rounded bottom. He didn't know if he touched her for himself or for her, but he couldn't stop the caress. His hands went to her hips, slid up under her shirt, and massaged the ribbon of skin there with the pads of his fingers. "Are you certain, Tansy?"

She nodded. "I'm pretty sure I can get him."

He bent his head to the nape of her neck, scraping his teeth back and forth. "I know you can, baby. Find him for us." She would never know what it cost him to say it, but he forced the words with conviction, when deep inside, his belly was back to knots. He couldn't summon the ice when anything concerned her, not even when he needed it most.

Tansy didn't hesitate. She cupped her hands around the small ivory hawk. Instantly the energy swarmed over and into her mind. Images poured in along with the thick sludge that she'd long ago come to accept with murder. She kept her palms very close, almost brushing the ivory game piece.

He'd drawn a card and the murder was very precise. He had to follow specific steps in order to get the points his team needed, now that they had a real chance to win, thanks to Stallion's screwup. No imagination involved in this one, no creativity. The victims were always picked well in advance, but usually they got to at least choose how they wanted to "do" them.

"You're not happy, are you?" she murmured aloud.

Kadan edged closer to her, skin to skin, wishing they were both naked and he could slide against her, distracting her from being sucked too far down the tunnel where the wailing victims waited and the killer grew stronger.

Tansy tried to push past the killer to find the threat she was looking for, but Hawk was upset. He was a careful

man and he didn't like the way the play was laid out. He
wanted to contact the referee, usually forbidden unless the
murder had to be forfeited. His team members were upset
with him, but they weren't the ones carrying out the details, and it wasn't fair. He was good at what he did, and he
followed every script down to the last detail—until this
one. The instructions were just too precise, and he didn't
like it. The ref was probably trying to get Team One back
into the game after Stallion screwed up so badly.

The Reaper was especially angry, getting in his face.
He wanted to win this round, and when the Reaper insisted
they do something his way, the others always went along.
Well not this time. This was his game and the play had to
be fair.

Kadan stiffened. He knew that name. He'd come across
the Reaper a few years back running a mission in Afghani-
stan. Big man. Competent. Cold eyes and hands like Nico
when he held a gun. He started to tell Tansy, but he didn't
want to break her concentration. He could track the Reaper.
Marine. A lot of combat experience. What the hell was he
doing running with a bunch of murderers? Over the years,
they'd fought a few battles together, and the man knew his
job. Kadan had respected him.

Had he been enhanced? Kadan didn't think so, not at the
time. That had to have come later. The man hadn't been a
stone-cold killer, not then. So did that mean enhancement
could push someone a little twisted over the edge? Jack and
Ken Norton had often speculated about that, along with
some of the other GhostWalkers. Maybe it wasn't the same
man at all. Kadan hoped not; he'd been a good soldier.

Tansy pressed closer to the hawk figurine, allowing her
gloved hand to brush the individual feathers. He refused to
let the Reaper intimidate him; he used the Internet, finding
the guest book the ref had given them to put a message on.
The guest book was a best-selling author's, and only an
automatic reply would get back to him. He would check the

next day for the ref's reply. When it came, Hawk was unhappy. There could be no deviations. Follow instructions exactly or lose all points.

"I've got you," Tansy breathed the words aloud, fighting down excitement. She had to stay calm and not allow any vibrations on that anchor thread that ran to the puppet master. She began a slow, inch-by-inch crawl along the tunnel, desperately trying to ignore the shocked gasps of the victims as Hawk entered the house through a second-story window and, following the dictates of the card he'd drawn, went into the young boy's bedroom first and made short work of him. The two girls were next.

Tansy closed her eyes, her breath ragged as she tried to slip past without looking in, but it was impossible. One child was around eight, the other no more than five. At least he was merciful, not drawing it out. They were dead before they were aware of the intruder. Hawk crept down the stairs, glancing at his watch, careful of the time. The adults were in the first bedroom. He killed the man instantly, before he woke the woman.

Fear burst over Tansy in waves. He taped her mouth and hands and proceeded to stab the dead male repeatedly while she watched, sobbing and pleading, terrified of him. He didn't speak, but grabbed her and dragged her back upstairs, first throwing her on the bed with the little girls, allowing their blood to coat her gown. Tansy could feel his distaste for the task, but he dragged her to the little boy's room and shoved her onto that bed. She was moaning now, in shock, trying to reach her child.

Hawk hesitated, caught the woman by the hair, his distaste for his task growing, but determination won out. He'd gone this far, done everything he was supposed to do for his team. *Your fault, lying, cheating whore. Look what you've done.* He waited until the horror of the repercussions of her infidelity registered, and he took a snapshot of her face, then he shot her between her legs, in both breasts, and finally in her wide-open mouth. *You shouldn't cheat on your husband, bitch, not when he's serving his country.*

Bile rose, but Tansy fought it down. She was too close to lose now. This had been a hit, pure and simple. She was certain of it. She'd seen hits before, knew what they felt like. Hawk maybe wanted to win a game, but somewhere, someone had wanted this victim, this woman, to suffer for her infidelity. This killing wasn't random. Someone had chosen her. "The dead man is not her husband," she murmured aloud, just in case Kadan wasn't following the information she was trying to share with him. "Check, but I know he wasn't her husband. She was having an affair and the husband wanted her punished."

She was looking beyond the murder, focusing on that thread that gleamed like silver, fat and shiny and much thicker than normal. The puppet master had to be in contact with his killers whether he wanted to be or not. He was the "ref." The man running the game. And he was running it for profit. *Contract killings.* He had his own team of hit men, and he played them all like fools. He was military, had been in some way part of the testing. Neat freak. Worked for Whitney. She was close to him now.

Clever, clever girl. I don't usually indulge whims, but you have to learn that bad girls get punished. Mommy and Daddy are going to get a little visit from my friends. The voice was chilling.

Kadan reacted instantly, her safety net, her guardian, standing between her and the man in the shadows. He caught both wrists and yanked her hands outward and away from the hawk, leaving it sitting on the table, a terrible reminder of the killing of an entire family.

"For revenge," she whispered and buried her face in his shoulder.

She was too weak to stand, and as she collapsed he caught her behind her knees, lifting her against his chest. She leaned over and was sick, staining the floor red. Kadan took her through to the bedroom almost at a run. Her skin was clammy, her face nearly gray.

"Tell me what she needs," Nico said, coming up behind him.

"I'm afraid to let her sleep. I think the puppet master is a dreamwalker."

"I have some powder," Nico said. "An old Lakota remedy. It will keep her in a deep sleep and stop any dreams, good or bad. It's been in my family for hundreds of years."

Kadan placed Tansy on the bed and fished quickly for the pills that would help to ease the pain already beating at her skull. She turned away from him, coughing, and there was blood on the pillow.

Nico pushed past him and laid his hands on Tansy's body. "Pull out my crystals; they're in my jacket in the hall closet. Let's make her more comfortable and put her to sleep. No wonder you don't want her doing this. This is tearing her up."

"She got important information," Kadan said, coming back into the room with the crystals, "but the puppet master is definitely tracking her. I have to find a way to guard her dreams."

"Give me some time to heal her with the crystals, and I've got enough powder for a few days. That should give Flame and Lily time to give a direction and we'll eliminate the threat."

Kadan sank down onto the bed beside Tansy, where he could watch over her and help Nico at the same time.

CHAPTER 18

Tansy woke in Kadan's arms. He was wrapped around her so tight she wasn't certain where she left off and he started. He was literally sprawled over her. One thigh lay wedged between her two bent legs, and his arm was around her waist, his hand over her breast. She noticed that even in his sleep he seemed to protect the injured side of her, careful nothing brushed against the laceration. Even the sheet was tented with pillows. He'd thought of everything to make her comfortable.

She didn't remember falling asleep. There had been so much pressure in her head, pain stabbing at her. She couldn't stand the light or any noises. Somehow she'd gone to sleep, and there'd been no dreams, almost a first for her. She rarely slept at night, and now she was afraid the puppet master might find her in her dreams. She'd been afraid to close her eyes, yet dawn was creeping through the window, she felt fine, and she'd obviously slept with Kadan wrapped protectively around her.

She shifted her body experimentally. Instantly his hand

tightened on her breast, his thumb stroking over her nipple.

"Don't move."

His voice was a blend of smoky sex and black velvet. His breath was warm on her shoulder and she felt his mouth skim over her back.

Truthfully, she didn't really want to move. She loved lying in his arms, feeling decadent and lazy, loving her naked body cuddled so tight against his. Every stroke of his thumb sent ripples of arousal from breast to thighs. It was a wonderful way to wake up.

"Where are the others?"

He licked her warm skin, grazed his teeth over her neck, taking his time just nibbling, his eyes half closed while he just absorbed the feel of her. "Does it matter?"

"No." Her answer came out a little breathless. His hips rocked against her, rubbing the hard length of his shaft along the curve of her bottom. The sensation was delicious.

"They went home to their women. Gator's wife is researching, and he wants to see what she found for us. They'll be back soon. I thought it would be better for us to be alone when you handle the other game pieces. I noticed it makes you uncomfortable when they see you afterward, although Nico was a huge help and I've asked him to be certain to be back by this evening."

His hands moved, cupping and kneading her breasts a little more aggressively, tugging at her nipples, rolling them between his thumb and forefinger until she was stiff and aching for him.

She closed her eyes, arching into him. "Thank you for being so thoughtful. I can't help but feel vulnerable afterward, and it is hard to have anyone see me like that. Half the time I don't know what's going on around me. And I'm always afraid I might end up fragmented and institutionalized again."

"You won't. I'll always take care of you."

She smiled at him, aching inside, wanting to believe he would always be with her.

"Stay still, baby." He levered himself over her so he faced her on his side, keeping her injured hip safe from jarring.

She loved his face, the hard angles and planes, his strong jaw with the dark shadow, his sensual mouth and straight nose. Most of all, his dark blue, almost black eyes. He wrapped his arm around her waist and pulled her closer, positioning himself so he had easy access to her breasts. "I love how warm and soft you are," he murmured, tracing a finger along the shape of her lips, down her chin to the valley between her breasts. "I love the thought of eating you for breakfast."

Her womb clenched. Liquid heat pooled. She loved the way he wanted her. His focus was always intense and complete. Wholly on her. He could make her wet just by looking at her.

His tongue teased her nipple, first licking, as if she were an ice cream cone, then harder flicks, before his mouth settled, hot and greedy, sucking strongly. She couldn't stop the ragged cry that escaped, or the way her body involuntarily pushed deeper into the heat of his mouth. He alternated between hot licks, small stinging bites, and sucking, so that her body just kept coiling tighter and tighter and she was left gasping for breath.

She held him to her, cradling his head, stroking his hair, sometimes yanking when another bite sent fire sizzling through her bloodstream. She watched his face, those incredible lashes, the concentration, the lust rising dark, almost frightening in its intensity. She loved that in him—the way he craved her, the way he needed her to give herself wholly to him. He made her feel beautiful and sexy and so wanted. At the same time she was so desperate for his mouth and hands and his body. The mix of emotions was incredibly sensual.

Kadan lavished attention on her breasts, teasing and stroking, his tongue a sensual weapon, his teeth erotic, his hands magic. He kissed his way down the curve of her breast, licking at the underside and trailing more kisses along her rib cage.

"You're so soft and warm, Tansy. I love the way your body responds to me." His hand was well ahead of his mouth, moving down her soft body to the junction at her legs, testing her wetness, her desire for him.

Kadan wanted to take his time and feast, a leisurely exploration of shadows and hollows, finding every hidden sweet spot, every trigger. He wanted an intimate map he could use to pleasure her. And he wanted *this* for himself. This absolute giving to him, her body open to every sensual thing he wished to do, her giving herself to him without reservation. She trusted him; whether it was instinct or not, or the connection of their minds, he didn't know, he didn't care—he knew only that she put herself entirely into his hands and gave him her body.

He moved over her, taking in every inch of her with his hands and tongue, tasting and teasing, dancing his fingers across her body until she was rewarding him with shivers of pleasure and soft moans she couldn't repress. He didn't want her to be silent. He needed to hear every sound, see and feel every response. His teeth raked again at her nipple and she choked out a strangled cry. His tongue flicked and curled around the peak and then drew it into the hot depths of his mouth. Each hard flick of his tongue sent sensations crashing through her, rushing to her womb, where his hand lay over her lower stomach and he could feel heat and the bunching of her muscles, while his mind shared every pleasure.

He licked his way over the slope of her breast again, down through the valley, and tasted cinnamon. Sheer pleasure rocketed through him. There had to be some kind of aphrodisiac in the lotion she used on her satin-soft skin.

His, all his. Every last inch of her. She arched into his mouth, pressing herself deeper. He slid his hand down lower, over her damp mound, his thumb sliding into slick heat, finding her hard bud and rasping over it with the bristles embedded in the pads of his fingers. Her breath came in ragged, breathy little moans, and her hips writhed and bucked in need.

He didn't let the flames licking over his skin or the wildfire burning along his shaft hurry him. He wanted to drive her into a frenzy. He wanted cinnamon candy for breakfast. Her scent called to him, and every nerve, every cell responded. He spread her thighs apart, and looked up at her. She looked sultry, face flushed, eyes glazed with a hot, desperate hunger. He lowered his head.

His tongue lashed at her, sending lightning whipping through her body, white-hot, threatening to consume her. Tansy nearly bucked from the bed, but his arms pinned her down and he continued his greedy feast. His teeth scraped and tugged, his tongue teased and probed, and then his fingers joined in.

She cried out, unable to stop the pulsing pleasure pounding through her. Lightning zinged from breasts to womb, spilling more cinnamon candy into his marauding mouth. He took her up, winding her into a tight coil of desperate need, until there was only heat and fire and the sinful ecstasy of his tongue and teeth.

He pressed tight against her hard, aching bud, and the sensations heightened; flames flashed like a firestorm, and she lost her breath and most of her mind.

"I love the way you taste," he murmured, licking at her hungrily.

His fingers plunged and curled, pressed deep and stroked, driving her wilder, pushing her to the very edge of the precipice, but never quite allowing her over it. She teetered there, reaching for the orgasm, but he refused to give it to her, drawing the pleasure out on a torturous rack until she shuddered and moaned and heard herself begging for release.

"What is it you want from me?" He breathed fire into her spasming womb.

"Please, Kadan . . . *please*." All she could do was writhe under his wicked mouth.

"Is this what you want, baby?" He rewarded that breathy plea. His fingers pushed deep, right through the tight folds. She could feel her muscles grip desperately. And then his mouth was on her tight, hard bud, already inflamed with need, and he suckled while his fingers thrust deep. He used the velvet bristles on the pads of his fingers ruthlessly, twisting against her swollen, sensitive nerve endings, and she screamed, her body clamping down in a vicious spasm, again spilling cinnamon candy into his waiting mouth.

He kissed the insides of her thighs and her stomach, then leaned down to lick at the offering still spilling around her rippling sheath, before he came up onto his knees and pressed the broad, flared head of his shaft into her hot, slick entrance.

"Easy, baby," he whispered when she arched into him, trying to impale herself on the thickness. "You're so fucking tight. Let your body accept mine." He worked his way through her soft folds while her muscles gripped and strangled, nearly milking him right then.

"I need . . ." She couldn't get anything out. She just desperately needed to be filled.

"I know what you need."

He sank deeper and deeper into her folds, until he was buried completely and his tight balls rocked against her buttocks. The sensation only added more flames, burning hotter, scorching them both. He blanketed her body, stretching out, wanting every inch of her skin against his. His lips found her throat, his hands her breasts, fingers sliding possessively as he licked at her pulse and nibbled his way to her mouth.

He rocked his hips gently, pressing down, the thick length of him rubbing along her swollen, stretched muscles, sending more lightning shooting down her thighs and up her belly to her breasts. His fingers pinched and tugged at her nipples, so that the lightning forked out and shot back to her clenching, slick sheath. She shuddered beneath him. And then he filled her mind, flooding her with everything him.

She pulsed around him, her body relaxing a little as her muscles became used to the stretched, burning feeling of his penetration. He took a long, slow stroke, pulling back and driving through the tight folds. Instantly electricity sizzled and arced through her as his shaft rubbed against engorged flesh. She gripped his upper arms as he levered himself over her, keeping that slow, steady, torturous rhythm that brought her right to the edge again, but kept her from falling.

Kadan looked down into her face, into her eyes. She was his. It was there in the depths of her gaze. That unconditional giving of her body to him. More than her body. Each slow stroke of his shaft, driving through the stranglehold her muscles had on him, sent waves of pleasure rocking through him, but this was so much more. When she touched him, when she was with him like this, the cold of his soul was gone completely. She brought heat and fire and melted the ice, or at least pushed the monster in him so far down he couldn't find it. She gave him her warmth, her heat, so that they burned together. So that he was alive.

Tell me you love me. Say it out loud. He kept the same torturous rhythm, while her body writhed under his and her hips bucked upward, desperate for relief. *Say it, Tansy.*

Her hands caught his face. Her gaze stayed locked on his. "I do love you. Every part of you. Can't you feel it when I give myself to you? Feel me, the way I need you."

She moved her body in little circles, squeezing her muscles, so that it felt like velvet fists massaging and kneading his sensitive shaft, suckling at him like a tight mouth, hotter than hell and just as sinful. He heard his own hoarse cry mingling with her ragged moan, and he gave up all pretense of control. He thrust hard and deep, over and over, his hips in a frenzy, reaching for the ecstasy, racing toward it. His head felt like it might explode, his blood boiled, his balls drew tight and hard, and still he pounded into her.

He drove deeper and harder, over and over, because she loved him and, God help him, he needed that love—was desperate for it, desperate to show her how he felt in return. He felt her tighten around him, and he gripped her harder, holding her helpless, pinned beneath him while he drove into her again and again. Her mouth opened wide and her eyes went opaque. She screamed and her body pulsed and clamped down, ripping his seed from him, suckling so strongly the sensation washed up his spine and nearly exploded out his skull. She drained him, taking every hot pulse of his body and milking him for more. Her body shuddered again and again in rhythm with the powerful jerking of his. Her womb rippled and convulsed around him, gradually lessening in strength and then fading as they lay together, gasping.

Kadan collapsed over her soft body, fighting for air. He nuzzled her throat as he rolled to the side, one arm still tight around her. He'd never come like that before in his life. He'd never felt that surge of love and emotion tied so tight with lust and desperate need. He'd never even imagined he could feel like that, and a part of him didn't trust such good fortune. She'd said she loved him, but he was in her mind, and there was something he couldn't quite put his finger on that shook him.

He kissed her again, wanting to be whole, wanting all doubts gone, and not certain how to achieve that when he couldn't find the way through sex.

"When I can walk, I'm going to take a long, hot shower," she announced.

He bent his head to her breast, pulling the soft mound into his mouth. He suckled for a moment and then bit down, needing to leave his mark. She gasped, a soft little cry of protest, her body arching closer to him, but she didn't stop him, rather her hands caressed his hair while she held him to her as if she knew what he was doing.

Kadan, standing in the doorway of the living room, watched Tansy through half-closed eyes. She sat curled up on the couch, legs drawn under her, long hair sliding around her body like so much silk. As usual, she hadn't bothered with makeup and she was barefoot. She wore his button-down-the-front shirt and he could just see the outline of her breasts and the darker nipples through the thin material. There was something very satisfying seeing her in his shirt and knowing she wore little beneath it but his mark.

If he crossed the room and took her to the floor, he had the feeling she'd be more than willing, even though she was exhausted. She sipped at her tea and flipped through a magazine, but her eyes, when she lifted them to his face, had more violet than blue in them, and he suspected her mind wasn't on him—or the floor. Her brain was fitting pieces of the puzzle together. Or maybe it *was* on him and he was coming up short.

"You okay, baby? I ended up being a little rougher than I intended." He rubbed his shadowed jaw and knew her thighs were chafed. He needed her back with him; he was not yet willing to have her go down that dangerous path again. Nor did he want her thinking she might do better than be with a man who had done nothing but bring chaos back into her life.

"I'm better than fine." She smiled up at him, but there was something sad in her eyes and her smile was wistful.

His heart did a funny twist in his chest, and deep inside,

everything stilled. Even the way she sipped at her tea was sexy to him, and yet she seemed so far away, as if she was distancing herself. The one thing he couldn't have with her, the one thing he would never be able to live with—was distance.

He leaned one hip against the wall, his eyes never leaving her face. "I can't remember ever having a home. I never expected to have my own woman or live in a house with her." He crossed his arms over his chest and regarded her without blinking, using his cool, catlike stare. "When this is over, are you going to marry me?"

He had her full attention now. She blinked rapidly and her lips parted slightly. He had the urge to kiss her, but he stayed where he was, never taking his eyes from her face.

"You already asked me that question and I said yes."

"No, I told you we were going to get married. I bullied you until you said what I wanted to hear. I want to know if you're really going to marry me."

Her tongue touched her full lower lip, the pouty one he often found himself staring at. She remained silent, a little shell-shocked, and although he knew he shouldn't, he touched her mind, needing to know what she was thinking.

She had been in a hospital for several months after a breakdown. It could happen again. What kind of genetics would she pass to her children—their children? Would he even want children with her? And her father, what about him? She had to wear gloves almost all the time, would that become an embarrassment? What about her work? She loved being far away from people, where she could just exist in peace. What about his work? He was a born warrior and would never be happy doing anything else. How much time would they have together?

More than anything she wanted to be with him, but was it right for him? Could she do that to him? Be selfish and take what he was offering her even though she had no idea what could happen . . .

"Stop."

Her gaze jerked up to his. She looked frightened.

"Can you love me the way I am, Tansy? Can you live with a man like me? That's what you should be asking yourself, not all that other nonsense."

"How would we live?" She sounded sad, almost forlorn. Her fingers wrapped around the tea mug until her knuckles turned white. "Like this? On the run? As long as you're with me, you'll never have a real home, Kadan. Whitney isn't going to stop and we both know it."

"You didn't answer my question. Can you love me the way I am?"

"You know I already do, but that isn't the point, Kadan. You push so hard sometimes, and whether you think so or not, my concerns are legitimate. You'll wake up one day and wonder why you ever wanted to be with me."

"So it's settled then. You'll marry me. Say it."

"I already said it."

"Well say it again. I want to hear commitment in your voice this time. For me, divorce is not an option. I want that same commitment from you. No matter what happens, no matter what we face, we do it together. We fit. You fit me and I don't want to be without you. I don't like you sitting over there, mulling over whether or not you're going to stay with me once we're done here. I want to absolutely know you're mine—that there's never a question, never a doubt that we belong. So tell me. Say it out loud."

Tansy kept her gaze on his face. He sounded so tough. So hard. His face could have been carved of stone, his body sculptured from steel, so very still. When he ceased all movement, he became part of his background, every part of him completely motionless—waiting. For her. He looked as if whatever she said didn't matter, as if she couldn't shatter him into a million pieces, but his mind was in hers and she knew better. She knew air might be flowing through his physical chest, but deeper inside, where ordinarily he was safe from anyone seeing him, he was holding his breath—waiting. For her.

"I love you, Kadan. I want to be with you always. And I don't bully so easily. I'm not afraid of you, and no one pushes me anywhere I don't want to go. I'm committing myself to you—to us. So yes, I'll marry you when this is done. I have no idea what kind of future we'll have, but even if I only get a small part of you, I'll have the best part."

Kadan couldn't move even if he'd wanted to. For a moment he had the strange sensation of falling on silken sheets and into her warm, soft body, of sharing her skin and sliding into the sheer intimacy of her mind. Everything in him settled.

"Okay." It was the briefest of words.

He had no idea what else to say. He could show her, but he couldn't say it. She didn't seem to mind. She flashed a sassy grin at him, just as if she caught glimpses of how much she meant to him; he hoped so—she deserved to know.

"At the end of the day, when we sit in our rocking chairs, Tansy, and watch our grandchildren play, I can promise you, being with me will have been worth it." Because he was going to devote himself to making and keeping her happy, and in a lot of ways he was very single-minded.

"Are we going to have grandchildren?"

"I want everything. I never thought I would have a home or a family, and with you I have both, but you made me want it all. Lots of grandchildren."

She took another drink of tea and regarded him steadily over the cup. "And when you're off doing your thing with the boys, am I going to be at home alone with the children?"

He wasn't going to lie. "This is who I am. I can provide

a safe home with others like us, with GhostWalkers. We all help one another. You won't be alone, but I'll be leaving for short periods of time frequently and we have to live in a safe environment. We have no choice."

"I don't worry about being alone. I'm good at it. When you're gone, I can do my photography work up in the mountains." She flashed him a small, seductive smile. "You can come looking for me."

"You can stay where I put you," he corrected. "During the times I'm gone, you won't be able to go to your parents, where I can't protect you and our children from Whitney or anyone else who might want you for their own reasons."

"That makes sense when we have children, but certainly before, I can still work."

His jaw tightened. "You can be in a safe environment."

"And my photography?" Her voice dared him to tell her she couldn't do something she loved.

"When I come back, we'll both go. I'm good at carrying equipment. Trained for years in it. I'll have dinner ready when you get back to camp every night."

Her eyes lit up, and he knew he wanted to see that look on her face for the rest of his life.

"Good then." She surprised and pleased him, capitulating without further argument, as if she knew that when it came to her safety, he couldn't compromise. "I'm not into big weddings, but I'm a fairly traditional girl, and torturing you with a formal dress and tux sounds like a good idea, just so we start off right."

He blinked. A muscle ticked in his jaw and there was no way to stop it.

Her smile widened.

"You aren't nice."

"Just making sure you know what you're in for." She tilted her chin a little with a mixture of challenge and defiance. "Did you tell Tucker and Ian the puppet master threatened my parents again?"

"Of course I did. We've stepped up security. Three more of my team members are arriving today to help Tucker and Ian, although the location is secure and I doubt they'll really need it. I wanted you to feel comfortable with their security. Did you want to call your mother today?"

She looked away from him, carefully setting the tea mug on the end table and plucking at imaginary threads on her jeans. "I think I'll wait another day or so."

"She'll be worried about you," he persisted. "You've always called her. Your mother is as much a victim here as you are, Tansy." He kept his voice low and gentle, a stroking caress rather than judgment.

"I know she is. I just don't know what I'm going to say when she wants me to talk to my father. I'm not ready for that, and I don't want to say or do anything that would hurt her."

He wanted to argue with her. The longer she waited, the harder it might be for her, and if she didn't call, her mother would become more upset and probably ask more questions, but her hurt was too raw, too painful, and he let it go. He'd force the issue another time for her sake, but not now, not when she was so pale and her eyes looked like two bruises. He crossed the room and took the seat at the opposite end of the couch, reaching for her bare foot and pulling it into his lap so he could begin a gentle massage.

"Are you up to giving me details about the puppet master and Hawk? I've been compiling notes and we have quite a bit already." He worked his fingers along her heel and up into her ankle and calf. "Once we finish that, I think I can find the others just by identifying the ones we already have."

Tansy's face stilled; her gaze jumped to his face, and any semblance of a smile was gone.

"No. We're not done until I handle every piece and

gather as many clues as I can. We have to be certain who these men are. We can't take a chance of identifying the wrong person, or leaving one of them out there to kill more people."

"I'll find them," he said, his voice confident.

Her eyes flashed silvery violet, and she drew her leg back toward her, trying to get her foot back. His fingers tightened around her ankle, holding her in place. Tansy shoved her hair over her shoulder and glared at Kadan. "My leg is injured, not my brain. Quit treating me like I'm about to break in half."

He appeared unmoved, other than lifting an eyebrow. "Maybe I'm the one about to break in half. The last thing I need is for some freak to be trying to play mind games with you." While one hand held her tight, the other began to massage her foot again.

Her glare deepened into a scowl. "This isn't about you. We're supposed to be finding killers, remember? If I can handle it, then so can you."

His hands stilled on her foot, his eyes darkening like a thundercloud. "You're feeling very sure of yourself now that you think I can't—or won't—retaliate."

Her heart jumped. She had been sure of him, of the way he was treating her like a porcelain doll. A ghost of a smile teased her mouth before she could stop it. She liked this side of him, all ferocious and ready to pounce. "You won't."

He leaned forward, hand spanning her throat. "Maybe not this minute, but your hip will heal soon and then you aren't going to be so lucky."

She turned her face into his palm, scraping at it with her teeth and then pressing a kiss in the exact center. "I'll be lucky. Whatever you do, I think I'll end up enjoying it."

Her voice sank into his groin, hardening his shaft so that his jeans were suddenly far too tight. Worse, she was right. What was he going to do to her? He'd never strike her, and if he tried anything like turning her over his knee, it wouldn't be a punishment, not the way his body went hard the moment he touched her. He couldn't even say he'd withhold sex—he'd never last.

Heat slid into his brain at his next thought, and he shared it with her. *I'll spend all night just bringing you close and never letting you get off.*

She blushed, just the way he'd known she would, the color creeping up her neck into her face. She looked slightly shocked, a little too innocent, and very much as if she believed he might actually resort to his threat. "You're so wrong, Kadan." She couldn't wipe the goofy smile off her face, and that would just encourage his perverse behavior. *You're probably very capable of using sex to control me, and worse, you'd probably enjoy yourself while you were at it.*

I'd say the probability was extremely high.

Why that would make every nerve ending in her body come alive, she didn't know. "You're so wrong," she repeated, shaking her head. "Seriously, Kadan. You have to understand me. There's something in me that can't let this go now, not until it's done. I've always been like that. My mind won't leave it alone."

"It's getting too dangerous."

"It was always dangerous. You know that. You knew it when you came looking for me and when you offered to let me out of this entire mess. Nothing's changed since then."

"Everything's changed." His jaw tightened. "I . . ." The damn word wouldn't come out, but his heart hurt, gripped in a vise. Everything had changed. Before he'd had nothing to lose; now he had everything to lose, and everything was sitting right beside him on the couch.

"Kadan." Her voice went soft, silky, sliding over him like the touch of her fingers. "Life is a risk. You know that better than anyone. You have to be who you are, a warrior, a man who risks everything to serve others. I have to keep doing what I do. I chose this path and I'm on it now. I can't be less than who I am any more than you can."

"Damn it, Tansy, you're asking me to risk *your* life. Your *sanity*. You didn't see yourself last night when I carried you bleeding to bed. You had a seizure and you couldn't even open your eyes or stand noise. If Nico hadn't been here, I have no idea what I would have done."

She waited a heartbeat, just looking at him. Once his eyes locked with hers, she leaned toward him. "I love you, Kadan. I'm not going anywhere. For the first time in my life, I've been able to touch someone without wearing gloves. I've been able to use my talent again when I thought I'd never be able to. Yes, immediately afterward, I'm having repercussions, but the exercises you've given me are working. I don't have the headaches constantly and I can sleep at night. To me, you're a miracle. You always will be. Tracking is important to me. I want to be able to do it when I need to, and I believe I can get to a place, with your help, where I can. Until we figure it out, of course we're going to run into some rough patches . . ." She paused when he made a derisive growling sound, but then continued. "I want to be able to help too, to give back and stop murders when no one else is able to do it."

"I don't like it."

"I know you don't. I don't like you putting your life on the line either, Kadan, but I understand why you need to do it, because I have the same drive."

He shook his head. "I don't have anything else. I could never make it in normal society. We both know that. You've seen inside of me. You recognize what I am. You, on the other hand, have a million other things you can do."

Tansy leaned back in her seat. "You know one has nothing to do with the other. You're arguing because you're afraid for me."

"And for me. I can't lose you."

"Then you'll just have to find a way to protect me. I

believe in us. You brought me back so much faster this last time, and I was really far in. We're getting better and better at it. I think the stronger we are as a couple, the stronger a team we'll be when I track."

"I'm never going to win any arguments with you, am I?"

"Probably not, not when it's something that matters to me, but I won't argue with you often," she promised.

"This would work much better if you just did everything I said, Tansy."

She flashed him another smile. "It's going to work just fine."

"All right then." He managed to keep his face entirely blank, but his fingers sank deeper into her calf, massaging her muscle. "Let's get this done. In order for me to eliminate both teams successfully, as well as the puppet master, we have to have all the identities and try to get them all in the same day. As for the puppet master, he's going to be the most difficult, but I have an idea."

"Did someone go to the site of the snake's murder and hunt for a camera? That was a huge mistake on his part."

"We're on it. Let's profile the last two, and if we get as much information as you did last night, I should be able to start hunting them as early as tomorrow. Lily and Flame are both researching for us, and I can put both of our GhostWalker teams on standby. They'll all help. Time will be everything."

"Do you want to go into the kitchen?"

"No. I'll bring the last two pieces in here. And your gloves. I'll get Nico's powder and your pills too." He set her leg carefully aside as he stood.

He needed to take a breath where she couldn't see that just the thought of her touching those game pieces made him break into a sweat. He had thought that he could control her, control the situations they were in, but he was finding having a partner meant giving up some of his control.

She sat in the same place, her chin on her drawn-up knee, looking too fragile to go after killers, but he knew she wasn't; she had a steel rod for a spine and more heart than most. When he handed her the gloves, she tangled her fingers with his.

"Kadan. Kiss me."

He didn't hesitate, leaning down to capture her mouth with his, loving her, tasting her fear, her belief in him. He cupped her chin and took his time, savoring her taste, knowing she needed him inside of her the same way he needed her. Then, because he couldn't resist, he opened a few buttons of the shirt she wore—*his* shirt—and leaned down to bathe the mark he'd made on her with his tongue before pressing kisses over it. He felt her shuddering breath, and something in him eased.

He carefully buttoned her up again. "Tell me what you're planning."

"I'll find him this time and try to observe, but at some point he'll spot me. I'm going to let him and see if he makes a mistake." She rested her forehead against his. "Hang in there with me. I know it will be hard, but just trust me. I'll need you."

He had to be honest. "I don't know if I can, but I'll try."

"This time, you hold the piece in your palm, be the table. I'll cover it with my hands and try to pick up impressions. If I have to, I'll touch the top of the piece and see what I get. That way, you can remove it the moment it's necessary."

Kadan liked the plan. He controlled the situation, and he needed to feel in control when she was putting herself in danger. He nodded and settled himself next to her while she pulled on the gloves.

Tansy took a breath, let it out, and laid her palm over Kadan's open hand where the ivory scorpion lay, tail poised to sting. Waves of rage poured over and into her, flooding her mind. Anger pulsed through her and with it the desire to strike back, hard and ugly. Hurt something. Someone. She had the impression of a woman cowering on the floor crying. A child in the doorway sobbing.

His head hurt, the pressure unbearable. He didn't want to hurt them. Not them. What had he done again? He tried not to hear the sounds of their weeping. She would leave him this time. She *should* leave him. Next time he might kill her, and he never wanted it to be her. He needed to find the others, tell them he had to go next, take a turn out of order if necessary, or move his timetable forward. *He couldn't hurt her ever again.*

The others understood him, the terrible voices that drove him. Maybe he would have been okay if he'd stayed in the military, but somehow he'd lost control of his temper. Every day, it just seemed to escalate until he couldn't stop rampaging. One wrong word and he had to pound something; if he didn't obey the voices, the pain in his head was unbearable. The satisfaction of feeling his fist slamming into flesh was becoming too short-lived. Now he needed to take it all the way when this happened. He had to find someone to pour his rage into—but not *her.* Never her.

He gathered her into his arms, rocking her back and forth, trying to comfort her, trying to comfort himself. There was blood on his hands—*her* blood. He'd gone to three counselors, but nothing helped, certainly not the medicine they'd given him. If he touched her again, he was eating a bullet. He had to find a way to stop the rage that consumed him. His head hurt so bad, vises squeezing until he thought his head would explode. And the voices, whispering all the time, telling him he was nothing. And that one voice that never let up, not for a moment.

Angela, I'm sorry. Take Tommy Jr. and go to your par-ents. Get the hell away from me until I figure out what's wrong. He needed to say it out loud. She probably feared leaving him. And he was afraid too. If she left and he got angry, there was no telling what he'd do. He wept silently, terrified for all of them, but the pain in his head was relent-less, and he needed to find someone to pound until the hurting stopped . . .

Tansy frowned. The faint whispers in his head held a familiar cadence. Was the puppet master actually taking part in driving this man to murder? He wasn't like the oth-ers she'd tracked. This man was ashamed and scared and filled with remorse. He was desperately fighting to keep from giving in to the madness. He had a wife and child. He didn't want to harm anyone, but he couldn't stop himself. The voice and the relentless pressure in his head caused ter-rible rages. Was the puppet master the voice?

"Don't," Kadan cautioned. "Don't give him any more to track you with." He watched her eyes, the way he always did. She was moving further away from him, the violet completely taking over the blue and the silver encroaching on the violet, until her eyes shimmered with that strange opaque that signaled she was deep inside the tracking lane.

Tansy didn't respond, didn't act as if she heard him. Her mind was completely focused now. He couldn't follow her, only read her thoughts, and she was on the thread of that voice. It was faint, the strand so thin, but razor-edge sharp, a bite cutting into the walls of Scorpion's mind, causing pain and enraging him with the relentless pressure. She stayed very quiet, letting her mind travel along the thread, careful not to disturb it until she found the second thread that led directly to her prey interlocking with the first.

Impressions swamped her mind. A shed. Benches and tables with cutting tools. A man sitting, his hands busy shaping the perfect piece. A masterpiece, museum-quality really. Few could ever top his skills in carving. Each detail so precise. He peered at the specimens gathered around him. Drawings. The live one in the glass cage. The dead one pinned to the table. Scorpions of various sizes. He needed this one perfect. It took work and discipline, but he had never minded either, rather he valued the traits.

This one had probably been a mistake, but he'd had no real choice at the time. Scorpion had maybe one to two more murders in him and then he'd probably kill himself. He didn't like making mistakes. He placed his tool on the table and moved it a couple of centimeters. Precise. Absolutely precise. Tansy drew in her breath sharply. The puppet master had OCD. His work shed was immaculate, every tool labeled and placed in an exact, designated spot. Nothing was out of place. Even the shavings were caught in a small container, so that not a speck was on the table or the floor of the shed.

This was his private residence and she doubted if it was on base. She tried to look around to see anything that might identify where he was. The longer she stayed, the better the chance of alerting him, but she wanted to give Kadan something more to go on.

She could make out windows, four panes darkened, but she could still see out. He must have been looking outside while he carved the ivory. He was humming off-key. And he was "pushing" at Scorpion, slashing at his mind with deliberate, painful strokes to provoke him. The man had no filters, and too much testosterone flooding his body, making him more aggressive than normal, his genetic altering deliberate.

A mistake. He made another careful cut into the ivory. He had chosen Tommy because he was already aggressive. His psychic talents were already strong as well, but like the others, Tommy had failed his psychological profile, not, like the others, due to his violent tendencies, but Tommy had them, buried beneath the surface. He'd thought he could bring the aggressive tendencies out and manipulate Tommy as easily as he did the others. He'd been wrong. *Wrong.* He detested mistakes and never allowed them, yet Tommy was living proof. He should have listened to his instincts and waited just a little longer to find the right candidate.

Tansy stroked a finger along the back of the scorpion, following the movements of the puppet master's fingers. Up the curved tail, feeling each groove. There was something there. *A watch.* A very distinctive watch.

You're getting to be a nuisance. Or maybe you're just lonely. Are you lonely, Tansy? Tell me where you are. Talk to me. I tried to visit you, but no one was home. Are you going to be waiting for me?

Tansy forced down fear and stayed still, breathing in and out, following the pattern of Kadan's breath. Kadan was there in her mind; she felt him, yet he didn't yank her out of the situation as he always had done. He waited with her, believing in her, and that gave her the confidence to carry out her plan. She wanted to keep the puppet master talking, hoping he would make a mistake while trying to draw her out.

He believed himself stronger, a better tracker, but she didn't think so. He manipulated eight men, but he didn't track killers. She'd been doing it for years. His ego was going to be his downfall.

I know you can hear me. Are you enjoying our little game as much as I am? I've found out quite a bit about you. Things you probably don't know about yourself. I have access to several very secret files. I'd share if you were interested.

Deliberately she stirred, sending a vibration along the thread, somewhere between apprehension and curiosity, spinning her spider's web to catch herself a fly. The puppet master would want to talk. He'd never had the opportunity to show off before. This was his big chance. He couldn't let her live long, of course, but while she was alive, he could share his superiority. Someone would know.

Tansy let him make the connection stronger, sending his energy back along the thread to find her. And with his energy came more information. She saw the box on the table, the bold, precise lettering. James R. Dunbar.

Kadan opened his hand and dropped the scorpion. They had him.

CHAPTER 19

Kadan sat at a small booth in the bar, Jeff Hollister and Gator across from him. Nico had already staked out the high ground just in case they needed backup. Jeff was a California boy, born and bred for surf and fun, with his bleached blond hair, dark tan, and ripped body. He looked at home in the bar, a trendy place overlooking the crashing waves below. Directly behind Kadan sat his prey, drinking a cup of coffee and reading a newspaper.

"You're always braggin'," Gator said aloud. "You're so full of shit. No one can hold their breath underwater that long, bro. Fifteen minutes, what a crock."

Jeff hitched forward. "I heard of a guy, local legend around here, owns a scuba business. Rumor has it he can hold his breath easily that long."

Kadan snorted loudly, derisively. "Talk about a braggart. I heard of that airbag. Talks himself up so people go to his business, but I could outlast him any day of the week. On my worst day that blowhole couldn't compare." He shoved himself away from the table, standing. "I'm going to start my own business and run his ass right outa this town."

Jeff and Gator laughed at his joke and Kadan waved and sauntered off. Behind him, he heard a chair scrape and felt the other man following close. Kadan went out into the night and inhaled, dragging information into his lungs. Frog had taken the bait, if it was Frog, and Kadan was certain Flame and Lily had found their killer. He was ex–Special Forces, had applied for the psychic enhancement, supposedly been turned down, but had disappeared for special training for months. He'd resurfaced with a team and run some missions, but his team had a bad reputation for trouble. In the end, he had been discharged and now ran a scuba diving business for tourists.

Kadan paused with his hand on the door of his SUV, to light a cigarette, something a diver wouldn't do.

"Hey, man." Frog came up beside him. "I heard you inside, talking about free diving. I do a little of that. I like to go down without gear."

Kadan grinned, a cocky smirk. "Gear's for wimps."

"I've got a boat right on the dock," Frog persisted when Kadan turned away. "You want to go man-to-man and see who can hold their breath longer? Or are you scared?"

Kadan allowed his face to darken and his eyes to smolder. "No one can beat me under the water. I'm a fucking fish."

"I'm a shark. So let's do it."

Kadan slammed his door shut and snapped away the cigarette he hadn't smoked. He didn't bother to look around; he could feel the GhostWalkers, his team, closing in to back him up. He went with the ex-SEAL, following him along the dock until they came to a high-powered boat. He stepped on without a qualm, showing off a little, that same cocky smirk on his face.

"You really think you can beat me?" Kadan asked.

In answer, Frog started the boat and took off over the

waves to open water. They passed a small fishing boat just a few miles offshore and Frog killed the engine. Without a word he stripped off his shirt and tossed his shoes aside. He waited for Kadan to do the same before he started the boat again and began angling it back toward a small inlet.

He slowed the boat considerably, weaving through the water as if going through a minefield. Kadan glanced into the water and his gut tightened. A small colony of the dead stared back at him. This was Frog's own private playground. Frog stopped the boat, reached into a cooler, and swung around.

Kadan was on him before he could complete the turn, catching the wrist of the hand with the small needle protruding through his fingers. "What's wrong, Frogman? You have to drug me to beat me? I'm not one of your civilians who trust you."

"Who are you?" Frog demanded.

Kadan held him close. "The executioner." The knife concealed in his other hand came up, sweeping across Frog's throat, cutting deep. He shoved the body face-first into the sea, right over the top of the man's victims as they stared upward just inches from the surface of the water. Kadan wiped the knife clean, slipped it into the sheath, retrieved his shirt, and tied his shoes around his neck before going into the water. The fishing boat picked him up. Nico gave him a hand into the boat.

"At least seven victims in the water. We need a cleaner in here fast," Kadan said.

"I already radioed them," Nico answered.

"One down," Kadan announced.

Kadan lifted binoculars to his eyes and stared down at the woman walking out of the bar, her legs showing to their best advantage in a short tight skirt and high heels. She had a sway that said she was on the prowl and a body that promised heaven. Her husband, Ken Norton, stood a foot away from him, a scowl on his scarred face as he watched his wife open the door to a sleek little low-slung car.

"He took the bait," a voice droned into the radio.

That would be Jack, Ken's twin brother. Both men were GhostWalkers from the SEAL team and lethal with or without a weapon. Both were protective and possessive, and Kadan couldn't believe his ears when Ken announced that his wife, Marigold, was going to lure the Italian Stallion out into the open for them.

A very handsome man, large and well muscled, followed Mari from the bar, gliding across the parking lot fast, coming up on her from behind. He grabbed her arm and swung her around, slamming her against the car door, shoving his knee between her legs. "You bitch, you can't embarrass me like that and just walk away. You were flirting with me. You're nothing but a rich bitch cocktease."

Kadan felt the sudden tension in all the men. Ken's face hardened, but he didn't break cover. The rifle went to his shoulder in a smooth, practiced motion, and Ken never missed.

Marigold leaned back against the car and smiled lazily up at the Stallion, one hand barely lifting off the top of the vehicle to signal the GhostWalkers to stand down. It was too public. There were others in the parking lot.

"Hey, lady, you all right?" That was Ian. He looked imposing, carrying himself like a man who knew how to fight and didn't mind doing it. He began walking toward them.

"Mind your own business," Stallion snapped, but he stepped back enough to allow Marigold to yank open her door. She fumbled with the keys, dropping her purse, then slammed the car door and roared away.

The Stallion picked up her purse, flipped Ian off, and unhurriedly sauntered to his car, whistling. He got in and sat for a moment, looking through Mari's purse. "Yeah, rich bitch, you're going to get a visit from a real man tonight." The bug in her purse picked up audio with no problem. He drove out of the parking lot whistling.

"Pull back," Jack said. "Team Two, he's heading your way."

Kadan was already in the SUV, Ken and Jack leaping in from either side.

"I'm taking that ass out," Mari hissed into her radio.

"You walk away," Ken instructed, his voice pitched low and firm. "Put the car in the garage just as we planned and walk away. We'll do the rest."

"He rammed his knee in my crotch," Mari bit out between clenched teeth. "He rapes women and then he kills them. I read Flame's report on this guy. I'm—"

"You're going to follow the plan," Ken snapped. "This is a mission and we run it by the numbers, we don't make it personal. Walk away."

There was an edge of a threat to his voice now, and Kadan rather admired it. He might have to use that particular tone for his own woman.

Mari muttered something under her breath and Ken shot his twin a small grin. They followed Mari's car out to the edge of the city. The house had been well scouted, far back from other houses, where no one would hear or see anything. A perfect place for Stallion to spend the night tormenting a woman. He would come calling and he would feel safe.

"I'll take this one," Ken said as they watched Mari walk away from the garage and into the trees where Nico waited for her with her rifle.

Kadan shook his head. "I can shield. We don't want him warned. It really doesn't matter who kills the son of bitch as long as he's exterminated. I'll take him down."

"That son of bitch put his fucking knee in my wife's crotch. I'll cut his heart out."

"We stick with the plan. I don't blame you," Kadan said. "I'd feel the same way, but we stick with the plan."

Jack nudged Ken. "I'm telling that little hellcat you married that you were going to deviate from the plan and make it personal."

"You keep getting me in trouble with her, and one of these days you're going to wake up with your throat cut," Ken said.

Kadan slipped out of the car shaking his head. He wasn't the only one with woman problems. He waited in the bedroom where both Mari and Ken wanted to be. There was no moon, and he put on soft light in the living room and a night-light in the bedroom as a tempting beacon. As a further lure, he added music, not too loud, but loud enough that if Stallion came calling, he would think Mari wouldn't hear him as he entered.

"He didn't wait long," Jack said. "He's driving up without lights, heading around to the back of the house."

"I've got him," Nico intoned.

"In my sights," Mari reported.

Kadan waited in silence, the familiar calm taking him. He welcomed the ice that set him apart. No nerves. Much easier than facing Tansy tracking the killers. He preferred this way. Quick, clean. It was done.

Noises indicated Stallion had entered through a window down the hall and was padding toward the bedroom. Kadan stepped to the side of the door. The knob turned and the door creaked as the intruder pushed it open and stepped into the room. He didn't notice the tarp on the floor, he was too intent on the sleeping form in the bed.

"Hey, bitch. I got your invitation and came to party," Stallion announced, taking a step toward the bed and the rolled up blankets.

Kadan came in behind him, a shadow only, his hand flashing with a quick, deep slice, and Stallion staggered, tried to turn, gurgled and dropped to his knees, then face planted. Kadan stood still waiting. It took a few minutes before the pulse was gone. "It's done. We need the cleaner."

There could be no discovery before their schedule was complete. He wiped his blade clean and walked out to join the others.

"Two down," Kadan said.

"There is no way he's going to fall for this," Gator said. "The man would have to be an idiot. Come on, Kadan. We need another plan."

"If necessary we'll go into his house and slit his throat, but get your Cajun ass out there and tie yourself up."

"Why do I have to do this?" Gator demanded.

"Cuz you're such a pretty boy. Our photographer isn't going to fall for one of us as the tied up model," Nico pointed out.

"Dumbest plan you've ever come up with," Gator grumbled. "Offering myself all trussed up like a Christmas turkey to a serial killer who likes to torture people isn't too smart."

Nico flashed a small grin. "Thought he wasn't going to take the bait."

"Well I happen to *be* the bait, and I saw the video of the rats eating those people alive. I'm not going to go out that way," Gator declared.

"Don't you worry, Bondage Boy," Nico assured him. "I'll have a bullet trained on him the entire time." He frowned a little, muttering beneath his breath. "Hope my rifle doesn't malfunction, been acting up a bit lately. I keep it around for sentimental value."

Gator suggested something anatomically impossible and stalked off. Kadan signaled to the others to get into position. Flame had tracked the high-end camera and found that Snake had his own photography business. Kadan set up an appointment to photograph a low-budget male bondage series for a private collector in an abandoned warehouse.

Snake took the bait without hesitation after finding out

no one would be there but him and the two models, late at night. It was extremely low budget and they weren't paying for much other than the bondage props. Snake's voice had indicated immediate interest, and he'd been seen twice scouting the location earlier in the day, noting how remote it was.

Gator and Jeff took up their positions, shirts off, barefoot, Jeff tying Gator as Snake strode in. They introduced themselves and Snake set up his lights and camera.

"Make it tight. You want this to look real," he said. "I'll tie you," he added and caught up the ropes. "We're going to have fun tonight." He knotted the rope, pulling until Jeff's circulation was cut off.

"Hey, man, too tight," Jeff complained.

Snake drew a knife and grinned. "That's the least of your worries tonight. I'm going to film the real thing, slicing little pieces off of you. People pay big money for films like this."

"Yes, they do," Kadan said quietly from behind him. The knife slid in, a kill stroke. Kadan helped the body fall to the floor. "Three down."

Blade was a man with a huge superiority complex. He wanted control and he wanted to be in charge. He enjoyed being cruel and publicly humiliating others. Kadan doubted very much that he'd take public humiliation well. Kadan hadn't worn a uniform in a long while, but he donned his, immaculate as always, and with Gator and Ian, entered the bar where Blade was known to hang out.

Blade held court at the pool table, women hanging around him and several men standing respectfully to one side. When he missed a shot, Kadan snickered. Gator and Ian both grinned, shaking their heads, turning away in dismissal to lean on the bar and whisper. Several of the women noticed the three broad-shouldered men and moved away from

Blade to investigate the newcomers. It didn't take long for Blade to realize he was no longer the center of attention. He threw his pool cue down and stomped over, shoving one of the women out of his way. The woman stumbled and would have fallen if Ian hadn't caught her.

Kadan reached out in a blurring motion and casually and quite brutally slapped Blade. "Keep your hands off the lady."

Blade's face turned cherry red. A sound escaped his throat, much like the roar of a freight train. He'd been Special Forces, enhanced, his body in shape, he hadn't even seen Kadan move and the blow had rocked him. A few of the men he'd ridiculed in the bar snorted derisively but hastily stilled their laughter when he glared around the room. Opening and closing his fists, he jerked his head toward the door.

"You want to take this outside?"

Kadan looked him up and down, his expression remote, dismissive. "You're not worth my time. I just came in for a cold brew. Someone else can teach you manners." He turned his back and swallowed the rest of his beer. "You ready?" He glanced at his watch. "I've got to be at the old airstrip in about twenty minutes."

Ian and Gator drained their glasses and they swaggered out, leaving Blade smoldering, furious, poised on the edge of violence.

"He's on you," Jack's voice said softly. "Following about a mile back. You hit the son of a bitch pretty hard, bro. There's no way he isn't going to try to kill you."

"Stay on him, Nico," Kadan said.

Jack, Ken, and Mari were all also snipers with reputations. Blade would have four rifles trained on him when he moved in to confront Kadan. Gator and Ian would be backing him at a much closer range.

Once at the old airstrip, Kadan slowed his vehicle, allowing Gator and Ian to bail out, running along the brush, crouched low to make their way to the hangar where they both got into position. Ken, Mari, and Nico had already gone high. Jack joined them as soon as he was able, coming in from the north and finding a nice limb to stretch out on.

"In position," Nico said. "He's approaching."

"I see him," Kadan said, and turned, a scowl on his face as the car roared up, sending plumes of dirt into the air.

Blade burst out of the car, slamming the door. "You son of a bitch. You think you can just bitch slap me in front of everyone and walk away clean?"

"No, I thought you'd follow me," Kadan said, his voice as cold as ice.

Blade paused, hand gripping his knife. He looked around, suddenly realizing that he was alone with someone who had eyes like twin glaciers. "Who are you?"

"The name's Kadan. Kadan Montague. I've been called Bishop in some circles. You give the GhostWalkers a bad name. You give every soldier a bad name."

Blade's face lost color as he began to back toward his car. "Why'd you bring me out here?" he demanded and threw the knife.

Kadan dove for the ground, rolling, coming up right at Blade's feet, knife sliding upward in a standard figure eight, cutting arteries along the way. He kept moving, getting away from the pumping streams of blood, his face dispassionate, his heart rate never going up. He watched the man die and then he turned and walked away.

"East Coast Team down," Kadan announced. "The jet's standing by, let's move out."

Ryland handed Kadan the binoculars and pointed toward the small cabin near the lake. "Lily and Flame have been working around the clock to get us as much information as possible on these suspects, but the one called Hawk, we can only speculate is the same Hawk the Reaper teamed up with a few years ago. We just don't have enough on him to be certain. But there's no doubt that this one is Scorpion. He's holed up here by himself, pounding on a heavy bag and running every day. He looks to be in bad mental shape." He glanced again at Kadan. "I did what you asked me to do. Did you clear it with the general?"

Kadan nodded. "I'll go in and have a chat with him. It's the best I can do for him."

"Nico's in place," Ryland said. "Keep him away from the door and outside if possible."

Kadan took a packet of papers from inside his jacket, slipped his gun in his belt at his back, and checked for his knife. "Nico, if you have to do it, take him out clean, no pain."

Nico didn't respond. He always took them out painlessly, one shot. Kadan was reluctant to eliminate Tom Delaney, Sr., and Nico understood why. The man had a wife and child and a good service record, complete with plenty of medals. Murder had never been his choice and he fought it—was still fighting it.

Kadan made his way down to the cabin. Walking. Giving Scorpion plenty of time to see him coming. Tom Delaney turned to watch him approach, his body covered in sweat, his face a mask of pain, knuckles bloody from hitting the heavy bag without gloves.

"Tom Delaney." Kadan made it a statement as he nodded his head in greeting.

Tom shook his head, a look of relief on his face. "I wondered who'd come for me."

"Kadan Montague, sir. If you don't mind, I'd like to propose something to you."

Delaney reached down toward a cooler.

"Please don't do that, sir," Kadan said. "Nico has a gun

on you and he never misses." Deliberately he used the name of a sniper most on Special Forces teams would recognize instantly. "I'd like you to hear me out."

Delaney straightened slowly, keeping his hands out away from his body. "You know what I've done."

"Yes sir. And I know what was done to you. Your profile was tampered with when you applied for psychic enhancement. You should never have been placed in that program. When you were enhanced, they also did genetic enhancement, raising the levels of hormones to make you super-aggressive. We know that you fought it. Unfortunately, the person who chose you for this program needed an eighth player for his game of murder. When you weren't cooperative, he began to use your own mind against you. You get headaches and bleed from your nose, mouth, and ears, right?"

"How do you know that?" Delaney looked around and lowered himself slowly to the wooden bench behind him, his hands still out in front of him in plain sight. "My head feels like it's in a vise and I can't control myself. I'm afraid for my wife, my son." His breath came in ragged gasps as he fought to keep from breaking down. "I go crazy. I killed someone, beat him to death, and for a little while the voices stopped. But they're back again. I tried to get help. I went to the veterans' hospital. I'm afraid for my family, for others, but they just gave me some drugs. I begged to go into the hospital."

Kadan had read the report on his desperate cry for help. "You were programmed, both genetically and psychically, to murder, and you've fought it."

Delaney shook his head again, pressing his fingers tight against his eyes. "I couldn't control it. I don't really remember beating that man to death, but I did, with my bare hands." He flexed his fingers. "I tried eating a bullet, but I couldn't. I kept thinking if I could get help . . ."

"He's in your head. Pressuring you to do what he wants."

"Who?" Delaney's head snapped up, his eyes hard.

"I'm going to get him for you," Kadan said. "In the meantime, I'm offering you one chance. If you fail, you're terminated. No second chances, no talking, I'll put a bullet in your head and you'll never see it coming."

"I don't trust myself. Just do it now. It's a relief. I don't want to hurt anyone else. I hit my wife. Damn it, I *hit* her, with my fist. I could hear myself screaming to stop, but I couldn't. And her face, when she looked at me . . ." He closed his eyes. "Just do it, man."

"I want to have you transported to a hospital. A doctor will try to undo or counteract the damage done with the genetic enhancement. Once I terminate the man pulling your strings, the pressure as well as the voices in your head should be gone. We can't get back the man you killed, but you can do your best to make up for it. You were a good soldier. The papers in this packet say you still are. As far as your wife and child will know you are on a mission. If you succeed, you'll come back to them, but you'll remain under the general's command and serve your country when needed. If you don't succeed, you will be terminated immediately and you will be buried with full military honors. Your wife and child will never know what happened to you and will receive your insurance benefits as befitting the widow and family of a fallen soldier."

"Why would you do that for me?" Delaney asked suspiciously.

"Because I've had to kill four people today and I'll kill four more by tomorrow morning. You're worth saving, and I don't want to have to look into your wife's eyes and know I didn't try. I don't want to have to go home to my woman and have her know I didn't try. I signed on for psychic enhancement, but no one asked my permission for genetic enhancement. Whatever happened to you could just as easily have happened to me."

"In return for this offer, what do I have to do?" Delaney

sounded wary. He was a soldier, Special Forces, and his every instinct would be to keep information to himself.

"You have to do exactly what I laid out for you. I don't need you to tell me anything about how you got into this or who did it with you. We'll take you to a hospital at an undisclosed location. You will be allowed one phone call to your wife where you will tell her you were called up for a special mission you can't talk about. Tell her you love her and to wait for you, to give you one more chance. Let her know you'll probably be gone several months. Cooperate with the doctor. I won't lie to you: We don't know how to undo the genetic enhancements; the doctor will probably have to counteract them in some way. I have no guarantee for you other than my word as a fellow Ghost-Walker that I'm telling you the truth."

Tom Delaney turned his face away, but not before Kadan saw him choking with emotion. "Let's do it then," the soldier said gruffly. "And if it doesn't work, promise me you won't let me leave that place alive."

"You have my word on that." Kadan motioned him to stand and turn around, indicating that he put his hands behind his back. "It's safer for you. You'll have guns on you all the way to the transport vehicle. They'll knock you out so the voices can't reach you."

Tom Delaney stood quietly while Kadan put handcuffs on him. "Look man. I know I don't deserve it, but if something goes wrong, tell my wife I really loved her. She has to know I really love her and my boy."

"I'll take care of them. You have my word."

Kadan led him back toward the top of the hill, where Ryland had a van ready. Ryland gave Delaney no time to change his mind or think about things; he knocked him out with one swift shot of the air syringe.

"The puppet master is a dreamwalker. You're certain he can't get to Delaney that way?" Kadan asked.

Ryland shrugged as he watched the van head out toward the waiting plane that would take Delaney to the small up-to-date facility Lily had built in the mountains of Montana. "It's Nico's concoction and he says no dreamwalker can get past that barricade."

"Five down," Kadan said and climbed into the SUV.

Jason Sturges, aka Bull, weaved his way cautiously through the animal pens, making his way in the dark along the narrow paths between fences. The steers pawed at the ground and bellowed occasionally, restless and distressed over the unfamiliar scents and the intruding shadows flitting through their territory. A few stomped their feet and pushed against the fences, rattling the boards with their heavy weight.

Bull smiled and crouched a little lower, listening to the waves of restless cattle. The man who was trying to blackmail him was somewhere near the lower fences. He could tell by the way the curious cattle swung their heads. He knew animals and he knew how to fight. Confident, and rather amused, he inched toward the lower pens where the bulls were kept.

Come alone, the voice had whispered hoarsely on the telephone. Hell yeah, he'd come alone. Maybe he should have invited a couple of his teammates to come along for the fun, but sometimes a man just needed to have his own good time. He'd have bragging rights after he killed his blackmailer. Anyone dumb enough to mess with a bull deserved the horns. Inwardly he laughed at his own joke and kept pressing forward, following the call of the cattle.

"Gator's directing the cattle," Nico reported into Kadan's ear. "He's herding Bull your way. I can't always get a clear shot. He's got a lot of cover."

"Tell Gator to keep him moving. I want him in motion at all times so he's easier to spot."

The report on Bull had been astonishing. As a soldier, he had a good reputation, was reputed to be excellent at his job, and had no damaging reports in his file. As crazy as the man was, Kadan had expected to find a few rumors floating, but Bull was either lucky or good, and Kadan had the feeling he was just that good. Flame had uncovered an alarming pattern of deaths on Bull's team. Nearly every mission a man was lost. His team had the highest loss rate of any team in the service, yet no one had questioned that each downed man was a legitimately explained death.

Sturges had been a serial killer long before he'd been enhanced. Flame had covered his high school and college years. There'd been dead students every year, and again, he'd never been so much as suspected, but Kadan was certain the man had been killing for years.

"He's close now, Kadan, and he's aware something's up." Nico said. "I don't have a clear shot."

Kadan hadn't expected less of Bull. The man was highly skilled and a GhostWalker. He couldn't fail to have radar. Sturges was in his sight now, moving slow, a gun in one hand, a knife in the other. He moved with a fluid ease, light on his feet, covering territory but staying in the shadows and keeping the cattle between him and everything else.

Without warning the man sprang, leaping into the air, twisting and firing several shots in Kadan's direction. Bullets hit around him, but none came too close. His instincts were more than good; Sturges had a sense of survival. He was back on the ground, flattening himself against the pens while the cattle stirred restlessly, running from one side to another, forcing Gator to struggle to keep them contained.

"No shot," Nico reported calmly. "He's fast, he's good, and he knows he's cornered now. He'll be dangerous."

Kadan said nothing, rolling beneath the fence, worming his way through the cattle, using his elbows to propel him, relying on Gator to keep the big steers from stepping on him. The mud and straw stank, drowning out any scent the other man was giving off.

Without warning Bull charged the fence, at the last moment rolling under it, not leaping over, giving Nico nothing to spot. Sturges almost landed on top of Kadan, his knife slashing across Kadan's back, kissing skin and laying out a burning brand that stung like hell. Kadan rolled, coming up to meet the other man, the two bodies slamming together hard, each locking the other's wrists so they knelt, shaking with power and strength, gazes locked as well.

Sturges hissed, recognizing the GhostWalker and for the first time realizing he really could die. He allowed one elbow to bend and rocked back, trying to throw Kadan. The grip on his wrists was relentless. He couldn't move either hand. He lunged forward with a head butt. Kadan shifted as if he'd been waiting for the move. Using Sturges's forward momentum, he flung him forward and up into the air. His head topped the fence and the cattle for just one split second.

Nico squeezed the trigger and Sturges fell, landing hard, his arms and legs flopping loosely while the cattle milled around him and blood pooled in the straw.

Kadan retrieved the knife and gun. "Rye. Send in the cleaners. That's six and we're on the clock."

"It took a little bit of time to locate these two, and we got lucky," Ryland said, moving through the vineyard. "Flame hacked into the Reaper's computer and found this little hideaway the two own together. Apparently they've set up a range for target practice. She saw an invoice for some hefty equipment. When I say target practice, I'm talking moving targets, like we use in the urban training."

"So what are they doing?" Gator asked.

"They've built quite a small city back here. We did a series of aerial photographs and the buildings are mostly shells."

"A stage." Nico glanced at Kadan. "They practice the murders here, so they can perfect each one before they carry it out."

"The details matter," Kadan said. "They're serious about getting the most points possible for each allotted murder. That's like the Reaper. He's a perfectionist and would be very serious about winning if he entered the game." He looked around at his team. "This," he waved his hands toward the compound, "is a perversion of everything we believe in. Our training, every soldier who went through months and years of training to *save* lives. They've warped the skills given them and the training practices, in order to perfect murder. They disgust me, but don't for one moment think they don't know what they're doing. I know the Reaper. I've worked with him and he's good. Better than good. You can't afford one mistake."

"Do we know what kinds of psychic or genetic enhancements either of them have?" Nico asked.

Ryland shook his head. "There's no documentation. Not in any files Lily could find on Whitney's computer or in any of the ones Flame hacked into on the suspects themselves. There isn't a whisper among the teams, either. We're going in blind."

"Do we have a clue what the winning team gets once the game is over?" Gator asked.

Kadan shrugged. "It's the title, no matter what else. The common bond they all share is ego. They want, no, they *have* to feel superior. It made no sense to put Tom Delaney in with the group. He didn't fit. He has the aggression, but he isn't a killer, not like these men."

"Lily says they consider the rest of the world sheep and they're the wolves. The more they kill, the more they need to kill," Ryland said. "I didn't understand and probably never really will."

"I don't want to understand," Kadan said. "And this," he swept his hand in an arc to indicate the small estate, "this is an abomination. They're training to murder just as they trained for missions."

There was ice in his voice and he felt the familiar cold settle over him. He welcomed the ice flowing in his veins, the cold part of him that became mechanical, that worked like a well-oiled machine when needed. And he needed the warrior out and fully functional.

"They'll know we're coming," Kadan warned. He would know. He had to assume the Reaper would know. "This is their home turf. They know every trap, every mine. And they'll be waiting for us."

Nico, Jack, and Ken gave a brief salute and split off, heading for their assigned positions. Gator, Kadan, and Ryland continued forward, moving apart and working their way through the vines into the orchards, where there was more cover, but more chance of an ambush.

Kadan inhaled and scented sweat. He went to ground, easing his way along, skin changing to the color of his surroundings. A thin wire stretched across the narrow trail. "Watch yourselves, I've got traps. Push them toward me."

He let his senses flair out, a strange sixth sense that had always been with him, long before he'd been enhanced, a type of radar like a cat's whiskers. The enhancement had amplified it, giving him the ability to "see" images in sound. How close. How far. Large or small.

"One's on you," Jack hissed. "Move."

A bullet rang out, thunked into a tree stump a hundred yards to his right. Kadan was already rolling to his left, into a shallow depression, and scooting forward. The man in the shadows had to be Hawk. The Reaper would never have exposed himself to Jack's sight, not even briefly.

"How was he on me?" Kadan asked.

Voices erupted throughout the orchard. The sound of running and branches breaking came from several different areas. Kadan knew it was Gator, deliberately throwing sounds to disrupt the Reaper and Hawk from the hunt.

Kadan slipped into the brush, keeping his body the color of his surroundings. He went up a tree, using his bristles to hold him while he climbed, careful to keep from shaking leaves.

Hawk moved along a narrow trail, gun in hand. He had marked the place where Kadan had gone down, but he couldn't find him. Kadan inwardly frowned. He was completely camouflaged; he knew he was. He hadn't shaken a bush or tree limb. How the hell had Hawk spotted him?

Hawk turned his face up to the sky and screeched, the sound a perfect replica of a hawk calling. A large red-tailed hawk spun a long circle overhead.

"He's using the hawk's vision," Gator called, excitement and admiration infusing his voice. "He can see what the bird sees."

Hawk turned toward the tree where Kadan clung to a branch just above his head, and the killer found himself looking right down the barrel of a gun. He died that way, watching the bullet come to him, drive him over backward where he sprawled out on the ground.

"Not anymore," Kadan said and leapt from the tree, landing in a crouch just feet from the fallen body. "Seven down."

The earth shook and rumbled; dirt and debris geysered into the air. The blast was loud, throwing Kadan off his feet and forward. Before he could push back up, another blast rocked the earth, followed by a third and fourth. Smoke poured around them, swirling thickly. Kadan sent out his radar and it bounced back to him. The Reaper was running.

Kadan went after him, trusting his warning system to let him know if he was nearing a trap. Twice he detoured from the trail, sprinting at full speed, hurdling several bushes when he was certain he was coming up on a trip wire. Automatic gunfire sprayed the area and he dove for cover. The Reaper was firing blind, and he was some distance away.

Through the smoke it was impossible for him to see Kadan clearly, but certain Kadan was following, the Reaper was keeping the GhostWalker off of him.

The moment the firing stopped, Kadan was back on his feet running. His radar told him the Reaper was a hundred yards ahead. He put on a burst of speed, and instantly his warning system shrieked. He made another dive, rolling as he hit the ground. The earth shook, and another series of blasts sent dirt and smoke into the air.

A motorcycle roared to life, and Kadan burst through the smoke to see the Reaper fishtailing through the dirt toward the far ravine. Kadan set off at an angle, running fast, gun out, firing at the tires as he sprinted across the open field. The Reaper responded with automatic weapon fire, aiming under his shoulder, but not really taking the time to do more than try to slow Kadan down. He clearly had an escape route planned and was using it.

The bike plunged over what appeared to be a drop-off and was out of sight. Kadan didn't slow down, streaking across the field to reach the edge of the slope leading to the deep ravine. Heavy brush and trees grew in haphazard fashion covering the walls of the deep cut through the mountain. If there was a trail, it was man-made and the Reaper knew it well. Kadan didn't hesitate and followed him in.

The ribbon of a track was pitted and covered with grass and a few rocks. Someone had taken the time to try to make something that resembled a path. Kadan followed it, but even with his speed, the bike was pulling away from him. The Reaper knew the ravine, every twist and turn, and Kadan had to take care not to break a leg or go tumbling headfirst to the bottom. Branches hit him in the face and brush tore at his arms, but he ran all the same.

He spotted the Reaper going up what looked like a very steep side, powering the bike over rocks and shrubs to get to the top. He disappeared for a moment and then turned the motorcycle back, pausing at the top of the ridge to stare down at Kadan.

Kadan paused, ready to dive into cover if the Reaper lifted his gun. The Reaper stared down at Kadan, a cocky smirk on his face, and then jerked his middle finger high into the air.

Kadan gave him a small salute for the soldier he used to be. There was no way for the Reaper to know he'd been herded straight into a trap, but Ryland had planned the assault perfectly.

The sound of two rifles was simultaneous. The Norton twins fired from opposite sides, and both bullets struck the killer in the head. The body toppled from the bike in slow motion, and rolled back down the slope into the ravine.

"Eight down," Kadan said softly.

CHAPTER 20

"Where the hell is Tansy, Nico?" Jeff Hollister asked. He spun around in a wide circle and then crouched down to examine the dirt, looking for tracks. "She should be right here."

Nico hurried toward a slight slope. "We wove the dream carefully, and we should have pulled her into it when we opened this sequence."

"I told her exactly what to keep in her mind when she drifted off to sleep and I recorded every detail. Kadan agreed to play it for her as she went to sleep. She has to be here."

Nico ran along the top of the narrow ridge. "She's not here, Jeff. Something's wrong."

Jeff frowned and closed his eyes, searching through the dreamscape. "Not another living person. You're right, she's not here. Something went wrong. Wake up."

Nico found himself in a recliner, Jeff across from him. Gator stood between them, guarding their bodies as they dreamwalked. He regarded them with alarm. "You couldn't have killed the son of bitch that fast."

"We lost her. She wasn't there, Gator," Nico said.

Jeff hit the arm of the chair with his fist. "The only answer is, while we were spinning our dream, Dunbar spun one she was more familiar with and pulled her in before we could draw her into ours. He has her. We have to get to her immediately. She'll be under his control. She doesn't dreamwalk."

"Get Kadan on the phone. He'll know if she has recurring dreams," Nico said. "Hurry. We don't have much time."

So much blood. It rose like a river, the current strong, threatening to pull her under. Tansy gasped and turned, looking in all directions, trying to find Kadan. He'd held her; she remembered the feeling of being safe in his arms. His velvet voice whispered to her; she felt his mouth against hers, so tender she ached inside. She knew he was beside her, *knew* it, but she could no longer feel him.

A shadow moved in the distance, striding toward her, taking the shape of a man. He waded through the blood, an evil grin on his face. She gasped, fighting for air, unable to move, afraid to speak, to draw attention to herself. Around her, she heard the wails of the dead.

"You're dreaming, Tansy. Wake up," she murmured, a litany of hope, but not believing for a moment that she would.

She even closed her eyes and prayed—that when she opened them, the shadowy figure would be gone. Instead, he was closer. A man of medium height, nondescript, he would get lost in a crowd. Not handsome, but not plain, a man with intelligence in his eyes who gave off a kind of cunning energy she recognized. Her heart sank. The puppet master.

"Tansy Meadows, how nice to finally meet you." He stood a short distance from her, his eyes running over her face, drinking in her fear, looking more feral than any animal she'd ever photographed. He was a predator, skillfully camouflaged in a sheep's skin.

Tansy straightened, lifting her chin, her heart beating fast. "You."

He smirked. "You were fairly good at keeping me out of your dreams. I was surprised what a worthy adversary you really were. Not quite my equal, but very good."

"Why would you think I'm not your equal?"

"I found you. You couldn't find me."

Her eyebrow shot up. "A reporter found me. You read about me in a newspaper and guessed. But you can't find my parents and you didn't track me by yourself. I, however, tracked and found you. Your safe little home just off base is not so safe. Your little shed where you carve your illegal ivory pieces for your game of murder is now *my* domain. And I know your name, *not* by cheating, but by being the elite tracker that I am. I found you, *James R. Dunbar.*"

Tansy took a deep breath, forcing herself to keep a look of utter contempt on her face when she was quaking inside. There'd been a plan. It didn't involve wading through blood, but she remembered, there had been a plan, and Kadan had whispered she would be safe.

Fury twisted Dunbar's face. He turned bright red, his face mottled with color. "You bitch."

"Why do men always resort to calling women bitches when we kick their asses? I found out a lot about you, Dunbar. For instance, you have an amazing amount of money in an offshore account. It seems your puppets don't have a clue you're raking in the dough while they do the work. You take contracts and kill for money. I'll admit it's rather brilliant. You actually designed your own killers. You dream up a little game, prepare the cards with specific victims right down to the exact details on how they must be killed, and you direct your puppets to do the killing for you. Even if they got caught, you'd walk away clean."

The red faded from his face, and his features turned crafty and a little pleased by the flattery. "You are a clever girl. I underestimated you."

She shrugged. "Most people do. I'll bet they underestimate you all the time." She had to keep him talking while her mind struggled to remember the plan. She wanted to stay at a distance from him, but she couldn't move and he was easing closer.

"I think you underestimate me, Tansy," Dunbar said. "You found me out when no one else ever has, not even Whitney . . ."

He was close—too close. Tansy tried to draw back even as she forced a smile. "I *knew* you'd worked for Whitney. You were in the original enhanced psychic program, determining who went through and who didn't. You handpicked your killers based on their psychological profiles. They flunked, didn't they? They would never have made it through, but you changed it so they looked good."

As hard as she tried, she couldn't move her feet, they were frozen in place. Her heart accelerated, the roaring in her ears increased. Her palms went clammy. *What was the plan?* Why had Kadan sent her here and then abandoned her? She clamped down hard on her runaway thoughts. He would never do that, and to think it—even for a moment— meant she was panicking.

Dunbar nodded. "Whitney never suspected, even when I put in suggested genetic enhancements for each of them." He flashed a little smirk. "Designer killers. I like that."

His smugness bothered her. He might not have killed, but he was more responsible than the ones he'd orchestrated to carry out his plan. He'd profited from the murders. "You made a mistake with one of them. Your scorpion wasn't so easy to control. He isn't a murderer."

Again his face flushed. She'd definitely pricked his perfectionist ego. "I made him into one. He'll do whatever I want." He indicated her feet with his chin. "You made a little mistake of your own, Tansy. This is *my* dream, not yours. I initiated it, not you. You delivered yourself into my hands." He winked at her. "Ultimately, I win."

Her mouth went dry. "Maybe. We'll see." *Wake up. Tansy, wake up. Kadan, where are you?*

Dunbar waded through the blood toward her, stopping just an arm's distance away. She couldn't move. There was no point screaming. The dead were already wailing loud enough, trying to warn her, but they didn't need to bother. Somewhere inside, she knew he had her trapped.

Everything in her stilled. Kadan. Her one regret. Did he know she loved him? Would that be enough for him to realize the truth about himself? She could never love a monster, and deep down, he thought that was what he was. She hadn't had enough time with him to show him the truth of who he was.

I'll love you forever. She sent the whisper out to his mind, hoping it reached him. Her beloved warrior. Whatever had gone wrong wasn't his fault, but she knew him, knew he would carry the guilt for the rest of his life.

"I really didn't want to use this dream, but you visit here so often. I didn't want to get blood on my clothes. It really bothers you, doesn't it?" He waved his arm in a half circle to encompass the lake of blood with so many victims crying out for justice. "Who are these people to you? Nothing at all, but you make yourself suffer for no reason in an effort to appease them. You can't save them. Someone wanted them dead for a reason."

"Money."

He shrugged. "Or revenge. It doesn't much matter. Someone was going to kill them. Why not gain from it? I wouldn't have killed you, you know. I found I looked forward to our little game, but I can't have you knowing who I am."

He stepped close, right in front of her, so close she could smell him in spite of the overwhelming scent of blood. It took an effort not to gag—or cry out in fear. She forced herself to be still, to gather her strength to fight.

Dunbar shook his head. "It's my dream, remember? You won't be able to fight. You aren't a dreamwalker."

He struck then, astonishingly fast, his hands spanning her throat, thumbs digging deep, cutting off air. He was very strong, something she hadn't expected. When she tried to struggle, to fight him, she couldn't lift her arms any more than she could move her feet. Her lungs burned. Her mind began to panic.

Tansy fought down the terror and forced her brain to function in the short time she had left. Her mind reached for his. He was controlling the dream, and that meant he had found a trail leading to her, or he couldn't have drawn her in, but she had the path that led to him. She followed it, trying not to succumb to the black edging around her and the white dots that swam in her vision.

She struck hard in his mind, ripping and clawing, shredding walls, trying to rip the dream apart. She attacked him using the same method as his attacks on Tom Delaney, clotting the blood, beating at the skull, shrieking until his mind was filled with pain and devastation. Dunbar screamed and let her go, grabbing his head with both hands.

"You bitch." He grabbed her again, throwing her forward, grasping her by her hair and shoving her down—down—holding her head so she couldn't break free.

She went under, the red blood thick and dark, pouring into her mouth and nose, flooding her mind and lungs, rising like a tidal wave, her worst nightmare. Hands reached for her, pulling her deeper; faces stared blankly, horror in their wide open eyes.

She knew she was dying. There was no way to think, no way to fight. She reached for peace, let it happen, refusing to give him the satisfaction of seeing or feeling her terror.

Kadan lay beside Tansy, listening to her breathing. It was the only way he could monitor what was happening to her. He wasn't a dreamwalker, and it was his job to guard her body while she was in Jeff and Nico's care. Something had gone wrong. The rhythm of her breathing had changed completely, until she was nearly hyperventilating. She was frightened. He shared her mind, although he couldn't enter the dream.

Jeff and Nico had assured him it would be safe. They would pull her into the dream they spun and hope the puppet master took the bait. There would be plenty of cover for them. Dunbar wouldn't know they were there until it was too late. He'd never get close to Tansy. They'd kill him and be back very fast. Once done, they'd alert Ryland. He was standing by in Dunbar's house, ready to destroy the body. If they failed, he would dispose of the man the moment he awakened. The details of the dream were still playing on the recording, Jeff's hypnotic voice designed to draw Tansy into the dreamscape he'd created.

Kadan hated the loss of control. He wanted to be the one protecting Tansy, standing between her and danger, yet he could only sit in a room with her body and wait for her. He wrapped his hand around her wrist, needing to anchor her to him when she seemed so far away. The phone rang. His heart jumped and he swept it up instantly, listening with dread to Jeff's theory.

"She's definitely in a dream. She's distressed. Her heart rate went up; she's breathing faster and shallow," Kadan reported. "I'm going to wake her up."

"You can't just wake her up," Jeff said, alarmed. "We don't know what's happening on the other side. I need to know what she dreams as a rule. Does she tell you?"

"Sometimes it's vivid enough that when she wakes up, it's still in her mind and I get images. Will that help?"

"Tell me. Don't leave anything out."

While he related the details of Tansy's nightmares, Kadan kept his gaze glued to her face. His hand shook as he held her to him, pulling her wrist against his chest and holding her palm over his heart.

"I trusted you with her, Jeff. Bring her back to me. I'd never survive intact without her." God help them all, because that was a threat. Kadan took a deep breath and let it out, trying to find a place inside of him that was warm. There wasn't one.

Jeff didn't bother to reply to him. He hung up, leaving Kadan more desperate than ever. There'd been a terrible sense of urgency in Jeff's voice. He could hear Nico in the background urging Jeff to hurry. It was silent in the bedroom once again; the only sounds were the clock ticking and Tansy's frightened breathing. He had talked her into this, dreamwalking with Jeff and Nico, promising her she would be safe. He had sent her off without him, trusting his friends, and they'd lost her.

He stretched out beside her and gathered her into his arms, trying to comfort her, even though he knew her mind was somewhere else. When he tried to enter her mind, there was a void, as if she had been yanked from him to another realm.

I'll love you forever. The words whispered in his mind and they sounded like finality. His heart jumped and he sat up abruptly, his dark gaze on her face.

"Get off her!" Jeff Hollister burst into the lake, diving deep, grasping Tansy by the shoulders and kicking his way to the surface.

Nico slammed hard into Dunbar, driving him back and away so that he lost his grip on Tansy. The two men fought,

hand to hand, their bodies close together, each man straining for the upper hand. Nico had the physical strength, but
it was Dunbar's dream and he was trying to control it. Unlike with Tansy, however, he couldn't control Nico.

Jeff burst from below, surfacing almost at their side,
pulling Tansy with him. He swung her into his arms and
raced for shore.

"Keep him alive. You can't kill him," Jeff yelled. "If
you do, the dream collapses and she's trapped here. We
won't be able to revive her."

Dunbar broke free and tried to wade away, hoping for
enough distance that he could end the dream. Nico refused
to let him go, wrapping his fingers like a shackle around the
man's neck and jerking him over backward into the sludge.

"Hurry up, Jeff," Nico called, concerned that Dunbar
might be able to find a way to wake before they were able
to kill him. Everything depended on reviving Tansy.

Jeff reached down and felt for a pulse. There was none.
Swearing, he tipped her head back and began CPR.

Kadan watched the emotions chasing across Tansy's transparent face. Sweat dotted her forehead and around her
mouth, and fear crept into her expression. When he took
her hand in his, her skin was clammy. She felt unnaturally
cold. Suddenly her body shuddered and arched. She gasped
audibly for breath. He actually saw fingerprints on her
throat, pressing deep, and she struggled, desperate for air.

Heart slamming against his chest, he fought to find the
fingers, to try to pry them loose, but there was no way to
find invisible, intangible hands. Her face reddened, her eyes
opened wide, then just as suddenly she was free, dragging
hard, audible breaths into her lungs so that her chest rose
and fell.

Kadan found himself inhaling when he hadn't realized
he had been holding his breath. Tansy flinched, her mouth

opening wide, eyes wild with terror, then she looked like she was holding her breath. A minute. Two. She struggled at first, her body straining against an unseen hold, until she just slipped quietly away, out from under his hands, her body going limp, the breath stilling in her lungs. Her eyes closed.

Kadan felt his own heart stop. "No!" He pressed his palm against her lips, checking for air. His fingers tried to find a pulse. He tried CPR. He even hit his fist over her heart, frantically trying to start it. Nothing. He tried to fill her mind with him, but there was only emptiness.

"Tansy, no." His eyes burned. His throat felt raw. "Fucking don't do this." He shook her again, trying to find a way to revive her. Her body remained limp and lifeless in spite of the air he tried to breathe into her. In spite of the stimulation to her heart and mind.

Kadan roared like a wounded animal, lifting her limp body into his arms, cradling her against his chest. Cold spread like an encroaching glacier, desperate to put out the firestorm of wild grief tearing through him. His heart shredded in his body, his mind went from clarity to chaos, thunder crashed in his ears, and for a moment, all civility was gone and he was standing primitive and stark in his raw, unrelenting agony. Only one other time in his life had he felt so utterly lost as a human being. He had sworn never to go there again, never to kill in cold blood, but the monster inside him was loose now, craving, needing, *demanding* vengeance.

Tansy. Don't leave me. Baby, please. I'm begging here. He buried his face against her throat. There was no heartbeat, no warmth, no gentle hands to touch him.

He remembered a once-innocent child begging his mother, his father, even his brother and sister. *Don't leave me.* But they had, and with them, they'd taken all the warmth in the world, leaving an ice-cold killing machine behind. Last time, he'd known his enemy. This time, who would pay?

He placed her body carefully on the bed again and knelt there for a moment, his hands framing her face. He hadn't touched his family, but he wasn't going to let her go without telling her. Saying it aloud.

"I love you, Tansy. With everything in me, good and bad. I absolutely love you."

He swallowed the last of the fiery grief clawing through him and stood, allowing the arctic cold to consume him, inhaling, drawing the ice into his veins and lungs and into his mind, welcoming the glacier taking him over, and then he began to assemble his weapons.

"Don't you die on us, Tansy!" Jeff yelled. "You're not going to die on us." He slammed his fist hard on her heart, turning her on her side, trying to drain her lungs. "It's not real. You can't let him kill you this way."

Nico jerked Dunbar close to him, face-to-face, staring into his malicious eyes. Without warning, Nico slammed his forehead hard against Dunbar's face, shattering his nose, driving the man backward and down. Before he could fall, Nico caught him by the throat, his fingers—with their superhuman strength—choking the air from the man. He dragged him across the macabre lake, wading through blood and victims as if they weren't there, to throw Dunbar on the ground beside Tansy.

"Don't let this son of bitch move," he ordered and crouched down beside Tansy.

Dahlia, his wife, had always been the one to focus energy, and then Nico had done the healing with Kadan, but this was a dream, not reality. Whether or not he could heal on his own outside the dreamscape world didn't matter—he was certain he could here. Tansy had woven the dream, and the puppet master had used it against her, but Nico could twist the dream for his own purposes, just as Jeff could.

He rubbed his hands together, gathering energy from the violence so thick in the surrounding air. When he'd acquired a pool large enough, he focused the energy between his palms, aiming it directly at Tansy's heart and lungs. White light burst from his skin, shining around each individual finger. The light hit Tansy's body, rippling over her like a wave. Her limp body shuddered.

"He's fighting us," Nico said, his voice flat and calm, wanting to scare the puppet master. "Kill him."

Dunbar's eyes widened in horror as Jeff's fingers tightened around his throat. "You can't," he gasped, his voice hoarse. "I'm holding the dream."

Jeff looked into the man's eyes, shock blossoming. "He's lying, Nico. This is Tansy's dream. She pulled him into her dream."

"Are you sure?" Nico asked.

"Oh, yeah, I'm sure."

Jeff released Dunbar and then swung his hand hard, the edge slamming into the puppet master's throat, crushing the larynx and smashing the trachea. "See you in hell, you bastard," he muttered.

Dunbar fell back, gasping for air, strangling, his face turning a mottled purple.

"This is her worst nightmare," Jeff explained. "It was powerful enough to supersede anything the rest of us were doing. She's a dreamwalker as well, which is why she's so good at what she does."

The moment Jeff broke Dunbar's hold on Tansy, the light soaked into her body. She shuddered, coughing. Gasping. Fighting to draw in air.

"Wake up, Tansy," Jeff ordered.

Ryland slipped into the neighborhood like the ghost he was, easing his way through the streets until he found the house he was looking for. The backyard was protected from the rest of the houses on the street, and he went up and over the fence and through the landscaping to the small toolshed. It took only minutes to open the lock and go inside.

The shed was amazing. Each wall was lined with shelves holding every kind of nut and bolt and screw possible. Tools hung neatly, each clearly labeled. There wasn't a speck of dirt anywhere. On the table were Dunbar's carving tools, the various blades razor-sharp and laid out neatly like surgical instruments. Beside the tools was a small piece of ivory, the shape of a frog emerging.

Ryland searched through the drawers and found a laminating machine and thick card stock. There was an index box of cards already laminated, and each card had precise instructions detailing a murder: the name or names of victims, address, how the victims had to be killed, and the time frame allotted. There were points awarded for each detail, and at the bottom of the card, there was the total number of points each murder could accumulate. Ryland had found the actual game, along with a website he was building for an online game.

Dunbar, being as neat and as precise as he was, had filed the game cards already used along with the total points for each team in the index box. The points were totaled in a fussy little hand and attached to the team's cards. In another drawer were drawings and notes on a proposed video game, titled *Murder Game*. There was no doubt that Dunbar had his cover already in place should any suspicion fall on him. The man was so precise, Ryland wouldn't have been shocked to find a neatly signed contract for each contracted murder filed away, along with a ledger and books for his banking.

On the floor beside the table was a wastepaper bin, and he could see a torn box with "James R. Dunbar" written clearly on it, the label Tansy had spotted. Ryland let out his breath. He was in the right place. There was no mistake. He made his way through the backyard until he came to the house. Shrubbery and flowers were well manicured. The lawn was mowed and the patio in the back was extraordinarily clean. Each window was screened and the screen was free of dirt and debris.

Ryland pried one loose and set it aside to be replaced later. The window wasn't locked, nor did Dunbar have an alarm, a testament to how safe he felt—how superior. There was no need for such things. The man probably believed it would only make him appear more innocent should any of the murders ever be traced back to him. With the proposed video game in various stages, he might actually get away with claiming the serial killers had seen his idea and had decided to implement it for their own purposes.

Ryland slipped through the window and eased his weight onto the floor. Dunbar was reputed to live alone, with no pets. He was a man who would never want dog or cat hair on furniture or clothes. Each room was immaculate, everything in its place. Ryland made his way to the bedroom.

James Dunbar lay on his bed in full uniform. He stared unseeing up at the ceiling, his body jerking and shuddering, in the throes of his dream. Ryland crept up beside him, knife out, waiting. Minutes ticked by. Dunbar's eyes suddenly bulged and wheezing gasps escaped. One hand waved in the air and then went to his throat as he choked and fought for air. Ryland stepped up, a dark shadow, looming over the figure on the bed. The eyes found him, there in the dark, and recognized death when they saw it. Ryland cut his throat.

"Puppet master down," he whispered softly, and walked away.

Tansy woke gasping for air, her throat raw and swollen, her lungs burning. Her heart pounded in her ears, and for a moment she was completely disoriented. Her chest hurt, felt bruised and battered, as if someone had been pounding on her. She touched her throat as she turned her head searching for Kadan.

He stood across the room from her, his back to her, strapping on a belt and shoving knives and guns into every conceivable loop. He pushed extra clips into a zippered pocket and reached for more.

She opened her mouth to call to him, but nothing came out, her throat was too raw and damaged. She reached with her mind, connecting, wanting him, needing him, only he wasn't there. In his place was something else, something not quite human. Ice-cold. A machine bent on destruction. Where there had been cool logic and distance, there was now utter chaos. He was no thinking person. Tansy doubted if he even knew what he was doing. He simply reacted. His warrior persona was his most familiar, and he took it like the chameleon he was, wearing the outer skin when his mind was fragmented.

He thought I was dead. He had probably watched her die. Her heart clenched. She couldn't imagine watching Kadan die. Tansy pressed a hand to her heart. He'd probably tried to revive her. She was fairly certain her chest was bruised.

Kadan. She sent his name to him wrapped in love as she sat up a little unsteadily.

He didn't turn around, the ice block in his mind an effective barrier.

She reached again, filling his mind with her, with the scent and taste of her—of cinnamon. Of love. She poured warmth into his mind. His entire body could be ice and she'd find a way to warm him. She tried to stand, needing to go to him, her body swaying weakly.

A small corner of his mind thawed just enough to let out raw pain. It burst from him in a rush of agony, so intense, so strong, it drove her to her knees. Kadan whirled around, gun in his fist, his eyes piercing cold, remote, distant, sorrow etched deep into the lines of his face.

Kadan. She whispered his name again, calling him back to her. She pushed her way deeper into his mind, filling him full of erotic images, of heat and love and her wrapped in the same skin with him. The scent of cinnamon grew stronger. *Look at me. Really look at me.*

His glacier-cold eyes flicked over her face, still remote, still distant, as if he didn't know who she was, as if he didn't see her. His hand tightened around the barrel of the gun.

She pulled herself up, hanging on to the bed. His mouth stiffened. His mind rejected what he was seeing. She forced her taste into his mouth, her scent into his nostrils, deeper, into his lungs. *Breathe me in, Kadan. Let me in.*

Fear flickered in his eyes and he took a step back. He shook his head slightly. He wasn't going to let himself feel that raw pain, no matter how real the hallucination was.

Tansy smiled at him. Gentle. Warm. She stepped closer, pushing aside the gun to move in close to him, to circle his neck with her arms and press her body, soft and pliant and so familiar, against his. He stiffened, both hands locking on her hips to push her away. She could feel the outline of the gun pressed tightly into her skin. There was only a thin shirt between them, and her warmth slid into the palm of his hands.

Does this feel like a hallucination? She stood on her toes and lifted her face, finding his mouth to brush her lips back and forth persistently over his. *Does this?*

He didn't move. Didn't blink. His eyes, like a cat's, remained wide open and staring, focused on her face, but he wasn't seeing her. The denial in his mind was loud. He wouldn't go there. He wouldn't feel.

With one hand wrapped around the nape of his neck to keep him close to her, she unbuttoned her shirt with the other. His arm was heavy, but he didn't resist her when she cupped his palm around the warm, soft, inviting mound of her breast and pressed her hand over his to hold him there. *Is this a hallucination, Kadan? Come back to me.*

He blinked. She felt his mind move against hers. Tentative. Raw anguish. Fear mounting to terror. A tendril of hope. He inhaled, drawing the scent of cinnamon deep into his lungs, as if he could trust his sense of smell, but not his mind. The cold receded just a little more.

His hand moved against her breast, an involuntary reflex. His thumb brushed over her nipple, sending a shiver of awareness down her spine. She went up on her toes again and kissed his mouth. "Kadan." His name came out. A croak. Her throat protested, but she got his name out, aching for him, for that man crouched behind a wall of ice. A man shielded by the cold.

And then he crushed her. His arms whipped up and around her, nearly breaking her ribs with their strength. The gun landed on the chair, and the momentum of his body took her backward until she hit the wall. He enveloped her, his body so tight against hers she could barely breathe, his mouth in the hollow of her shoulder, his face wet against her skin. His body shuddered, wracked by silent sobs. He held her for a long time, just held her, without speaking, his mind in a turmoil, wild and unrestrained.

When he moved, his hand whipped up to span her throat, this time gently, but his thumb tipped her head back and he took her mouth, and there was nothing gentle there. He was rough, possessive, taking over, wanting to crawl inside her.

Tansy went pliant and accepting, kissing him back, letting his marauding hands tug away her shirt so he could slide his hands over every inch of her skin, whatever he wanted, whatever he needed. His mouth left hers, trailing kisses over her chin, down her throat, to her breast. She circled his neck with one arm and arched into him, a little helplessly as he took, frantic for the taste and feel of her.

"I have to be inside you right now," he whispered hoarsely. "Right now, Tansy."

The urgency in his voice, the mesmerizing need and desperation, had her tugging at his belt, his jeans, shoving them partway down his hips even as his mouth pulled strongly at her breast and his teeth tugged at her nipple. She was suddenly nearly as frantic as he was, her body clenching and dripping with liquid heat.

He lifted her, hands hard on her bottom, fingers digging deep as she wrapped her legs around his waist and locked her ankles tight. She could feel him pushing at her entrance, driving through tight folds to stretch her with his invasion. He didn't give her time to adjust, but thrust upward as he dropped her down hard, her sheath enclosing him like a tight fist. She dug her fingers into his shoulders, throwing her head back, a moan escaping.

Kadan turned, angling her body so her back was against the wall and he could slam hard and fast, pounding deep in a frenzy of need to be part of her, to know she was alive, surrounding him with silken walls and scorching fire to melt away the last of the cold. He didn't allow himself thought. He wanted only to feel. To know she was alive by touch, by sound, by scent. He didn't trust his own mind, but his body knew hers, his hands and his burning, aching shaft as he thrust into her over and over.

"Look at me," he commanded. He needed to see her eyes. Her eyes always told the truth.

Tansy's gaze immediately jumped obediently to his. She looked sexy, eyes glazed with passion, her expression almost tortured as he rocked her body over and over with his pistoning hips. Her breath came in ragged gasps and her breasts bounced, but, as always, she held nothing back from him, moaning softly, her muscles tightening around him, riding his frantically bucking body with the same matching fervor as he rode hers.

Heat rose from his toes up his thighs to center in his

groin. The fire raced through his bloodstream, burned in his belly and up through his chest, until it filled his mind with a rush of pleasure so intense it burst behind his eyes like streaking rockets. His body jerked and her muscles tightened to a stranglehold, gripping him with her fiery, silk-lined sheath. Jet after jet of hot seed soaked deep, triggering more violent ripples around him.

Kadan pressed her against the wall, his face buried in her throat while he gasped for air. Mostly he just savored the feel of her in his arms, his body surrounded by hers. When he could breathe a little, he managed to get to the edge of the bed and lay her down, his body collapsing over hers, still buried deep, holding her hips locked with his.

"I swear I'm going to live here—fucking live here forever. I'm not letting you go, Tansy. I'm staying inside you, part of you, where I know you're safe every minute of the day." He buried his face against her breast, the warm, soft, inviting flesh she never kept from him. Never hid from him. "I thought you were dead. I held your body in my arms and thought you were dead." A shudder ran through his body.

"I know," she whispered, her hands caressing his damp hair. "I'm so sorry, Kadan."

He shook his head, his shadowed jaw sliding sensuously between her breasts. "You shouldn't be with me. I don't know what I would have done. I looked at myself and saw all those killers standing right beside me. I *wanted* to kill. I even needed to."

The shame and guilt and absolute loathing in his mind broke her heart. Tansy caught at his head, jerking him up, so that he was forced to look at her. "You're *nothing* like they are. Not a single part of you. You feel so much, so deeply, and your mind shuts that off to protect you. You aren't a cold, unfeeling monster, Kadan, you never have been. That part of you is necessary, it keeps you from losing your mind. It's a protection. Without it, you couldn't do the things you need to do to keep the world a safer place. I know that sounds silly and trite, but it's still the truth." She brushed her mouth gently over his eyelids. "I love you exactly the way you are. I love that cold warrior who keeps this man—*you*—sane and alive and coming back to me."

"What if I had hurt someone?"

"Who?" she demanded. "Who were you going to hurt?"

He looked confused. "I don't know. Someone."

She smiled and leaned up to kiss his nose and each corner of his mouth. "You were on automatic pilot. You didn't know what you were doing, only that it needed action. I'm in your mind. I see you better than you see yourself. You couldn't handle the grief, and the warrior took over, but he wouldn't have harmed anyone."

"You don't know that for certain."

"I do, Kadan. Partnership is trust. I trust you completely. I give you everything I am. My body, my heart and soul, and my mind. I trust you to see *me*. What I want, what I need, who I am, deep down where no one else can see. And if I'm your partner, your true partner; you have to trust me to see the real you even when you can't. I do the things you ask because I know I can trust you to keep me safe, to tell me the truth. You have to love me all the way, give yourself to me all the way, or let me go."

His heart slammed hard in his chest. "You have me, Tansy."

"Then believe in me when I tell you that cold part of you is a guardian, not a monster. Yes, you have killed, and you're capable of killing, you do your job, but you don't kill for fun or pleasure or because it makes you feel powerful. You are not a monster and nothing will ever turn you into one. That line is not blurred for you. You would have come to your senses and put your weapons away and crawled into your mind where no one could see and grieved for me. You *were* grieving; you just didn't let yourself feel it."

He blinked and there was love in his eyes. Tenderness.

Joy. "I don't deserve you, but I'll be damned if I give you up."

"I won't let you give me up."

Kadan kissed her hard, his mouth rough, then tender. "You're naked and I've got all my clothes on."

"And weapons," she pointed out.

"Sorry about that." His hips began a slow seduction, moving in long, languorous strokes. "I'm not leaving your body, not even long enough to take my clothes off. We're going to be like this all night, and then tomorrow, you're going to come with me to Montana and we're getting married."

She tugged at his shirt until he levered himself up enough to let her pull it over his head and toss it aside. "I think we need a little more planning time for a wedding."

"No, we don't." He licked her ear, teasing with his tongue. "I'm not waiting. And then I'm tying you up in a locked room naked, no clothes, and spending our honeymoon torturing you with pleasure until neither of us knows whose skin we're in."

"That's the plan?" She shoved at his jeans and the open belt to get more room as his hips pushed deeper into her, filling her with heat and fire.

"That's the plan," he said firmly. "So don't bother wearing panties under your wedding dress."

CHAPTER 21

"You haven't told me you love me, Kadan," Tansy said.

Around the room people milled and talked and laughed, some swaying to the soft music and others crowding around the table of food. Kadan ignored them, centering his complete attention on Tansy. He lifted her left hand, thumb feathering a caress over her skin, and then he kissed the wedding band he'd pushed onto her finger just an hour earlier. "I showed you last night."

"You haven't *said* you loved me," Tansy reiterated. "You know, those three little words you like to hear me say."

"I told you the other day when that bastard wrapped his fingers around your neck and choked the life out of you." There was an edge to his voice, his eyes going midnight dark.

Tansy scowled at him. "I was dead. I don't think that technically counts."

Kadan swung her into his arms because he needed to feel her close to him. He couldn't talk about her being dead, not even joking—not yet. The music was soft and sexy, and he pulled her tight against him, one hand sliding down the curve of her spine to rest on her rounded bottom as he swept her around the room.

He pressed his lips against her ears. "I've asked you twice if you were wearing panties. That should tell you something." His tongue flicked out in a lazy swirl and then his teeth bit down on her earlobe.

She laughed softly, bringing instant joy to him. "It tells me you're thinking about sex, not our wedding reception. Stay focused here, my man."

"I'm perfectly focused." His hand did a small circular massage, pressing lightly so that her body fit more snugly against his.

She turned her face up and kissed his throat. "I love you very much, Kadan Montague."

She didn't move away from him or demand he remove his hand. She danced closer, melting into him. He slid his palms up her back and encircled her protectively. His eyes burned. His throat closed. Tansy. His wife. She was his *wife*. His other half. She was and always would be his home.

He turned her around on the dance floor, struggling to find some balance with the emotions pouring in. She said he felt too much and the ice protected him, shielded him. At first he hadn't wanted to know how much he felt for her, but now that emotion, that terrible love that clogged his throat and made his heart ache, was his world.

"I want children," he murmured in her ear. "I want to feel them growing inside you, and see them feeding at your breast."

"Just remember it might inhibit your penchant for sex on the kitchen table," she teased.

Kadan drifted around the dance floor with her, lost in their world, barely aware of the GhostWalkers, the general, and her parents in the room. No one mattered to him but her. "I'll just have to be more innovative."

She turned her face up to press kisses along his throat.

"I love you so much, Kadan. And you have to tell me, say the words out loud. It's our wedding day. And every anniversary and the day each child is born."

Laughter rumbled in his chest. "You drive a hard bargain, lady."

The song ended and another began. They hadn't broken apart, neither wanting to let go of the other. Kadan felt Tansy stiffen and knew before he turned who would be standing behind him. He forced a polite smile as he looked down at Tansy's mother, careful not to look at her father.

"Tansy?" Don Meadows stood there, his hand out, waiting for his daughter to dance with him while Sharon smiled expectantly up at Kadan.

Kadan felt Tansy's reluctance, but she turned to her father and obediently placed her hand in his. Kadan took Sharon into his arms, but his eyes followed his wife around the floor. She smiled. She spoke to her father, but when Kadan touched her mind, she was silently weeping. No one could tell, certainly not Sharon, who chattered away about how happy she was to have him for a son-in-law. All he could think of was getting back to Tansy and holding her, comforting her. She suddenly looked over her father's shoulder and sent him a small smile and Kadan's heart clenched.

He had married the most courageous woman he could imagine. She would stand with him and stand for their children. It wouldn't matter what Whitney, or Violet, or anyone else threw at them, they would be make it as long as they were together.

He guided Sharon across the room, bent to drop a brief kiss on her cheek, and then took back his wife.

Pulling her into the protection of his arms, keeping their bodies close, he leaned down, his lips against her ear. "I love you, baby, more than anything in the world. I absolutely love you." And when she touched his mind, there was no doubt.

Keep reading for a sneak preview of
the next exciting book
by Christine Feehan

ℬURNING
𝒲ILD

Available May 2009
from Jove Books!

Jake Bannaconni swore viciously as he swerved the sleek, purring Ferrari to miss the Buick pulling right out in front of him. Downshifting, he was around the car and gone, the Ferrari a silver streak on the treacherous mountain road. Ahead of him, on the switchbacks, he caught glimpses of the Porsche he was pursuing. The low sporty car was swerving all over the road, traveling insanely fast on the steep, narrow ribbon of highway. Thanks to his "other," Jake had amazing reflexes and vision, and that advantage allowed him to push his car to the limit in an attempt to catch his quarry, even on the narrow, twisting mountain road.

A quick glance in the rearview mirror revealed his face was a granite mask, hard lines etched deeply, his gold-green eyes twin chips of ice, glittering menacingly. It didn't matter that he could scare anyone with a look, he truly felt murderous in that moment. He didn't care about the two occupants of that car, both falling down drunk, pawing each other obscenely in front of everyone at the senator's party, but he damn well wasn't going to let them destroy his child.

Shaina Trent, society's darling, jet-setter, life of the party and precious do-anything-for-Daddy daughter of Josiah was carrying his son. How could he have been so damned careless? He had known exactly what she was when he had bedded her. He had known both his family and hers had wanted the alliance. Each family suspected that he was the very thing they'd been seeking all along—a shifter—and they wanted his bloodline to boost their fading abilities. And they wanted to regain control of him. He should have suspected something when Shaina had thrown herself at him—after all, she'd never looked at him before, always acting as if she were far above him.

He downshifted and put on a burst of speed as he caught another glimpse of the Porsche sliding sideways around a turn. His heart went to his throat. The driver was so drunk he stayed in the wrong lane. Jake doubted either realized he was in pursuit. Shaina leaned toward the driver to massage his neck flirtatiously.

Jake cursed himself for geting into such a predicament. Desperate to find a way to shackle him, the two families had made an alliance, and, like an idiot, he had fallen into their trap. A part of him even felt guilty and thought he deserved exactly what he got.

He had deliberately slept with Shaina as a way to get back at her father, yet Shaina had been using him just as he had been using her. He hadn't been stupid enough to believe her when she told him she was on birth control, but he had been fool enough to use the condoms she produced. What none of them had figured out yet was that he would gladly burn in hell before he would accommodate them all.

Planned pregnancy was the oldest snare in the book. It was too late now; he had to live with the consequences—and so would the rest of them. Both families—and Shaina—had seriously underestimated him. He had planned his revenge for years. He had everything in place. It wouldn't take much to ruin either family financially, and he wasn't above buying freedom for his child.

Jake slammed his open palm on the steering wheel in an agony of recrimination. He knew better, but he just couldn't resist thumbing his nose at Josiah. But they would never have his kid. It didn't matter whether the boy was a shifter or not. Jake would find a nurse, a decent one, to come in and raise him right. He sure couldn't love the boy, but eventually he'd find someone who could.

A muscle jerked along his jaw. He'd always been savage, clawing and fighting his way out of the cage they'd tried to keep him in. They wouldn't have a chance to cage his child. His son would never know that unnatural, deceitful life. A nurse wasn't a perfect solution, but it would be the best he could do for the kid.

He couldn't trust Shaina to keep the unborn child healthy, so here he was in California, chasing her down, the jet standing by to take her back to his ranch where his guards would keep her out of trouble and away from drugs and alcohol until the baby was born. He had a team of doctors at his disposal, the best his research could find in Texas, and he was going to make certain the kid had the best possible start.

Jake swore viciously again. Shaina could drive off a cliff for all he cared, but he made it clear that he owned her father's company, had bought up the stock, and he would ruin them all if they dared cross him. The child was his, bought and paid for. Shaina was not going to endanger it. He had turned the tables neatly, ruthlessly, finding a bitter pleasure in all their shocked faces.

Shaina, damn her, had no right to drink herself silly and poison the unborn baby. She had no right to go off with a drunken fool when she was so close to delivery. She had thought herself safe, a thousand miles away from his home state, never dreaming he would be concerned enough about the baby to track her down.

With each passing mile, he shortened the distance between the Ferrari and Porsche, closing the gap steadily, relentlessly. He could see the convertible now, weaving all over the highway, crossing the center line, changing lanes, tires squealing in protest around every sharp curve. He was right above them looking down and he saw Shaina move her hand to caress the driver's lap. The Porsche swerved again right into the other lane.

Suddenly his heart jumped again, and an icy shiver feathered down his spine. He caught a glimpse of a little Volkswagen Bug puttering along, two turns ahead, coming right into the path of destruction. Jake actually called out a warning, totally helpless to stop the inevitable.

The collision rocked the ground, shattering the peace of the night, a cacophony of terrible noises he would never forget. Grinding metal, the scream of brakes, the force of the vehicles coming together, folding like accordions. The sight and sounds sent chills down his spine. Sparks flew, the convertible tumbled over and over, spilling gas everywhere. The Volkswagen, a compacted scrap of twisted metal, slammed into the mountain, flames licking its length and up along the dried grass.

The smell of gas and flames and blood hit him hard. Jake hesitated long enough to report the accident from his cell phone. Leaping from the Ferrari, he sprinted toward the closest car, the crushed Volkswagen. The road was strewn with shattered glass and metal fragments. Shaina and her new boyfriend lay motionless on the ground in the distance, blood running from them in streams. Neither had been wearing a seat belt, and both had been thrown several feet from the car. He doubted if anyone could have lived through the force of that head-on collision, but something propelled him forward in spite of the flames moving quickly along the road.

Gas was everywhere, in every direction, even splashed along the mountainside where the Volkswagen had tumbled end over end. Inside the Bug, two occupants were hanging upside down, held by their seat belts, heads and arms dangling limply. He wrenched open the nearest door. It was already hot with the flames licking at it from the flaming grass on the mountain. With superhuman strength he tore it open, and reached inside to unsnap the seat belt. The body fell into his arms.

It was a woman, covered in glass and blood, but still alive. Aware he had no choice, no time to examine her first, he lifted her out, closing his ears to her cry of pain. He ran a distance from the cars to deposit her in the grass. Blood was pumping from a terrible gash in her leg and he yanked off his belt and wrapped it tight around her thigh, just above the gash.

When he turned back, the Volkswagen was already engulfed in flames. He had no hope of getting the other victim out. He sent up a silent prayer that the occupant had been killed instantly. Resolutely, he turned toward the convertible. He had covered half the distance when an agonized cry froze him in a fragment of time that would remain etched in his mind forever.

"Andy!"

The woman he had rescued somehow managed to get to her feet, which was a miracle, considering her injuries. She stumbled back toward the Volkswagen. For a moment, he could only stare incredulously. She had broken bones, was covered in ragged deep gashes, her face a mask of blood, yet she was running back, right into a wall of flames, and she ran with astonishing speed.

For a split second, pure shock held Jake frozen to the spot. The gasoline on the road had ignited. The flames actually licked at her legs, yet she continued on toward the fiercely burning vehicle. The woman had to have known the car was going to explode at any moment, yet still she ran toward it.

Jake cut her off just a few feet from the car, snatching

her up into his arms, sprinting away from the intense heat and building conflagration. She fought like a wildcat, kicking, scratching, the blood making her so slippery he lost his hold more than once. Each time he dropped her, she didn't hesitate to turn back, her eyes on the burning car as she tried to run, then crawl, back toward it.

"It's too late," he cried harshly. "He's already dead!" Ruthlessly he flung her to the ground, covering her body with his own, pinning her down while the earth beneath them rocked with the force of the explosion.

"Andy." She whispered the name, a lost, forlorn sound wrenched straight from the heart.

In an instant, all the fight went out of her. She lay motionless in Jake's arms, small, completely vulnerable and broken, her eyes staring up at him unseeing. Again, time seemed to stand still. Everything tunneled until he was focused wholly on her eyes. Enormous, tilted like a cat's, aquamarine with dark orbs, unusual and mesmerizing, now haunted. She seemed familiar—too familiar. He knew her, and yet he didn't.

For the first time in his life he felt a strong protective urge welling up out of nowhere. He became aware of the gathering crowd staring down at the woman as others came upon the scene. Instinctively he shielded her, barking orders to check the overturned convertible, to ensure ambulances and the police were on the way.

He worked furiously to stem the flow of blood pouring from the woman's temple and from her leg. A part of him knew he should be thinking instead of Shaina and the child she was carrying, but his mind was consumed with the woman he protected. All he could do was silently vow not to allow her to slip away as she so clearly wanted to do.

Her grief-stricken green eyes begged him to let her go. Where had he seen those eyes before? He looked into them again, drawn by some unseen force. Almond in shape, pupils round and black, the irises a rare aquamarine, the blue-green surrounded by a golden circle. Unusual. And yet he knew those eyes. Where had he seen them?

"Let me go."

She knew then that his will held her when she wanted to slip away. Jake found himself leaning close to her so that his mouth was against her ear, his breath warm against her skin. His golden eyes glittered ruthlessly, mercilessly into hers. "No." He said the word implacably. "Did you hear me? No." He denied her a second time, his white teeth snapping together in finality as he applied more pressure to the pumping wound in her leg.

She closed her eyes, tired, and turned her face away from him as if she had no fight left in her. The ambulance was there, paramedics pushing him aside to work on her. A short distance away, firefighters draped a blanket over Shaina's friend. This was one accident Shaina's father could not make go away with his money.

More paramedics were working desperately at Shaina's side. It took him a minute to realize they were taking the baby—his son. His heart in his throat, he waited until he heard the triumphant cheers. The child was alive, more than they could say for the mother. He waited to feel emotion, any emotion, at Shaina's death or his son's birth. He felt nothing at all, only a sense of contempt for the way Shaina had lived and died. Silently cursing his own cold nature, he looked down at the woman lying so still, her dark eyes staring past the paramedic to the burned car. He shifted slightly while they worked on her, to block her view.

Jake followed the ambulances carrying his son and the woman to a small hospital. Although the place seemed a little primitive by Jake's standards, the overworked staff seemed to know their jobs.

"I'm Officer Nate Peterson." A young highway patrolman thrust a cup of coffee into his bloody hands.

Her blood. It was all over him. Jake's shoulders sagged

and all at once he was immensely tired, but he needed to find out if she was still alive.

"Can you tell me what happened, sir?" the officer asked. The young patrolman was shaking so badly he could hardly hold his pen. "Andy and I were good friends," the man admitted, choking back emotion.

"Tell me about him," Jake asked, curious about the man who inspired such loyalty that a woman would run through fire to save him, even with her own terrible injuries. A man who could make a patrolman shake and hold back real tears. Jake could *feel* the genuine emotion pouring off the other man. He looked around the hospital and found others looking just as distressed.

"His name was Andrew Reynolds and he was twenty-five, best mechanic in town. He could fix anything with an engine. I was best man at his wedding only five months ago. He was so happy that Emma married him. *They* were so happy."

Emma. That was her name. "Is she still alive?" He held his breath.

The patrolman nodded. "As far as I know. She's in surgery. Did you see the accident?"

Jake crumbled up the paper coffee cup and threw it in the trash can. "They were drunk. I followed them from Senator Hindman's party. Shaina Trent, the woman, was carrying my child. She didn't want him and had signed him over to me, but it didn't stop her from drinking and partying with her friends. I was worried because both of them appeared to be drunk. I'm sorry, I don't know the man."

Jake gave the rest of his statement as clearly as possible, knowing the skidmarks would bear him out.

Jake overheard a young nurse crying in the hall and he walked over to her on the pretext of comforting her. "Are you all right?"

She sniffed several times, her eyes bright and a little

interested when she saw him. Jake stuck out his hand and patted her shoulder. "I'm Jake Bannaconni." He knew the name would be recognizable and when her eyes widened satisfaction settled in his belly. "Can you tell me about the woman? Is she alive?" He looked at the nurse's name tag. Chelsey Harden.

Chelsey nodded her head. "She's in surgery. She's only twenty-one. I don't understand how this could happen. She called me earlier today and said she took a pregnancy test and she was so happy. She was telling Andy tonight at dinner. I bet he didn't even have a chance to know." She covered her face for a moment and broke into sobs.

Jake patted her shoulder again. "I take it you two are friends."

Chelsey hiccupped and blew her nose. "Very good friends. I went to school with Andrew and he introduced us. Now she has no one. Andrew's parents died last year in a car crash and Emma's died when she was a teen. They only had each other. It seems like some kind of curse or something, all these car wrecks." Her face whitened and she covered her mouth with her hand. "I'm sorry. Your wife was killed as well. I'm so sorry."

Jake shook his head. "We weren't married, but we were having a child."

"He's going to be fine. He's a little early, but he's very healthy," Chelsey hastened to assure him.

"How long will he have to stay here?"

Meaning how much time did he have to set things in motion. He had a vague idea what he wanted to do, but no real plan. It was obvious the staff felt sorry for him. His pregnant girlfriend had run off with another man. Shaina was in the news all the time. The paparazzi loved her and of course Jake wasn't unknown to them, but Shaina's exploits were always food for the gossip magazines and she loved the spotlight.

The world believed that she'd left Jake brokenhearted.

In truth, they had despised one another. Her father had filled her with conviction that the Trents were so far above the Bannaconnis—Jake in particular—that she felt she had lowered herself to sleep with him. Not that she hadn't enjoyed it and kept coming back for more, but the tabloids only knew what Shaina wanted to feed them. Now that she was dead and sympathy surrounded him, Jake knew he could use that to his advantage.

"You'll have to talk to the doctor, but for a preemie, he's healthy. Maybe a week, but I honestly couldn't tell you." Chelsey let out a soft sigh. "Emma really wanted a family. It was so important to her and to Andy, because they didn't have anyone at all, so they kept saying they would have a big family."

Jake raked a hand through his hair. He should have his son immediately transported back to a hospital in Texas and return home. This wasn't his mess to clean up. But he knew he wouldn't. He had looked into Emma Reynolds's blue-green eyes and something had opened up in him, something nameless he didn't understand. But regardless, he couldn't walk away.

A man approached and Jake was instantly aware of Chelsey straightening, immediately changing her demeanor to a very professional face. So this was a hospital administrator. Someone had recognized Jake and they were sending the big guns to make certain he was comfortable with his son's treatment.

"You're burned, Mr. Bannaconni, on your hands and arms. You need to have that taken care of."

"I didn't even notice," Jake said truthfully.

He sized the man up as his burns were treated. Dignified. Sincere. This was a man who had too much work, too little time off, and who believed in what he did. And he was fiercely proud of his hospital—Jake could tell that the moment the doctor began showing him around—yet apparently had little money to bring in modern equipment.

Jake seized the moment, striking where he knew it would do the most good, murmuring about a sizable donation for the care his son had received, asking questions about his child, how long he'd have to stay, what the repercussions of an early birth were, and what he could do to better help the hospital care for him. Finally he managed to turn the conversation to Emma Reynolds and how terrible he felt for her situation. What were her injuries? Did she need special doctors? He would be more than happy to fly in who or what they needed to help.

Dr. John Grogan, head of the hospital, tried to convince Jake that Emma Reynolds wasn't his responsibility.

Jake looked very grave. "I'm well aware the rest of the world might think that, but it was my girlfriend and her lover who are responsible for the death of Emma's husband and for her injuries. She has no one else. Taking care of bills or making certain she has anything she needs is the least that I can do for her." He glanced around and lowered his voice another octave. "I'd prefer if no reporters know I'm here or that my son is still here."

Grogan nodded. "We're a small hospital, Mr. Bannaconni, but we're very discreet with our patients."

Jake let out a relieved sigh and slumped a little to show how tired and upset he was. "Please let Emma's doctors know I'm willing to help out. I need to see my son now, if that's possible."

The first step toward becoming involved in Emma's life was accomplished. He let himself be led to the nursery where he was forced to wear a gown, mask, and gloves to stare down at the wrinkled little boy who lay naked in small incubator with lights everywhere.

"How is she today, Chelsey?" Jake asked as the young nurse came down the hallway toward him. "I've just come back from seeing my son and thought I'd peek in on her."

Emma's room was the first room closest to the nursery. She was pregnant and the OB doctor wanted easy access to her if she began to miscarry after her traumatic ordeal. It was easy enough for Jake to use the excuse that she was so close to his son to look in on her. Emma had been unresponsive to the doctors and nurses, but when he walked in, her blue-green gaze would jump to his face and stay there.

Chelsey sighed. "She doesn't talk to anyone, Mr. Bannaconni. We're all a little afraid for her. But I heard the baby was doing better. He's breathing on his own now and it's been only three days."

"Yes, he seems much better, although they tell me he should be gaining more weight." Jake paused with his hand on Emma's door. So far no one had ever stopped him from going in. Today he wanted Emma to give the staff her permission to allow him to help her. "I'm going to try to give Emma a reason to live today. You gave me the idea the other day when we talked."

Chelsey patted his shoulder and this time her smile was flirtatious. "I hope you can find a way to get through to her."

Jake smiled back, letting his gaze slide over her with a man's interest. Chelsey's breath caught in her throat and she gave him a little wave as she sauntered off, her hips swaying more than usual. Jake pushed open the door to Emma's room and slipped inside.

As he closed it he heard Chelsey giggle. "He's so hot, Anna. My god, when he smiles I think I'm going to orgasm on the spot."

He glanced at Emma and knew she heard. He closed the doors on the laughing nurses and crossed to her side.

Emma held her breath. He was back. She could go far away from the others and not have to face the reality of being completely alone again, not have to think of her beloved Andrew as dead, not have to deal with losing his baby, but then this man would come in and sit down, filling the room, filling her head with the scent and sight of him, compelling her to live again. He forced her back to the surface every time where there was no escape from the terrible grief that overwhelmed her.

Silently she pleaded for him to go, to just let her be in the half-alive, half-dead state that protected her from feeling. But once his gaze focused on her, it didn't leave.

"How are you today, Emma?" He always sounded intimate, talking to her as if they were best friends—more than friends, closer. He used the pads of his fingers to stroke back her hair. "Are you feeling any better?"

Each time he touched her, no matter how light, she felt as if electricity arced between them, zapping her alive again, so that the fears and the sorrow were closer than ever. And he held her there, gently but firmly, forcing her to look at her empty life while unimaginable grief poured over her, holding her prisoner.

She didn't answer him. She rarely did, just looked mutely up at him begging him to let her drift back into her safe little cocoon.

Jake dragged a chair to the side of the bed, spun it around, and straddled it. "I named the baby this morning. I didn't ever think much about the naming process, but I wanted to give him a good name, something that he'd be happy with even as an adult. I found a baby name book in the waiting room."

She couldn't look away from his face. His tone was soft and low and very intense, but there was something that was a little off. She couldn't tell what it was. His gaze never left her face. He reminded her of a leopard with his golden-green eyes and his unblinking piercing stare, so focused on her there was nowhere to hide.

He leaned forward. "He's so little, Emma, I swear I could fit him in the palm of my hand. It scares me to think of taking him home when I don't know the first thing about taking care of a baby. Does it scare you? You're going to have a baby. Did they tell you that? That the baby is still alive with only you to protect it?"

Her breath caught in her throat and her hands moved to cover her stomach. Was it true? She could feel her heart pound, hear it thundering in her ears. She'd willed herself to die, she wanted to die, and she would have taken her baby—Andy's baby—with her. She closed her eyes briefly, afraid she'd heard wrong.

Jake sighed softly and ran his fingers through his hair as if in agitation. "That's what scares me. There's only me to be the parent, to give the baby a good home, and I'm so far from the real deal." That admission slipped out and his voice rang with truth.

She swallowed—hard. Her throat convulsed. It took effort to part her dried lips and she had to reach for her voice. When it came it was thin and shaky and nearly unrecognizable. "Are you certain? About my baby? Are you certain I didn't lose it?"

He leaned closer to her. Jake Bannaconni. She'd heard his name spoken in hushed, awed whispers, but she still couldn't figure out why she knew him. What was it that was so familiar about him, and why did she feel as if his will held her own?

"Your baby is fine, Emma. The doctor said even with the blood loss, the baby appears to be healthy. There are no signs that the pregnancy will terminate. You're going to be a mother."

Tears burned behind her eyes again. Her baby. Her precious baby was safe. She wasn't entirely alone and there was a small piece of Andy growing inside of her. "Thank you for telling me about the baby. I was afraid to ask and no one thought to tell me. Just my head, my leg, a million other injuries and . . ." She trailed off and stared, blinking up at the ceiling, tears welling in her eyes.

"Andrew," he supplied gently. "I'm sorry, Emma, we both have to live with what happened. And we both have babies to raise by ourselves." He flashed a small smile. "I have the feeling you'll be much better at the parenting part of it than I will."

"You'll be a good father," she reassured. "Don't worry so much." How in the world was she going to take care of a baby?

Jake picked up Emma's hand, his thumb moving along the back of her hand. His touch was achingly familiar. "Have they said when you can get out of here?"

Emma shook her head. "Where would I go?" The thought of her apartment, her home with Andrew, was too much for her to contemplate. She couldn't face going back to the apartment and trying to pack up Andy's things.

"We'll deal with it later, when you're feeling stronger," he assured. "I called my lawyer and asked him to look into insurance for you and a settlement of some sort. At least to get the ball rolling. I know you don't want to think about money, but it will be important when you have the baby."

Emma lifted her lashes, allowing her gaze to drift over his face. There was something about him that haunted her, commanded her, drew her like a magnet when she wanted to be left alone, to simply disappear. No one else compelled her as he did. She knew him. The memory of him nagged at her, yet she couldn't place him.

She could remember the events leading up to the accident, sitting in the car, so excited, her news of her pregnancy on the tip of her tongue, but she held back, determined to wait until they were at the restaurant and she could see Andy's expression, watch his eyes and his mouth when she revealed they were going to have a child. He'd died without ever knowing. She hated that. Her gaze flicked again to Jake's face. She knew he was Jake because he told her, not because the memory of him had returned.

She didn't remember the crash. She remembered after,

when there was pain and fire and Jake staring at her, stopping her from following Andy. His eyes fascinated her, pulled at her, like a predator searching for prey. His focused stare made her uncomfortable, yet in some strange way comforted her. Maybe if her head ever stopped throbbing and the doctors backed off on the pain medication she could think more clearly, but right now, his personality was too strong and she couldn't think for herself.

"How do I know you? I looked into your eyes and I know you."

"I'm sorry. I'm the man who pulled you out of the car." He looked down, taking his hand away from hers and rubbing at his temples as if he had the same headache she did. "I couldn't get to your husband. The fire was everywhere."

She saw burns on his hands and her heart jumped. She reached out and drew his hand to her. "Is this from pulling me out of the car?"

He drew back, something inside him shaken from the touch of fingers on his skin. It wasn't sexual. He responded to women sexually as a rule and this was something altogether different and he didn't trust the feeling at all. "Yes." His voice came out more gruffly than he intended.

Emma let out a small sigh. "I'm sorry you were hurt."

"Emma," Jake said softly, "what matters is that you and the baby are safe." He regretted pulling away from her when she'd voluntarily reached out to him.

Chelsey opened the door and popped her head in. "You need anything, Emma?" she asked, but her gaze devoured Jake.

Emma's face closed down, her eyes going vague. When she didn't respond, Chelsey frowned and looked at Jake. He rose and patted Emma's limp hand.

"I'll get you a few things from your apartment, Emma," he said deliberately. "I'll be back this evening." He nodded toward the hallway and Chelsey followed him out. "I'll need her key and the address," he told the nurse.

"I don't want to get into trouble," Chelsey said.

Jake stepped closer, leaning down as if to keep their conversation totally private. His voice was low and compelling, but he knew the heat of his body and the scent of his cologne enveloped her. Chelsey inhaled and a small shiver of awareness went through her. "I wouldn't let you get into trouble. Emma has to snap out of this and if she has a few things familiar to her, it may help. You're just helping her friend and you saw that she didn't object."

Chelsey nodded and hurried away, to return with the key and small piece of paper with the address on it.

"You're a good friend to Emma," Jake said as he pocketed the key and walked quickly away before she could change her mind.

He found the building with little problem. He stood in the doorway and surveyed the small apartment. Small? Hell, it was tiny! The furniture was old and worn with use, the china was chipped and cracked. The couple had nothing. He stalked through the four rooms. This entire apartment would fit into his master bedroom. Frustration grew with each step and he paced back and forth, prowling like the caged cat he was. There was something here he couldn't quite put his finger on. Something he needed to understand, *had* to understand. It was a burning drive in his gut and Jake Bannaconni was a tenacious man.

Everything was very neat and clean, so much so that he found himself throwing out the dead roses in the little vase; they seemed an obscenity in the atmosphere of the apartment. He paced restlessly again, quick, fluid steps of sheer power. There was a key but he was missing it! He halted abruptly. The pictures. Pictures were everywhere—on the walls, the desk, the small bureau, and there was an album sitting on a coffee table.

He studied one of the photos. The couple was looking at one another, as they seemed to be in every other picture, as if they had eyes only for each other. Their expressions were genuine, love shining brightly between them until it was almost tangible.

Jake traced Emma's lips with a gentle fingertip. He had never seen two people who looked so happy. It was in their eyes, it was in their faces. Emma took his breath away. In most of the pictures, she wore little or no makeup.

She was very small, almost too slender with an abundance of flaming red hair framing her fragile heart-shaped face. He had never had the slightest attraction to skinny women, he preferred lush curves, but he couldn't stop staring at her face, her eyes. He touched her picture again, tracing the outline of her face, his other hand gripping the cheap frame until his knuckles were white. Abruptly he put it down.

The kitchen was filled with baked goods, even bread, obviously made from scratch. The bathroom held two toothbrushes, one white, one blue, side by side in a container. There was a pregnancy test kit right next to the small soap dish. In the corner of the mirror, someone had written "Yes!" with lipstick.

In the bedroom, without a qualm, he went through their clothes. Andrew's shirts were a bit threadbare, but every button was in place, every tear neatly repaired. Every shirt was clean and ironed. He found a jacket with tiny embroidered stitches on the inside seam. "Someone loves you." He stared at the words, feeling a yawning chasm of emptiness welling up inside him.

Jake Bannaconni was elite. He had superior intelligence, strength, vision, and sense of smell. Muscles rippled beneath his skin, flowing like water, fluid and controlled. He was one of the youngest billionaires ever reported by *Forbes*, and he wielded vast political power. He had the savage, animalistic magnetism of his species and the ruthless logic to strategize and plan boardroom battles. He could mesmerize people with the sheer strength of his personality; he could attract and seduce the most beautiful women in the world, and frequently did so, but he could not make them love him. This—this *mechanic*—had commanded love from all those around him. It made no sense.

What had made Andrew Reynolds so damned special that he could inspire that kind of love? That kind of loyalty? Hell, Jake couldn't claim love or loyalty from his own parents, let alone anyone else. As far as he could see, Reynolds hadn't given his wife a damned thing, yet everywhere he looked he could see evidence of their happiness.

He touched Emma's brush, strands of red hair gleaming at him like spun silk. His gut clenched. Longing nearly overwhelmed him. More than longing. Black jealousy assailed him. He'd heard his kind had that dangerous trait, but never once in his life had he ever experienced it. The emotion, so strong, so intense it left a bitter taste in his mouth, knotted his gut and put a killing edge to his already volatile temper. Andrew and Emma's life was fairy tale. A fucking fairy tale. It wasn't real. It couldn't be real. She didn't have decent clothes. Every pair of her jeans was faded and worn. There were only two dresses hanging in the closet.

He found books on birds everywhere, an amateur design for a greenhouse aviary drafted by a feminine hand. He folded the drawings carefully and slipped them inside his coat pocket. He spent another hour in the apartment, not really understanding why, but he couldn't pull himself away. He was a man who needed freedom and open space. He was intensely sexual, seducing women and bedding them whenever, wherever he wanted. He'd never considered having a woman of his own, yet looking around that tiny apartment made him feel as if all the money in the world, all the political clout, all the secrets of what he was and who he was, all of that was nothing in comparison to what Andrew Reynolds had had.

Jake closed and locked the door. Someone had to look at him that way. Not just someone—Emma. He couldn't walk away and leave her. The thought of another man finding her, possessing her, sent rage careening through his mind. Inside, he roared a protest. Emma should have been nothing to him, but he couldn't get the sight or scent of her from his mind.

He wanted the damned fairy tale. He could be patient. He was methodical and completely ruthless. Once set on a course of action he was implacable, unswerving. No one, nothing, stayed in his way for long. A grim smile touched the slightly cruel edges of his mouth. He played to win, and he always did. It never mattered how long it took. He always won. He wanted what Andrew had had. He wanted Emma Reynolds, not some other woman. Emma. And he would have her. Nothing, no one, would stand in his way.

Penguin Group (USA) Inc.
is proud to present

GREAT READS—GUARANTEED

We are so confident you will love
this book that we are offering a
100% money-back guarantee!

If you are not 100% satisfied with
this publication, Penguin Group (USA) Inc.
will refund your money!
Simply return the book before
March 6, 2009 for a full refund.

NEW IN HARDCOVER

From #1 *New York Times* bestselling author

Christine Feehan

—•—

DARK CURSE
A Carpathian Novel

—•—

Born into a world of ice, slave to her evil father, Lara Calladine knew only paralyzing fear as a child. Only by escaping with her mysterious gifts unbroken would she survive to claim her great Carpathian heritage as a Dragonseeker...

penguin.com

M264T0408